The Quarry

Winner of the
Flannery O'Connor
Award for
Short Fiction

Stories by

Harvey

Grossinger

The Quarry

The University of Georgia Press

ATHENS AND LONDON

Published by the University of Georgia Press

© 1997 by Harvey Grossinger

All rights reserved

Designed by Erin Kirk New

Set in 10 on 13 Aldus by G & S Typesetters, Inc.

Printed and bound by Thomson-Shore, Inc.

The paper in this book meets the guidelines

for permanence and durability of the Committee

on Production Guidelines for Book Longevity of

the Council on Library Resources.

Printed in the United States of America

01 00 99 98 97 C 5 4 3 2 1

Library of Congress Cataloging in Publication Data

Grossinger, Harvey.

The quarry : stories by Harvey Grossinger / Harvey Grossinger.

p. cm.

ISBN 0-8203-1896-5 (alk. paper)

I. Title.

PS3557 R655Q37 1997

813'.54—dc20   96-30803

British Library Cataloging in Publication Data available

For Sue, who never wavered,

and for my daughters,

Ruth and Rachel

The living and the dead glide hand in hand

Under cool waters where the days are gone.

Out of the dark into a dark I stand.

—James Wright, "All the Beautiful Are Blameless"

Acknowledgments

Some of the stories in this book first appeared in the following publications: "Dinosaurs," *The Chicago Tribune*; "Hearts & Minds," *Western Humanities Review*; "Home Burial," *New England Review* (a much earlier version was published in the *Antietam Review*); "Leisure World," *Cimarron Review* (a much earlier version was published in *Ascent*); and "Promised Land," *Mid-American Review*.

I wish to thank the editors of those publications and to express appreciation to the Maryland State Arts Council for a Literary Work-in-Progress Grant.

Many people over the years have contributed to the writing of this book through their encouragement, affection, insight, and sustaining friendship. All of them, in their own way, have enriched these stories. Among them I'd especially like to thank Sue Edlavitch, Marc and Nancy Diamond, Gaye Denis-Passes and Harold Passes, Bill Loiseaux, Ellyn Bache, Charley Cree, Richard McCann, Joyce Kornblatt, Chuck Larson, Kermit Moyer, Mary Ellen Henry, Alan Crooks, and my parents, Sidney and Hannah Grossinger. I am very lucky to have such compassionate and generous friends and mentors.

Lastly, I need to thank Bob Geller, a former English teacher of mine at Mamaroneck High School in Mamaroneck, New York, my very first reader, who pointed the way back in 1966. I hope you are around to see what you started.

Contents

Dinosaurs   1

Hearts & Minds   31

Home Burial   69

Leisure World   91

Promised Land   119

The Quarry   153

Old age ain't no place for sissies.
—Bette Davis

Dinosaurs

The birth of the solar system, the demise of the dinosaurs, the melting of the polar ice caps: haunting cosmic mysteries emerged from my grandfather Zolly's mouth in a tone of grave wonderment. In the early fifties, when I was in the second grade, he'd tell me—sitting on a black leather club chair in his living room, puffing on a hand-rolled cigar, a cut-glass ashtray balanced in his lap—that the nighttime sky was sprinkled with diamonds, God's diamonds. When I was in the fourth and fifth grade, a time when boys my age were busy building plastic Nautilus submarines and Flying Fortresses, Zolly was buying me dinosaur models and geological maps of the earth's crust. If I had a heavy cold, he'd sit at the foot of my bed and spread Vicks VapoRub on my chest and nose. "Know where you come from, the sages of Israel advised," he'd tell me, his pale, green irises as small as buttons. "The giant lizards are the blueprints of the past. Study them."

Zolly dropped by with library books for me to read when I was in bed with the mumps or chicken pox. He had me memorize the names of dinosaurs and the ages in which they lived, then he'd grill me whenever he and my grandmother Manya came over on the weekend in the summer for a swim in the oil-slicked Long Island Sound and some shish kebab or broiled swordfish steaks. He'd bolt his supper and then quiz me on the Mesozoic Era or the Pleistocene Period. He'd even slip me a few bucks when my father wasn't looking.

When I was six my grandparents sold their red-brick house in Pelham Bay and moved into an ornate, rent-controlled building near University Heights, a few blocks from NYU and the Hall of Fame for Great Americans. They had a sunny top-floor apartment with parquet floors, a zinc stove, and a clothes wringer in the plant-filled kitchen. The place always smelled of simmering peaches and lemon oil. Zolly stacked heavy cases of seltzer bottles and celery tonic behind the dumbwaiter, and he wrapped his panatelas in white butcher paper and kept them in the cupboard. The stuffy, high-ceilinged rooms were filled with dark Oriental rugs, lamps with flame-shaped bulbs, heavy mahogany sideboards, and rose-colored tufted upholstery. Manya hid sachets of powdered viburnum in the wide walnut dressers.

Zolly always liked to stand at the front of the first car when he took me by subway into Manhattan. In the morning we'd go to the Museum of Natural History, where we'd cruise luminous marble corridors filled with the osseous remains of saber-toothed tigers and iron-plated reptiles. A cathedral of bones, Zolly called it. I can remember him taking my picture with his old Polaroid Land camera as I stood in the pleated footprint of a woolly mammoth. Before leaving he'd fire questions at me, and if I answered them to his satisfaction we went straight to the gift shop, where he bought me fossil puzzles and stegosaurus piggy banks and pterodactyl mobiles. Tired and hungry after a few hours of walking and talking, we would go to the Horn & Hardart for lunch, or to a steamy dairy restaurant on Amsterdam Avenue where I always ordered *latkes* and tangy applesauce and watched the darkly dressed old Jews inhaling their cold borscht and eggplant and noodle *farfel* at crowded tables.

It was my younger sister Delilah who phoned and told me that Zolly had died in his room while watching *Hill Street Blues*. I wondered aloud how he had felt the past week. "He sounded so-so last Sunday morning," I said dolefully, as if that illuminated something. I heard Delilah's breath catch. I was suddenly light-headed and felt a stabbing pain behind my eyes.

"Lenny," she asked gently, "are you still there?"

"Why didn't anyone call me last night?" I snapped at her.

"Daddy phoned from the funeral home but your line was busy. Things were hectic; it must've slipped his mind."

I nodded tentatively, as if she could see me. I knew this had been coming, but that never made anything easier. "I'm thinking," I finally said. "Was Zolly alone?"

"I told you he was watching TV," she said between coughs. She told me she had bronchitis. Her voice trailed away and I heard shouting in the background. My girlfriend Martha, curled naked and tanned in the water bed beside me, sighed. Her brassiere dangled from a hanging pot of African violets. "I'll tell you something, Lenny," Delilah said.

"Don't—tell me later." I heard my stomach churn. "What are the arrangements?"

She ignored me. "The blood flow to his brain had recently gotten worse. They think he might have died from a ruptured aneurysm. Some days he thought he was Eddie Cantor, then he had a spell doing David Dubinsky. He'd think he was at a Sacco and Vanzetti rally in Herald Square. He started walking through the house in the middle of the night, calling for Manya."

I pulled the quilt over Martha's behind. Little gurgling noises were coming from her mouth. I could hear the traffic outside: the gears of plows and four-wheel-drive jeeps, the horns and chains of passing cars and school buses. I peeked through the curtains; last night's snow was powdery, like laundry suds. Then Leakey, my Great Dane, started barking to be let out. "How's Dad doing?"

"The way you'd expect, I guess. But it was a bummer for Bernice," Delilah said. Bernice is our mother. "She found Zolly in his La-Z-Boy recliner when she went in to give him his pills."

The last time I saw Zolly was in La Guardia Airport. It was getting on toward midnight and he couldn't stop yawning. My father was on his knees undoing Zolly's boots. On our way into the terminal Zolly had slipped off the curb and freezing slush had filled his socks. His clawlike feet were the color of mackerel. My father reached a hand up and swept the damp, stringy hair from Zolly's broad forehead.

I massaged Zolly's shoulders and teased, "You'll be a new man soon, Papa."

He bowed beneath my hands. "Don't humor me, Benny."

"It's Lenny," I said softly. "I'm right here, behind you."

He moved his head slowly from side to side. "Where the hell were you? Don't hide from me next time."

My father turned to watch a poodle-haired stewardess in knee-high boots run past. "Hot stuff," he said, rubbing his temples as if he had a headache.

"Everyone's in a big rush," I said.

"Lenny, you've got quite a pot on you. Would it hurt you to drop a few pounds? You need a heart condition at forty?"

I touched my belly. "The doctor says I have a slow thyroid," I said.

He frowned. "Last year you said you were big-boned." I crouched down and brushed mud off the cuffs of Zolly's corduroy slacks, and he smiled, holding my hand in his for a moment. There were thin violet lines along his wrist, and his watery eyes burned with illness and decay. A black comb was sticking out of the breast pocket of his shirt. His gaze rested on my briefcase at his feet and he mouthed my name impressed into the burnished leather: "Leonard A. March."

My father squinted into the glare of a recessed light and gestured with his hands for me to say something. "Lenny, talk to him for God's sake."

I touched Zolly's thigh. "Are your legs cold, Papa?"

He tilted his big head sideways and stroked his jaw. Spittle gleamed at the corners of his mouth. "I can't tell anymore. My circulation is for the birds. Your father will explain how I sit in my pee since I can't feel the wetness. I reminded myself last night that I'm going to give you a bit of money."

My father gripped my shoulder. "He wouldn't be so sick if your grandmother had lived."

"He's ninety-two, Dad," I said.

He squeezed the withered rabbit's-foot key ring in his free hand. "It's all been downhill since then. The guy used to be a goddamn powerhouse. He kept the most precise ledgers you'd ever want to see. Remember how he could swim in the ocean? Like a goddamn shark. Promise to shoot me if I get like this."

My father has an album of frayed sepia photographs of Zolly when he lived in Chicago that I'd thumbed through as a boy. They showed a young man riding the fierce Lake Michigan waves in the middle of the winter, his glossy black hair piled high on his head, alive in the brutal wind. When I was growing up, Zolly taught me how to swim in the gentle surf at Orchard Beach. *Shmendricks* swim in pools, he always told me; a *mensh* swims in the ocean. In the rest room, with his bathing trunks dropped to his ankles, he would clean the toilet seat with a single sheet of tissue paper. When I asked—as I always did—why he didn't tear off more paper, he sighed like a man falling into a deep sleep and told me he was saving the city money. "I hate waste," he'd say in a raw Slavic accent. At his bakery he copied phone orders with pencils sharpened down to their pink erasers.

Zolly looked asleep, his head dropped to his chest. I checked the time on a digital clock suspended by wires above a treadmill and rowing machine on a revolving pedestal. A chinless man with soaking red hair and blue crescent earrings held out a folded sheet of paper and asked me for some spare change. It was a *Jews for Jesus* leaflet. I handed him a buck in dimes and quarters and he gave me the peace sign.

"Even at this hour," my father said irritably, throwing his topcoat over his arm, "the *shnorrers* are earning a living."

"Why don't you drive Zolly home and hit the sack?" I said. "He looks exhausted and this delay'll probably take most of the night. I've got plenty of stuff to read."

He lifted the brim of his felt hat slightly and leaned close enough for me to smell cigar smoke on his breath. "Stay here," he said directly into my ear, and left to see if my plane was still grounded in Pittsburgh due to the weather.

Zolly stared at the baggage carousel and tapped his cane against the chrome base of a standing ashtray. It struck me that everything about him had dwindled. His once big hands were now starlike and matted with wiry gray hairs, and he had trouble catching his breath after walking short distances. Bending, my father told me, put a strain on his heart. A slim, spare woman with auburn curls sat down across from us and began humming "Memories" with her eyes closed. We could see the tops of her stockings when she crossed her legs. Zolly turned and winked at me. He clutched my wrist. "Where've you been hiding? I don't care for being around strangers."

"I haven't gone anywhere, Papa," I said. "I'm right here." I stooped beside him and tied his shoelaces.

"And my Benny?"

"He went to check on my flight."

"Again?" His breath smelled like boiled milk.

"Again."

His face sagged. "With Benny everything's an emergency. Did you have words?"

"He lives to worry, Papa." I kissed the top of his head. His cottony hair had thinned into the shape of a halo. The gray of his skull was visible beneath his skin. "Don't give me a hard time," I said, running my fingers over his hand.

"I'm not his responsibility," he said. His croupy breathing came in high, sharp wheezes. "You remember my cousin Milo? He lived in Chicago, near the stockyards, in a hole without a radiator. It gave me the whooping cough. I boarded with him when I first came over from Europe. Everything there stank like Poland."

With his heels drawn against each other, the taps on his wet saddle shoes scraped the concrete floor. Since Manya died fourteen years ago he had hardly left the house. They were on a junket in the Bahamas—a sixtieth anniversary gift from their children—when she had a stroke. Zolly had been out of their stateroom since early morning, sunning himself and playing dominoes and three-card monte. When he went in to get Manya for the buffet lunch, he found her on top of the chenille bedspread, her lips having already turned blue. She'd been reading an Agatha Christie mystery, her finger poised to turn the page. She was airlifted by helicopter to a hospital in Nassau; then Zolly had insisted on hiring a nurse and chartering an executive Learjet and having her flown to Kennedy, so she could be treated by Jewish doctors. Manya was driven by private ambulance to Montefiore Medical Center in the Bronx, where she died from renal failure five days later. We buried her in an old cemetery a few miles from Crotona Park, in a family plot Zolly had purchased the day before they were married, and after the funeral he sat on a mourner's stool in my parents' house and stared out the kitchen window. He spoke to no one.

I remember coming into the kitchen a few days after the funeral and asking him if he wanted company. He looked up at me and smiled sadly. His face was disbelieving and mottled, and his liquid eyes were wreathed with twisting hairs. I told him to eat something and I put water on to boil. I gave him a tangerine and watched him peel the rind in one long coil. When his tea was ready he stirred two teaspoonfuls of sugar into his glass and tipped the tea into a saucer, sipping it through a lump of sugar wedged between his crooked yellow teeth.

He traced the marbled grain of the wood in the maple breakfast table with his finger, and I remembered how he would stick that same finger inside my shirt collar and tickle my neck. The lines in his hands were like badly crumpled paper. When I turned to leave he reached for me. "It's all right if you want to stay, Lenny," he said. "I like having you here."

I poured myself a glass of tea and sat down across from him. His eyes were restless in their milky, purple-veined sockets, and his fists were clenched. In profile, with his high, pointy cheekbones and his nose curled like a snail, he looked like I knew I would someday. People had always said our faces were exactly alike, Sephardic-looking, troubled. Both Zolly and my father had ears like satellite dishes and palms as wide as saucers. When I was a child I used to imagine that I could sleep in their hands. They were both six-two and swaybacked from years of braiding dough into *challah* and pumpernickel. The three of us had leathery complexions etched with fine, sword-shaped fissures, coarse brown hair, and reddish-brown quill beards that stirred in a stiff breeze. The three Freuds, my ex called us.

I cut him a slice of prune *babka* and we talked about the family. Zolly rarely reminisced about his childhood, and when he did he sounded angry. His father, a dairyman from a market town along the Dnieper, near Kiev, was mauled by a wild boar and died from rabies when Zolly was twelve years old, and he said he couldn't remember much about him, except that he hardly ever spoke to him. "One time he told me about a pogrom, when the drunken Ukrainian peasants came with their dogs and whips and pitchforks and beat everyone with long sticks that had rusty nails in them. He said he hid with his baby sister in a boarded-up cellar filled with parsnips and mushrooms. His father lost an eye and his mother was violated by those pigs. Your great-grandfather was a hard man, Lenny, he didn't even let me touch him. Kissing was for ninnies and mama's boys. I hated him for that, and I still do. Can you imagine? All I've got left of him is the sound of his voice when he was hitting me with his strap. Nothing pleasant remains in my memory."

I felt suddenly bleak then—reminded of all the misunderstandings I'd had with my father, and the week-long silences which always ended in dubious truces orchestrated by Zolly, who told me to take back whatever I'd said if I didn't want to suffer from a bad conscience later on, when I was a man.

He rolled the band of his Longines wristwatch around his hand. I could almost hear him thinking about Manya. "Manya wouldn't put up with your not eating and moping around," I said.

"I miss my wife already and it hasn't even been a week," he said, his voice cracking. "When I had a fever she always made me marrow broth and apricot candy. Who'll pick me out a decent tie to wear? Coming into her kitchen was like getting a hug."

He was constipated for weeks at a time, his grief settling in his colon. He relieved himself with stewed rhubarb and soap-water enemas. Finally he moved into my parents' house, and spent his days listening to his Edith Piaf and Mario Lanza albums, his nose buried in the *Wall Street Journal* and *Barron's*, or he languished in front of the Zenith, eating Swanson's TV dinners and watching crime shows and *Sixty Minutes*.

My father returned and cursed the airline. "We made the trip for nothing," he said.

He told me the plane wouldn't be leaving Pittsburgh for at least another hour. I managed to convince him to head back home, and at the boarding gate he engulfed Zolly and me in his arms. I was distracted by a commotion over someone's backpack that had set off the metal detector. I exhaled forcefully and turned to look out the tall arched window. All I could see was the blur of snow blowing across the sulfur beams of the runway.

With my face slightly averted, both of them pressed against me, straining to kiss my cheeks. A plane taxied into view, letting in a blast of light. In the shadows of the smoked glass I was wearing what my ex called my haunted look. If someone had taken our picture, we'd have been caught—our smiles vaguely ethereal—in a pose of abject rigidity. I heard Zolly make a noise like a purr, and felt my father's big warm hand around my back, squeezing my shoulders.

I phoned Northwestern and told the chairman of my department that I was going home for my grandfather's funeral. While I packed, Martha picked up some dress shirts for me at the dry cleaners. At noon she drove me to O'Hare, where I waited almost three hours for my connecting flight out of Seattle in a noisy snack bar with a spectacular view of the runways. It snowed all during my trip. From the airport limo, my parents' L-shaped house, nestled in a web of barren hawthorns and willows, appeared tranquil. A *yortzeit* candle burned in a glass on the screened-in porch. I paid the fare and tipped the scowling chauffeur—he'd ranted at other drivers and wore a plaid tablecloth on his head like Arafat.

Delilah's old Dodge Dart was parked in front of the fire hydrant across the street. Two boys in hiking boots and high school varsity jackets were shoveling snow out of the driveway. The shovels made dull, scraping sounds when they hit pavement. I nodded at the kids and the taller one gave me a thumbs-up gesture as I slipped and caught myself before falling on the flagstone footpath. It was as slick as a luge track. "What's happening, man?" the shorter one shouted.

My stomach was queasy from all the coffee I'd had on the plane. I took a few deep breaths and knocked. Bruce Zellner, my older sister Sylvia's husband, opened the door and peered at me as if he couldn't place my face. "Remember me, Zell?" I said.

As soon as I stepped in the doorway my glasses fogged up. I fingered the silver wire of the frames as I wiped the lenses on a handkerchief. After I resettled them, I offered Zell my hand. He arched his back and made a clucking sound. Bruce was a head-and-neck surgeon with a thriving Westchester practice. He was one of those humorless fitness fanatics who always gave the impression that you were fortunate to be in their presence. Beneath a slate-blue blazer, his oxford shirt was unbuttoned at the throat, and a *mezuzah*, coiled in a patch of graying hair, dangled from a gold chain. His brass belt buckle looked like something that would go over the head of a horse.

"Hey, buddy," he said, pumping my hand. "Condolences."

"Thanks." Before letting go of his hand I glanced at his knuckles; the horny joints looked as rutted as screws.

"If you don't mind me saying so, Len, you look pretty heavy. I know, you have no time for exercise and eat too much junk food. Am I right or am I right?"

I left him standing there waiting for an answer. In the kitchen my mother was humming "A-Tisket, A-Tasket" as she shelled Brazil nuts over the sink. A lazy Susan filled with sour cream and chives, horseradish, and nubs of gefilte fish on colored toothpicks was on the butcher block table along with some half-filled bottles of Manischewitz. She stepped on the pedal of the garbage pail and groaned, seeing my damp pants and shoes. "Leonard, darling," she said, waving. I tried to kiss her. *"Don't!"* she yelled, covering her mouth. "You'll catch my strep throat. We have an epidemic in Mamaroneck. How do you like this crazy weather? Trust me, we'll have snow for *Pesach.*"

I was startled at how pale she was—her skin looked as colorless as fluorescent light. She had freckled bags under her eyes and her minklike hair was brushed into a crooked part down the center of her scalp. It seemed to me that her washed-out gray eyes had moved closer together. Her nails were longer than a stripper's.

"Delilah said you found him. That must've been awful."

"I can't get over it. It was like not having any air to breathe." She reached up and smoothed my collar. "I called 911, but it didn't matter. The poor thing was already among the dead when the paramedics came running in. It was a difficult few months; you cannot imagine how he had changed. Now, maybe your father and I can get some sleep. Come then, let's find him. You know what a worrier he is. He's probably convinced some terrorist's hijacked your plane."

Everyone was downstairs in the finished rec room. Standing clumsily in the doorway, I felt like a piece of furniture. Delilah, in designer paratrooper clothes and turquoise aviator glasses, crouched by the ancient Betamax, flipping through tapes. She blew me a kiss. I worked my way through the family and neighbors, accepting their sympathies, dodging questions about my job and social life. My father was sitting on the black Naugahyde love seat with Sylvia, a magazine rolled in his hand. She was opening a pack of Salems. A hoop of blow-dried hair fell into her eyes when she reached for a lighter on the petrified-wood coffee table. She held the cigarette as if it were a joint.

"What can I tell you, Lenny?" my father said, his voice rising. "When Zolly stopped eating smelts and herring two years ago I could read the handwriting on the wall perfectly."

"You could?" I said.

"Of course he could," Sylvia insisted.

He nodded at us, remembering the past two years. Steam from the kitchen had descended the stairs and spread like a soggy blanket over the crowded room. Heat rose from the ducts on the carpeted floor. A trio of men in herringbone overcoats came down the stairs. Each of them carried a pot of poinsettias on a plastic tray. My mother was making shame-shame with her fingers to a woman in a frosted hairdo with faint blue streaks flowing from the center of it. My father went to greet the men bringing in the plants.

I motioned for Sylvia to stand up. "Where're the twins?" I asked, putting my arms around her. She had always been a knockout, the most popular girl in her class from grammar school on. She'd lost weight since I'd last seen her, and small wrinkles, almost like embossed coins, had erupted at the corners of her mouth and eyes.

"They're spending an extended spring break in Delray Beach— at Bruce's parents' condo," she said, lighting another cigarette. "They don't need this at ten years old."

I glanced sideways at the bay window; the snow had stopped and the bottom of the sky was dimpled by the rising moon. People plodded across the front yard. "I miss him," I said.

She muffled a cough. "I've forgotten him. I mean, how often did we have anything to say to each other? He paid no attention to Delilah or me; you were the only one who was special to him. I don't think he said more than hello and goodbye to me since I went away to college. He acted like he was on Valium."

"Don't sound so bummed-out, Syl," I said derisively. "I'm the only one who had any time for him. I shared things with him. You and Delilah were always off somewhere."

Her eyebrows lifted. "Just be thankful he wasn't leashed to some fucking machine for another year," she said. "Or being fed through a gastric tube. That would have freaked you and Daddy out for good. I know you'd love for me to go through the motions of grief, but I deal with this kind of family crap all the time."

"My, my," I said. "Haven't we gotten terribly cynical in middle age?"

She laughed, her eyes glinting, and kissed my lips. "Can you blame me? Oh, don't be so serious, Lenny. By the way, speaking of family crap, have you heard from what's-her-name?"

"I bump into her at the library occasionally. She's engaged to an orthodontist from Highland Park."

"I never warmed up to her," Sylvia said, her shoulders slumping. She ran her fingers through her curls. "Zolly said she was some hot dish; he called her your tootsy. Jesus—I can remember when he used to call *me* a floozy. He said her knockers could drive a man crazy. All your babes turned him on."

An old woman came over and seized my hand. "Aunt Frieda?" She gave me the once-over and turned to Sylvia. "How do you like that? He doesn't even recognize me." She pinched my cheek and asked her, "Did you ever see such a handsome face?" Sylvia shook her head no, and Frieda waddled off.

When Sylvia went to get a drink, I maneuvered myself through the milling relatives, making my way to Aunt Goldie, my father's sister, who was sprawled on the corduroy chesterfield with the scroll-like arms and the lavender doilies fastened to its back. Her pink-fringed slip showed over her bruised knees, and her feet were wrapped in Ace bandages. She was holding a magnifying glass and fanning herself with Zolly's obituary. My parents stepped behind me like a team of mountain climbers.

"How're you feeling, Goldie?" Her neck looked swollen.

"Don't ask, *boychik*," she shouted in a tinny voice.

"Goldie takes what, Ben," my mother asked, "ten medicines a day?"

"At *least* ten," he said, counting with his blunt fingers.

I followed my father's back as it disappeared into a crowd of relatives. Cousin Helen, Goldie's daughter, waved at me from the wet bar. Helen had once been a shapely woman. Now her legs were as thick as logs and clusters of veins ran in her shins like Roman numerals. Jed, Helen's husband, blocked my father's path. They squared off for a moment as if they were going to spar, then embraced. Jed had a flowing beard like Moses and could've passed for a biker.

My mother and Goldie started talking about me as if I weren't there. "Zolly used to take Lenny to the history museum and Hayden Planetarium," Goldie said. "They loved going on the rides."

"The museum's not the same as Coney Island," I said.

"How Lenny used to love his pot roast and *kasha*," she said, ignoring me. "Just like my father. He was such a bashful man."

"Are you starting to cry?" my mother asked, searching Goldie's puffy face.

"Yes," Goldie said. "I mean no. I cried plenty already."

"Please, Goldie. Don't start up again. And for your information, my Leonard was a picky eater. Helen was the decent eater."

"But Zolly," Goldie said proudly, her hair wild with grief, "may he rest in peace, was a wonderful eater. What a loss."

At my back I heard ice cubes rattling and fierce breathing. "Guess who?" my father thundered. He handed me a glass of cream soda.

Sitting in a wheelchair was my Uncle Mickey, Zolly's youngest brother. His legs were bundled in a woolen afghan and his hands were twisted in his lap like frozen mittens. On his swollen feet were penny loafers cut open near the front for his gout. He was wearing tiny earphones plugged into a Sony Walkman.

"Say hello," my father said, jingling change in his pocket.

"I don't need coaching," I said.

"Mickey," my father yelled, "it's your nephew." He squatted down and pulled Mickey's torso around in the wheelchair. Then he yanked the earphones out of his ears and I heard Johnny Mathis singing "Chances Are." Mickey looked baffled. I kneeled down and kissed his cheek; his breath reeked of smoked fish.

He touched my wrist with trembling fingers and grinned; there were shreds of pipe tobacco on his blackened molars. "My brother wasn't active in the *shul,* but he was a regular person, a good mixer. He never missed *Gunsmoke.*"

"Mickey," Goldie shouted, waving her cane in his face. "My rheumatism is killing me today."

My father whispered in my ear, "You look bushed. Go take a shower and unwind."

"I'd just like to talk," I said wearily. "In private."

He blinked and poked my chest with his index finger. "After twenty years you're in a hurry to talk? After supper we'll go see Zolly and then we'll talk, just you and me. Okay?"

After showering and shaving and staring at the cracked fossil posters still tacked to the wall above my old desk and built-in bookcase, I lay on the hooked rug and meditated in the dark. After only a few minutes my metrical breathing grew shallow as my ex's naked behind impinged upon my centering exercises. I recalled my yogi's guidance on how to focus a wandering consciousness and tried to project myself onto a deserted Alaskan glacier. I wanted to masturbate but was terrified one of my aunts would blunder into my room in search of a toilet.

When I told Zolly I was going to major in paleontology—I was a sophomore at Washington University—I felt sure he would be delighted. Instead, he started calling me one of the *Luftmenshen*—men who talk in the air, who don't have their feet planted firmly on the ground. It turned out much to my surprise that he had always wanted me to go into business with him and my father, or if that wasn't my cup of tea to at least become a doctor or a lawyer and make a good living. He seemed disheartened when I told him what my academic advisor had told me: that studying the past was, in the purest sense, an effort to uncover something lost in ourselves, a chance to literally walk in the footprints of all our ancestors. "Another one lost in the clouds," Zolly said, shaking his head. "I thought I had *already* taught you that a Jew without a lot of history isn't a Jew worth knowing. Now it's time to behave like a grown man." He left phone messages for me in my dorm requesting that the "*Luftmensh*" call back at his convenience. When he and Manya went on vacations—to Las Vegas, to Hot Springs, Arkansas, to Miami Beach every February, to Israel in 1973 (I was doing graduate work in Minneapolis by then), a few weeks after the Yom Kippur War—he addressed letters and postcards from *Yad Vashem* and *Masada* and the Eden Roc Hotel to the "*Luftmensh*," care of my department. When I grew to lament a working life spent ruminating about the black hole of extinction, he had no easy advice to give me, and said that loss was what life was all about.

It had pained him when my ex and I split up. He told me he thought she was a girl who seemed fairly crazy about herself, and that he liked immodesty in a woman. She was built like Cher, with glowing copper hair and large calico eyes primed to soar out of her face. She taught Russian and mail-ordered her clothes from an L.A. boutique. It blew me away when I found out that he'd been sending her perfume and flowers and plants—My Sin and black-eyed Susans and droopy philodendrons—every few weeks after we'd started dating. Around her he was vain, like a boy flexing his muscles. He taught her pinochle and casino and warned her about the diseases carried in nonkosher foods, in shellfish and pork. She was charmed by what she called his Old World manners. He flattered her, and she flirted with him, feeding on his admiration.

My ex moved out of our lakefront townhouse two springs ago. I was on my way to a conference at the Smithsonian, and she was helping me pack. We were in the laundry room, folding underwear and rolling socks, when she suddenly announced that she felt trapped by my needs, sealed in coarse sand like one of my fossilized Gobi Desert lizards, petrified skeletons so small they could fit in your hand. She sounded furious when she told me how intense I was, and how bullied that had made her feel. She said I needed to be more laid-back, that I wasn't a fair listener. When I reminded her of how she'd come home from departmental meetings so wired and bloated that only a belt of Maalox and a Xanax could calm her down, she broke down in sobs and had a migraine that lasted for the next two days. Finally, I was able to persuade her to see a marriage counselor, but the one she chose—a fish-eyed, cigarillo-smoking social worker whose campus office was filled with jazzy punk-art magazines and fluffy Amish pillows—traded snide, confidential-feminist lingo with her. She used the words "lifestyle" and "gendered" and "personality disorder" in every sentence. When my ex told her there was something wanting in me—that I spent more time thinking about the pathological conditions in long-extinct organisms than I spent thinking about her—the therapist concluded that I was paranoid and phobic because I was more interested in dead things than living ones. Still, it was her clinical opinion that couples who split up needed closure, and they could find that by remaining caring friends. When I told Martha that, she couldn't stop laughing. The day I got tenure my ex and I went out to dinner at her favorite Indian restaurant, and when I awoke the next morning with heartburn and the runs, she was gone.

Zolly appeared at my door one evening about a week later—less than twelve hours after I'd told him over the phone that my wife and I had separated. He'd flown to Chicago without telling anyone, in order to find out firsthand what had happened to my marriage. "Just like that?" he said, when I told him she had left without even leaving me a note. "On the spur of the moment? What's wrong with her?"

"Why the hell not? She's a very contemporary woman."

"What did your parents say?" he asked gravely.

I lowered my voice. "I haven't told them yet."

"Be calm, these things work out. Lousy times are to be expected in any marriage. You need to find a rabbi to talk to."

"A rabbi? *Please*—don't make me laugh."

He hesitated. "What do you want from life, Lenny?"

"Nothing," I said, miserable.

"Then I'm not surprised this happened."

To save face, I suddenly invented another man.

He grabbed my shoulder. "Were you mean to her? I pray to God you don't have any problems pulling your weight in the bedroom?"

I shook my head. "Christ—if anything, she liked a little rough stuff. She just said she needed space, that she wanted to meet new people. She said we were getting boring."

He looked glum. "Boring? This is *eppes* some explanation! So she makes like a tomboy and monkeys around with a different fella? You weren't two-timing her, were you? I told you a husband can't ride two horses with one behind."

"That goes without saying," I said, suddenly dismayed that I *hadn't* cheated on her.

"Lenny—I wish you would have had children."

"Knock it off, okay? Are you trying to make me feel worse?"

"Your father would know what I'm driving at. We want to pass things down to another generation—I don't know, wisdom, tricks, even money if we're lucky enough to have saved some."

"There are certain things you just have to accept, Zolly. Thank God she hadn't wanted any children yet. Imagine the headache *that* would have created."

"Well, it makes *me* feel terrible that you don't have your own family. I don't get it. I wish she would explain it to me."

"More than likely she would, but please don't ask her to."

"I taught you to never leave a mess, didn't I?"

I shrugged pitiably.

Zolly stayed in Chicago for a week. He paced around the house for a couple of days, drinking Lipton's tea and reading the draft of a paper on the eohippus—a fossil horse from the early Eocene epoch—I was planning to deliver at the Field Museum. I used some free passes I had won in a departmental Super Bowl pool and took him to a Bulls game on Sunday afternoon. He polished off a couple of Polish sausages and slept soundly during the entire second half and overtime. For weeks I'd had reservations at the Cape Cod Room of the Drake Hotel for my ex-wife's thirty-seventh birthday. The night before he left we went there for dinner. Zolly wasn't all that impressed with the service. Our waiter, a fussy young man in a dark maroon jacket, looked steamed when Zolly asked him if the shrimp cocktail and turbot were fresh. Afterwards we saw Dustin Hoffman in a revival of *Death of a Salesman* at the Goodman Theatre with the tickets I'd bought to surprise my ex. Zolly kept whispering to me in the theater that guys like Willy Loman were *shnooks* who got exactly what was coming to them.

When I came downstairs it was past seven and an argument had erupted between Uncle Micah, my mother's younger brother, and Uncle Serge, my father's older brother, a blowhard in a waxed flattop who had a nose and mouth shaped like wire pliers. After a few minutes everyone jumped into the debate, citing newspaper and magazine articles they'd seen or heard about, quoting the opinions of celebrated professors and pundits remembered from *Meet the Press* and *Face the Nation* and *MacNeil, Lehrer.* Before I sat down, Serge demanded to know if I sympathized with the PLO.

I told him I thought the West Bank dilemma was hopeless, but that the diplomats were working night and day on it.

"Working on it my ass. You're an educated man, and that's all you got to contribute on the subject?"

I nodded feebly.

"They hate the Israelis in Washington," he shouted. "And the news guys, they're even worse. A bunch of self-hating Jews like that Robert Novak character."

"Don't holler so much, Serge," my father said. "Nobody in their right mind wants another war in the Middle East."

"Ha! The goddamn State Department is pure Ivy League. You think those Yalies want us in their country clubs eating whitefish and *bialys*? The crazy Arabs won't be happy until they throw every last one of us into the sea. Even Zolly knew that."

"Serge—are you speaking for the Arabs now, too?" Uncle Micah said. "Or for yourself?"

My mother had had enough food catered to feed a dozen grieving families: slabs of brisket and breasts of veal, casseroles of potato *kugel* and stuffed derma, side dishes of wax beans and sauerkraut. Sylvia and Bruce had left to go see a movie in town. A place had been reserved for me between Delilah and Ginger, her new boyfriend. Ginger worked in a drug-rehab center and wore a three-piece suit and a braided ponytail.

I smiled and looked down. Circles of fat swam in the sour red-cabbage soup. "Can someone pass me the salt?" I said.

"Salt," Goldie cried, "is bad for your blood pressure. It ruins whatever decent metabolism you got."

"What isn't bad for you nowadays?" my mother asked.

"Are you aware, Lenny," Goldie bellowed, "that your Zolly was the first man in his line to hire colored people? All the *shvartzers* loved him."

"Papa took nothing for granted," my father said. "He thought of the future. He was a pioneer in his business."

"He should be in the *World Book*, if you ask me," Cousin Milo said. Milo had flown in from Chicago only a few hours before I had.

"What a story," Serge said. "You make him sound like Albert Schweitzer. He was loaded, he could afford to be a big shot."

"He struggled and worked his *tochis* off," my father said, pointing his finger at Serge. "Show some respect for a change."

"He was too good for this world," Goldie said, sobbing.

Uncle Mickey smacked his lips over a bowl of *shtchav*. He made noises in his throat like a dog coughing up a bone.

"I'm not bad, but my brother was some pincher," Aunt Frieda said, showing everyone her thick hand. "He had strong fingers like a kosher butcher."

"I had a little clothing store on the corner of Hoe Avenue and

East 173rd Street," Uncle Moe, Goldie's husband, said. He was smearing white horseradish on a slice of *challah*. Moe was shaped like a cello—he had an enormous behind and a thin neck. His fuzzy eyebrows were like caterpillars. "I knew just how to take in Zolly's pants, how he liked his cuffs should fall. He hated too much starch in his shirts. It gave him a rash under the arms. All the time we lived with him and Manya he never raised the rent on us. Never even a dime. And he was quite famous for being a heavy tipper at the big Chinese restaurant on Southern Boulevard. The Chinamen all called him Mr. Zolly."

Serge dropped his knife and fork and laughed. "Spare me."

"*Please*—enough already, Serge," my father said.

Serge's face and crown glistened with sweat; his fingers were laced across his big stomach. "Don't boss me around, Benny. You forget I'm your older brother."

"You just don't want to hear any of this," my father said.

"Honey, tell them how handy Zolly was with a screwdriver," Goldie said to Uncle Moe.

Serge threw his napkin on his plate and left the table.

"Serge—I wouldn't trust that louse with a crummy nickel," Leo Epstein said. He was Mickey's brother-in-law, my deceased Aunt Ida's brother. "Gussie, you went and married a real *momzer*." Leo's cataracts looked like panes of frosted window-glass.

"Ben," my mother said gently, "go say something to your brother."

"Say what? I don't have to tolerate such foolishness from him. For more than fifty years he's resented his father and me and Goldie. The hell with him."

Aunt Gussie leaned over her plate and waved her hand at my mother. "Bernice—must I tell you that with Serge everything's a production?"

"People are people, darling," Moe said. "Nothing adds up."

"I'm tired of being the one in the middle of everything," my father said, glowering at everyone.

He told my mother he had no room for cake and ice cream, and asked her to save him some *rugalech*. "I'm taking Lenny for a ride," he said, tossing me my parka, and we started for the door.

Once outside, my father put on a pair of black earmuffs. I turned around to look at him, but his face had disappeared into the collar of his dove-gray topcoat. He made harsh grunting noises behind me and slipped on the ice. Rock music—"Born in the U.S.A."—blared from down the street. He pointed to the garage. "Let's take the Bonneville," he said. "The heater doesn't work so well anymore in the Cutlass. Here, take these. You drive for a change." He handed me his rabbit's-foot key ring.

The funeral home was a three-story, umbrella-shaped building linked by tunnels to a limestone pavilion full of tubbed bonsai trees and glaring cobalt floodlights. Con Edison repair crews were digging in the Boston Post Road; twisted cable lay everywhere. The neighborhood around Besser's had changed in the past few years. All the residential side streets were named after poets. Goldlake's Delicatessen was gone, as were the Rexall Drugstore and Robard's soda fountain. Driving there we passed The House of Tahiti, a pagoda-shaped Polynesian restaurant on the site of the demolished Knights of Pythias lodge. Flanking the mortuary was a Century 21 franchise and a Subaru-Isuzu dealership.

I backed the car into a diagonal space between an El Dorado and a hearse with lace curtains on its windows. My father went around to the trunk and checked the bumper and tailpipes. He pulled his gloves off with his teeth and kicked snow off the tires.

"I didn't hit anything," I said. "I hardly recognize the place."

He stood up. "Mamaroneck's a regular city now; you can't expect to see it all in one trip." His face glowed in the jagged beams of the floodlights; his collar was spiky with snow. Down the street a neon sign flashed the time and temperature from the wall of a Pier 1. "Zolly called this the Jewish section of town since he got his lox and sable at Goldlake's."

Inside, my father scribbled our names in a spiral ledger open on a rosewood secretary, as if we were visitors instead of immediate family. The place was decorated in solid shades of brown and gold, and smelled of soggy cigars and cologne. The odor of wilted flowers lingered in the air. "*Flowers* in a Jewish funeral home?" I said.

He shook his head. "Nothing's the same anymore."

We threaded our way through several dozen mourners grouped

around a silver coffin and a wailing family. We passed three gray-faced men in overcoats talking casually in front of a room filled with caskets, as if they were merely browsing. A barrel-chested man wearing soft shoes and a knitted *yarmulke* appeared out of a stairwell and directed us to an elevator whose walls were lined with velvet drapes. "Sunrise, Sunset" funneled through the concealed speakers.

Zolly's coffin was beneath three chandeliers dangling from parallel crossbeams. It was moored like a kayak on stilts. My father walked over to the heating vent and waved his hand in front of it, making sure that warm air was coming out.

I drummed my fingers on the coffin lid. "Do you mind if I open it for a minute?"

He took a deep breath. "Serge was out of town yesterday when I bought the coffin. I know he'll make a stink about it. He's not happy unless he makes a federal case out of everything."

"Screw Serge," I said. "He's not the Gestapo."

He shook his head. I opened the coffin. Zolly's head lay on a light blue pillow. He was closely shaved, and his face was powdered pink. His hands were dry and chalky; there was a speck of dirt beneath his left thumbnail. On one arthritic finger, almost smothered in hair, was his wedding ring. He had on his tortoiseshell wire-rim bifocals, and was dressed in his royal blue sharkskin suit, black suspenders, and the nut-brown tie dotted with tiny gold seahorses that I'd bought him for his birthday many years before. I leaned down to kiss his cheek; it was cold.

"Christ. Sometimes I wish it was thirty years ago," I said, looking over my shoulder at my father.

"It won't ever be thirty years ago, Lenny."

"I just wanted you to know how I was feeling."

He nodded. "And besides, what makes you think it was such a picnic then? You were a kid, what did you know? Your life is someplace else now, but we've all had a lot of time to get used to Papa's death, watching him waste away on us the past year or so. He'd sit around in front of the TV and drift. He hated his useless body, Lenny. He had the works: kidney and prostate trouble, bleeding colitis, even a bum ticker. It's funny, but I would have figured him for a killer stroke, or the big C. Someone dying of old age can put a family through the wringer, take my word on it. I only thank God he didn't have a bad case of Alzheimer's on top of everything else. I feel terribly responsible for some reason, like I should've done something."

"You shouldn't blame yourself," I said, closing the coffin. "You were a good son. Take my word on that."

He made a sour face. "It'll be a relief when we get him in the ground tomorrow."

"I read the will before dinner," I said. "It surprised me."

He sat down on the mourner's bench and pressed his fists against the padded cushion as if to propel himself. He leaned toward me a little. "Can I ask you what you're going to do with all your loot? First—follow my advice and find somebody you can trust. Those investment guys can take you to the cleaners."

"What loot?"

He smiled and scratched at a mole beneath his eye. "*What loot?*" he said mordantly. "How come everything's a question with you? Papa left his entire estate to you, including his portion of the business. We're full partners now. I want your honest input, Lenny. I'm seriously thinking of merging with another line of bakeries. I've already fielded serious offers. We'll be a chain, like McDonald's."

I was flustered. "You must be kidding? I mean, the will simply said I got whatever he owned, and I just assumed he had a few dollars stowed away and maybe some life insurance. I thought you automatically got his share of the company. I'll write it over to you— it's all yours as far as I'm concerned. All I heard growing up was how you two busted your rear ends for years and barely managed to break even. How the overhead was crushing and the profits went into machinery, medical insurance, and the pension plan. Jesus—is there anything else I should know?"

He flushed and ran his hands through his hair. "I make no bones about it, Lenny. I worked like a bloody horse, six days a week, sometimes sixteen hours a day. Not like some men I know with soft jobs and big paychecks. Most people break their asses for nothing all their lives. We're not a wealthy family, but I'm not ashamed of being comfortable. I've earned it."

I could see snowflakes swirling into the parking lot. For a moment I wondered if he thought *I* was ashamed of him. He went over to the window. The moonlight shone through the slatted blinds and lay in curved stripes across his chest. I suddenly felt anxious, as if I were on display, and had a crazy notion that Zolly was watching my reaction from inside the coffin, through a one-way mirror, like the kind they have in police shows.

He pivoted about gracefully. "I'm sure you remember Zelig Fuchs, Papa's cousin? He lived in Mount Vernon when you were a boy."

I nodded. "The fat cop? He's the one who had all those Dalmatians running around his backyard. He must be a hundred years old by now."

"Close, Lenny. Zelig's way up in his nineties. He's a filthy rich ex-cop now, he lives like a sheik on a golf course in Boca Raton. He was a homicide detective, a powerful lieutenant with serious connections. We used to call him a fixer. Papa's business—the small bakery on Tremont Avenue he ran with Mickey—was going under, and with Zelig's influence he was able to get a big loan when the banks turned him down. Certain agreements had been made. He welcomed this opportunity, Lenny; he was ready to take advantage of a chance to get ahead of the game. In those days *nobody* could afford to be idealistic. You do a *shmear* to get a *shmear*. When Papa had some trouble paying back the vigorish, he drove a truck for Zelig's friends and smuggled whiskey and molasses in from Quebec."

"What's the score?" I said. "How much are we talking about?"

He held his arms out. "A nice bundle, kid. Six figures, never mind the business, plus some beachfront property in Miami Beach and a thick pile of Israeli bonds."

"This is great," I said. "The family will think we rooked them out of Zolly's money. Who else knows about this?"

He made a harsh, throat-clearing noise. "Don't worry, Serge always talks like he's piss-poor; he'll sic his army of fancy ambulance chasers on us. There's no way that bastard won't contest the will."

I closed my eyes for a moment and felt my heart knocking about like a cornered bird inside my chest. My hands were clammy, and I was afraid I was on the verge of an anxiety attack. "I can't deal with this," I said, rubbing my forehead. "My grandfather in Dutch with the shylocks, running errands for bootleggers and crooked cops. It's unbelievable."

"Believe it," he mumbled, dropping his eyes.

"Why was I kept in the dark about all this? Didn't you try to convince him that his will would cause trouble between you and Serge?"

He was looking off into space; his flannel shirt was stained with perspiration. "C'mon—what's done is done; it's all in the past now. Papa doesn't need me defending him. He was a generous man and it was fortunate he had something for us to fall back on. Be proud of him, Lenny; what matters most is how much he loved you. There are things in our life—mine and Zolly's—that are none of your business. Why do you want to open old wounds?"

The skin on my skull was so tight I had trouble blinking. "Because I want to know the whole truth, that's why," I said.

He squinched his face and patted the air between us. "The whole truth, is it?" he said nervously. "Well, there are two reasons why I didn't mind that he left everything to you. First, for starters, there's no law against it. And second, it made him happy, it's what *he* wanted. Serge can go to hell as far as I'm concerned. As for Zolly's days smuggling booze and running with racketeers, he wished that part of his life be kept a secret. Despite what you may think, he was a tyrant, and he treated your grandmother like she was his maid. He always wanted his way, and no matter how much money he made it was never enough to make him feel secure. For sixty years he acted like he couldn't afford a shoeshine. All his life Zolly griped that the competition was breathing down his neck, trying to knock him out of business. He had a closed mind and was always climbing all over my back. He smothered me, and for a long time I hated him. You always put him on a pedestal, and he adored you for it. It's taken me a lifetime and many disappointments to realize that fathers are not above the weaknesses of their children."

He paused to blow his nose into a monogrammed handkerchief. I

went over to the window and watched a pair of crows bathe themselves in the snow on a burled telephone pole. He started talking
again, this time in a measured, subdued tone—about the risks Zolly
had shouldered in order for our family to grow and prosper—and
I couldn't shake the feeling that my father wished he were talking about *me*, as if I were the one who had died and left behind a
past richer and more daring than the timid and ordinary life I had
always led.

"We're driving Papa to the cemetery tomorrow," he said. "A rabbi's going to say *Kaddish* over him. I want you to join us at the *shul*
first."

"What for?" I said. "The last time Zolly went to temple was for
Delilah's *Bas Mitzvah*. He used to tell me that the God of Abraham
and Isaac was like a blind umpire calling balls and strikes."

"Grow up," he said, his voice lowering. "You know nothing of
the world's compassion. Everything is so belittled in your way of
looking at things. You're not doing this for Papa, but for me."

"I can't—it's a sham," I said. "It wouldn't feel right."

"You were always such a bad sport," he said, a shadow of disgust
crossing his face. "I blame my father for that."

On the way out of the funeral home he told me I should look at
the pile of clothes Zolly had left. When a blast of cold air hit me I
panicked and stumbled; something hard melted in my will. I felt
like a little boy, the snow frigid against my pants. He helped me up
and whistled slowly, checking my face for bruises. I told him in a
shaky voice that I would accept his judgment on all matters relating
to the burial and Zolly's estate. He put his arm around my hips and
squeezed.

He began removing snow from the windshield with his bare
hands. I started the engine and put the defroster on; then I got the
ice scrapers out from under the front passenger seat. "Don't knock
yourself out," I shouted. "I'll do that."

A light fringe of snow lay like a *tallis* on the shoulders of his coat;
white steam puffed from his mouth. "Put that thing down," he said,
"and look at the stars."

An icy wind bored into my face. "It's freezing, Dad."

"I know. But tell me, Lenny. What do you see?"

I blew on my hands and studied the murky sky. "It's pretty cloudy. There's the Big Dipper, I guess. Is that Venus or Jupiter?" He threw his arms up in a pleading gesture, his palms cupped, grasping at the falling snow. "Nah, nah," he said impatiently. "I mean—what do you *see?*"

I braced myself for his pained look. "I give up. Tell me."

He pressed his hands against my ribs and tucked me under his arm. "A wonderful mystery," he whispered, pinching my cheek between his thumb and pinkie like he'd done when I was a boy.

We buried Zolly next to my grandmother in a Bronx cemetery surrounded by a wilderness of empty warehouses and vacant lots. It was almost noon before we arrived, a convoy of flatbed trailers bearing Army field artillery having slowed traffic down on the Hutchinson River Parkway to a crawl. It had snowed during the night, and the rock salt crackled under our boots as we picked our way along the pathways to their plot. The misty air tingled with the bite of winter. Two gravediggers sat on the hood of a dump truck, leafing through a *Penthouse*. The interment lasted no time at all. Outlined in a circle against the tinted bronze light, the rabbi, an arthritis sufferer with a wreath of red hair—who glided across the snow-washed ground with metal sticks, as if he were cross-country skiing—led us in the mourner's prayer, and then my father, with rime forming on his goatee and a blank expression on his pale, oval face, asked if anyone wanted to say anything. Uncle Micah choked back tears and told everyone that Zolly took people as he found them, and in his opinion *that* was a marvelous quality to have had. Uncle Micah's eyes, cloudy through his thick glasses, were bathed in clear liquid. I felt dazed, my knees buckled slightly, and for a few seconds I wanted to yield to my anxiety and flee. To keep my balance I focused on the speckled granite and cut-stone tablets, their wind-bleached Hebrew letters like brittle bones. The women were wrapped in furs and shawls, the men in black skullcaps and leather-palmed driving gloves, camel's hair and navy overcoats ballooning behind them. Moving forward in slow, plodding steps, delicately placing pebbles on the casket, the mourners were like figures in a snowy paperweight.

———

The following morning I watched the silent snowflakes settle against the skeletal trees. Defying the weather, a few of the branches were alive with buds. My face, reflected in the small, rain-streaked glass, seemed to float above the house. In the window, what appeared to be tears on my cheeks were merely beads of snow. I climbed stiffly out of bed and went across the darkened landing. I stood at the edge of Zolly's room, staring at his bed, and saw my fingernail scratches of thirty-five years ago on the walnut head-board. I entered on tiptoe and peered into the walk-in closet; it smelled of talcum and mothballs. Dead flies were hanging in a spiderweb from the ceiling, and paint was flaking off the walls. On the floor, beside his beach thongs and Weejuns, were some of Manya's hatboxes, a copper samovar, a can of Butcher's wax, a beauty parlor hair dryer, a bundle of racetrack tout sheets, and a stack of paint-by-number dinosaurs I'd done as a child. A pair of his false teeth floated in a glass of baking soda on a nightstand next to his bed. I stripped off my pajamas and stared at myself in the full-length mirror nailed to the back of the bedroom door. I looked flabby and battered, with a maze of violet stretch marks across my thickened hips and belly, patches of psoriasis, like frost, on my el-bows and knees. Zolly's smudged fingerprints on the glass were like splintered fossils petrified in quartz.

I changed into one of Zolly's long-sleeved white shirts, the collar stiff as bone, and found a paisley silk necktie and a pair of woolen argyle socks in the cedar bureau with the cut-glass knobs. From a shelf below his trousers and belts I took a pair of oxblood wing tips. Next came the suit, a vested blue Hickey-Freeman with narrow gray pinstripes and a missing button, and a wide-brimmed felt hat. When I finished, I stared somberly at my reflection in the mirror and had the eerie sensation that I was two people. My pulse was racing so fast I had trouble focusing. I stood in the silver glow of the window and couldn't shake the knowledge that Zolly's life had been superior to mine—that he had made things *happen,* provided for a family, had seized his life somehow. The realization that what little I knew about the dinosaurs was more than I knew about my own family struck me like a permanent burden, and a wave of bitterness passed over my heart. I stood there for a long time, as still as the gathering snow streaming blindly from the veiled translucent sky, and strained to hear myself make a sound like living breath flowing down a current of time—watchful, feeling as if the world were just about to turn.

There's something the dead are keeping back.
—Robert Frost

Hearts & Minds

When I was nineteen my father went out for a pack of smokes and never came back. My mother and I were in the dining room, sitting around the walnut drop-leaf table on what would have been my sister Dinah's sixteenth birthday. We were watching a news special about the hostages in Iran and licking envelopes and postage stamps for Jimmy Carter's second presidential campaign when my father left, to buy some Pall Malls, he said. He'd been drinking tequila and crushed pineapple out of a canteen while he rolled joints and lectured us about how he was all for nuking Khomeini back into the Ice Age. "We ought to jump up and smack some shit into that sorry-ass peckerwood," he said, slamming the door behind him. My mother barely lifted her head from the messy table.

After a few days she told me she had a pretty good hunch that after he had lost his shirt betting on NBA games he went and gambled away most of my college tuition money on blackjack, and was now probably overcome by feelings of remorse. As far as school was concerned, the money wasn't such a big deal to me at the time. I was a junior-to-be at the University of Florida, and though I was an above-average student I spent most of my time there hustling sorority chicks and playing five-on-five basketball in the student gym. Besides, I'd planned on working for a year or so and then backpacking in South America with my best friend Ollie for at least six months before heading back to Gainesville. Ollie's old man was a senior 747 pilot for Pan American, and he had promised that he could get us free round-trip tickets to Lima.

My mother casually brushed aside my suggestion that my father had been shanghaied by angry legbreakers. "No way, José," she said. "He's probably holed-up somewhere, feeling sorry for himself. Only bankers and oil executives are worth kidnapping. Besides, what'll we ransom for him? His Phil Ochs and Paul Butterfield albums? His Moroccan hookah?"

There were many things over the years that had baffled me about my shy, affectionate father, but chief among them I guess would be the way he struggled to cement the shattered fragments of his turbulent nature with words and phrases that often had little connection to how he had always lived his life. For some reason he got a kick out of calling himself a fatalist. "The die is cast," he'd gravely say, his blue-green eyes swimming past me, the silver roach clip my mother had sent to him for his birthday, during his tour in Vietnam many years back, tightly pinched between his nicotine-stained fingers. "There's an inevitable pattern to human existence."

As I grew older I found all this exceedingly strange, since he also avidly embraced what he called the "incongruous certainty" that the history of man was a heartbreaking chronicle of sudden, catastrophic events. When I reminded him that he never had much of a stomach for coincidence, he fired back that paradox was at the very center of his life. Clearly agitated, which he was often enough during that time, he told me that he had an insatiable craving for the absolute beginning of things—which I took to mean anything he wanted it to. Leaning down to speak to me—his pale, tremulous eyelid jumping like a goldfish, a big sweaty palm like a steam iron on the curved vertebrae of my lumbar spine—his small black morbid pupil narrowed like a mouth and sucked me in. And I would have been lost for good in there, had it not been for the sly glimmer of recognition shuffling between us—a wry glint reminding me that he knew in some discordant chamber of his foolish head that we were no more than broken shards of clay.

Breathing deeply through his long teeth and stoical smile, he told me that despite his agnosticism he actually believed in some form of religious salvation, though I know it made him feel sullen and ashamed that he couldn't account for blind chance and our family's hard luck. Once, after a long drowsy day of smoking reefer at the beach, he drove his lime-green Willys jeep through the picture window at Jordan Marsh and got slashed to ribbons. Were it not for the fast-talking paramedics lunching at the Burger King across the street, he would have bled to death on the spot. As it was, when they got to him he had no blood pressure to speak of and only a few arrhythmic pulses. They put lines in his veins and somehow managed to resuscitate him.

He was in surgery for almost seven hours, coding twice. His gut was sliced open like a melon, and the trauma surgeon labored over his exposed abdomen for most of the night, picking gritty pieces of windshield out of his liver, mesentery, and small intestine. It took more than two hundred sutures alone to close the jagged wounds in his scalp and forehead. For weeks afterward he was snugly swaddled in layers of antiseptic gauze and thick brown bandages. When I told him he walked like Lon Chaney, Jr., in *The Mummy's Curse*, he came at me with his arms extended, as if he were going to strangle me. As luck and mercy would have it, the painkillers he was on made him compliant and droll. Gaunt and hollow-eyed and loaded on codeine and Black Russians, he kept on repeating that it was *fortuitous* he had a full head of wavy hair— fortuitous that he wouldn't need to wear a wig, fortuitous that his livid scars wouldn't show.

But that wasn't the worst of it. Plowed into by an old Chinese woman driving a black Mercury convertible (we were sitting on a bench at a Coconut Grove bus stop, eating Good Humors and waiting for our father to finish his business at the bank), my younger sister Dinah and I hovered near death in Jackson Memorial's pediatric intensive care unit for almost a month. None of the doctors thought I'd pull through, but somehow I managed to survive a ruptured spleen, a lacerated pancreas, and a pair of collapsed lungs, plus multiple rib and leg and shoulder fractures, while Dinah, whose only sign of critical injury was a bloody ear and a ring-shaped bruise on her temple, suffered total brain damage. She was only seven. It was in all the South Florida papers. For three years she vegetated in a state-run rehabilitation hospital for head-injury victims, and then quietly died from respiratory and renal failure brought on by a raging fever of unknown origin. Fortuitously, at least as far as my parents were concerned, there were no machines to disconnect, no feeding tubes to detach.

My parents, Etta and Max, hadn't been getting along during the nine years since Dinah's death. They went straight from their period of mourning to one of estrangement. Instead of saying that we were sabotaged by unlucky karma—instead of simply blaming the old lady and working hard to get past it—they needed to find fault in each other. So I wasn't terribly surprised by my mother's delay in contacting the authorities about his disappearance. At that point in their marriage they mostly left each other alone. My mother pierced ears and sold bargain jewelry in a Coral Gables shopping mall. She went out to clubs with her divorced women friends and drifted toward depressed divorced men who humiliated her. My father was into peyote and jai alai. He switched jobs every few months and spawned exotic get-rich schemes; whenever he was on to something new, or sealing a fresh deal, he said he could feel himself starting to molt, his skin turning inside out. In essence, taking chances with other people's money turned him on. Though I continually worried about him, it was actually a tonic, a relief, not having him around for a brief spell. Then, after he'd been gone for almost six weeks, my mother finally relented under the weight of my pleas and called the Metro-Dade police department in order to report him as a missing person. The cop she spoke with said they didn't have the manpower or money to be hassled about marital abandonment anymore; they had more than they could handle with all the robberies and assaults and drug murders going down. He said my father would come home when he was hungry and horny. When she started cursing at him, the cop told her to write the governor a letter and hung up.

For years now I've wondered how my parents would have reacted if I had died instead of Dinah. Her death had opened up an enormous canyon between them, a chasm so vast and perilous they were unable to reach across to one another. By now I've asked myself dozens of times if anything can mitigate the sorrow of losing a child. It seems not, since everything they did and said after the accident— toward me as well as toward each other—was soured by an undercurrent of permanent bitterness. The evening after we buried Dinah, I watched them from my bedroom window as they wobbled in grief around the backyard, the oppressive, woolen air full of gray-white smoke from their cigarettes. She raised her face and said something to him, and I saw my father pull a handkerchief from his pocket and wipe the sweat from his cheeks and neck as they moved in slow motion toward each other. They paused a few feet from one another and stood in a pool of fading sunlight for a few minutes. They were so still they could have been a pair of hypnotized deer. Then slowly, and with grace, he reached out to touch her and she spun away from him, and something with the air-hammer force of the Florida heat flashed through my spine. Although it forever went unspoken between us, I knew a door had slammed irretrievably shut in our family and that they were finished with each other.

The police came over a few mornings later, after I'd twice called myself and apologized to the grumpy watch commander for my mother's short fuse and rudeness of the day before. I told him about the strain she was under, and he grunted his understanding. I had just finished my bowl of oatmeal and wheat germ, and could feel a gentle trembling in the nerves in my body as I watched her pour coffee for the detectives and then open the refrigerator door and pull out a pint of half-and-half and a can of almond macaroons. She was wearing blush and mascara and frayed cut-off jeans, and one of my father's paisley ascots was tied around her throat. She had an air about her, the defiant strut in her walk of a major-league slugger, and her skin radiated an odor I likened to wild vanilla.

The detectives had a rap sheet on my father and cited back to her his prior arrests: vandalism and trespassing, mementos from his salad days in SDS; thirty unpaid speeding or parking tickets; possession of an unregistered derringer; fencing hot stereo equipment and VCRs; battery on a Hare Krishna at the Orange Bowl during half-time of a Dolphins game.

"Sounds like a righteous citizen," the potbellied detective said, grinning at my mother. He had a bullet-shaped head and his tie needed ironing. "You think he welshed on a debt or something?"

"I wouldn't be surprised," my mother said. "He's done it before."

"Let's talk women," the other detective said, pushing up the sleeves of his plaid sport jacket. "A weasel like this always has a cookie or two stashed around somewhere."

My mother went to the sink and turned on the swan-shaped faucet with her back half turned to us. She squeezed some lemon-scented Ajax onto her palm and soaped her hands and wrists. The sun was shining in on her through the window and her face glowed in a way I had never seen before. For a moment I had a strange sensation that I had absolutely no idea who she was. "Don't be silly," she said, squinting into the circle of yellow light. "I don't care who he's planking. I just want to know where he is."

"I mean like, lady," the plump detective said, "be straight with me. Why get bent all out of shape if he isn't making off with your money or jewels? Why bother looking for him under every stinking rock in Dade? It seems to me you and your kid are better off without him."

There's no accounting for love, my mother told them.

The cops waltzed through the motions for a month, and then she hired a private investigator to find him. When she told me I was both surprised and secretly elated. It confirmed what I felt inside my skin: that she really did love him after all, and that something durable and unyielding in their life together had somehow managed to survive the calamity of Dinah's death. The detective she hired, a bruiser named Paris France of all things, made a living hunting down senile retirees in Miami Beach. She got his name from a librarian friend at the Opa-locka Public Library who had dated him a few years back and had twice employed him to find her mother in Little Havana. He worked fast and cheap, the librarian told my mother. She said he looked and talked like a Pensacola redneck, and that he played marimba and congas with a Latin jazz quintet at a popular dive called The Bay of Pigs Club, in an alley off *Calle Ocho*. I knew the place; there were topless go-go dancers in wire shark cages on either side of the slanted, strobe-lit stage. The place was usually jammed with sleek University of Miami women, lawyers and law students, bunches of seething anti-Castro Cubans in tiger fatigues and maroon berets.

We were sitting on our porch just shooting the breeze—France, my mother, and I—a spangled milky light spilling into the Everglades. He showed us the bronze St. Jude medallion around his thick neck. "The patron saint of lost causes," he explained, smiling.

France was wearing baggy camouflage pants, mud-spattered Desert boots, and a bleached denim work shirt and leather bolo tie. Squinting at us, he rolled a cheroot around in his mouth. Particles of half-chewed hamburger meat stuck in the gap between his crooked front teeth. He was supposed to be part Samoan, but his square pinkish face made me think of a boiled canned ham. He lived and worked out of a purple Winnebago with black thunderbolts painted on the fenders and roof. He said he was a jujitsu master—that he taught a course on self-defense for widows at Miami-Dade—and I noticed the calluses on the edges of his huge hands. He caught me staring at the tattoo of a striking cobra above the name *Maybelline* on his upper arm. Before I could work up the backbone to ask him where he got it he said he was with the AirCav in '65, in the bloody Valley of the Drang, and that he'd taken a round from a Chicom in his belly. He had spasms and seizures and was vomiting blood and almost died from sepsis and shock. He said he developed the peritonitis because the slopes dipped their ammo in water buffalo droppings.

"Let's get down to cases now, Mrs. Hirsch," he said, rubbing ash into the glazed periwinkle-shell ashtray in his lap. He took a calculator out of his front pocket and placed it on the wrought-iron table between us.

My mother twirled her tiny pearl dove earrings. "Well, now," she said, hugging her knees, "what would you like to know? I mean, what information do you need right off?"

"The works," he said resignedly. "I use a special technique of

thought waves to locate people. Like telepathy. So the more stuff I
know the better. It enables me to think like them."

I could tell right off he had roving eyes. She told him a few things
about my father I didn't particularly see the point in mentioning—
how he'd withheld his taxes for more than ten years and was never
audited by the IRS, his burning of hundreds of draft cards in Washington Square Park—and he told my mother she shouldn't throw
her bread down the toilet searching for a hump like my father. He
mimicked Lawrence Welk. "Uh-one-anda-two, be smart and ditch
the crazy dude."

"Thought waves my ass, man," I said, my heart racing in my
throat. "Who should she throw her bread away on then? On a turkey like you?"

France looked unfazed; he hardly seemed to be breathing. My
mother's eyes darted in their sockets and I heard the flow of tension
in her voice when she said, "Your father doesn't own me, Sonny.
And neither do you."

She looked hard and cold and I braced myself for her anger.
Instead, she glanced at France and ran her tongue over her upper
lip, her perfect front teeth showing in a teasing pout. She drew
my hand and France's together as if we were exchanging wedding rings. He offered me his tentatively. I shook it; it was bony and
very warm, like a newborn's. He fingered his plumed, ash-blonde
sideburns and tugged at his collar. France was thick-necked and
wet-mouthed and his shifty, recessed eyes were the shade of pale
watercolors.

My mother gave him a recent color Polaroid of my father. It was
taken near Cape Canaveral, in February, at a truck stop, and across
the highway was a Dairy Queen and an auto wrecker with rusty
cars and Greyhound buses up on blocks. In the photo my father
wore Ben Franklin spectacles and the diamond-like tie clasp with
the signs of the zodiac on it that I'd given him for his birthday.
Knotted in a ponytail, flaming copper hair gushed from his large
head; the ageless hippie, he called himself. When I was a boy my
father was built like a pole vaulter, thinly muscled, six-three with a
needle-straight torso. Now he was flabby and his deeply lined Slavic
face was layered in fat. The veins on the backs of his legs were as

bunched as grapes and his behind rolled when he moved. I had had a crampy feeling in my gut like the beginning of diarrhea a few minutes earlier as I watched France paw through my father's belongings. He drew his lips back when he saw the Australian bush hat and machete and Starlight Scope, the torn Vietcong flag and bayonet with the hammer and sickle on it. He asked me in a calm, impersonal voice when my father had been in Nam.

"Sixty-eight," I told him, "but he rarely talked about it. He was with the 26th Marines at Khe Sanh. If I asked him about it, he said his memory was a blank. He did his whole tour on dexedrine and hash."

"Fucking-A no-man's-land," France said, shoving some sticks of Juicy Fruit in his mouth. "That was a shit load of trouble. Everyone got whacked one way or another." France then called the war a lobotomy.

It was humid out, and the hazy evening sky simmered with mosquitoes. Opaque, lightless clouds shifted slowly along the tangerine-colored horizon. The air smelled loamy and saturated with ozone, and June bugs swarmed over the imitation Japanese lanterns bolted on either side of the front door.

"I'm a professional, Mrs. Hirsch," France said in a rich tenor voice, "and thus I'm obligated to offer you my best professional advice. Drop the foolish sentimentality and protect your interests. There are many poor bastards like your husband for whom just like that"—he slapped his hands together, crushing a glowworm—"a large part of their life is over. Don't torment yourself so much."

He looked sideways at me when he said that, and turned his pious eyes down flirtatiously. I knew what he was thinking beneath his doleful smile, but I resisted the urge to see my father as a helpless victim of his past. France had a boozer's map of broken capillaries in his cheeks, a blunt, socket-like jaw, and what looked like a surgically repaired harelip. His trained, pumpkin-colored hair was brushed flat and glistened in the razor-cut style favored by greasers. It was powdered with dandruff. A pencil with a broken point was cocked behind his ear.

"But you think you can find him, don't you?" my mother asked.

"Hey—not to worry, not to hurry," he said, smiling, and touched her back, checking, I was sure, to see if she was wearing a bra. "I'm the original good hands people. I like to keep a low profile, but I work twenty-four-hour days, Mrs. Hirsch."

"What's the deal?" I said. "Too devoted for sleep?"

"I'm an insomniac—like that guinea Sinatra."

They made small talk for about an hour—France absentmindedly jotting notes on an unlined blue graph pad, his jagged, smashed fingernails sticky with motor oil and engine gunk. He told her he liked to be paid in cash or by certified check, with some good-faith money down as a deposit; he said his current mailing address was in Pompano, care of The Randy Pelican, a motel on A1A. My mother brought out a pitcher of pink lemonade and poured a few jiggers of Cointreau into it. I was drinking seltzer with grenadine and a sprig of spearmint. You had to hand it to him; France had his *shtik* down pat. While she babbled on and on about my missing father's dismal habits and disreputable friends, he peered up at her every few seconds from his phony note-taking with dark and dreamy crocodile eyes, and he made these plaintive bubbling noises in his throat, as if he were a mourning dove or a pigeon, and sharply rattled the melting ice cubes in his glass with a snap of his hairy wrist.

She sent me back into the kitchen for the pecan brownies and Sara Lee banana-apricot cake. I stood in the doorway for a few moments before coming back outside. In the dimness I could see France leaning over her, lighting her cigarette and staring into the front of her dotted-swiss dress as she bent forward to receive the match. I saw the coral lipstick marks on the filter tip when she exhaled the smoke in jets through her nose. He turned and fixed his lizard eyes on me, as if he knew all along that I'd been watching them, and for a moment I hated my mother for having exposed us to the indiscreet probing of a depraved loser like France. I stared at her but her shameless, glistening eyes flicked past mine. My mouth was swollen and parched, my arms slack at my sides. Slumped against the door post, I was punch-drunk as a boxer out on his rubbery knees, as if a chemical keeping the oxygen working inside my brain had been drained from my tissues. She crossed her slim, moon-white dancer's legs and dangled a straw-colored wedgie on her prehensile, plum-polished toes. In this soft crystal light I was shocked by the rich voluptuous batter of her skin. As they talked I could hear the sound of a squirrel's tooth boring like an auger into the oak baseboard of the porch.

It turned out that France was a former bunko and vice cop, and he did what all the dicks on TV do: he checked out the Miami flophouses and showed my father's picture to the hookers and pawnshop owners he employed as snitches. He told my mother he would reach out to some dirtbags he knew on the street who owed him favors. I would have been shocked had he come up with a lead that way. My old man was a chiseler and a moocher, hardly a crook. He wanted to cut a stylish figure, to curry glamour, to feign a kind of off-beat, worldly splendor. It was all bluster and a diversion—he lacked the capital and connections for a serious wager. But he was always *shmoozing* hotshots who weren't afraid of taking risks. He won some diñero at the dog track and opened an antique sporting goods store that sold crossbows and flintlock fowling pieces and Bowie knives. He spent years perfecting a disposable pencil that glowed in the dark and automatically dispensed lead from its center. The sporting goods store filed for bankruptcy—he was in hock to a renegade Liberty City narc named Rocco Alcoa, but managed to square things with him somehow—and the pencil hardly dented the glutted ballpoint pen market.

In between flakey ideas he engraved mausoleums for a living, or worked as a courier for some brokerage houses downtown. He was someone who couldn't succeed at anything but who thought he could and persisted in acting as though he might. When we lived in Lower Manhattan he took me to East Broadway and Mott Street greasy spoons, and he counseled me to have the courage to trust my imagination and explore the unknown. He gloated about getting his parking tickets fixed and flirted with Ratner's saucy cashier who (he swore) tucked a loaded Mauser into her girdle. On Eighth Avenue, west of Times Square, and down by the Port Authority, he pointed out all the strip and homo and porno dumps, and told me the world was filled with dispirited and forsaken men. He took me by subway to the worst neighborhoods in the city, to the South Bronx and Bedford-Stuyvesant, the tenements like blitz-torn London, and warned me that the revolution was coming. I had no idea what he was talking about but I loved the rich swagger in his voice at those times, his piercing stare, his brisk agile stride—as if he didn't want to displace anything inside his body. Be skeptical, he always said, and take risks. Whenever one of his ventures didn't pan out—and they never did—he told me it didn't pay for Jews to trust in the Almighty.

───

While France looked for my father and diddled with my mother, I worked at my great-uncle Birdie's delicatessen. Birdie was my mother's mother's brother and he felt, I gathered, that it was his responsibility to teach his fatherless nephew how to get along in the world. When he arrived at work in the morning, an hour before we opened for breakfast, the first thing he did was check the till. Then he opened the Wells Fargo safe behind the meat counter and went over the previous night's deposit slips, reading the messages that Anthony, the night manager, had left for him. When I worked the early shift, Birdie knew he could always find me in one of the family-sized rear booths, gabbing with Ace and Holister, his two West Indian short-order men, and some of the waitresses while I ate my blueberry blintzes or corned beef hash and soft-boiled eggs. Birdie would sit and join us for a glass of hot tea and a prune Danish after he had yelled at everyone that the place looked like a pigsty and that business was down because of it. Frowning, he'd lean across the table and run the back of his warm hand over my cheeks, as if he thought I had a fever. Holister would tell Birdie that he had an Antiguan "customer" in town who demanded his constant attention, and then he'd ask him for a raise and some time off. Birdie'd make a hard swallowing sound and mutter, "Un-huh, un-huh, I wonder what she looks like," and everyone would laugh. Flicking ash from his Perfecto onto my empty butter plate, he'd flash me a look and bellow, "Sonny!" in his commanding baritone. "You need a summer shave and haircut. I don't want your beard in the white-fish salad."

My lower back was killing me and my neck ached as well, as did my damaged shoulders. I was ashen from sixteen-hour shifts. Behind the cold cuts stacked like rolled coins and the smoked salmon streaked with thin brown veins, I prepared party platters and triple-decker club sandwiches. When a parade of stoned teenagers wandered in close to midnight for knockwurst and beer, it was my job to check ID's. I catered *Bar Mitzvahs*, baby showers, and circumcisions, baked mandel bread and fruit-filled tarts and lemon poppy-seed cake, suspended rows of huge waxy salamis from the deli's oaken rafters, played five-card draw and craps on the metal stockroom floor with the staff: with those good-natured show-offs Ace and Holister and Bishop Carver (a fountain and dessert man); with Basil, the preening, six-foot-eight-inch health salad and cole-slaw man, who had fuzzy eyebrows with a flash of white in one of them and a receding fringe of graying crinkly hair, and claimed to be a tribal prince back in Sierra Leone; with Boris Foxman, the lanky Latvian frankfurter and *knish* man, who carried a tin flask of vodka in his Levis and reeked of beets and malt all the time; and with the meek though endlessly squabbling Indian and pencil-thin Thai busboys, who were taking accounting and marketing classes at Florida Atlantic. Most of my friends were gone, doing Europe for the summer or holding exciting internships with county newspapers and local businesses, or working as counselors and getting laid at the sleep-away camps they themselves had once gone to as campers. When I wanted to be by myself, I'd take my breaks in the mouse-infested cellar where Birdie kept the large, black-labeled cans of sauerkraut, Heinz baked beans, and Thousand Island dressing, and spend an hour or two in seclusion, staring dully at *Playboys* or scraping the mustard and mayonnaise tins with enormous rubber spatulas.

No matter how strained things were, nothing had managed to penetrate my illusion that love could move mountains. What else would you expect from the child of ex-radicals? At one time or another my mother had told me how they had met on Cape Cod, at a Buddhist commune just outside Provincetown, where they harvested radishes, kale, and withered onions, and studied Zen. My father during those days wore a shapeless navy-blue beret and a grubby goatee, and he fancied himself a beatnik; he was finishing a junior year internship—they called it field work—required of NYU sociology majors. A high school dropout, my mother was a precocious flower child—on the lam from her screwball parents who lived in Evanston, Illinois. Her father, an eminent though detested astrophysicist at the University of Illinois, and later at Northwestern, browbeat all his guileless graduate assistants into doing his numbing research, and then he torpedoed their postgraduate fellowships or grant applications if they refused to sleep with him. Her mother grew up in Lincolnwood, spoke Yiddish and Polish like a Warsaw native, was smart and indolent and sky-high on diet pills and bloody Marys most of the time. (When she was blind as a prairie dog and in her dotage, my grandmother told me that she'd inhale the briny scent of her father's smooth skin and lime shaving soap left on his barber's razor after he left for work in the morning and tingle all over with pleasure.) For many years my great-grandfather Zev—a one-time alderman and stickler for Chicago etiquette—had owned an acclaimed prime rib and veal chop restaurant in the Loop. It was a high-octane, old-style supper club, a swanky club notorious for its Machine and Syndicate clientele—with leggy cigarette girls and whirring ceiling fans and a bow-tied piano player in the cocktail lounge, and starched blood-red tablecloths and napkins as big as diapers on the black oak tables. There were private, smokey, cavelike party rooms upstairs.

My father shyly approached my mother in a Barnstable head shop and asked her out to a Patrick Sky concert. Photos of her from the time when I was an infant show a willowy young girl wearing baggy overalls, love beads, and black lace mantillas, with wooden clogs or sandals—leather thongs twisted into the peace sign—on her dusty, bare feet. Later she wore demin hoop skirts or bellbottoms, ladybug-tinted sunglasses, and tie-dyed pullovers with Buffalo Springfield or Iron Butterfly or The Mothers of Invention stenciled on the back, and she pinned carnations and wild camellias in her wreath of plaited titian hair. She moved into his drafty St. Mark's Place apartment a month after they were first introduced. They were the only people living in that vinegar-reeking slum who weren't either Greek or Ukrainian. I was born in a grimy bay of the emergency room at Bellevue, surrounded by nodding heroin addicts and puking derelicts from the Bowery, only hours after Alan Shepard had ridden a Redstone rocket into space. My mother was seventeen when she gave birth to me, having walked the twenty blocks to the hospital because she had no change for carfare. My father had forgotten to leave her a few bucks when he left early that morning with school friends to listen to Socialist speeches at a Union Square labor rally. He came to see both of us at the hospital later that afternoon. My mother said I was wrapped in a crocheted receiving blanket that her cousin Tasha from Chicago had sent to her, and that my father rocked me in a caned rocker for about an hour— humming Woody Guthrie tunes until I fell soundly asleep—and then off he ran to work. He made rent money playing the ocarina and Jew's harp with an Irish folk sextet at a grungy coffeehouse on MacDougal Street, down the block from Washington Square Park.

I thought of them as they were back then when I was chopping bell peppers and cabbage for salads, or boning thick slabs of belly lox, or unloading crates of cream soda. The parents of my childhood believed deeply in the healing power of faith. They memorized haiku and used bohemian expressions; we ate our meals sitting on tatami and their conversation was peppered with aphorisms from Confucius and *The Tibetan Book of the Dead*. Along with Shirley Chisholm and Jimmy Breslin they marched on Gracie Mansion in the bitter sleet to protest the exploitation of municipal hospital and sanitation employees. They left me and my sister with friends for weeks at a time and hitched south to take part in sit-ins and freedom rides. My mother always joked that my first lullabies were "We Shall Overcome" and "Kumbaya." They belonged to a Waverly Place poetry society and a Black Panther study group. The modish teak magazine rack in the bathroom of our apartment was stuffed with *The East Village Other* and *Ramparts*. When he had some extra dough—a windfall, he called it—my father took me and my

mother to hear Vaughan and Rollins and Monk and Davis at the
Village Vanguard, Dave van Ronk and Richie Havens at the Fillmore
East. (I later learned that this "windfall" came from my grandparents in South Florida—usually a fat check for one of our birthdays.)
Regardless, something happening was always on the boxy mahogany console—Les Paul and Stéphane Grappelli and Dexter Gordon,
Lester Young and Wes Montgomery smoking at the Half Note, The
Yardbirds when they had Eric Clapton and Jimmy Page. My parents
picked the phonograph up cheap (as they did most other things) at
a Sunday afternoon flea market on Delancey Street, near the Williamsburg Bridge. My grandmother, a Miami Beach sophisticate,
called them panhandlers, scavengers.

To smother the fried eggplant and goat cheese smells floating
up from the dark and dingy stairwells, my mother burned honeysuckle and hyacinth joss sticks in ruby-colored smoked-glass candlesticks, and the psychedelic living room walls in our sixth-floor
walk-up were covered at one time or another with posters of Ho
and Lenny Bruce and W. H. Auden and Country Joe and The Fish
and Diane Arbus freaks and grinning Buddhist monks in silky saffron robes smoking reefers. Stolen and overdue library books—*The
Stranger, Siddhartha, Subterranean Angels*—and anti-Klan leaflets
were scattered all over the swirly linoleum floors and blocky Salvation Army furniture. They each read a few verses of Homer or
Virgil to me before I went to sleep each night. In a battered wicker
valise there are crinkled sepia prints of me playing potsy with my
father in front of the Electric Circus, of me napping with Dinah and
Fred Astaire, our snow-white Angora, in a rusty red wheelbarrow
in Tompkins Square Park, of the four of us eating Wiener schnitzel
and Yorkshire pudding and pistachio ice cream cones at Expo 67.
When I was six they took me with them to the moratorium in
Washington and chanted mantras with Allen Ginsberg as he tried
to levitate the Pentagon.

After the Tet Offensive my father suddenly dropped out of graduate school, quit his dreary job checking facts at a publishing house
on Madison Avenue, and, while dressed in a colorful dashiki he had
shoplifted from the big Altman's over on Fifth, went downtown and

enlisted in the Marines. He arrived in Vietnam believing he could prevail over the steely hearts and minds of his fellow jarheads and persuade them to drop their M-16's and embrace the Viet Cong in a clasp of brotherhood. Instead, he became a remorseless predator and won two Silver Stars for valor and a Purple Heart for taking a frag from a mortar round in the back of his thigh.

The Brownies he sent my mother from China Beach showed a scrawny young man with a menacing Trotsky beard and a haunted gaze beneath a dark mantle of frizzy hair. He looked like a scowling and embittered conscientious objector type, one of those indignant Quakers who mopped floors at a V.A. hospital with a broom wrapped in a wet dishtowel. The background was crowded with shirtless Marines either crashing in the sand or surfing. In creased snapshots from a firebase he called the Twilight Zone he wore thick nightfighter cosmetic on his cheeks, and he had chalked *BOMB 'EM & FEED 'EM* across his helmet. His impenetrable, drugged-out eyes burned with the opiate rush of the war. We had black-and-whites of him doing push-ups and sit-ups in a giant Chinook, playing checkers and casino in his hooch, sitting on a moped beneath the silver belly of a C-130, eating raw fish and rice with his long tapered fingers in some burned-out ville in the Mekong Delta. In his steel-hardened flak jacket he carried a folded 8 x 12 full-color glossy of my mother—coiled hair like Rapunzel's in spilling blonde ropes on her pale, freckled shoulders, her chin up like a fashion model, her small breasts straining against the lacy, lilac-fringed cups of her brassiere. Where other men wore bandannas cut from camouflage parachutes, or long Comanche feathers, or baseball caps, or stuck one-eyed jacks or the ace of spades in their helmet bands, he wore a pair of my mother's mesh pantyhose around his head to protect him from evil spirits. For her birthday she received a white *ao dai*, plus a package of gloomy paperbacks—Strindberg, Schopenhauer, Dostoyevski—and a crazy note written in his large backslanting hand concerning the possibility of universal repentance and the sickness of the modern soul. In the ink-stained letters he'd written to her from Quantico after being shipped home from Vietnam, he'd only wanted to talk about spooks and apparitions and blissful hallucinations. After his discharge my parents packed up their green Valiant convertible and we moved back to Hialeah, a mile or so from where he grew up.

———

On a drizzly Sunday evening, after a typical July rush, I was preparing a carryout order when a women with a reedy, liturgical drawl asked if she could get a quart of shrimp salad and a few *bialys*. It was Zelda Klein, the mother of a couple of mop-haired kids I remembered from Hebrew school. We made some light conservation and I inquired after her sons. Her ice-blue eyes were messianic.

Five nights later she was waiting in her ebony Fleetwood for me to get off. The vanity plates said *SHALOM*. She rolled down the window and said she'd been sitting there for three hours. "The Girl from Ipanema" was on the cassette. Bracing myself, I asked, "What for?" She didn't bat an eye. She said that her husband, Ted, was in Tallahassee, on business, and opened the door for me. She was wearing a cream-colored sundress with spaghetti straps and was twisting her hair around her index finger. As I slid in beside her I had a sense of my brain swelling inside my head.

A dog started barking as we rolled onto her gravel driveway. "That's Putzi," Zelda said, "my Chow Chow. He won't bite."

The crimson clover and bougainvillea blossoms around her house needed pruning. A limestone gazebo with bird feeders was built alongside a cantilevered sundeck, and a basketball hoop sagged above the garage. She showed me where the scarlet hibiscus and Spanish moss had cascaded through the glass roof of a caved-in solarium—damage from last fall's brutal hurricane. I followed her into the house. Putzi came over for a scratch. He emitted a nasty mackerel smell and had gentle tan eyes. The living room was furnished with matching nutmeg chesterfields and glass-fronted bookcases filled with atlases and dog-eared dictionaries and encyclopedias, with terra cotta planters and table lamps whose opaque shades reminded me of dragonfly wings. On the glossy maple floors were ribbed cotton durries Zelda said she'd found in a New Delhi bazaar.

A pair of braided-nickel candlesticks holding white Sabbath candles were on a cherry credenza. We stood kissing in her darkened bedroom for a couple of minutes. She made a laughing noise in her throat when our teeth clicked together, and unhooked my belt. After undressing she knelt beside me and pushed my head down between her knees. My shoulder muscles were so tense they felt on the verge of cramping. Her fingers drilled into my neck. She was high-waisted and bony; fine, scroll-like veins crawled up her thighs. I felt so swollen with desire that I forgot to breathe for a minute and lost my erection. She rolled away from me like a pro wrestler coming out of a hammerlock and rested on one elbow, stroking my stomach. There were off-yellow scallops of crimped skin beneath her jaw, roughened pouches beneath her eyes.

"I don't know what's the matter with me," I said mildly.

She turned on an overhead recessed light and squatted over me, fishing a pack of L & M's and a book of cocktail lounge matches from a black satin purse. A sickle-shaped cord of old surgical stitches curved halfway around her ribs. Her blood-red fingertips whitened as she pressed on the edge of the night table. A book on biorhythms was open on its spine. She shifted slightly and a gold locket swung like a tiny pendulum between her flushing breasts.

"You must think I'm a real cock teaser," she said, holding the cigarette like a joint.

"I don't think that," I said, feeling edgy.

"Oh treasure, you probably don't even know what it is."

The smoke made me suddenly light-headed. I moved clumsily and fell across her calves. "Anything busted?" I asked, trying to make a joke out of it.

She made another noise in her throat and eased her weight from her hip to her belly. A small, jagged ligament pulsed gently in her neck. I touched her thin biceps; her smallpox vaccinations reminded me of tiny etched skulls.

"Have you ever been seduced by an older woman?" she said softly, and ran her tongue over her front teeth, licking some particles of tobacco from her lips. Her naughty eyes were full of mischief.

I shook my head, *No.*

"It's not really my style, that is, wooing virile young men into my seamy marriage bed," she said. A bright crescent of lip gloss ringed her mouth. "I just thought I'd pretend I was Anne Bancroft in *The Graduate* for the evening. You catch my drift?"

I caught nothing at the moment, either of her drift or anything else, but since I didn't want to appear like a dimwit I made a kind of chesty, congested grunt and nodded so emphatically I was sure she thought I knew exactly what she was talking about. She returned my nod with one of her own and slid a whiskey-flavored thumbnail into my mouth. Our noses were so close together I could smell the stale reek of Sunday's seafood salad on her breath. I angled my thighs so she couldn't see my erection coming back. She rolled over again, fingers resting against my leg, and told me her story: Ted's numerous infidelities, her chronic anxiety and panic attacks, their mutual addiction to laxatives and Miltown, her botched hysterectomy. A Dixie cup filled with pills was on the night table, along with an antique rotary phone.

"I was so easy at your age," she said. "Ted said I reminded him of Rita Hayworth and I melted on the spot." She said he had seduced her simply by saying that with her shoulder-length, fluffed-out red hair and pinup body she looked like Hayworth in *Gilda*.

"I missed that one also," I said.

"Never mind," she said. "I bet Max never told you we used to make it in high school."

I shrugged. "Oh yeah? He told me everything about his life but he never told me that."

"Well, there you are. Sex was the only thing between us. We climbed all over each other in my daddy's Galaxie. Your father was a great bullshitter. Every new song or book he liked was labeled groundbreaking, and if he didn't care for it he said it was mush, or trivial, or decadent. He was always talking about being on a quest for something he called 'the truth.' Max had absolutely no tact; your grandparents had spoiled him rotten. He went around with this superior, asinine expression on his face, and if he didn't get his way he'd sulk for days."

"He's run away," I said. "I think he's gone for good."

"That sounds like him. He always had a talent for disappointing people. It must break your mother's heart." I could hear the gloom and neglect in her voice.

"Maybe he's just crazy. Maybe he can't help himself."

"That's too convenient. I have cancer. Here, I'll show you." She nestled against me and put my thumb to her breast and had me caress the hard knot where her breast and armpit joined. Her hair had drab ash-colored lights; it was graying above her ears. "There are malignant floaters, diseased tissue, growing inside my chest wall now," she whispered.

"I'm sorry," I said dully, and felt stupid after I said it.

She was squinting at the open skylight above our heads. "After my first operation the nurses came around every few hours and checked my vital signs. They woke me up in the middle of the night and in the early morning to record them. Whenever I asked them if I was going to be all right they'd say my vital signs were stable. That's how you know if you're going to survive. My life was falling apart, my husband couldn't stand to touch me, but I was a regular Rock of Gibraltar. Everything was fine until a few weeks ago. Who'll want me after the surgeon's finished this time?"

Moonlight streamed through a gap in the blinds. I started to say something but she put her hand over my mouth. "I've never had anything of great importance in my life," she said, "and now I'm going to croak before I'm fifty. You know, many of my friends are actually quite happy. It's amazing, isn't it, people actually being happy? God—I must sound like a wretch."

"What does it matter?" I said softly. I felt worn out from the strain of whispering.

"It all matters, Sonny. Only young people invest in nihilism. It *all* absolutely matters. You know, I would have thought Max Hirsch would have had it together by now. Money, cars, the whole bit."

"My mother thinks the war drained something out of him, out of both of them," I said, feeling it all start to come loose in me. "That's why they came back home. She said he needed to be in a place that appreciated the creative spirit. They believed that anything was possible in Florida."

Her cigarette was poised above my face. She sighed with her

mouth closed. "Whatever you say," she said. "In my book Florida never changes; it's a state of mind." She had an unfocused look in her eyes, as if the room were spinning and she was ready to pass out.

"He started fucking around with people who were out of his league and got his ass kicked," I said. "The truth is everything changed after Dinah's accident. When I told my father I wished we could go back to how things were before, all he could say was that he never got anything that he really wanted out of life. That made my mother feel great."

Zelda said, "And you? How did it make you feel?"

I shrugged. "I don't exactly remember."

"I'm sure he didn't mean it that way," she said contritely, as if she were speaking for him.

"He meant it. Why say it if it isn't true?"

She took a long drag on her cigarette and said, "Look, you said he was feeling real shitty, and that can work on people in strange ways. You should cut him some slack; it's better not to be so bloody disapproving at your age. You'll have nothing to say when you're middle-aged."

"He always told me the problem with life was that we had too many choices. I don't know what to do about him—or my mother—anymore."

"Do what? What in the world do you think you can do about it? It's not your job to watch out for them," she said impatiently. "Couples separate all the time. It's not the end of the world. Don't be such a responsible son."

My heart was pounding in my nose. Her attention was fading. God knows how much dope she was on. She got out of bed and turned on *Dallas*. "Ted has a bleeding peptic ulcer," she called to me from the bathroom. "The rotten prick's going to need surgery if he keeps drinking."

I remembered that Ted Klein was a big man with springy silver hair and a nose like a ball-peen hammer. He looked like a greeter in a casino.

When Zelda came back into the bedroom she was wearing fresh blush and a lavender muumuu; she had her hair up in a striped towel. "He's the managing partner in his high-profile corporate firm, and spends our money buying his hens imported lingerie and expensive gold pins and pearl bracelets. Last year he was banging an assistant district attorney; this year a novice public defender. I met her at some lawyer's picnic I got dragged to. A desperate young woman, with a lisp and crooked teeth. He's well past the Rita Hayworth stage. I know my Teddy well; he wants a blow job every other day as well as insider information. Thank God my daddy saw fit to leave me a trust fund." She yawned then, pointing her garish toenails.

We watched TV for almost two hours, *noshing* on cold leftover Chinese takeout and drinking Blue Nun and jasmine tea from flowered demitasse cups. We rested on the edge of the bed—legs hanging—for a few minutes. She told me how Ted had knocked her up the summer after she'd graduated from high school. They never even discussed her having an abortion or putting the baby up for adoption. They were married by an uncle of his, a judge in Orlando, when she'd first started to show, and she followed him back to Durham for his senior year and law school.

"I didn't know you had an older kid," I said. "I only knew the twins."

"The baby was stillborn, a girl," she said, with no trace of emotion. "I should have gotten a lawyer and immediately filed for an annulment. But I was stupid and afraid."

She said she went to college part-time for six years and got a degree in secondary education. Ted and her mother and grandmother bullied her into quitting her job teaching junior high school art after she had the boys. She said it was their contention that wealthy people didn't teach in public schools, and she gave in to them without a fight.

"You're going?" she asked when I came back from putting the dirty dishes in the sink. Tony Bennett was on Johnny Carson, singing "Bewitched, Bothered, and Bewildered."

I told her it was time for me to go. Tomorrow was my day to open the deli.

She took a swallow of the wine. "But what if I'm not ready for you to go just yet?" she said lecherously. "I have an itch for you between my legs." She slumped back against the pillows, pouting, and lifted the muumuu to her thighs. "Stay, honey. I want company, Sonny. Look, we don't have to do anything. Just get into bed."

"No—I'd better not."

She pulled down my zipper and tugged at my shorts. "Jesus, you're so big, lover," she said demurely, clicking her tongue. Her look was inflamed.

I shrank away from her. "What was that for—fun?"

"I'm just a shrew," she said, reaching over to her purse and pulling out a fifty. "Here, call a cab."

"I don't mind walking," I said.

She stood up and kissed me on the ear. "I mind," she murmured. "Treasure—please turn on the floodlights. *Ciao.*"

Zelda came by the deli two weeks later. She was dressed in a short leather skirt and spike heels, and told me she was saved. The growth was benign—a simple mass of dilated lymph vessels. There was no sign of new tumors anywhere. "How come you never called me?" she said.

I told her I did call the hospital, twice, but they wouldn't give me any information about her condition, and I was afraid to call her house. I told her I had come to the hospital to see her, with a box of cherry-filled chocolates and a bouquet of yellow and blue violets, but developed cold feet when I thought I'd heard laughing male voices, Ted's and her sons' no doubt, coming from her room. I told her I felt like a jerk, sneaking around up there in the bright lime-green corridors with my little gifts in my hands, sick people in shabby bathrobes and indecent pajamas gliding past me in wheel-chairs. When I couldn't think of a plausible excuse to give them for my being there to see her, I fled, dumping the flowers at the nurses' station on her floor and devouring the chocolates myself, later that night, alone.

"The hospital is a terrible place," she said, her eyes drifting. "Germs and pain, and the hideous smell of disinfectant everywhere.

They kept me there for three days because I started running a high fever. Nobody with any brains wants to get sued these days."

When she removed her sunglasses I was shocked to see a pair of bruised rings encircling her puffy eyes like an aurora. Had Ted belted her? I wondered. I wanted to ask her what happened but froze. "I look appalling, I know," she said. "And it's not what you think. I got dizzy and walked into a door frame the other day."

"Dizzy?" I said, an unexpected, aggrieved tone creeping into my voice.

She held my wrist firmly. "It's low blood sugar, I swear. Ted didn't lay a hand on me. He knows I'd shoot him in the face with his own gun."

Birdie and Basil were over by the soda fountain watching us talk, Basil in his knee-length apron and Birdie shading his eyes with a loaf of pumpernickel. He shook his large bald head wearily.

Without wanting to, and certainly not knowing why, I worked myself up into a sort of desperation over this woman. What had begun as a diversion on both our parts had soon turned into something else. She picked me up after work and we made love along the banks of mosquito-infested canals, the dank South Florida air as sticky and thick as molasses. With frogs and crickets making a racket all around us, we screwed on plaid summer quilts zippered with mold. She took me to a renovated, thirties-style European cinema in South Miami and we saw some old favorites of hers— *The Four Hundred Blows, Breathless, Belle De Jour*. We ate our breakfasts at a Denny's in Hollywood and our suppers at an International House of Pancakes off I-95 in Broward County—spots, we were sure, where neither of us would be recognized—and we spent a three-day weekend at the Red Lion Inn on Palm Island, Al Capone's winter home, balling away. We went to the Parrot Jungle and Sea World and took lazy hypnotic strolls on the beach in Fort Lauderdale, watching the sun set a blasted orange beyond the freighters and oil tankers inching forward on the horizon. We lolled on our stomachs in the warm cloudy water, her small bright breasts drifting under my eyes like whitened jellyfish, our bodies imprinted in the muddy emerald surf by the withdrawing tide, and rubbed each other's feet and back. We must have looked and sounded strange to the dilatory lifeguards perched beneath the flaps of their wide canvas umbrellas. We splashed into the shallow water, the oyster-colored, slow-moving clouds unraveling above us like spools of ribbed yarn, and sent out gleaming sheets of spray. We smoked some decent pot and drank chilled sauterne out of a thermos and ate chicken salad sandwiches and persimmons for supper and sang old Broadway musical numbers like "The Impossible Dream" and "The Age of Aquarius"—surrounded by hundreds of indolent college kids capering on sand as white as cream, all of them as bleary-eyed as we were and doubtless feeling that they, and not us, were somehow at the very center of the universe.

For a month I was dazed. France had had no luck in pinning down my father's whereabouts, and I'm not sure how hard he even tried. I decided to have it out with him. He was a man dead set on domesticity. He was stretched out on the fishnet hammock in the backyard, sunning himself, a khaki Ghurka hat pulled low on his forehead. A role of custardlike fat sloped over the waistband of a pair of my father's frayed Bermuda shorts he was wearing. The black curls on his round belly were matted in greasy tanning lotion. His spindly brown legs, crossed at the ankles, hugged the wizened trunk of the baby fig tree. An empty stein of Guinness dripped brown foam on an *Enquirer* folded in the acacia. He was sucking on an Italian ice in a pink cup.

"This just isn't working out," I said in as raw a voice as I could muster.

He shifted in the hammock and showed me a muscle as dark as tinned cheese. "What's the deal on the chick you're bopping?"

I stared at the pockmarks on his face. "Stop busting my horns," I said.

"Don't get so bent out of shape, huckleberry," he said, fixing his reddened eyes on me. "We all need a piece of something strange now and again." He rolled a barbell out from beneath the hammock and started doing curls.

"You must really think you're goddamn Charles Atlas or something," I said.

"Fungoo," he said, laughing. He clicked on the portable radio next to the hammock and moved the tuner to the far left, pausing at an FM station playing Brazilian bossa nova. "Hey, sport, you like Stan Getz? What about José Feliciano? Oh yeah, come on baby, light my fire."

"Just leave my mother alone, understand, dufus?" My head was starting to throb from squinting into the sun.

He smirked. "You must think you're a real bad-ass. Don't bite off more than you can chew. You know, no man can have a woman who doesn't want him."

Mel Torme came on the radio, singing "Mambo Italiano." I wanted to tell France to go screw himself, but my voice died in my throat. He turned his wide body away from me and rolled off the hammock. He went over to the garden sprinkler and opened his mouth under the nozzle and let the current gush over his nose and beard. He didn't so much walk as scuttle, like a hermit crab.

Later that evening I passed my mother's bedroom on my way out to see Zelda. The door was open and I watched her put her leg up on the ladder-back chair and run the perfume bottle between her thighs and lightly touch the skin above her stockings. A hairpin with an onyx mounted on one end was snaked through her braided ponytail.

I lingered in the kitchen and waited for her to leave. After a few minutes I went outside and sat gloomily on the porch. A faint blush of phosphorescent light showed through the platinum sky. The air smelled of sandalwood. With tropical suddenness a gust of biting horseflies came out above the drooping palmettos. My parents had come a long way from their days frugging to live music at the Cafe A Go-Go and studying yoga with a swami from Bangladesh. As much as I tried, their lives eluded me.

An older couple walking a Labrador retriever stopped in front of the house and turned around. Our neighbor, Ida Fink, an Auschwitz widow, was putting a *yortzeit* candle on the windowsill. Across the lawn my mother's laugh was acoustical, as if it were reverberating within the diamond-tiled walls of an indoor pool. She and France were sitting in my father's gunmetal Buick Roadmaster, listening to "I Got You, Babe." They sang and bounced rhythmically to the sounds coming from the radio, and their voices fit together perfectly.

———

The postcards started arriving on the first Wednesday after Halloween. They were mostly the extra-large, decorative, brush-textured, greeting kind, with his name scribbled on the inside above some Old Testament proverb or maxim from St. Paul. The mail was the ideal way to communicate with me and not with my mother, since it had always been my job to collect it every day from the mailbox. The first one was sent from a dude ranch in Yuma, Arizona, and spoke glowingly of his having competed in a calf-roping contest. His penmanship was neat and precise and written boldly in peacock-blue ink. He told me to study hard and exercise daily, and to meditate on Buddha. He said it was a better world than people thought.

In the following months I received picture postcards from Sequoia National Park, a Hopi reservation, Haight-Ashbury (a nighttime scene of the acid heads queued up to see Janis Joplin and Big Brother and the Holding Company at the Fillmore West), a West Hollywood all-night cinema that only ran W. C. Fields and Marx Brothers and Laurel and Hardy films, and from Goshen, Indiana, where a fierce-looking man in a grizzled Hasidic beard sat in a huge Mennonite buggy with his wife, six children, and two sheep dogs. He wrote that he was living off the land like a trapper, eating horse chestnuts, wild strawberries, and turtle eggs, and catching cutthroat trout by hand. He said that he'd broken out in shingles after a heavy cold, which had caused his testicles to ooze and crust over in scabs. There was a small postcard from the Grand Coulee Dam folded inside an air-mail envelope. On it he said he was newly engaged to a woman from Moscow, Idaho, named Freedom who talked dirty during intercourse and screamed like a man being kicked in the nuts when she climaxed. He never gave me a return address or a phone number where he might be reached. Had he, I would have taken the opportunity to remind him that he was already married and had a family to take care of.

When I showed the postcards to Zelda she toyed with her teacup and curled her lips. "People, life, everything is so damn messy, Sonny," she said dismissively, covering my knuckles with her lacquered nails. "Nothing ever stays the same. If I think too much about my past it turns my stomach and gets me depressed. Worry about your own head."

"But I should do something," I said.

She looked at me skeptically. "Do? I don't think he cares what you do. Even if you do nothing at all." There was an ironic edge to her voice that confused me even more.

I decided to show one of the postcards to France. The Winnebago was in the shop for a brake job, so we drove in his ex-partner's Land Rover to an Art Deco bar near Biscayne Bay called The Dancing Crab. When I said I didn't know he had had a partner, France grinned behind his sunglasses and said I'd never asked. He ordered a margarita and a plate of mussels from a waitress with smudged copper makeup, and then asked her what time she got off work. She arched her thick black eyebrows—they looked dyed in India ink—and told him to get bent. I ordered a basket of crab fritters and a glass of sangria. A five-piece zydeco band was playing, and a trio of redheads in glittery G-strings and rhinestone pasties took turns slithering up and down a silver pole.

It was happy hour and the curved bamboo buffet was jammed with lawyers, gas company executives, and software types from Xerox and Wang. I was curious to see what it would take to turn my father around. "It's personal," I told France when he asked me what the deal was, and handed him a manila envelope. I added that I respected his judgment and trusted his discretion.

"Piss on discretion," he said. "And don't be yanking my chain, huckleberry." He held up his drink and growled, "L'chayim." He took a sip and grimaced as if he'd swallowed something spoiled. Before opening the envelope he said he was going to be a hard case, that he worked for my old lady, not me. "I'm too f-ing old for any Rootie Kazootie shit from you or anyone else."

Inside the envelope was a blown-up photograph of my father and Freedom sitting on a huge black Harley, smoking dope. Max was wearing bib overalls and small hoop earrings. His gray-veined scalp was trimmed down to a burr and his GI dog tags hung on a beaded string around his neck. He looked sleepy and pale and his Hawaiian shirt was stained with perspiration. IN-A-GADDA-DA-VIDA was tattooed on both of his forearms. Freedom looked like one of those Soviet-bloc hammer throwers. She was wearing a sleeveless white undershirt with *Let It Bleed* embroidered in red across the front, and had wide heavy legs and amber hair in cornrows. It looked like jagged pink sores were running down the front of her shins. There was also a charcoal sketch of them. He wrote on the back of it that they'd camped at the Little Bighorn and had their profiles drawn by a wasted Vietnam vet in a Sioux headdress, rattlesnake leggings, and deerskin moccasins who claimed to be the great-great-grandson of Sitting Bull.

"You look worried," France said.

"I'm just thinking," I said haltingly.

He scratched his jaw and looked me over as if he'd just remembered who I was. "Well—I can't read your mind, huckleberry."

"I don't know what to make of it all," I said.

I sensed a kind of apprehensive logic in France's hard, empty stare. He put his soft, moist hand on my shoulder. "He can take care of hisself," he said. "He made it back to the world, didn't he? He don't need you or your mother or nobody. Sometimes a fucker gets all jammed-up inside, there's nowhere to turn. No lie—your old man's got an attitude problem; sooner or later he needs to unload his shit and get his asshole squared away. He needs to get hisself to join one of those Vietnam vets' groups, like A.A. Fucking Assholes Anonymous. Don't *you* be a dumb-ass dipshit and waste your life having a bad conscience. Let it all go."

My skin was burning when France had finished speaking, as if he'd slapped me across the face with the back of his beefy paw. I didn't know what to say to him. That thinking about my father made me feel an unnameable shame? That I had absolutely no idea where any of us were heading, and it hardly mattered if I did? Dinah's death, I understood, was only a bitter fraction of all this accumulated grief, and it had been foolish of me to think that I could have sheltered my parents from ruin. The truth was that all of us were in one degree or another smitten by our shared misfortune, that we would never be able to let any of it wither away, and that my father, unlike my mother, had slipped far beyond the point where whatever I might have done earlier, to either console or soothe him, made little difference anymore. I didn't need to look at France to know that he was grinning at me. I'd seen his gap-toothed smirk enough times these past few months to know that there was a lush dark quality to his sneer, something foul and corrupt and decayed, that it was etched with malice, a withering, self-assured mockery. In the end I just stared at his big putty-textured face and said nothing.

———

  For months I was morose, plodding through my daily existence as if I were semi-conscious. Without Zelda in bed beside me I had trouble sleeping, and behaved badly at work the next day, barking orders at the befuddled busboys. That fall Birdie had advanced me some money and I went and bought a used Suzuki, and when Ted wasn't around I took her on all-night cruises up and down Alligator Alley. We went to the Breakers Hotel and the Everglades, and spent a weekend in Key Largo drinking mescal in a reggae bar. (As time passed Zelda was less and less worried about scandal.) We went to chamber music recitals at the amphitheater in Boynton Beach, drove up to Daytona and watched the stock car races. We bought each other presents. She gave me a Pentax camera and a fancy tripod, and blushed when I said I wanted to take pictures of her in the slinky new underwear I had gotten her at Lord & Taylor's for her birthday—chiffon slips and dark nylon stockings with seams in the back, black and blue satin bras (strapless) that bit into her flesh, frilly panties with embroidered hearts and scallops on them. (I'd managed to take a candid of her bending over in the claw-footed porcelain tub, shaving her long white legs with a disposable razor—

her clean wet body wrapped in a heavy purple bath towel, a half-affectionate expression on her wan face; and a posed shot of her turned seductively sideways, her eyes half shut, hair pinned in a chignon, dressed in nothing but a sheer pink slip.) And she liked to cook—homemade rigatoni tossed with navy beans and basil, deviled eggs with caviar, grilled rockfish with leeks, garlic, and shallots, angel food cake served on ivory dessert plates with morning glories painted by hand on the pleated border. When I talked about my parents she tried to sound encouraging, even optimistic, but I could tell by how she looked at me that hearing about them too often made her feel very uncomfortable, even embarrassed, and there was a barrenness and thickness to her voice that was unmistakable. I told her that once or twice I'd picked up the phone at home and heard a man's voice above the Ravi Shankar album I'd given my father for his birthday a few years earlier, talking to my mother about universal ecstasy and "getting cleared by Jesus." The edges of the man's gravelly voice sounded blurred, distant. When I worked up the nerve to confront my mother with my growing suspicion that she was keeping his whereabouts hidden from me, she said I was delusional.

In the moonlight, Zelda's dyed silk caftan matched the bronzelike indigo of the sky. A vase filled with nasturtiums and dahlias sat on the cedar dresser, on top of a crumpled copy of *Vogue*. Moonbeams danced upon the narrow hemispheres of her bottom. I was holding her when the phone rang. She smiled up at me in her sleep and rolled over on her stomach. "I'll get it," I said, reaching down under the bed. Ted was marlin fishing in Barbados and never called home when he was out of the country.

My father's voice over the telephone was broken. I looked back at Zelda, now half-turned from me, the starlike, coppery moles on her back like a connect-the-dots puzzle. "Are you there, Sonny?" he said, his words coming in a burst. I heard shouting, the thud of bodies being slammed.

"Where are you?" I shouted. "What's going on?"

"Get bent, dipstick," I heard him yell. Then, to me, roughly, "Some mother with an Iron Cross wanted to use the phone. He better not mess with me. I'll grease his Nazi ass."

"Calm down, take it easy. How'd you get this number?"

"A guy answered the phone at home," he said warily. "He sounded mucho pissed. He gave me this number to try. Am I interrupting something? Are you all right?"

Unwinding myself from the sheets, I felt chilled. Instead of tracking down my father, France must have been tracking me. For a second I wondered if I should tell him that I was screwing the same woman he screwed at my age? Would he appreciate the symmetry? Instead I said, "Everything's cool. Where the fuck are you?"

"A strip joint," he mumbled. "It's ski-world outside, snowing some serious shit."

"But *where?* Are you alone?"

"In ZZ Top, Wyoming," he said, laughing. "Some low-rent redneck dump. Ain't no soul brothers here. Freedom's in the crapper. It's her time of the month."

I heard shrieking noises in the background, like electric guitars and saxophones. Zelda stirred in the bed beside me. She coughed and made a choking sound in her sleep.

"You think if I come back to your mother that's best for you and her, don't you? C'mon man, what do you think? Be a stand-up guy with me."

I didn't answer him right away. I hoped he wasn't on acid or something worse. "I can't answer that question," I said.

I heard a slapping noise. "I guess it's real serious with that dude over there. I wish she'd've told me herself."

"He's a number one scumbag," I said. "It's only a temporary thing."

"Can I ask you something else then?" He was sighing now, half-mumbling into the mouthpiece. His voice sounded very distant.

"Ask," I told him.

"I need to know if you hate me."

"Christ knows I don't hate you." I said. My teeth were chattering slightly.

He snorted into the receiver. "What're your plans?"

"I don't know exactly. I haven't made up my mind. What about you? How are you living? Do you need money or clothes? What can I send you?"

"Fucking-A. What about *me?* Jesus," he said wearily. "I get along, score some speed now and then. I think you'd really like Freedom. She's very laid-back; even lived in Martinique for a while. She was in the Air Force for ten years and did a tour at Tan Son Nhut. Remember when I told you how the gooks smuggled all kinds of groovy shit down the Ho Chi Minh Trail? They were thick as thieves with these samurai cowboys from Special Forces. Grunts were always spreading shit about kickass colonels making *beaucoup* dollars trading in morphine and antibiotics with the pussy ARVN and Saigon police. Freedom says that even the potlicking brass were smoking dope and dropping acid during the war. Making all kinds of whoopee with the VC. She says she wants to write a book about it. I know your mother'd like her. Hey, you think she'll ever forgive me?"

"There's nothing to forgive," I whispered.

"Outstanding," he said scornfully.

"I'm not joking. You haven't done anything to forgive you for."

I heard his breath catch. "I suppose there's no point in my coming back there or anything? I mean, it'd be a waste of everyone's time. Why don't you come out West and be with me and Freedom? We're moving to an ashram in Oregon, near the Snake River. Do the whole sixties thing all over again. Power to the people, go nuts one more time. You know, drop out and turn on. Man, you should really see the Bad Lands. My life is kind of like them, the stuff of my life inside me. I miss you."

"Me, too," I said.

"I'm a loser, Sonny. Do you remember what your mother used to call me when one of my businesses failed? 'An idiot with a nickel's worth of talent. But without the know-how.' She blames me for Dinah, and, maybe, who knows—" and he broke off. Then he started crying.

"It's not your fault. Christ, it just fucking happened. I was with her. I mean, maybe it was my job to protect her." I told him over and over again that it was all right, that I wanted to see him, that he should come home with or without Freedom. "Look—why don't you cycle back to Florida and I'll . . ."

But he wasn't there. While I was shifting the receiver to my other ear I heard a click. The line went quickly dead. It could have been the last beat of his heart. Zelda turned under the quilt and the sheets rustled like a breeze blowing among palm fronds, exposing a dark triangle in the crescent of her abdomen. The six-bladed ceiling fan ticked on and cool air rained down over us.

Careful not to wake Zelda, I got up from the bed to wash my face. The hallway and bathroom were walled in framed stanzas from Milton's *Lycidas* and Blake's *The Four Zoas*. A round crack in the vanity mirror had radiated like a spiderweb the past few weeks. The flimsy glass was streaked with apricot face powder. Out the oval window I could see elusive summer lightning flashing above the treacherous cypress bogs to the west. Vast star clusters, like spilled milkweed seeds, were sprayed across the sky. There were raindrops on the slithery and steamy palmetto leaves, like enormous tears.

When I came back into the bedroom Zelda was up, leaning on an elbow. She turned the edges of her mouth down and looped an arm around my ribs when I sat down. "What's wrong?" she murmured. She moved her fingers slowly along my spine, caressing it.

"My father called," I said, and ran my hand up and down her thigh in a lulling rhythm. I put my hands behind my head on the pillow and closed my eyes. When I opened them I saw that my own curved and somber reflection was shining like a nimbus in the mirrors of her pupils. "He says he wants me to be with him, but I know that's only a line. He doesn't want me anywhere near him. I'll only remind him of everything he wants to forget. Now he's saying he wants to relive the sixties."

I saw the change in Zelda's face, the way she made her chin firm. She said, "Poor lamb, he's blinded himself to everything. The dirty little secret is that the sixties were really awful. The war, assassinations, race riots, everyone was drugged out of their fucking mind."

"I don't know," I said. "I don't want to make things worse. I don't know if I'm feeling anything. I'm afraid that my attachment to him is permanent and that I'll wind up being just like him, stuck, never able to separate myself from him. Whatever I feel about him, love or hate, it doesn't matter—I ache all over."

"It's hard to draw the line sometimes when it comes to parents," she said softly, angling her wide hips against my belly.

Outside the house, garbage cans rattled like gunfire as cats scavenged for food. "I want you," I said, and crawled securely against her, Zelda's long body warming to me, bending to me.

She rolled her eyes to the tops of their sockets. "It's normal," she said, taking my face and holding it for a long time before kissing my lips, "for people to fall in and out of love. It can even happen to us."

A bolt of lightning arced across the moon-drenched sky and the bedroom was filled with shimmering white light for a few seconds. In the flickering muted darkness I imagined I saw our straining forms dissolving outside the window, spools of ghostly blue smoke. What abiding truths, I wondered, were there left for me to acknowledge and tell Zelda? That I'd grown to understand, if not entirely embrace, that what she had begun to call our "quaint affair," this transient attraction and appetite we had for one another, would soon subside, would soon eviscerate itself, as would, no doubt, my mother's and France's. That try as I might to deny it, I knew that the settled harmony of our lovemaking would at first sag and then, as we tried vainly to rescue it, bitterly break, fading, finally, into eddies of regret—wounding ridicule, harsh words, enmity. But I was sure I would not (could not) go back to the kind of heedless and haphazard life I'd led before I met her, and the brutal clarity of that left me frightened and bereft.

And though I knew I would most probably hear from my vagabond father from time to time—for a pep talk, for funds—I also knew that there was little chance I'd ever see him again—that secretly I harbored a terrible desire, my wish that he would stay very far away from us. He was locked into a way of life where the only thing left for him to do was what he was doing. I'd had enough of all this. Perhaps only then—with his corrosive presence not always around to eat away at me—I would be able to shrug off this crippling habit of picking over my parents' seeping wounds. And then: would I have the nerve to disavow what I had always thought of as my unhappy family's inexplicable tragedy—have the nerve, that is, to relinquish some cherished part of myself to silence and fate, and move on into the unchartered future?

I lightly kissed Zelda's pale russet mouth and loose rose-scented hair and felt her warm whistling breath on my own. There was a grainy, mole-flecked discoloration in the hollow of her collarbone, the reddish-brown spots like stippled velvet. She held my hand for a moment before smiling shyly and letting it fall gently to her breast. The lids of her unopened eyes were still sharply rimmed with turquoise liner. I tucked a few matted strands of hair behind her ear. When I was sure she was asleep I slipped out from beneath the silky burgundy sheets and went to sit by the open, double-glazed window. There were slivers of gold and green paint on the windowsill, tiny scratch marks on the window frame. I could feel the cool scented wind rising among the orange trees. The sound of rainwater dripping against the shiny ferns and grapevine was meditative, strangely reassuring. She slept soundly then, still smelling of glycerin and lemon soap, her painted toes curled outside the Shaker quilt, oblivious to the thunderstorms that kept me awake for the rest of the night.

Home Burial

For weeks I imagined I could see him coming off the plane, carrying souvenirs. In my mind he looked the same as the day he left—broad-shouldered, trim, deeply tanned. The picture of him they printed in the newspaper, one of those sawtooth-edged Brownie snapshots that always made the day appear gloomy, had been taken years earlier, on Utah Beach, a few days after the invasion of Normandy. Behind him, on the sand, you could see the rows of dead soldiers covered with ponchos.

My father came home from Korea when I was fourteen. Not exactly Korea, but San Francisco, where he'd spent the past four months at Letterman Hospital recovering from pneumonia and malnutrition. It was Election Day, 1952, and everybody in my neighborhood had been wearing Stevenson buttons for months while at the same time saying he didn't have a prayer against Eisenhower. My Uncle Eli kept telling me and my mother how Adlai would have had a fighting chance if he hadn't always looked like he'd just emerged from a drugged sleep. I couldn't have cared less who became the next president. Our local newspaper had a front page story on my father; they called him a war hero. The paper said he had crawled out of his foxhole on the slope of a hill and destroyed two enemy machine-gun nests that had pinned down his company.

Later he was captured and endured eleven months in a diarrhea-soiled toolshed as a prisoner of war. Sick from dysentery and beri-beri—his belly and joints were bloated, his feet and gums swollen and bleeding—he'd been left to rot when his captors abandoned camp. A platoon of Marines out on a midnight patrol had discovered him, along with the remains of some twenty of his men.

We met him early, soon after sunrise, with the golden bars of sunlight splayed across the rusted tin freight hangar at Mitchell Field. To pass the time on the ride to the airport I'd played the game of memorizing license plates my father had taught me. There were still traces of fog out, places where the sun hadn't burned through yet. The Bronx River Parkway was full of wet leaves and the air was heavy with smoke. We drove with the windows down and the wind sounded like surf at the ocean. Above the sounds of traffic the gleaming chrome radio in my Uncle Eli's maroon teardrop DeSoto crackled with static. He moved the dial and turned the volume up when he heard Peggy Lee singing "Just One of Those Things." My mother, riding up front with Uncle Eli, could not stop coughing. She'd been hacking and wheezing for more than a month now, thanks to the ragweed and mold spores.

The whole time my father had been missing my mother would go upstairs and hide in the bathroom whenever the phone rang. She'd run water in the tub or flush the toilet three or four times— anything to drown out the sound of my voice. We'd been in the breakfast nook finishing our French toast when the phone call came informing us that my father had been found alive. She held the receiver an inch or so from her ear and her expression was pure amazement. Watching her, my mind was blank. Her mouth was open halfway, and she was taking short, urgent breaths through it. Although she never said it, I knew she'd given up hope of ever see-ing him again. Her self-control was all for my sake, in order to shield me from the inevitable. To tell the truth, whenever the phone rang—this despite my knowing that the Army always sent an offi-cer around to deliver an official account of how and where a soldier had been killed in action—I thought it would be news of his death. But my worst fear was that he would never be found at all. Relieved when the caller was my Aunt Sophie or a neighbor, I would go into the living room and salute my father's picture, which sat on top of the mantelpiece. It was a formal photograph, taken before I was born. In it he wore a dark pin-striped suit and a wide necktie, and his black hair was piled back in waves. His somber brown eyes seemed focused on something behind the camera. It was impossible to know what he was looking at, but there was an intensity in his gaze, a surge of concentration in his eyes, that I couldn't get out of my head. Before the phone call I'd been secretly hoping for, this photograph of someone I'd never known entered my dreams like a ghost and came between me and the face I remembered as my father's.

The night before we went to meet his plane, my mother took me out for supper. The Shanghai Cafe was one of those places with bad air, hazy blue light, and starched red tablecloths that smell of spilled drinks and soy sauce. It was on a narrow street across from the RKO Proctor where my father used to take me for Sunday matinees during the winter. I looked at my mother's hands as she read the menu. Her skinned knuckles were wrinkled. She put the menu down and took a pack of Old Golds out of her purse, and lit one up.

"You look tired," I said. "Anything wrong?"

She turned her face to me and smiled. "You're like your father, Noah," she said, and rubbed her wrist as if the veins inside of it were hurting her. "You shouldn't expect too much from him at the beginning."

I had a funny sensation just then, a nervous rush that made my stomach cramp. "I don't get it," I said. "When you came back from California you said there was nothing to worry about. What are you hiding from me? What's the big secret?"

She looked at me and smiled in a way that seemed forced and full of something else I didn't care to find out about. A sullen waiter wearing a black bow tie took our order of egg drop soup, moo goo gai pan, and rainbow shrimp.

"I'm not being evasive, Noah. I thought I told you he'd be different for a while."

"All you said was that he wasn't acting like himself."

She moved the glass ashtray around with her finger. "He's *not*," she said, and leaned back and touched her temples. "I'm going to need your help with him."

"Sure," I said.

Her face sank. "You know what I mean. Why are you being so difficult? We have a situation here."

"I'm not trying to be difficult," I said.

She sipped at her gin rickey and blew jets of gray smoke out of her nostrils. "You'll see," she said stiffly. "Sometimes there are things a lot worse than dying."

I wondered how she could even think that, especially after what he had gone through. "Are you saying he should've given up?"

"*Please*, eat," she said, though it was clear she had no appetite. She crushed her cigarette out in the ashtray and fiddled with the gold snap on her purse. We were sitting in a cramped booth encircled by panels of faded rosewood and fancy carvings of dragons and serpents and warriors on horseback. Shreds of lo mein were stuck in the dimpled vinyl buttons.

"What do you think *we* should do then?" I asked.

"It doesn't matter what I think," she said, her fingers searching in her pocketbook for another cigarette.

"Don't say that," I said. "To me it does."

"I just think," she said, "that we need to take one day at a time." She sat back and put her palms down flat on the table as if she were going to push it away from her.

"I'm sure he'll be okay once he's back home," I said.

She shook her head. "I'm not sure about anything, Noah. It'll be a whole new beginning for us. Please don't drill me with questions I can't answer. I know I can count on you to give me a hand with him."

"You can depend on it," I said.

She hesitated when I said that, and instead of speaking reached over and slipped her hand into mine. Her fingers felt like ice. The bar up front was jammed, and the clatter of falling cutlery came from the kitchen. She flinched with each unexpected noise. "It's just not that simple, is all I mean," she said, and her whole body seemed to lift in exasperation.

I spooned into my soup and tried to be ready for whatever was coming next. I felt helpless and frightened. Watching her, I remembered how I used to sit up in bed at night after my father had tucked me in and read me a story. I'd hear his shoes scraping against the staircase as he walked downstairs, then I'd hear my parents talking in whispers through the heating register in my room. Now, she bit into her lower lip and stared reproachfully at a squabbling elderly couple in evening clothes who sat nearby. When a baby began to make a racket in the booth behind us, she seemed to shudder inside her clothes. When I asked her to please talk to me, she leaned over and streaked a finger across my forehead as if she were writing a message to herself.

On the drive out to Mitchell Field my mother and Uncle Eli argued about what my father's doctor had told them about his condition. Mostly they spoke in Yiddish so I couldn't eavesdrop. Eli was my mother's brother and he owned a Rheingold distributorship in Mamaroneck. After World War II my father had had trouble finding work, so he'd taken a number of different jobs until he could find something he could build a future on. He'd enrolled in evening accounting and business courses at Fordham University, not far from the zoo. People used to say that my father was a natural salesman, that his element was conversation. For some reason I have it in my head after all this time that he loved to work with his hands. I have a memory of him doing the grouting in our bathrooms and puttering in the garage. He managed a busy liquor store on the Grand Concourse a few blocks from Yankee Stadium before it was sold to a company that built mortuaries, and then he went to work for Eli. At the time we were living in the Bronx. With someone around he could trust, Eli was free to play golf twice a week at his country club. After a couple of years he made my father a junior partner, and we moved from the run-down apartment building on upper Broadway, a few blocks south of Van Cortlandt Park, into Westchester County.

They were discussing money now—I knew the Jewish word for it—and my mother's neck and shoulders had stiffened. She set her purse on her lap.

"What do you want from me, Irene?" Eli said in English.

"I don't want anything," she said. She opened her purse and took out a crumpled pack of cigarettes, then pushed in the lighter on the chrome dashboard with her thumb. Half of the nail was chewed away.

Eli looked at me in the rearview mirror. "Your mother thinks I want her to sign something so I can have your old man's stake in the company back. Christ, I'm simply trying to protect the both of you. Haven't I always come through?"

Her head was turned sideways and I could see that her teeth were gritted around the cigarette. "Oh, all right, Eli," she said, and cut him off with a sudden laugh. "Who asked you to protect us? Let's just get there. I've had it with these business discussions."

An egg truck with Pennsylvania tags had jackknifed across the median strip and the Southern State Parkway was strewn with yolks and shells and crushed powder-blue cartons. A large-finned police ambulance blocked traffic in our lane as the trucker was taken from the cab. He was hoisted onto a stretcher and covered with sheets, and two men in green hospital attire rolled him into the rear of the idling ambulance. The cops were still sitting in their cruisers, and Eli leaned his head out of the window and did his Milton Berle imitation that made them grin and shake their heads at him. Looking out my window, I could see that part of the trucker's head was gone.

A freckled medic with a bandaged throat wheeled my father down the cargo hold. His lap was draped in olive blankets and his gaunt face was as white as typing paper. The air smelled of gasoline and burning rubber. A heavy Army nurse with close-cropped silver hair grabbed me by the elbow and blocked my path to him. In a flat John Wayne drawl she said I'd better wait a few minutes, in order to give him a chance to adjust to the surroundings. My mother stood beside me brushing down the front of her coat. She

held her other hand up like a visor to shade her eyes. "Phil," she
said three or four times. "It's Irene, Phil. Irene and Noah."
Eli edged past me, breathing heavily, and I had a prickly sensation
in my spine between the shoulder blades. He turned around and
told me to give him some room, that he needed to ask a few questions, find out what was what. My mother had looked good when
we left the house, she had made herself up for the homecoming.
She was wearing a new calico dress and open-toed strapless navy
pumps. Her reddish-brown hair was marcelled and pulled away
from her face in a way that made her round green eyes appear even
rounder. Now she was sobbing and her mascara had started to run.
My father's head turned slowly, and I remember his moist eyes
straining to focus on something diagonally across the runway. A
helicopter with camouflage markings had landed about fifty yards
from us. Suddenly he made a high, piercing moan, the grimace on
his face hardening into a puzzled frown. My mother jerked as if
she'd been plugged into a socket.

In a few minutes I was given permission to embrace him. He
smelled funny, like burnt meat. His checks were a grid of healed
cuts, and his sticklike arms were badly broken out in jagged patches.
My mother brushed her lips across his trimmed sideburns; I could
see her bowed head in the polished shine of his combat boots. The
scalp around his hairline was oily and raw, and his nose was bent,
as if it had been broken more than once.

I looked at my mother—standing unsteadily while Eli held her
by her elbow, listening to what the nurse had to tell them about my
father's care—and tried to imagine what her frame of mind was.
They raised their eyebrows at each other when the nurse spoke
about his bedsores. The sun glowed silently, and high passing clouds
made shadows on her face. Slowly, a bit distracted I thought, she
flicked her hair off her eyes. She was looking over the nurse's shoulder, making eye contact with the horizon. She didn't seem to hear
anything the nurse was saying.

I listened, nodding mechanically, pretending to understand. My
mother's mouth was slightly open and I could hear her teeth clicking. I wanted to ask what I was supposed to do, how I could help. I

was restrained by my fear of the truth—that someone would tell me all too clearly that there was absolutely nothing I or anyone else could do. That my father's condition was final, that nothing was possible anymore. I wondered if my mother had grown suddenly astonished by the weight of that prospect.

There was a commotion when three Marines in starched battle fatigues walked over and saluted my father. He just sat there as serene as an owl. To the indifferent eye he simply looked bored, or sleepy. One of the Marines shook Eli's hand and said they were veterans of Inchon. Then he held his arms out and pretended he was a dive bomber. The other two acted as if they had pom-pom guns, flak noises coming from their throats. My mother forced a smile but I could tell she was holding something back. The Marines had tattoos of naked women on their forearms. Then they all started talking at once—brainwashing, the H-bomb, fallout shelters—things I'd heard about in school. I looked my father in the eye and made a face at him, one he used to make at me when I was little. I curled back my cheeks and slid my lips back over my upper teeth. Then I bounced around and slapped at my chest and armpits and made believe I was peeling a banana. I made screeching sounds like Cheetah in a Tarzan movie.

The Marines got a big kick out of me and one of them gave me a Three Musketeers. About a hundred feet in front of us a cargo plane had taxied to a stop and was unloading caskets. My mother wrote something on a memo pad as the Marines saluted my father once more and left. She asked the nurse about my father's eating habits; her voice was barely audible over the diminishing echo of the plane's propellers. My father hadn't budged. His eyes looked so cold I imagined you could crack ice cubes out of them.

"We'll take it from here," Eli said to the nurse, and he took hold of my father's wheelchair.

A few days before he left for Korea, we'd gone fishing for flounder and bluefish off the corrugated iron pier in New Rochelle. The dark blue-green water rippled over a sandbar, like windchimes gently tapping in a muffled breeze. Rusted oil drums drifted in the tarlike sound. I could still see the plume of copper smoke that rose from his ivory pipe when he baited my line with redfin minnows.

Smiling, he stroked my hair and told me it was my job to keep things going at home. Whenever he caught something, big or small, he extracted the hook as quickly as he could and threw the squirming, bleeding fish back into the water. Now, walking behind him and Eli and my mother, I felt as if I were following his body in a funeral procession, as I had followed my grandfather's three years earlier.

Back out on the highway my mother made a throat-clearing sound and asked me how I was doing. Before I could answer, Eli said I seemed fine. "Never better," I said sharply.

Eli chewed me out for being fresh, then stopped to talk with the fork-nosed man collecting tolls. My father started shaking when we zoomed across the Triborough Bridge. It was windy out, and the water below was sudsy and black and hundreds of seabirds seemed to hang suspended between the silver spans.

"Eli's just trying to help," my mother said without conviction. I could see her rolling her thumbs in her lap.

"Tell us what's on your mind," Eli said.

"Well, Noah?" she said. Her tone was edgy, fretful.

I glanced over at my father. He had his hands in his pockets and seemed to be watching the country glide past the window. There was something thick going over me in waves. I shrugged and told them I wasn't sure what I was thinking. I wasn't lying; he looked the same as the day he left. For a minute or so there was total silence in the car, then my mother pointed to her temple and cocked her thumb and forefinger as if she were holding a pistol and squeezed the trigger. "It's in here," she said.

"His nerves are shot all to hell," Eli said, his voice choked with cigarette smoke. "Every kind of lousy thing happens to men during war, but some can't forget them. What it adds up to is that an average man can take all kinds of pressure but then—*whammo*—everything that man is just falls apart into little pieces, and his brain turns to water. Your pop is just too damn sensitive for his own good. You can't help him by moping around. You've got to put it out of your mind."

"Getting over this takes time and patience," my mother said. "Not thinking about it will help."

"I don't know," I said.

She turned around and smiled at me. Her whole face seemed compressed into that smile. "He'll be all right," she said, in a hollow tone of voice I'd never heard her use before.

"Most men manage to shake it off and walk away from it," Eli said. "Give him time, Noah. He'll come around. I mean it."

"I hope you understand what we're saying," my mother said.

I told her I understood, but the trembling in my legs told me otherwise. I didn't believe for a second that not thinking about it would help. Instead, I told them I couldn't imagine him not being himself again. Eli then started telling a story I'd heard at least a dozen times; about how my father's infantry company had ambushed and destroyed an entire SS panzer unit in the Ardennes with bazookas and recoilless rifles. My father had won a Silver Star for that.

"I think Noah's had enough for today," my mother interrupted, ending the conversation.

———

We hadn't had him back with us for more than a week before I could tell they were already smoothing things over for me, getting me ready for the disappointment they were sure I couldn't handle. In their voices was the hemmed-in anger and resentment adults feel in the face of hopelessness. For the first few months my mother made me go with her to Friday night services at the synagogue, where I sat quietly and watched her pray for his recovery. I found it disconcerting that she believed God had nothing better to do than to answer her prayers, particularly when it concerned my father, a man who had had no use for religion. I asked her if all POWs had suffered the loss of their speech and memory. She must have sensed my growing despair, since she'd felt compelled to make him sound like some banished Biblical seer, one of those solitary messengers of heaven left wandering in the desert. When I told her I was bored with going to temple, she said it was important I understood that nothing could be taken for granted. Who could say for certain, she'd tell me, what he was thinking and feeling behind the immensity of his silence? Since I had no answer that would persuade her to see my side of things, I walked with her to Westchester

Jewish Center and watched her close her eyes and bend her head in earnest supplication.

Things hadn't changed that much in our neighborhood, except for the TV antennas that were sprouting up by the dozen on the rooftops. Sleek-fendered Buicks and Chevys with their tinted windshields and shiny chrome grilles and humpbacked trunks were parked up and down the block, and a Daitch had recently opened around the corner from my school. Horse-drawn wagons full of iced fish stacked in tiers or fresh fruits and vegetables in wooden crates were a thing of the past. We put my father into a Polish rocker on the small porch and waited for him to recognize things. I walked him down the winding hill from our house and showed him the new telephone and power lines that stretched along the New York Central commuter tracks. My mother and Aunt Sophie, Eli's wife, wallpapered the upstairs bathroom in the refurbished attic guest room where he would embark upon his convalescence. The attic was deep, cool and musty, with glossy heartpine beams and cedar-stained wood siding and brass lamps with maps of the American Revolution for shades. It reeked of Spic and Span and shellac. The double-paned dormer window had steel bars over it. My sixth-grade class picture was on the squat fruitwood hope chest that used to be in my parents' bedroom, and my father's frayed Yankee pennant was thumbtacked to the wall alongside a framed autographed photo of Joe DiMaggio. He had an L-shaped leather sofa bed, a Philco clock-radio on the round mahogany nightstand, a tortoiseshell hooked rug, two small gilt mirrors, a burgundy hassock, and a sapphire vase full of chrysanthemums and Chinese peonies, my mother's favorite flowers.

After school, when the weather was nice, I'd take him to the playground near our house, where he sat on the chalked foul line and watched me shoot baskets or play paddle tennis. Talk to him, my mother told me every day. So I did. About school and my friends and the people in the neighborhood I knew he had liked. In an effort to revive his memory, I told him the mournful stories he had once told me: about his penniless childhood in Batavia, Illinois; about his mother, dead from septicemia a few months after they'd moved to

Aurora; about his despondent father, who'd earned a measly living
working for mobsters, delivering black market rum to speakeasies
during Prohibition; and of his own dismal adolescence, boarding
with his mother's spinster sister in New Jersey, beside the Passaic,
after his father was killed by a hit-and-run driver. But he just
seemed to sink deeper into himself—the folds in the skin on his
neck a deepening shade of gold—a disbelieving expression on his
drawn face, his pitiless blue eyes so pale they were almost white.
I tried to expand and enlarge all the meager events of our daily
existence. Well, I'd say to him, what do you think? He looked desolate, as remote as a man in a coma, but for some reason I was sure a
wordless part of him understood what I was saying. In January I
took him tobogganing on a public golf course and watched him
catch snowflakes on his tongue. Once I thought I caught him checking around for something—he looked on the verge of speaking—
and I told him that his landscaper, Mr. Manicotti, had packed up his
family a year ago and moved back to his parents' house in Ozone
Park after his father had a stroke. He held out his fist like a boxer
getting ready to jab, and I could tell from the way the muscles in
his face were working that he was struggling to speak. Then he
strummed his flinty knuckles with his fingertips, an involuntary
gesture that could mean practically anything.

How do you help someone caged within himself? You convince
yourself that nothing can be taken for granted, you tell yourself
you're willing to try anything, but it's another thing entirely to
believe it. Satchmo, my Angora cat, remembered him. When he
wasn't nuzzling his head beneath my father's motionless hands, he
slept on his belly like the Sphinx next to where my father was sitting—purring, his big front paws out in front of his face. I took my
father fishing for yellow perch north of Valhalla, at Kensico Reser-
voir, off the sandstone dam glittering with mica. My mother packed
a picnic supper of turkey club sandwiches and potato salad, and we
drove to Bear Mountain State Park where I skipped stones on the
duck pond beneath a rising sulphur moon as he sat on a wrought-
iron bench and watched the startled birds scatter in midair. I held
his arm and we pitched horseshoes in the backyard or threw darts
into a rubber target against the house. I showed off my batting

stances—the exaggerated crouch I'd copied from Stan Musial, deep in the batter's box, a wrist-hitter's hitch in my swing. He looked at me warily, hunched stiffly in the Morris chair, holding a Hires root beer float in his hand, and I had the notion that he was holding back a laugh. I stood him up and we stooped together in the box I'd drawn with the end of my bat in the ground. Make believe it's Carl Erskine, I said. Get ready for the overhand curve. Beneath my hands the knobs of his shoulders felt like the heads of metal screws. When I bent down to flex his knees for him he flopped over, as if he'd suddenly lost all muscle tone. What do you see? What's out there? I was shouting now, gasping for breath. Do you know who I am? Who you are? Do you? Do you?

I awoke each day with a troubling feeling that something had been settled in my family that could never be undone. Talking to my father was like taking a stranger into your confidence; he'd look at me as if he'd never seen me before. He often slept with his eyes wide open, as if he had been frightened into sleep. And as for my mother, it soon became clear that some final thread of resistance to the truth of our future had given way. Usually a smart dresser, she began to look haggard. A dimpled tic flashed in her cheekbone whenever she looked into my father's solid, unresponsive face. She started wearing clothes she'd normally have given to the Salvation Army. Her housecoats looked linty and her nylons had runs in them. She'd only do her marketing after dark, driving five miles to a small grocery store open till ten. I'd hear her come downstairs two or three times during the night, checking dead bolts and door chains and turning the oven and burners on and off, sniffing for gas. For her supper she'd scald cans of Campbell's soup, and while we ate, sit sideways in her chair chain-smoking and drinking a tumbler full of straight vodka or rye. My father sat in his chair and every few minutes I reached across the table and straightened his terry cloth bib. At times he seemed baffled by his food. He'd move his knife and fork around his plate, turning over his brisket or cutlets or asparagus as if he were searching for something. After a while she stopped shopping and cleaning altogether, and it became my job to dust the furniture, vacuum the soiled carpets, and stock the empty refrigerator. She used sleeping pills, and her eyes, once as bright as topaz, looked permanently darkened, as if all the light in them had been consumed. An old woman's eyes, she called them.

One night in February, after watching the *Cavalcade of Stars*, I found her drinking a brandy in the darkened living room. Strings pulsed from the phonograph console, and Satchmo snoozed on an armrest of the brocade sofa. She stood poised on her toes, barefoot, like a ballerina, and gazed through the frosted bay window. Icicles hung like silver pendants from the Japanese maple in our backyard. Scattered rays of winter light pierced the curtains and sliced across her features like razor blades. She looked stranded, almost lofty in her isolation, and I trembled, seeing her as someone unbroken by what had happened, as someone other than my mother. She turned and smiled at me for the first time in weeks. "You have to stop doing this," I said.

She swayed to the lonesome cadence of a harp. "Don't I deserve a hug?" she said.

I felt snared in her beam of delusory joy. Behind her, out the window, headlights from a snakelike string of passing cars fanned out into the icy mist. Heavy snow was piled in our driveway. The other houses on our street were dark. For weeks she had grown quiet with me; it was as if her will to speak had been crippled by despair over my father's vast silence. I struggled to find some brief encouraging words. Her lips moved, and she motioned for me to come to her. She embraced me and hummed in my hair, and we paced the floor as if we were waltzing. An enormous dreamy mood engulfed us, and I shuddered in her arms like a small wet animal. We floated together, sustained by moonlight and dread, and I imagined what it might have been like being alive inside her. Beneath my fingers her ribs felt like piano keys. "He just needs more time," I said. "You know—day to day."

Her eyes looked weighted, numb. "It's no good," she said softly. "It won't work. I'm doing the best I can."

"Then I'll work harder," I said, taking her hands and squeezing them till I heard her murmur in pain.

There was a bit of movement in her face, as if a nerve were jumping from one cheek to the other and back again. Her eyelids stirred faintly at the sound of the wind chimes hanging from the wainscoting above the breezeway outside. A wide band of sleet had formed on the window. "I'm coming apart, Noah," she said, wrapping her arms around her chest. "I'm afraid it's too late."

"It's never too late," I insisted. "Life will be fine once we get the right breaks."

"But I have to live with him," she said, and looked around me, out the window. She hadn't had anything to drink at dinner, and I saw that her hands had started to shake.

"Why did he enlist again?" I said.

She said nothing.

"Answer me," I said.

She sighed deeply, as if something stuck inside her head suddenly loosened, and turned and faced me. "He didn't have to," she said, her voice low and thick. "He didn't have to."

The sound of waves pounded in my ears. "Why?" I repeated.

"All these questions," she said, raising her eyes to the ceiling. "These things are none of your business. I don't want to talk about any of it anymore. *Ever.*"

All right," I said, and in that moment the feeling I had always had for her changed somehow, and I understood for the first time the void between the way things were and the way I thought they used to be.

Passover came late in April that year. It was a mistake having the *Seder* at our house. Everyone tried to act as if it were important to continue the simple family rituals we had followed before my father left for Korea. "Magical cures are not unheard of," Eli said when I expressed my skepticism. "You can never tell what might bring someone around." A shrill voice inside my head kept saying that the best intentions were rarely sufficient in making bad things turn good.

Eli was windy and gruff during the service, and both bored and starved us with one of his digressive sermons on the Diaspora. He plowed through the entire *Haggadah* like my grandfather used to, and I remembered how my father would taunt them by disputing the translation and embellishing the text with his own exotic interpretation of Exodus. When Eli spoke of the Children of Israel foraging in the wilderness, he gave my father a watery glance that upset everyone. After the meal my cousins watched *Your Hit Parade!* in the family room while I stood with my forehead pressed against the windowpane in the foyer outside the Florida room and heard my mother and Eli argue about the business and money. Something had to be done with him, she said. She couldn't go on much longer like this; things were getting worse. Then she said that she was mostly worried about my behavior; she said that *I* was acting strange. I could've been knocked cold by that remark, and I wanted to burst in on them and demand that she take back what she'd said or else I'd do something that would fill her life with sorrow. My ears were tingling, and I felt the loss of my father like a missing limb. For some reason I didn't move, and they continued their crazy bickering for the better part of an hour—more talk about insurance premiums and investing in new equipment, talk I only half heard in my growing distraction—while my father sat there silently, decked out in an embroidered Israeli *kipa* and a new Harris tweed sport coat we'd bought him for the holiday. With a sudden jerk he knocked over my mother's cup, and hot coffee ran all over his trousers. He didn't make a sound.

By the summer he would grunt for food and water and let us know when he needed the toilet by wagging his hands wildly toward his bottom and letting out a bellow. On Saturdays I strolled him around the village for exercise. Occasionally we'd stop in the park to watch the shirtless Italian men play boccie ball and argue in the sun, then we'd go have a pizza or a stromboli for lunch. We huddled together like conspirators in my room while I categorized my baseball cards according to dozens of conflicting statistical factors. I strummed the hand-carved ukulele he'd sent me from Pearl Harbor and sang made-up Hawaiian songs to him, and on the laminated card table where my mother played Mah-Jongg Wednesday nights we played Parcheesi or Chinese checkers the best we could, which always meant me playing for both of us. Most days he sat like a statue on the porch—brooding, I imagined, though he was probably just watching Satchmo, who would wash his paws and ears while perched on the lip of the limestone birdbath.

It was Flag Day and I was showing him how to play mumbletypeg, when a green, beat-up Plymouth pulled into our driveway and a man wearing an Eisenhower jacket with captain's bars and carrying a black briefcase came up our walk. "Your mother's expecting me," the man said, holding out a sleek, fluttering hand for me to shake. He made eye contact with my father and gave him an exaggerated grin. The enamel of his protruding front teeth was badly stained, and his bristly black mustache seemed to have an electric current running through it, since the hair-ends stood at attention when he spoke. "I'm Captain Glaws," he said to my father, shooting me a hangdog look. "I'm your friend."

Captain Glaws was an Army psychiatrist, and he began coming by each Monday around the same time in the late afternoon. Previously—and only intermittently—my mother would take my father to a private clinic in Ossining, not far from Sing Sing, to see someone who specialized in his type of shell shock, but he charged too much and Eli's insurance policy didn't carry that kind of coverage. Captain Glaws was long-necked and balding and had a pleased look on his face all the time. He'd greet me with his bony hand extended and then pat my father's head as if he were a playful dog. Sometimes he'd let me sit in the Plymouth and shift the gears. The car reeked of waxy chocolate milk cartons, and the rubber floor mats were always covered with sandwich rinds and cigar wrappers. He would bring me packages of Yodels or Ring Dings and then ask me to beat it for an hour or two. Sometimes—it must have been his way of establishing intimacy—he would wear khaki chinos and a polo shirt and play catch with me in the yard before he went inside.

After a few minutes he'd start to look around for my mother, and a pained expression would come over his face if he didn't see her right away.

She would stand in the shadow cast by a copper lamp at the bottom of the landing, and make an entrance. He'd usually have his hands in his pockets, and he'd walk right up to her until his shirt touched her sundress. I would go behind the garage and watch him lead her by her bare elbow inside the clacking screen door. Outlined by the soft saffron glow of the citronella bulb, they moved about, circled each other, talking, smiling, arranging their gestures. She seemed to be modeling her clothes for him. He would say things to her that made her blush, and I'd see beads of spit erupt between his narrow lips.

A few times I came back from my walk to find them drinking lemon cokes or egg creams. Tommy Dorsey or Duke Ellington would be on the Victrola, and she'd be serving him wedges of rhubarb pie or strawberry *babka*. When I entered the kitchen she winked at me over his shoulder and shook her head in a way that said it was not a good idea for me to say anything now. They giggled with crumbs in their mouths and I was dizzy washing my juice glass in the sink. Something I only vaguely understood had a hold on her, and I was afraid that if I said anything at all I would only make matters worse without accomplishing anything. Like most parents, mine had worked hard to establish the kind of family they felt they'd never quite had themselves, a family that could weather all misfortunes, and now that family was gone. I knew my mother could no longer be a hostage to my father's illness, that some limit to her grief had been reached. Seeing her eyes returning to life, it was clear that I would be on my own in this, that all of us would be.

One afternoon I watched them talking outside. My father was in the backyard, napping in the hammock. Captain Glaws was leaning up against the fender of his car. He flicked her hair away from her eyes with his long, blunt-tipped fingers, and opened his mouth in a wide, imploring grin. She colored, and her whitened flesh seemed to bleed in circles beneath the surface. Smiling, she traced his mouth with her thumb. They went inside and I waited for almost an hour before following them. His jacket hung in the hall closet and his briefcase was on the ottoman. The easy chair my father always sat in had been moved to the other side of the living room. Captain Glaws was sitting in it, drinking beer from an earthenware mug, his skinny legs crossed at the ankles.

I knew it was coming, but I was stunned nevertheless when my mother told me she was putting him into a veterans hospital. When I protested she said, "Don't be silly, it's a nice cozy place," in a tone surely meant to be consoling but that in fact sounded scornful.

"Everything's all wrong," I said.

"Oh, Noah," she said gently, smoothing her skirt. "It's all done, it's history. He'll have no decisions to make. His life'll be certain, safe. Not like ours."

I wanted to put my hands around her throat. She looked old and mean and I turned my face away.

"What am I supposed to do?" she said, her voice rising. Her eyes were riveted on me. "Go ahead, tell me."

"I want things to be the way they were," I said.

"You must think I'm a rotten mother. No one knows how to act decently anymore. Life is too short, and I need to live for myself for a change. You can have a bad conscience for both of us. Wait till you're my age, then you'll understand what I'm talking about."

"Just tell me—why did he enlist?"

She turned to leave the room. "God," she said, her fingers steepled over her mouth and nose, her hooded eyes alive with anguish. "Because he'd rather have been in Korea than with me."

The window was open and the air was saturated with the smell of crushed honeysuckle. I thought of a summer vacation a few years back, at Lake George. My father and I had gone hunting for arrowheads and fishing for crappie and trout; after supper we'd listen to the ball game on his shortwave radio. My mother was sulky, and she spent her days in a webbed beach lounge, reading gothic romances and drinking gin-and-tonics. It was muggy and hot and the cabin we slept in had begun to smell like buttermilk. The murky nights were charged with the fumes of ionized air. One morning I found the picnic table at our campsite covered with black ants. My parents fought all the time—about everything. I must've blocked those two weeks out, because in truth nothing had ever been the same after that. When we came home they were tentative with each other, and with me. They both simply looked exhausted most of the time, and always seemed on the verge of sleep. One evening, while I washed our mess kits and strung them on a clothesline nailed to a couple of cherry birches, I watched their shapes silhouetted against the flickering mottled light inside the cabin. Sunset's swirling dust-cloud and spotted lilac cape had dragged its ermine skirt across the peaceful lake. My parents could have been a pair of pious Jews *davening* at dusk, but their voices sounded like simmering wasps. In a few minutes my father emerged. His face was flushed—something had taken the breath out of him, he looked staggered and frail. He smoked a cigarette and ordered me to get my things together and help him pack the car. I did what he said, and didn't question him.

The night before the day of his departure, I paused in front of my mother's open bedroom door. Out the window, descending clusters of clouds were like silky pearl corollas against the sky. Her shoulders were covered with the black lace shawl my father had given her for their anniversary a few years back. My heart made odd little jumps as she stroked her wiry hair. She leaned toward the rusting dresser mirror, dragging her antique bone comb of stippled garnet against a clump of tangles. The comb wouldn't come out, and the more she pulled the more snarled her hair became. I wanted to burst into her room and say that I could help her, that we could move away to another city, another state, that everything would work out. I wanted to tell her that anything was possible, that I would make it all right, that what it all finally came down to was love and trust and endurance. But when I saw her face arrested in the dingy glass it was impenetrable, a face ragged and faded beyond recognition. I looked away and felt my pulse drumming in the roof of my mouth. When I saw her later, in the kitchen, she was un-ruffled, almost serene, filing her polished nails into half moons. She looked at me with eyes burned clean of any purpose or hope, and I felt like a stranger—a boarder—in her life and home. I turned away when she asked me how I was feeling, and her voice was free of bitterness when she said that it was no one's fault we couldn't make a go of it.

For more than four years I visited him regularly in his hexagon-tiled cubicle at the VA hospital on the bluffs overlooking the Hudson. The hospital was cold and dark and always smelled of resin and mosquito repellent. It was my impression that he liked my coming, even though I knew that our time together made no ordinary sense. His ward was jammed with lonely looking men in olive pajamas who read comic books and watched game shows on a portable TV. Some had pot and whiskey and penknives smuggled into their footlockers. I brought him magazines he couldn't read, a clock-radio he never listened to, and Necco wafers and Indian nuts the other patients stole.

My mother divorced him after about a year. There were other men after Captain Glaws, good men I must admit, men recovering from divorce themselves, or from widowerhood or business failures; men, in other words, who were in the same boat she was. I don't hold any grudges toward her. After all, as she said, she had her own life to lead. She felt that her life had been quietly ebbing away from her, and she craved intimacy—who among us doesn't?—attach-ments that reached far beyond the transitory ones of the flesh. Heartache permeates every family in greater or lesser degrees, and I have no reason to doubt that she did the very best she could. She was distracted by her own deep needs, and who am I to judge her?

Later she eloped with a Dutchess County pharmacist—someone she'd met on an Israeli sightseeing bus in Eilat, at the southern tip of the Negev—who was still grieving over the loss of his wife and daughter ten years after their deaths in a car wreck on the Taconic State Parkway. Sidney was a shy, quiet man who reminded me of

Charlie Chaplin, and my mother seemed less anxious with him, if not entirely happy. She sold the house I grew up in for a nice profit and bought a vacation bungalow in the Poconos. In a very short time she became a woman I hardly recognized. It was as if when my father left her life for good I too became someone out of another time, a time she would've rather simply buried.

As a way of escape I joined the Air Force after high school, and never saw her again. Sometimes, in places like crowded elevators or supermarket lines or movie theaters, I suffer from pangs of regret when I smell my mother's perfume on the neck of a strange woman. When she died of a pulmonary embolism a few years later, a complication of a minor operation to repair a hernia, I was an MP stationed in Thailand. I received a formal condolence note from Sidney a few weeks after her funeral.

The last time I saw my father was on his birthday, the year I was discharged from the service. I was twenty-four and ready to try college. I'd gone to Macy's and bought him one of those stuffed animals made of polyurethane pellets and cellulose fibers. It was a snowy afternoon, and I was reading the sports section of the *Daily News* to him in the steamy arboretum while he picked at the plaster on the lime-colored walls. A line of glowing freighters was anchored in the icy river beneath the Palisades. He lay on his side, facing the window, and stared at the barren trees and high-voltage lines outside. His hair was matted and his beard was rough. He was wearing the silk tea gown I'd mailed him from Bangkok and clutching the stuffed cat on his knee. I was reading him an article on the Knicks when he let loose with a groan like Satchmo did after a runaway go-cart had smashed his spine on the sidewalk in front of our house. In his hand were the toy cat's translucent green eyes. He held me in his sad gaze for more than a minute, and the feel of his whiskers and dog tags against my face and chest when I hugged him has remained with me for all these years. It was like mid-August under the pure rods of fluorescent light. Talking wildly on into the night as snow fell in sheets outside, I did not think of ever abandoning him, till some orderlies came and took him back to his room.

This is the man
That lies in the house of Bedlam.
—Elizabeth Bishop

Leisure World

From what Judah Landau could see, there was only one dish of charlotte russe left in the revolving pie carousel. Tracking it, he swept a saucer of marmalade aside. "In *my* opinion," he said, jabbing his curved thumb in his chest, "Florida's going to the dogs. Every snowbird in Sheepshead Bay is moving down these days." He smacked the table with his other hand, scattering lemon slices, Equal packets, a thin pot of white horseradish in a cruet. His shaved cheeks were grooved with raw scabs.

Leaning forward, Zucker gave him an imploring look. "Pinkie—*again* with your wife's boyfriend? You didn't used to be such a mental person." Zucker had always called his younger cousin by his West Rogers Park nickname.

Landau shook his densely curled head. His sharp-jawed face was flushed, as if an electrical charge had been sent through it. He was having brunch with Maurice Zucker at the Bagel 'n' Things Cafe in the Royal Coconut Plaza. The place smelled of fried potatoes and perfume. Crowds of morning walkers were jammed into yellow rattan booths. Out the tinted windows garnished with *Chanukah* banners and spider plants, foursomes in bright orange and gold clothing waited to tee off on Leisure World's flat nine-hole course. An old man sitting on a sandstone bench threw bread crusts at a few brown ducks settled on the barren pond. Immaculate palm fronds stained the color of the ocean drooped in the blazing heat.

Zucker tested his tea with his tongue; he sipped it through a sugar cube. He wore a mourner's black ribbon on the lapel of his corduroy jacket; after a decade in a wheelchair, an uncle of theirs had died a few days ago in Del Ray from Alzheimer's disease. Landau had had a severe falling out with him years before at a Passover *Seder* and had refused to attend the funeral. The deceased was a forlorn eccentric who had accused Landau of swiping a precious family heirloom, a pair of braided glass candlesticks. "You want a fresh opinion?" Zucker asked, his whiskey-colored face fixed on his order of creamed herring and smoked chubs.

"Go ahead," Landau grunted, dark eyes shining inside thickly fringed lids. "I can take whatever it is." He rolled a lemon drop in his big lower lip.

"I hafta laugh, Pinkie. Look what gets into you." Zucker pointed at him with his spoon. "*Sable* monkeying around—I can't believe it for a second."

Landau bared his square teeth; he played with his empty mug. "I *know* the signals a woman sends out," he said condescendingly. He shifted in his chair and tapped the blade of his knife across his scaly knuckles. From his belly came the flat rumbles of lousy digestion. He karate-chopped at his plate.

An ambulance roared by outside, distracting them.

Zucker combed his woolly sideburns with his fingers. "Now just a minute, Pinkie—I'm not so young anymore. You need to refresh my memory."

"Needs-shmeeds," Landau said icily.

Zucker pointed at his wilted iceberg lettuce; he looked indignant. "Shush yourself already! You're always jumping the gun with everything."

"*Shush?* After what I saw?" Landau barked. "I'm not a greenhorn."

Zucker took a nibble of herring and tried not to make a face. It tasted like it had been frozen. "Troubles, troubles—are you asking for some kind of heart breakdown?"

Landau felt a bitter sensation rise in his throat. "I have my hands full at home," he said, fiddling with the cuffs of his shirt. His box-shaped head felt bloated, pumped up. "Where's the goddamn half 'n' half?" With his raised cup he signaled to a sleepy waitress with a clay-pot dome of frizzy red hair who sat smoking behind the cash register. She came over with a pot of boiling water and handed him a nondairy creamer. Her starched white uniform smelled of milk.

"That doll's got some knockers," Zucker said, scratching his chin. "The *goniff* who owns this dump likes them with big tits. I get a hard-on every time I come here. It's impossible to have a cup of tea in peace anymore. Women excite me more now than when I was a young man."

"For crying-out-loud! You're almost what—eighty-three years old?" Landau said.

"So? You think I'm a corpse yet?"

"Don't be such a smart aleck," Landau said. "We got terrific issues in the world, serious problems even heavyweights like Kissinger can't solve. No one knows from *gornisht*. From nothing. And I need to remind you that wives keep secrets from their husbands all the time?"

Zucker made a tunnel with his left hand, then drilled his right index finger through his clenched fist. "Live a little, Pinkie. Have some pizazz. It's Talmud; it's Torah," he cooed.

Landau tilted forward and sniffed at the blintzes stacked like logs on Zucker's dish. He felt parched, his insides were making him uncomfortable. "I need this aggravation like a hole in the head," he murmured.

Zucker's sagging tea bag drained in a black plastic ashtray. Landau, sighing like an old dog, fingered the thin wet string.

"Tsk, tsk," Zucker clucked. He blew a kiss at a quartet of women who sat down nearby. Butch cuts for the heat, toreador pants, pink Reeboks, squarish, blue-veined necks, eyelids the shade of astroturf. One of them made a noise like a bellows when she breathed.

Landau grunted at them and looked away. "Check the lousy hairdo on that heavy broad. She reminds me of Rod Steiger in one of those gladiator movies."

"It's a chemotherapy wig," Zucker said.

"Hey—pay some attention. Sable goes to the ritzy mall in Bal Harbour and comes home from the beauty parlor with painted nails and her hair in beads—a 'Nefertiti braid,' she calls it—and with a box of scented stationery she got at Neiman-Marcus with 'Ms. Sable Landau' at the top. *I'm missing!* When I mention this insult in a friendly way, she hands me some baloney about doing her own thing. What gives?"

"Bite your tongue," Zucker scolded. "Why behave like a stuffed shirt? Better you should feel lucky that you're married to such a modern girl."

"That's not my point," Landau snorted. "Between Sable and Stuie and Shelley, I get the message loud and clear. What the hell do I have to show for fifty years of breaking my balls? If we'd've stayed in Winnetka instead of coming down to Florida, at least I could've gone to Sox games in the summer. I'd've been far better off moving to the West Bank. At least I could have helped the Israelis kick Arafat's ass. Florida is for the birds." He filed his gritty, ingrown thumbnail with the edge of a matchbook. He looked at his handsome cousin from Lwów, the only member of his father's sister's family who had managed to survive Hitler's Europe: flirtatious and courtly, with his luscious red hair moussed with *Kölnischwasser;* a retired furrier who kept a condo in Evanston that he rented to glamourous celebrity professors.

Zucker grinned. "In the words of my granddaughter, 'Chill out.'"

"The last time I spoke to Stuie, that's what *he* said to me. He doesn't mind pissing my dough away on this screwball Hindu swami he goes skiing with in Wisconsin. Lazy so-and-so thinks I'm a regular Onassis. Did I tell you he's coming down next week for a few days? He's probably tapped out again."

"Please—stop with the complaining. You get so keyed up you'll need a tranquilizer soon."

"I'll tell you something else," Landau said, pinching Zucker's wrist. "This character Freud, he's the new head of the condo finance committee. He looks just like that half-breed Yul Brynner, who Sable always found irresistible. Don't worry, I've checked him out plenty already. He was a chiropractor in Philadelphia, and those phonies are strictly from hunger. Rip-off artists pretending to be real doctors. I heard he's got season tickets to the Dolphins and occasionally has lunch with Don Shula. The wise guy's even got an Apple computer in his apartment. Marvin Kaminsky lives next door to him, and he told me that since the man's wife passed away from Parkinson's disease three years ago he's got horny widows and divorcées coming and going. Marv says the guy holds court in the sauna and entertains the *alter kockers* with Polack jokes. He jogs on a treadmill wearing gold chains around his neck and brags about his jumbo certificates of deposit and his cognac collection. He told Abie Gerber that he took an El Al flight to Tel Aviv during the Six-Day War in order to shoot the Jew-hating Syrians. He swears that he has connections in the *Mossad* and that Golda Meir gave him a medal."

Zucker sucked his teeth. "You think that a chiropractor knows from the *Mossad*? What's got into you? Abie Gerber's a fat *shlemiel*. Freud probably wears a bag to shit in and has lifts in his shoes."

"The bastard looks like a million bucks, Maury. He's a goddamn six-footer!" Landau held his arms out to demonstrate.

Zucker's eyelids lowered, and he wiped his bifocals on a napkin. "Whew! He sounds like some operator. And you know for certain that this comedian is shacking up with Sable?"

Landau shot Zucker a hard, dimensionless glare.

But that's *exactly* what he was sure of. Not long ago he noticed a deep bruise on Sable's throat while she blow-dried her hair. Suspicious of enlarged or discolored moles, he immediately demanded she make an appointment with the oncologist. Unblushing, she coolly told him it was a hive from an insect bite. Landau wasn't buying it. "Since when does a spider have fangs like a snake?"

She sat on the edge of the bed, naked, and powdered her breasts with cornstarch. She yelled, half-laughing, "Then it must be one of those yellow-fever mosquitoes the HMO is always warning us about."

He leaned his face into his palms and admired her admiring herself in the satinwood dresser mirror. Her hipbones were as flat as sails, her veinless legs like marble pillars. She hadn't worn a girdle in decades, and had recently started buying her underwear in a Coconut Grove lingerie shop that catered to young women.

He said, "Why wear wool legwarmers in this crazy weather?" "Oh, please, Judah! It's the fashion." Unruffled, she clipped her toenails and painted them blood-red. The hard filings flew in the air like hailstones.

His frustration began to creep up his neck like a burning hand. "Who was it that scratched you?" he hollered. "I have a right to know!" She continued slathering Oil of Olay on her thighs and elbows; the ivory filigree cameo that Landau had given her for their fortieth anniversary dangled on a gold chain between her pear-shaped breasts. His ears were ringing; he hid his erection with a pillow.

She picked up her emery board. "Are your piles bothering you, honey? Maybe you should take a sitz bath with Epsom salts."

"Don't change the subject on me!" he said in a booming voice. Exasperated with her, he got up and slammed a housefly against the accordion closet door with his open palm.

Unfazed, Sable shimmied into a lavender leotard and left for her jazzercise class.

Landau began putting two and two together. It wasn't a week later when he spotted Sable and Leon Freud flirting on the wheelchair ramp in the swimming pool. She had eyes for him already, he thought. When Freud grinned at her, Landau saw that the roots of his teeth were green. He looked simonized; sweat pooled on his butternut skin in shivering droplets. Freud was hairless and lean; he had a thin, penciled mustache and rounded shoulders like an athlete. In the pool he swam with a sinuous crawl, his hands stabbing a path ahead in the rippling water. Sable kept fiddling with the straps of her bathing suit; she continually snapped the spandex around her wrinkled bottom. Freud had a tattoo on his upper arm in the shape of an upside-down menorah; he had a firm behind, like a target.

Afterwards, Landau phoned Zucker and told him what he'd seen: "A *Yid* with a tattoo; can you figure it?"

That night, before supper, Landau examined his own backside in the door frame mirror: floury, bell-mouthed, inert. He loathed the erosion of his body, his pale, ropy shanks, the coarse gray hair—it looked like lint—in his navel. His belly hung; his nipples protruded. He thought how Leon Freud's behind spoke to Sable—it sang to her. Landau's sang, too: of the thousands of meals he'd eaten across the table from her, of the skid marks on his roomy boxer shorts, of his carbonated rumblings.

Zucker tugged at Landau's arm. "Stop brooding. Haven't you approached Sable about all this?"

Zucker's remark puzzled him. "That's out of the question," he said sullenly, his congested face a garment of resentment. "You know how tough minds work in Chicago? I'm no bullshit artist. I'll make Freud divvy up when the time is right. I know the score. You think I want Sable should know I know?"

Zucker only pressed harder. "It's a terrible mistake you're making," he said affectionately. "You must unload yourself or you're asking for a serious nerve condition and fluid retention. Over at the new reform synagogue, in Plantation, they have an institute on all kinds of crummy family relations. Maybe even the chubby lady rabbi, the one with the Ph.D. in elderly psychology, would take the time to sit down with both of you—go ahead, invite that con artist Freud if you want—and make a useful recommendation."

What kind of *shul* was that? Landau thought. The place was a Mormon palace, with organ music and polished-bronze pulpits and prayer books printed in English. He raised his arms slowly behind his head and peered at his old cousin. "Not a chance, Maury. I'm a meat-and-potatoes Jew, from meat-and-potatoes Chicago. Don't think for a second I can't handle that *yutz* myself."

"*Shah!*" Zucker whispered, his thin, elastic neck craning from right to left. "My God—do you want everyone in Broward County to know you're hard up?"

Landau had a sudden taste of gloom in his mouth, like rancid borscht. He felt his stomach cramping, and with a raw, derisive laugh he peered sourly into Zucker's gelatinous, artificial left eye. "The hell with everyone! They probably know already. This Shangri-la

is the land of busybodies and know-it-alls." He signaled to the waitress to bring their check. "Here," he bellowed, slapping the bill in
Zucker's palm. "It's your turn."

The very next night, before eating, Sable found him pinching the skin on his heavy thighs, the purple vessels bunched like pitted prunes. He almost curtsied, covering himself with his freckled
hands.

"Judah," she said, "what's wrong? Give me a look." She tried to
pry his hands apart.

He cringed, giving off a pained sigh. "I smell the deckel burning.
Go—go! Turn off the light under the oven."

She smiled protectively. A complexion˙ like Redi Whip, he
thought.

"It's a sweet potato *kugel*," she said. "Darling, does your penis
hurt you?"

Landau crumpled to his knees.

"Judah!" she gasped.

"Don't shame me! Let me be!"

She crouched in a catcher's stance above him, her lips twisted
down at the corners. Landau remembered when they flew kites in
Grant Park along the lakefront, before the park was home to rapists
and bums. She would root for him whenever he played shuffleboard
against the bearded Jews in overcoats. As a boy he had played four-
wall handball at the YMCA and Sunday morning softball games
with her brothers Lester and Emile.

"Judah, did you lift something the wrong way and rupture yourself again?" Sable had on her *Leisure World Is A Place For Lovers*
apron. She grazed his whitened flank with her Press-On Nails and
his stiff hairs moved like cilia.

"Make supper!" he roared. "Go vacuum, the house smells funny.
Iron, set the table, argue with Dan Rather! Just don't fuss over
me!" He glanced between her parted legs, her nylons rolled below
her knees, and imagined he saw Freud's reddened face drooling out
at him.

She stood up, smoothed her skirt, patted her hair. "You lied to me the last time you came back from a checkup. It's your prostate again, I knew it. I'll go call the urologist's emergency number. For being such a big sissy you'll have to wear a bag now. *Gottenyu!*"

"Don't bother anyone," Landau said, propping himself up on one elbow. "The prostate's working like a Timex. You always made it clear I didn't know what a woman wanted—what *you* needed. Tell the truth, Sable, I couldn't satisfy you, right? And now, out of spite, you're getting even with me. You're just like Solomon, may he rest in peace." He lost his balance and spun over on his back.

Scowling, Sable yanked at her apron strings. Her thin arms, twisted across her waist, looked like an umbilical cord. "Not that nonsense with my father again? Go on! Please stop making jokes. Is there blood in your urine? Come, make a big sis so I can see." She went to the bureau and got him a Banlon shirt and a pair of beige chinos. "Put this on before you catch pneumonia."

He sat up. "Pneumonia! It's 80 degrees in here, the way you set the thermostat. Leave me be. *Go.*"

She stormed out of the bedroom, hurt, muttering in Yiddish to herself, and soon Landau heard her banging about in every room. Moving chairs, shifting the foyer area rugs. In a matter of minutes she was speaking in what he called her "official voice." She can't go anywhere around the apartment without the cordless phone, he thought. He heard Sable let out a *gevalt!* her younger sister Minnie could have heard in New Jersey. His shoulders slumped; by morning every Jew in South Florida would think he was cockeyed.

Landau soaked his blistered piles in a tub of hot salt water for twenty minutes or so, and decided he'd clear the air, see what Sable wanted from him. Her own checking account? Her own car? Money frozen in the bank he couldn't touch? It didn't much matter anymore. He'd do whatever was required to preserve order, maintain appearances. When the time was right he'd deal with Freud. He put on lime tube socks, rubber-soled sandals, and plaid Bermudas instead of the chinos and went into the kitchen. Congealing on a wooden carving board were the unsliced meat (it was a boneless French roast) and the *kugel*. A note taped to the Cuisinart said she'd gone to Burdine's for a brassiere special. Then Mah-Jongg at the clubhouse. It ended: *No point in waiting up. Remember to take your irritable bowel medicine. Sable.*

Landau slipped on a cotton Shaker sweater-vest and a feathered felt hat, and groaned at the sight of his dinner. Sable still took pleasure in cooking stupendous meals. Unlike so many of his neighbors, Landau was a huge meat eater; he was unafraid of hardening of the arteries, of gallstones, of having an expensive pacemaker implanted in his thick chest. He had no patience with hypochondriacs or exercise nuts or people who bought lottery tickets. He once told Maury that cholesterol had gotten a bum rap from cardiologists.

He went outside on the terrace. The ring of keys on his belt jangled as he walked. Wasn't this her regular canasta night? he wondered. He couldn't keep track of all Sable's activities anymore: *Hadassah,* the UJA phonathons, the Maccabee Garden Club, the Prime Timers outreach program for newly arrived Russian families settling in Greater Miami—she was the brains behind the sisterhood's major fund-raiser during *Purim,* the annual *Hamantashen* Shindig. It was all starting to make him wacky.

In the distance he could see the rigs rushing by on the interstate overpass. Cicadas rattled in the frangipani. He felt remote, ravenous, gassy. *Yortzeit* candles trembled in jelly jars on windowsills. The flowering hibiscus smelled like burning pine. "Sable must think I'm a dummy," he said out loud, startling himself. His mind wandered: Judah Landau the master plumber, the neighborhood handyman, a drain expert, a professional Mister Fixit who couldn't keep his own wife's pilot light going. Sable had an encyclopedia packed with grievances; she was a resentful woman. Landau's one-man business never made enough money, the kids had to walk around in cheap looking clothes from South State Street discount department stores when they were in grammar school (Sable had had no choice but to send them to a fleabag day camp in Skokie), he bought junky living room furniture at bargain basement prices that fell apart after a year, he carried home blind cocker spaniels from the pound that gored the mock-Oriental rugs with their burly claws, he couldn't afford High Holy Day tickets at the ultramodern synagogue—a polygon with stained-glass windows and a geodesic dome designed by Buckminster Fuller.

Landau remembered: the trouble began almost forty-four years ago, on their honeymoon, in a cut-rate, grime-encrusted Van Buren Street dive only one notch above a flophouse. Sable's father Solomon, a squat man with clout and connections, had a wild, drooping Cossack mustache and dressed like a stevedore—dungarees, a heavy, torn mohair sweater, a blue Greek fisherman's cap—and suffered from emphysema. Solomon ran a successful taxi fleet and who knew what else out of a goon-owned hockshop on Milwaukee Street. He had offered to treat them to a snazzy suite at the Belden-Stratford Hotel for a few days, plus the free use of one of his cabs. The place Landau rented instead was crawling with ants. Cobwebs heavy with dust coated the lampshades, and with the windows open the narrow streets below reeked of onions and kielbasa. The sheets smelled like Roquefort salad dressing, and the thick, resinous odor of dead flies moldering in the heat of the buzzing light bulbs permeated the two tiny rooms. Sable had started sneezing the second they arrived; she picked hairy balls of lint off the pillowcases. The watery redness in her eyes said he should have swallowed his pride and accepted her father's gift. Landau ran across the street to a Ukrainian grocery and bought her two boxes of tissues, Chuckles, an egg cream, a stale almond Danish ring, and a quart brick of Neapolitan ice cream. He had a five-day furlough and had just ridden twelve hundred miles in a cramped train for his wedding. As it turned out, he was too beat to do anything other than sack out.

He'd foreseen consecrating his conjugal duties with flying colors, and the next night, after blundering, he blamed Sable for everything. He ranted at her that she made him feel klutzy and ashamed. At first Sable ignored his complaining; she assumed he was simply exhausted from boot camp and the trip north. Then, almost consolingly, she urged him to use a lubricant (she fished a tube of Vaseline out of her traveling kit and held it out to him like a gift). Perhaps, he recalled her having said, he was in too much of a hurry.

Try slowing down, she suggested sweetly. Relax, catch your breath a minute, stop forcing so much—wait till she's ready for him. He turned his back on her. When Sable touched his shoulder he shouted, "What can I do?" He said it was all her fault; that she didn't know how to excite him.

Awakening in the early morning with sunlight streaming through the filthy curtains, he found himself smothering beneath Sable's hot thighs. Inflamed, he rolled over on her and lost control of himself when they kissed hungrily. For months afterward they lay in bed like mummies, wrapped in separate quilts, sadly bewildered, not knowing how to touch each other, adrift in their own separate distress.

———

The silvery lights around the malarial-looking canal were gleaming. From someone's open window Landau heard an orchestra playing the opening bars to "I've Got You Under My Skin." He stopped and watched a racing motorboat circle by in an immense corona of glistening foam, its droning engines drowning out the music. The air smelled reptilian, almost mineral. June bugs chirred in the anemic oleander. He saw the jagged, broken curve of a shampoo bottle in the bushes. An old man wearing a Sony Walkman who reminded him of a leprechaun struggled along on a pair of canes. Landau tapped the brim of his hat. "What does she want from me?" he muttered, frightening the old man.

He paused at a traffic rotary, inhaled deeply. The sun was going down, the thin clouds were fading in swirls of orange and varying reds and violets. Landau felt queasy, his bloated head swam. He went into the street without looking. He heard a horn and looked up. A girl with a spiky pink Mohawk was calling him an asshole out of a Stingray convertible. A black man with a bald head was driving.

"*Momzers!*" Landau yelled, moving swiftly to the opposite sidewalk. Everyone's out to nail me to the cross, he thought bitterly. He heard a kind of muted growling and noticed he was being trailed across the noisy shopping plaza by a Labrador retriever. The atrium had a broken fountain and was like a prison yard under its platinum floodlights. He entered a B. Dalton's and bought a copy of *Modern Maturity*. At an outdoor cafe he sat on a bamboo chair and had a cappuccino and a piece of *halvah*. "Stayin' Alive" blasted out of a Sam Goody. He stared at the hanging maidenhair ferns and didn't leave until some people from Leisure World he recognized waved at him to come join them. One of them was Martin Novack, a long-faced belligerent refugee from the camps, who gave an annual lecture after the *yizkor* service on *Yom Kippur* that he called "The Lessons of Auschwitz." In conversation—and Novack's guttural, high-pitched English gave Landau the willies—Novack only wanted to reminisce about his first wife and parents and the glamourous time in Vilna before the Nazi meatgrinder arrived. As if life was ever glamourous for the Jews in Poland or Russia, Landau would think of saying scornfully, his indignation stoked by Novack's muddled surges of sentimentality. But he never did. Softened, he thought he had always heard the grim irony in Novack's metallic voice, an accusatory and urgent tone that told him the poor stiff was probably expecting another pogrom at any moment.

He paused and read the carryout menu at Duck Chang's Cantonese Sampan and studied the live lobsters in their dark window tank. It suddenly occurred to him that perhaps Sable was testing him; that maybe she was using Freud simply for leverage, to get him to go out more, to take her to places like Club Med, or for a romantic weekend in Miami Beach, fox-trotting at the Fontainebleau Hotel, or for a gambling cruise in the Caribbean. She'd often mentioned wanting to drive up to Jupiter to see Burt Reynolds in a play. Landau could care less about a third-rate actor like Burt Reynolds. Landau didn't own any leisure clothes, and he didn't golf or play tennis or cards or swim laps. He hated sweating in the humid air, the stink of cocoa butter and insect repellent, and he missed the brutal wind and bleakness of Chicago, the icy black sludge a few days after a monster snowstorm, the black mirror of Lake Michigan. He knew a few nutty people his age who went in for scuba diving and snorkeling, but he couldn't imagine the pleasure they got from being underwater and nose-to-nose with transparent colored fish. At Tito's Spaghetteria he bought a slice of Sicilian with anchovy and peppers and a Brown Cow, and read an article in his magazine—"Herpes After Seventy." When he saw Martin Novack reading the menu at a table nearby, he quickly left for home.

In front of his apartment he folded his arms and hugged himself, bending alongside a hedge of amaryllis and orange impatiens. He cupped a petal and watched a wingless beetle suck at a leaf. The checkerberry bushes Sable had planted last spring were heavy with fruit. He opened the door and called her name, forgetting for a second that she was out for the evening. He put water in the teakettle and sat down on a stool in the kitchen. His head ached; his nose, at the large tip, burned. There were shooting pains in his ribs, acid bubbled in his gut. He flipped through last week's condo newsletter and the editorial page of this morning's Miami *Herald.* Dope killings, a gang rape in a swanky Boca Raton spa, child pornography in a Tampa day-care center, an armored car holdup in a Marriott resort outside Epcot. The phone rang, stopped, rang again. "Hullo. Judah Landau on the line."

"It's me," a voice whispered into the phone. In a crossed connection he heard someone with a Jewish accent ordering egg rolls, spareribs, and chicken chow mein.

Landau glanced at the wall clock above the range. "Stuie? Is that you?" He wondered if his mind was playing tricks on him.

"Uh huh," Stuie mumbled.

Landau's heart went flat. He hadn't spoken to Stuie in a couple of months. Sable said Stuie was very busy. Yeah, Landau had thought, the Illinois dropout who worked in the Art Institute souvenir shop selling Expressionist posters and Chagall calendars was too busy to talk with his old man. The last time they spoke Stuie told him he gave off bad vibes, that Landau's karma bummed him out.

"How've you been, Stuie?" Landau asked pleasantly.

"Okay, I guess," Stuie said.

Landau turned and looked out the window. A glistening band of perspiration ringed his mouth.

"I'm in Fort Lauderdale, Dad. At a Pizza Hut near the airport."

"I'll be damned," Landau said. "How come? You know I wasn't expecting you until next Saturday."

"Maybe you got the dates screwed up. Can you come get me?"
The phone buzzed in Landau's ear. He smacked the receiver in
his palm. "Sorry, Stuie, no can do. The Town and Country's in
the shop."

"Again? Shit," Stuie groaned.

"We got a rotten connection, Stuie. Catch a cab and I'll meet you
out front."

"The damn thing should be totaled," Stuie said. "How many
times has Mama told you to buy a new car? Twenty? Thirty?"

"Stuie—can't you take a cab for once?" Landau said. "What's the
big deal?"

Always with the fresh mouth, Landau thought. A year ago Stuie
had tried to convince him to get a "fully loaded" Volkswagen
Golf—tinted windows, a CD player and a cassette deck, dual air-
bags. Stuie drove a rusted Karmann-Ghia he claimed got fifty miles
to a gallon of gas and never needed an oil change. When Landau
told him he'd never buy a German car, Stuie insisted that cars and
beer were the two things the Germans were really good at. They're
pretty good at homicide, too, Landau muttered in response.

He took the garbage out and waited by the side of the road. A
heavy man in drugstore flip-flops and olive drawstring pajamas was
picking through a pile of newspapers; the dumpsters were filled
with crushed pizza boxes, disposable diapers, and sand wasps. Stuie
was always the sore spot. He knew Sable blamed him for Stuie's lack
of direction. According to her, he had yelled at him too much. He
had had no right to expect Stuie to stick his jaw in the way of
ground balls and wicked line drives. Is it my fault he's such a pansy?
Landau had grumbled. Had he *forced* Stuie to work in Brentano's
for ten years, selling paperbacks? She said he never got off Stuie's
back, but Landau argued that it was impossible to get a straight answer out of him. Here's a kid who flunked driver's ed. twice, he
reminded Sable, who, despite Landau's incessant coaching and pep
talks, made one bonehead play after another in Little League. In his
opinion, Stuie had gone straight downhill ever since he'd tangled
with those red-faced Irish head-knockers in Lincoln Park during the
'68 riots.

Shelley, on the other hand, was one of those smirking, high IQ types, but at least she had made decent marks so Landau hadn't minded that much when she joined the Peace Corps right after Michigan and planted corn and barley in Ethiopia for three years. It was okay with him if his daughter wanted to be another Eleanor Roosevelt, he always knew she'd straighten herself out. Shelley made serious money these days cutting deals for some high powered real estate developer whose impressive office was in the John Hancock Building. She drove a red Lexus and lived in a renovated three-story brownstone in Hyde Park. Shelley told her father she loved the high-stakes action, the rush that came from gambling with other people's money. He only felt miffed because her childless six-year marriage to a prominent North Shore periodontist was on the rocks. Sable had never cared too much for Roy—she thought he was inconsiderate and a bully—but Landau was flattered that Roy had scaled his diseased gums for nothing.

It exasperated Landau that Sable had never minded that Stuie didn't know from sweating bullets. She always said that he was ultrasensitive, that he was still finding himself. Who the hell has the time to be sensitive? Landau fumed. That kid's got some nerve—he *always* takes good care of number one. He let his mother break her back cooking and freezing meatballs and marinara sauce whenever they'd visited him, and thanks to her scouring the pigsty he called his "crib" her bursitis had acted up for weeks. He expected she'd always be around to tell him how to defrost a chicken or season a soup. Sable would love for him to patch things up with Stuie—be his pal. He'd told her a thousand times Stuie'd never give an inch. It galled him that maybe Sable wanted *him* to feel guilty down *here*, while at the same time Stuie and his faggy Northwestern psychiatrist were making a monster out of him on the money she made him send Stuie so he wouldn't have to rent in some dangerous Mexican or Vietnamese neighborhood. Stuie thought he was such a swinger, when the real truth was he didn't know shit from Shinola.

An hour later they sat drinking tea across from each other. Landau had sliced pieces of pound cake and arranged them on a tray. Stuie had a chili-bowl haircut with a cowlick at the top right of his scalp. His hair was greasy-looking, like seaweed. His complexion was sallow; he had small white eruptions on his chin. Landau detected a thickening in Stuie's speech, a choking noise. He wondered if Stuie had the clap, a drippy rash on his balls.

Landau slid his chair back against the oven. "Can you believe this steamy weather?" he said. 'I hope you're prepared for a real heat wave. We need a storm to cool us off. Did you bring a bathing suit?

Stuie shrugged. "I brought Mama a box of Godiva chocolates from some gift shop in Water Tower Place," he said, gesturing toward his khaki duffel bag.

"I can't get over how comical life is," Landau said, ignoring him. "I was talking about you earlier to Maury. It's almost as if my mind guessed you were flying down."

"Solid," Stuie said, lighting up a Viceroy. "Way it goes, I guess." He wore clothes Goodwill wouldn't take—soiled Army surplus pants, scuffed hiking boots caked with mud, a torn Black Hawks jersey. Landau had always hated the way Stuie dressed, his odd grease-monkey outfits.

"Still smoking that crap," Landau said. He frowned and waved the match smoke away from his face.

Stuie nodded, blew a smoke ring. His bottom teeth looked pulverized. They made Landau think of a row of tiny headstones. "Where's Mama?" Stuie asked, already bored with the conversation.

"What do you mean?" Landau asked suspiciously. Had Stuie come to Florida to put the arm on him? he wondered. Would Stuie be giving him the business?

"What does it sound like I mean, Dad?"

Landau heaved his shoulders, he chewed the stale cake ferociously. "Your mother's auditing an astronomy course at Florida Atlantic. I bought her a telescope."

"She said something about that," Stuie said. He coughed like a small dog. He went to the fridge and found some Velveeta and a hunk of Hebrew National salami wrapped in foil. He made a sandwich on a roll and poured a glass of skim milk in a beer mug.

Landau pointed to the counter. "You don't care for *kugel* anymore?"

Stuie looked stumped. "Wow—my head must not be on straight." He went and cut himself a square out of the pan.

Landau winced when he saw the sores on Stuie's knuckles. "When's the last time you saw a *Yid* doctor?"

Stuie put his sandwich down. "Give me a break, man." He had a halo of milk around his mouth.

"Go check in the mirror," Landau said.

"You don't have to be so *intense* all the time," Stuie said.

Landau dropped his fork and grabbed Stuie's wrist. "What's this?"

Stuie started to laugh. "They're just warts," he said. "Is there anything else?"

"Like what?" Landau stared at him.

Stuie smiled and pulled his hand away.

Landau took a deep breath and glanced away. "So—what brings you to the land of Medicare and paramedics? Did I tell you I took a CPR course at the fire station?"

"I didn't know I needed a reason," Stuie said amiably. "Besides, I won't be staying long." He had a way of looking aside when he spoke to his father. It drove Landau wild, and Stuie knew it.

Landau massaged his breast. "How long?" he bit off.

"Oh—a day or two, I guess. Let's hold off talking till Mama gets back."

"What do you want to talk about then?"

"I don't want to talk at all," Stuie said, yawning. "Hey—do you have any Old Style around here?"

"In Florida?" Landau said solemnly. "Don't ask. Silverfish and ants we got plenty of. And widows. I can't even get decent pastrami down here." He stood up and looked through the kitchen curtains; a laugh leaked out of him. "How goes things in Chicagoland, kiddo? Are you pulling in any moola yet?"

"You're acting very weird. C'mon—is something wrong with Mama?"

Landau sponged down the chrome sink area, ran the disposal for a few seconds. He tried to smile. "It's nothing, nothing. Just eat."

Stuie's teeth rattled like dice in a shaker. "What's the deal? Is

her angina acting up again? I know someone at Michael Reese she
can see."

Landau threw his arms up. "Pipe down! Lower your voice!"

"Then tell me what's going on."

"Nothing . . . she's normal. Her angina is fixed. You know your
mother."

Stuie's nose started to run; his eyes bulged mistily.
Landau was embarrassed. He wanted to slap Stuie like they did
in war movies. "Drink some ginger ale, Stuie; it'll settle your stomach. Maybe you need a few bucks or something? Don't tell me you
got some girl in trouble?"

"Who needs this? I came here to tell you I got my act together,
that I'm getting married. You really bring me down."

Landau felt suddenly hot, his mouth dry as matzo meal. Stuie
was as white as an egg. Squinting in disbelief, Landau cried, "*Mazel
Tov!* We didn't know you were seeing anyone special."

"You never asked," Stuie said gravely.

Landau snorted; he didn't know Stuie was even interested in
women. This would change Sable's tune, he thought. Maybe he
could even spare him some dough for a starter home in Morton
Grove or Glenview. Who cares if Stuie knocked the girl up, it was
better this way. He needed to learn to stand on his own two feet.
Teach him responsibility, be a father, a parent—experience firsthand what *that* crap's all about. He touched Stuie's hand for a second; it felt boneless and soft, like a warm kitten. "Does your fiancée
have a name, if it's not too much trouble to ask?"

Stuie looked up warily, made a noise in his jawbone like pebbles
crunching when he breathed. "Connie Perez," he said mutely.

Landau seemed flustered; this was too much. "She's *Jewish?* Like
the famous Israeli Peres?"

"*Consüela Perez*," Stuie groaned.

Landau stared at the fading light outside; he counted to ten.

"She grew up in Cicero," Stuie said. "Her folks split from Cuba
a month before Fidel came to power. They came down to Miami
about ten years ago and bought a flower mart in Little Havana. Her

father operated an elevator at the Knickerbocker Hotel for twenty years. Connie's a Ph.D. student at Loyola; her field is early childhood development. She's a disciple of Piaget."

"I read about that loser in *Newsweek*," Landau said. "Didn't he beat up his patients?"

There was an awkward pause, then Stuie said, "You don't know what you're talking about."

Landau tasted glue on his tongue. "I stand corrected. The guy's a regular *mensh*." The poor girl was going to need her education, he thought. Sable would bust a gut when she heard this cockamamie news. "You must be what, Stuie—ten, twelve years older than her? Señor and Mrs. Perez must be thrilled their daughter's marrying a Jew."

"Everything copacetic with them," Stuie said glumly.

Landau feigned interest. "How'd you get acquainted? She wants to teach slow learners?"

"That's total racist bullshit," Stuie stammered. He went on to lecture his father in a shrill voice about something he called the *problem* of environment. Landau thought a stranger—one of those varicose vein queens gossiping around the condo pool—would get the impression that he and Sable had raised some kind of *faygele* in the worst slums of Chicago.

"You sound like that great friend of the Jews, Jesse Jackson," Landau said, wiping his hands on a paper towel. "I'm pleased to see you're still an idealist."

"Why the hell not? A single act can change a life."

"What do I know?" Landau said, shoving his hair off his forehead. Another one of Stuie's hard-luck stories, he thought. Even his choice of a wife was an act of defiance, a childish tantrum. He had prayed he was finally finished with Stuie's nutty causes and petitions and social theories; he should have anticipated Stuie marrying a boat person. "It ain't easy being a dumb *sheeny* all your life," he said wearily.

Stuie made a tent with his fingers in front of his face. "We're both committed to running. I met her at the Chicago Marathon. We split the rent and utilities on this rowhouse in Rogers Park. She's talked me into going back for my degree, at night, at DePaul. We've even rapped about buying some land and moving to the Upper Peninsula and opening a Montessori school after I get my Master's."

"I'm wondering what that kind of degree is worth, Stuie? Do they even have a decent faculty at DePaul? It's a place for colored kids, right?"

"It's a living," Stuie said hoarsely.

"Maybe you have a picture handy of Miss Universe?"

Stuie dug into his tote bag and pulled out a creased Polaroid. Consūela was a tall, thin, dark-skinned young woman with razor-cut black hair. She wore a zebra-skin jumpsuit and a leather bomber jacket and reminded Landau of a rock video star he'd seen on cable once. He felt a depression sweep over him. He envisioned Stuie as the deranged head of an educational cult, out frolicking with his followers on the grounds of some boarded-up resort hotel along Lake Superior. He saw pink slips from the bursar's office sent to Florida, threats from collection agencies in *his* mailbox. He shut his eyes and tried to imagine Stuie at the blackboard teaching the alphabet to first graders, doing long division and fractions, explaining the nuclear arms race to juvenile delinquents.

"A Master's already?" Landau said. "If memory serves me, you couldn't get passing marks in your basic garbage courses at Champaign-Urbana. Back then it was music appreciation you were majoring in. You gave me such a headache with the blasting guitars and drums all the time."

"I was burned out then—strung out. The pills and everything. I'm very much in touch with my feelings now," Stuie said. "I'm back on my feet now. I'm motivated, *centered*."

Landau tested the kitchen floor with his sandal. "Sounds like a swell idea, Stuie. So, how much will it cost me?"

"Oh, God," Stuie said. Then he coughed—*caff, caff*—and clutched his throat like a man gagging on a piece of food. His temples throbbed like the gills of a large fish.

Landau grabbed his shoulders. "You want I should do the Heimlich maneuver on you?"

Stuie shook his head, *No*. "Put your mind at rest, Dad. I promise it'll cost you nothing."

"I wasn't born yesterday," Landau insisted. "You think I'm talking dollars and cents? Everything costs. We've got a big history between us. I'm supposed to forget that? You pissed away every nickel you ever earned or I ever gave you. A P.R.—just what your mother always had in mind for a daughter-in-law."

Neither of them said anything for a minute or two. Stuie kept picking at the crust of his roll with a blackened fingernail. The kitchen smelled of pickle juice. Landau opened and slammed the refrigerator door three or four times.

"She's *Cuban*," Stuie panted. "I told her, I told her." He'd lost control of his mouth.

"Told her what? Who's *her*?" Landau demanded, flapping his arms. "Try making sense for a change. Is that so much to ask?"

"I said no way, but they wouldn't listen. I must have been insane to go along with this. Where the hell is my mother?"

Landau shook his head and grimaced. "She's on a heavy date. Getting *shtupped*, I suppose."

Stuie didn't move. Then he shouted, "I can't believe you said that!"

Landau's pulse danced in his neck. "People are stubborn; they only see what they want to see."

Stuie's soft, liquid eyes seemed to shrink. "You've really freaked this time. I wouldn't waste my time going to therapy with you." He stood up and threw his food in the sink.

Landau had a wild urge to push it and Stuie down the disposal. "I'm aware of how it must pain you," he said dubiously. "Imagine how it must eat my heart out. Like a knife in the back after all these years. Look, your mother thinks you've got no direction in your life, that you're drifting. And she blames me. I can handle that unfairness, no problem. But what mother wants her son to be a zero? You're a nice kid, but it's hard to get a break without some natural talent. You've got my blood in your genes, Stuie. There's no smooth sailing for regular guys like us. It's a stinking world. Thank God we don't have to eat cat food for supper like a lot of old people in Miami do. I'll take her to Jackson Memorial to see someone with a sex specialty. Don't worry—I won't crap out on my responsibilities.

Judah Landau won't leave a mess behind him. It would turn your stomach to know what happens to people when they get old. Nobody gives a shit anymore. Nobody cares what we know about human experience. The kids in the malls and supermarkets are rude as hell. The doctors treat us like morons. Don't worry about us, go ahead with your plans, you got my blessing if you're sure about this girl. What do I care if you raise *goyim*—I'm done worrying about such things. I can see Miss What's-her-name on a chair in the center of a spinning ring of young men, dancing the *hora* at your wedding. Your mother will be glad to know that you're *centered*."

Stuie kicked the pantry door, breaking off a hinge. "Goddamn you! This was all *her* idea from the start. I wanted to just elope, but she and Connie got together and persuaded me I should tell you face to face. I knew you'd act like this, but she insisted that telling you over the phone would be discourteous. 'Don't be disrespectful to your father,' she said over and over again. And that I shouldn't expect you to change your ways at this stage. She swore that you'd be proud. But I knew what would happen. I knew you'd be the same *shmuck* you'd always been. Mama's known Connie for two years already. They hit it off immediately. They met when she came up to Chicago when I had my wisdom teeth pulled. Last July she sent Connie a silk blouse from Marshall Field's for her birthday and said it was from both of you. What's with you? You talk like a fucking creep. Making this stuff up about her out balling someone is sick!"

Landau fell back into the dishwasher. He felt as if he'd stumbled into a hole, as if he'd had the hell beat out of him. He grinned defiantly. The familiarity of his son and wife had suddenly assumed a new force, a strange new shape. In an instant of stoic illumination he saw that he was merely an accessory in the lives of his wife and children, and he knew that if he didn't do something right then he would slide down the dense well of his desperate mood and drown. He left Stuie staring into the sink, slammed the hall closet open, and found his reversible denim jacket. Once outside, he hurried, eyes down, along the mottled flagstone pathways of the condominium. He tripped on a crack, his sandals sinking into spongy soil. His heart was hammering. Bloodsuckers! Work like a horse all your life, and to what end, what purpose? For a retirement grounded in regret and bad faith; for a selfish kid who never bothers to kiss you and then eats you out of house and home.

_____

The Leisure World clubhouse loomed out of the darkness like a cruise ship. Ripples of light shone smokily through the tranquil mist. Vinyl state pennants snapped in the breeze, electric menorahs glowed a phosphorescent orange. Harry Belafonte singing "Day-O" came from the twin loudspeakers atop the gabled roof. Pale yellow citronella globes ringed the nearby shuffleboard courts. Frogs croaked, insects fizzed, and Landau heard faint splashes coming from the darkened swimming pools. When they arrived ten years ago, they'd been warned by the Haitian porters to be mindful of water moccasins that came out at night in search of tadpoles and ducklings. They had heard stories from their neighbors of spotted salamanders bigger than iguanas. For months Landau had lugged a bat around when they went out for an Early Bird Special or to a band concert at the shell in Pompano. Recently all the commotion was over baby alligators who'd gotten disoriented in the Intracoastal Waterway, found their way to the banks of the man-made canals, and could eat a Chihuahua or a grandchild.

He was overcome by cigar smoke and perfume. The huge rec room bristled with activity; mobs of talkers stood around pinochle and bridge tables, a line of women in matching flapper hats was practicing the Charleston, another group was doing the merengue. He found Freud holding court around a pool table, a cue stick balanced in his palm. Landau felt slightly sick; his pulse vibrated in his bones, it drummed behind his eyes. For a minute he stood and listened to Freud explain about barium enemas and polyps to four men in straw hats and Hawaiian shirts.

"Wiseass!" Landau shouted, pointing at Freud. "Outside, this minute! We got business to settle, Jew to Jew!"

"Do I know you?" Freud asked, in a voice as thin as a wire.

"Hah! You faker!" Landau screeched. A bald man in a T-shirt

with *I Love Leisure World* stenciled crookedly across the front made shame-shame with his quivering fingers.

Freud looked around helplessly. "Who knows this *shmo?*"

"It's that blowhard Landau!" a chorus of exasperated voices thundered.

"Judah—Judah!" Sable, colored Mah-Jongg tiles clutched in her fingers, blocked his progress toward Freud. "What's wrong with you?"

"Two-timer!" Landau roared, pointing at both of them.

"Leon," Sable said. "I'm ashamed for my husband. Judah, why are you doing this to me?" She reached to feel his forehead.

Freud's mouth went slack in disbelief. "This wild Indian is your Judah?"

Sable bowed her head sadly.

A very old man who looked like Albert Einstein stepped forward tentatively. "Mister, please go avay. You don't vant big trouble mit the owners association," he creaked.

Landau gave him the finger.

"It's not your fault," Freud said to Sable. "He's flipped out."

About thirty of them went outdoors. Rodents scattered, black wrought-iron chaise longues were dragged across the slate patio. Someone in a battery-driven cart offered to find the condo president. "Get one of the *shvartzer's,*" a hunchbacked woman in pedal pushers called.

"Your ass is mine," Landau growled, showing a balled fist.

"Judah! Compose yourself," Sable cried, slapping at his beefy arms.

Landau studied his rival in the cloudy, turquoise halo cast by the swimming pools: kiwi-green eyes, half-moon bifocals, canary-yellow shorts, white stretch socks with flying pheasants on them, a pale blue golf shirt. Freud's lips were smeared with some kind of orange sun grease. Suddenly Landau jitterbugged, he tried to cold-cock Freud with a left hook to the chin. He missed by a foot.

"Now just a minute, Judah. What's this all about? You act like I stole your parking space."

Landau dug his heels in and hunched down into a prizefighter's stance. "You must think I'm a goddamn patsy. I'm from the streets of Chicago."

"Excuse me, Mr. Marciano. But where do you get off making such a fuss? What should I do to make friends with you?" Freud asked.

"Landau, stop acting like a *putz,* control yourself," a voice urged from the darkness.

"Is this guy legit?" Freud asked, kicking off his Wallabees. "I must warn you that I boxed in the Pacific." He hopped around on his small feet, put up his dukes, and sparred with a pock-faced man wearing a cranberry AARP baseball cap.

Sable tore at Landau's jacket; she ripped the checked acrylic lining.

Maury Zucker, breathing hard, pushed between them. "It's okay, Sable. Look, Pinkie, it's Maury. Listen, buddy, you're a little dopey tonight. Try relaxing, give a big stretch with your arms." He said, loud enough for everyone to hear, "Pinkie needs a good long rest, Sable. He doesn't mix too well with anyone in Florida. He's got a psychosomatic condition that you and Mr. Freud are like . . . how should I put it . . ."

The assembled listeners gasped, men tapped their index fingers to their temples. Freud tucked his shirt back in his pants and grimaced at Landau in disgust. An old woman wearing a gauze pad over one eye called him *meshuggener.*

Sable clung to his neck like a pulley on a beam. "Judah," she cried. "I can't believe you'd think such a crazy thing!"

Landau turned and looked down at her. His chest made a rattling noise, like an idling bus. He searched the shadows: reverent faces, charred by the sun, bald heads like stone. He caught a whiff of wintergreen; the misty air was gummy with insect repellent. What surprised him was how much he could see, how definite everything had become. He scanned the crowd without saying a word, as if measuring the density of his silence. His eyes burned. Giddy with rage, he struck at something hard—a leg, a shoulder. Men were all over him now, like water bugs. Someone had him in a headlock, another in a full-nelson. Feet knocked his shins. He was hit across the face with something—a handball paddle, a mop. His nose was smashed, his whole head gave way from the pounding. Landau heard Sable shrieking at him—she wanted to know if anything hurt, if he had to use the toilet. She screamed that the doctors were on their way.

Zucker murmured, "Shh . . . shhh." He whispered in Landau's stinging ear that he should breathe easily, that everything would work out for the best.

Landau was breathless, his neck hurt. Wheezing, he saw double— two Sables gliding in slow motion, a spatter of gnats dancing above him. From the corner of his blinking eye he saw flashing lights; he heard sirens very close by. A mad elation had filled his swirling brain. He was suddenly beyond anger, beyond substance. His sore head roared like a furnace. He rolled to his side and soiled his Bermudas. Undigested food dribbled out of the corner of his bloody mouth; his moist, abysmal odor billowed back into his shattered nostrils. Someone had grabbed his wrist, firmly, told him not to talk; someone else waved smelling salts in his swollen face. He flailed his heavy arms when the paramedics put a mask over his nose. The needle under his sweaty skin sizzled.

Sable pinched his cheeks. She lightly blew on his nose as if it were a candle. "Judah, do you recognize me?" she whimpered forgivingly, over and over. She heard the crunching in his jaw when he exhaled.

Oblivious, Landau had slipped calmly away—as if his feet had floated off the ground. Everything seemed to lift out of itself. His head hung on the cloudless purple horizon like a planet. Then came a strange keening sound—a brittle strangled laughing that broke open deep within him. He rose higher and higher—his body buoyant in surrender—above the uproar, the wheeling skulls, the blurred faces—into a cold black space all his own.

An aged man is but a paltry thing,
A tattered coat upon a stick . . .
—William Butler Yeats

Promised Land

When I picked up the phone early this morning, Charley
Palestine's voice sounded very distant. "Bad connection," I told him,
clearing the sleep out of my throat. "Let me call you back."

"Lou's dead," I thought I heard him say.

I smacked the receiver against my palm. "Who did?"

"Exactly," he muttered.

For months now I'd been having my doubts about Charley's plan
to move to Florida. He was seventy-five, and in poor health. Zandy,
my wife, was losing patience with both of us. "You don't even notice the changes in him," she said to me with accumulated irritabil-
ity one night last fall. Whenever we discussed his moving, Zandy
would roll her coffee-colored eyes and say the whole scheme would
backfire on me. "He'll expect you to fly down on a minute's notice
and take him to the periodontist." This morning she made hissing
noises as I spoke to him. Since Zandy, I was amply aware, could
make a grievance out of anything, I contented myself with nodding
agreeably at her concerns, a gesture that only managed to tick her
off even more.

That afternoon I left my law office on L Street around 3:45 and
walked the five blocks to the HMO. Heavy yellow cranes and earth-
movers were chewing up downtown Washington. The sky, pitifully

bruised and overcast the past week, was already growing dark. The winds brawling in off the icy Potomac were cutting.

Charley looked beat. I was afraid his emphysema was getting worse. We were slouched opposite one another, on needlepoint-padded wicker armchairs, in the radiology department waiting room. "Where Have All the Flowers Gone" was being filtered continuously through the hidden Muzak speakers. I was slightly nauseated from the sushi I'd had for lunch. The waiting room, paneled in fillets of imitation maple, was lit for reptiles. Charley, his hands clenched in his lap, was talking, and I was listening. The Wildroot was pooled like Elmer's glue on his black mop of hair. When I came back from the men's room he sprang up and said, "Elliot, do you remember when they kicked our Giants out of the Polo Grounds?"

I smiled and tasted something bitter in my throat; gas was flowing through my bowels. "Who's they?" I asked, egging him on. "It's a mystery to me."

He shook his head mechanically. "Smart aleck," he sneered. "I can still give you a *zetz* on your heinie."

"Hey—come on now," I said, widening my eyes.

He squinted down at me and eased himself back into the armchair.

"Charley," I whispered, "nobody kicked them out. They wanted to leave. It was all about making big bucks."

"Hah!" He stared at me for a moment and grunted. His face was shiny, and his arms, once big with freckled muscles, looked soft.

I leaned forward and put my hands on his knees. They shook slightly. When he parted his lips I caught a whiff of scallions on his breath. "Please don't brood," I said.

He grunted again and scratched the dimple in his chin. When he was younger, people said he looked like Kirk Douglas. "Never mind all the malarkey, Elliot," he said. "I don't need you to tell me what happened."

"What's eating you, Charley?"

His eyes cut quickly to the salmon-colored carpet. After a minute or two he glanced back at me. He shifted uncomfortably, as if his clothes didn't fit properly. He'd had hip surgery about five years before and wore one of those lopsided orthopedic shoes on his left

foot. "For crying out loud," he said, coughing like someone who
had swallowed smoke.

"Yes?" I held my breath. He stared past me without expression.
I searched his face. He wasn't wearing his glasses and without them
his rabbity eyes appeared terribly wasted, the pupils deep as wells.
As long as I'd known him he'd had a habit of pulling down his lower
lip and fingering his gums when he was bothered about something.
His teeth were fluted and looked like they'd been in the bottom of
a fish tank.

I put my hand on his shoulder. "Tired?" I asked.

"Nah—it isn't that," he answered, uncrossing his legs.

"What then?"

"I'm past the age," he said quietly, "where I expect things to happen. I've decided to take matters into my own hands." He showed
me his calloused palms, then the backs of his bony hands. "It's about
time I took a risk."

Before I could respond, he was summoned by the nurse.

When we got out it was late. Lights were burning everywhere. He wanted to walk so we headed toward Pennsylvania Avenue. We passed a young man in a Redskins burgundy jacket holding out a tin cup who cursed at me when I ignored him. Charley
sounded like an idling bus when he breathed. I was conscious of him
watching me. He had black tufts of hair on his ungloved knuckles;
his nose was raw from the wind. Beneath a streetlamp his flesh appeared almost pulpy. I sensed that he'd lost weight the past few
months; his pants were beginning to look a whole size too big on
him. He stopped and asked a hooker the time.

Smiling slightly, Charley shook his head at her. I knew what
was going on. He was one of those people who always felt they
should've been able to do something whenever anything bad happened. Lately, when someone he knew passed away, he coped with
his grief by dredging up old losses. Today it was the Giants. When
they dumped New York, Charley moped around with a dazed expression for weeks. Years later we sat upwards of three hours in my

Opel and watched the steel ball of the wrecker demolish the Polo
Grounds. Zandy said we were behaving like children. She thinks
sports—and baseball in particular—are foolish and dull. When
Charley and I got there, work crews in yellow hard hats were busy
smashing the grandstands in the outfield. Grown men in business
suits were tripping over each other in the bleachers with hunks of
brown sod and murderous spears of box seats under their arms.
Charley was wheezing, I remember, and he clutched the steering
wheel like it was a life preserver. I was ready for him to have another heart attack. Afterward, in a smoky cafeteria on Morningside
Heights—a former Columbia hangout of mine jammed with seething undergraduates—Charley had cried like a baby.

There was a commotion outside the Treasury Department. Limos
were double-parked all over the street, and surly Park Police were
busy roping off the sidewalk. Out of the blue, Charley turned to me
and said, "You're like your grandfather, Elliot."

"Am I?" I asked, watching the traffic.

He grinned and said nothing.

The air was tart, the Mall misty and almost deserted. We walked
carefully—there were patches of ice everywhere. Some joggers
were out—mostly Marines in gray sweats—braving the chill. I
tucked my head deep into my collar. The wind was brutal all of a
sudden.

Charley paused in front of the Air and Space Museum. He bent
and nodded at an old woman bundled in newspapers on a bench and
asked me over his shoulder, "How's your sister getting along?"

"All right, I guess," I said tentatively, breathing hard myself now.

He turned away from the old woman and stared directly at me.
His whole face was creased from the wind, his eyes watery. "Where's
she living now?" he shouted.

"Bloomington, Indiana," I said slowly.

"Elliot? Is she happy yet?"

I shrugged. "Yetta's into finding herself, Charley. It doesn't matter what you or I or anyone else thinks. Besides, we don't talk that
much. She and Zandy never got along."

His brow furrowed. Stars had emerged over the Tidal Basin. He coughed violently, his cheeks turning bright red. "Are you all right?" I asked.

"I don't understand," he managed to say between coughs. "It's not like the old days. The last time I saw Yetta, she went around intimidating everyone, demanding that they stop eating meat. She had a very fresh mouth and was always disagreeable, and she let her hair grow under her arms. She smelled like manure."

"Ha, ha."

"I'm not making jokes, Elliot. Explain to an old man how a married woman leaves her husband with two little children and runs off with some *shiksa* pervert to write poetry in Indiana."

I heard myself sigh. The Washington Monument looked bleak against the dim skyline. A huge jet seemed to fall gracefully through the air, filling the night with noise. "Don't be such a prude," I yelled into the wind.

His mouth twitched. "I figured you'd say something like that. Why should I even bother to express my opinion to you?"

"C'mon, she has needs," I said defensively. "Jesus, between you and Zandy, Yetta can't get a break. You think it was a treat living with that scumbag Ralph? I'm amazed she stayed with him as long as she did. It's not been so easy for her."

"Dat's very interesting," he said in a hoarse voice, mocking me.

It had started to snow—almost invisibly—but the wind had picked up even more. Paper and trash were blowing everywhere. "Where's the funeral?" I asked, changing the subject.

"At Arlington National Cemetery. Tomorrow morning. Ten sharp. I never told you that Louie enlisted when he was thirty and was wounded in North Africa chasing after Rommel's tanks." He was watching a pair of muscular Doberman pinschers sniff each other on the museum's steps.

Drab figures in heavy winter topcoats shuffled past. I thought nervously of the drive home later. Images of Beltway traffic tie-ups floated across my mind as I trailed Charley up Seventh Street. He stopped on the gravel balcony that overhung the Hirshhorn

Sculpture Garden and pointed down at the snow-dusted Rodins. He waved to a security guard who approached us from the opposite terrace. "Are you coming, then?" he asked me, confusion in his voice.

"Sure," I said, leaning with my back against the railing.

He grimaced. The security guard walked by us and nodded.

"I mean it," I insisted.

He shook his head. It was really snowing now.

"Are a lot of people coming?"

He looked momentarily flustered. "What kind of a screwy question is that?" he said thickly, his eyebrows flecked with snow. "Who knows, maybe we'll be lucky and Alan King or Joey Bishop will show up and make a few Las Vegas jokes. Does it matter to you?"

"Of course it doesn't," I said. "I was just interested."

He thought a minute. "And don't worry about transportation," he finally said. "I've made arrangements already."

I tried to sound nonchalant and reminded him that I didn't worry about him as much as he thought I did. He took a step backward and gave me a phlegmy grunt. In this light he looked very cold and very tired. His twisted nose was beginning to run. He was moving his head—yes and no—and fiddling with the buttons on his coat.

I stared at my spattered shoes and felt embarrassed for some reason. Then I forced a laugh. When I looked up, he was off again. "Wait up!" I called. I hunched my shoulders against the wind and followed him. He turned on his heels and pointed at me, then stumbled backwards for a moment. I was sure he would slip on the ice and hurt himself.

"I made a silly mistake," he shouted. "Louie kept on saying he should've moved to Florida after that *putz* Reagan was elected. He had an interesting theory that heavy doses of radiation from the sun's ultraviolet rays gave cancer cells cancer. Don't make a face, wise guy," he said when I caught up with him.

"Come on, Charley," I pleaded. "Lou was full of crap."

He looked very annoyed. "You're a gloomy person, Elliot," he said almost blandly. "Terribly gloomy."

I was trying hard to keep up with him. His legs were no longer than mine, but he was the type of person who always liked to stay just a little ahead of his companion. Moving along slightly behind him, staring at his bent back and shoulders, I wondered what he was really thinking about.

We passed a group of Japanese tourists in trench coats. They were studying a Metrorail map with a miniature flashlight. I felt numb on the outside, my skin wrapped in glacial cold, but on the inside, beneath my clothes, I was soggy. Exposure to frigid, damp air wasn't the best thing for Charley's lungs, and the last thing either of us needed was a bad cold.

"I'm freezing," I said cheerfully, hoping to break his mood. "Let's go."

"I can't get over it," he said, pausing in mid-stride. "Lou was a professional guy, an intellectual in my opinion. He was a big reader, a terrific follower of current events. He was the first one to appreciate that cancer was a booming industry. He called it a capitalist disease. He'd slip articles for me to look at under the door. He had a line, 'Everyone's a winner,' that summed up his personality. The guy never made a fuss on account of his lousy condition. He never sponged on his pals. Lou had guts."

An image of Lou Bluestein flashed across my mind: linty navy beret, bushy Trotsky beard, Mantovani on the antique cherrywood phonograph, a dark apartment littered with overdue library books and esoteric journals and moldy carryout boxes from Big Wong's restaurant. I grabbed Charley's elbow and spun him around. "For Christ's sake," I shouted. "Lou was pissing blood for a year, you told me, before he had worked up the nerve to go see someone about it. He may have been a goddamn intellectual for all I know, but he was also a horse's ass. Yeah, sure, he was a nice guy, a charming socialist with elegant Old World table manners, but he also had hardening of the arteries and high blood pressure and was so damn fat I'll bet he wasn't able to see his own nuts for the past ten years. Like someone else I know, he never bothered to take care of himself. Instead of watching what he ate and visiting the doctor, he believed in pipe dreams."

Charley took a deep breath. I braced my shoulders for his anger.

Instead he just muttered, "Oh, boy," and nodded once or twice in disgust. "I know what you're thinking, Elliot."

"*Please*, Charley. I'm too goddamn cold for any heavy analysis or hysterics, okay?"

"You're thinking," he continued, meeting my eyes with a frosty stare, "that I'm getting soft in the head. Am I right?" He shuddered, and shifted his weight from foot to foot as if he were running in place. He was obviously freezing.

"No," I said softly. "You're not even close."

"But you implied it, Elliot. It's the same thing."

I threw my arms up. He looked animated, and a thin film of mucus covered his upper lip. My calves felt sore, as if I'd been doing wind sprints in the snow. I was conscious of his thick breathing, the way he seemed to lean sideways in the wind. He needed a hot shower and a shave and a haircut, I thought desperately, maybe a week or two at one of those geriatric California spas—as if that might solve everything. I suddenly staggered, felt a weakness in my ankles.

I noticed a break in the clouds and suggested we head back. The windshields of the parked cars we passed were covered with snow. He flashed me one of his concerned looks, announced, "I want more exercise," and took off toward Constitution Avenue. I followed his rear end, which was rolling and swaying like a small boat in heavy seas, and yelled for him to slow down. It had started to sleet; my hair was sopping and my corduroy clothes smelled like spoiled fruit. For an instant Charley seemed to pause and glance back at me. Then he slipped—a stooped figure in yellow streams of mist—waved his corkscrew arms, and caught his balance before landing.

I saw him lit up by car lights. His step appeared almost springy. I wondered why watching out for Charley had become my life's work. Then came the grating roar: "I'm not a corpse yet, Elliot! Do you hear me? Elliot?"

My head started to spin. He seemed to hesitate for a moment, as if waiting for an answer, stuck out his stomach in my general direction, then, head lowered, turned away and resumed walking. I felt cramped, and hungry, and had to concentrate to keep from falling in the snow.

"Charley! Charley!" I shouted at the frail silhouette receding in the pearly darkness.

When I was a little boy, Charley had made a meager living selling goods out of the trunk of his sea-green Nash. It was mostly things only refugees from Hitler's Europe wanted—wool socks and foundation garments, pots and pans and dishes, Fuller brushes, yo-yos and Spaldeens and tops and dolls for their children, straw brooms and ironing boards. Charley rented rooms in northwest Bronx Park, a short stroll from the Botanical Garden. It was a leaky ground floor apartment with peeling, lime-colored linoleum and shuttered venetian blinds caked with dust. The building was usually dirty, the air foul from kitchen gas and burning *yortzeit* candles, the white-and-black tiled hallways dim as a cave. Charley's wide bedroom window looked out at an expanse of clotheslines strung across an alley, his living room window at a bus stop.

I learned about Charley's history piecemeal. I knew he was born on the South Side of Chicago, and that his mother had died in a suspicious sweatshop fire when he was nine. He had no brothers or sisters, and never knew who his father was. For a few years he lived happily with his mother's brother's family in Blue Island, before getting thrown out for wising off to his Aunt Bertha once too often. He bummed around quite a bit after that, working at various odd jobs—pushing a pail and mop at Billings Hospital, delivering bread and milk and ice, hawking franks and soda pop at Comiskey Park— often sleeping on the floor at friends' places or hanging around skid row. Following a tip from a disgruntled *Trib* columnist he got loaded with after Cub-Pirate games, a Pittsburgh scout drove to see Charley play ball in an industrial league in Calumet City.

He had three mediocre seasons in the minors, playing mostly in Georgia and Tennessee. He had gaping holes in his game— shoddy field, weak stick, though very savvy on the base paths. Convinced he'd never make it all the way to the majors, and worn out from fighting with bombed hillbillies who called him *sheeny* and *kike* from the bleachers and dugouts, he decided to pack his duffel and make a fresh start elsewhere. He called his Uncle Jake at the kosher slaughterhouse where he worked to apologize for being such an ingrate, and then hopped a B & O freight train heading east the day after Roosevelt was elected to his first term and met my grandfather at a pick-up softball game in Crotona Park a week later. They soon became best friends.

In between real jobs—off and on he sold discount women's apparel and shoes at S. Klein's and Gimbels—Charley spent his free hours at the ballpark. My grandfather used to joke that Charley was just learning how to hit breaking stuff when Hitler invaded Poland, years after he had quit playing ball for money. Thirty years later Charley was indignant when I purchased a Volkswagen bug with the dough I'd earned over the summer busing tables at a country club. When I was in the third grade he finally went to work for my grandfather, a commercial painting and flooring contractor. For ten hours a day Charley would sit on an aluminum stepladder and answer service calls from a wall phone in my grandfather's cinder block office. My grandfather, a generous man with a gentle disposition—a man who valued quality over money, I was persistently reminded—took Charley and me to Sunday doubleheaders at the Polo Grounds. My father was enrolled in law school at Columbia then, and besides, he couldn't have cared less about baseball.

Much to my grandfather's delight, Charley took me on as an apprentice. He bought me a glove and a bat and a pair of black cleats. When I was nine he drove me to Cooperstown for an Old Timers' game. Imagine their distress when it became clear that I couldn't judge fly balls, was slow-footed, had no stomach for sticking my kisser in the way of bad hops. I stank something awful, but Charley encouraged me to keep trying. He never got down on me. In the fall we played catch on the weekends and watched the World Series on television, and during the winter he'd let me rub fragrant saddle soap into the enormous brown pocket of his mitt. I did it gingerly, with reverence, and doing it made me feel like I was in contact with big-league history. Whenever I got discouraged and whined to him about my lack of athletic talent, he spoke to me like a saddened uncle and either sharpened my spikes with his rusty pocketknife or

wound fresh layers of colored masking tape around the thin handle
of my Willie Mays-model Louisville Slugger.

When my grandfather passed away from cancer, Charley came
forward without being told and pulled the family together. He went
on long walks with my father and accompanied him every morning
to say *Kaddish* at the basement orthodox *shul* on Vyse Avenue, two
blocks from the Southern Boulevard El. Charley changed the oil
and brake shoes in the Bel Air, went to the A & P for my mother
every few days, made sure Yetta and I got our quarter allowance
each Wednesday after Hebrew school; he took us to see *Peter Pan*
and the Rockettes at Radio City Music Hall for *Chanukah*. I can
remember him and my father sitting by the open kitchen window in
their shirtsleeves many nights during that summer and fall, talking
about the big house in the suburbs we'd all be living in some day. The
house they always spoke about had a huge two-car garage and a backyard filled with swings and singing cardinals and luxuriant tulips.

That winter my father sold my grandfather's business after he
was hired by a big Washington, D.C., law firm. Before the deal was
finalized—the buyers were a large family of Lithuanian Jews living
in a red-brick house on Mt. Eden Avenue—Charley had warned my
father over and over again that *Litvaks* were notorious for being
clever sharpies who'd rob you blind if you didn't hold onto your
wallet for dear life. He said that with *Litvaks* you're always buying
the same horse twice. Astonished that my father would actually
abandon the Bronx, Charley drifted from sight for a few years. My
grandfather had left him a lot of money in his will, so Charley didn't
need to work. To kill time he drove a taxi in Riverdale part-time and
played the trotters at Yonkers Raceway. He mailed me birthday
cards written in Yiddish with ten-dollar bills in them, and then
called a few days later to make sure I'd gotten them.

He visited Israel with a group from his synagogue, then went
back the following year and became a *kibbutznik*. In '67 we received
a package of snapshots showing Charley—deeply tanned and finely
muscled—reading the *Jerusalem Post* on a park bench outside the
King David Hotel, at the Golan Heights, dressed in army fatigues and
blowing the *shofar* while standing atop a captured Syrian artillery

piece, praying at the Wailing Wall, wading in the Galilee with his black hair braided like a hippie's, in a white Nehru jacket shaking hands with a man who looked like Ambassador Abba Eban. When I was in college he sent me a rambling letter a week or so after Chappaquiddick. In it he told me about his medical problems—his glaucoma and emphysema and gum disease—and the widow he had been seeing for more than three years who had died from Hodgkin's disease a few months earlier. He said that being in Israel without her was too painful and that he'd be coming to Washington in the fall, probably for good, a week or so after *Succoth*.

Zandy and I were married a week after my freshman year of law school, and for a year we lived on the top floor of my parents' house in Bethesda. After returning, Charley rented a one-bedroom apartment in Foggy Bottom, not far from the White House. He used to love walking after rush hour in that part of the city during the summer. He said that Washington at dusk reminded him of an excavated village. Then, after finally getting settled in, he stumbled down a flight of stairs and knocked out his front teeth and broke his jaw. For months following the oral surgery he spoke with resignation and weariness about the past. All he ever seemed to talk about was how he'd wasted the best years of his life.

The accident damaged his coordination, and my father, who naturally felt terrible about the whole thing, finally took Charley to see some specialists up at Johns Hopkins. His problem was diagnosed as one of those neurological things that would just take time to heal in a man of his age, so my father convinced Charley to move in with us for a few months. Poor Charley—his breath always smelled of rotten apples, and he'd spend his days alone with his nose buried in the papers. Zandy's parents, and her mother in particular, a silver-haired woman who always wore slick leather pants that squeezed her thighs like salami casing, had a fit. Doris was the kind of woman who spent her days booking dinner reservations and playing golf and bridge and trampling over waiters. She was certain that Zandy would be exposed to something that would impair her ability to conceive children. For weeks there were bitter discussions between my parents and Zandy's, there were nasty things said about Charley in general. Who the hell is he anyway? my father-in-law demanded. Doris went on and on, with no evidence I might add, about Charley's imminent collapse and his smoking in bed. He occasionally smoked an El Producto, but never in bed. Nothing was simple.

Sadly though, Doris was on to something. After about six weeks or so, Charley started wetting his bed. He looked awful every morning, and wouldn't drink his prune juice or Ovaltine or eat his Cream of Wheat. He smelled like chlorine, his hair looked like he hadn't shampooed it in weeks, and his shirts were dirty. Then he got progressively more withdrawn, stayed in bed all morning, stopped answering questions. One day he set my mother's prized parakeets free. Their feathery remains were found days later by Hansel, my parents' brindled boxer. Charley'd play his Cole Porter albums at full volume before sunrise and wake up the whole neighborhood. My father was bombarded by complaints, including a particularly vicious one from a psychiatrist named Sugarman who lived down the street. When we took Charley to Friday night services, he fussed and passed gas. One night he crept down the basement steps and peed all over the fancy electrical sockets my father had rigged up for his power tools. On her way to do her ironing, Zandy discovered Charley on top of Angela, my parents' chubby Peruvian maid, in her snug sleeping quarters off the utility room, his enormous head buried between her bronze breasts, like a baby getting burped. My father, under attack by my mother at this point, had numerous discussions with Charley that always began and ended with my father saying, "You'll have to try and understand, Charley," and Charley giving off a kind of pierced look, his eyes staring over my father's shoulder into the distance.

My father pulled a few strings and got Charley into a snazzy clinic near Annapolis. I'd visit him on Saturdays, after my morning tax seminar. In the beginning his illness was as difficult to cure as it was simple to diagnose. Tests revealed a severe hormonal imbalance. His blood chemistry was all fouled up, as were his kidneys and thyroid. He had sprouted warts on his knuckles, and huge corns had bloomed like orchids on his toes and fungoid arches. They started doping him up after he smeared his feces in the coils of the hot plate I had given him for his birthday. I dreaded seeing him. The medication he was on—in heavy doses that could have calmed the Atlantic Ocean—relaxed him so much he forgot who I was. He always appeared half asleep, his face raw and blotchy, the surface of his eyes like gelatin. I thought a light breeze could blow him over. It was easy to see that he wasn't feeling any better, and his yeasty breath soured the room like spilled beer. He was always miserably barbered, with loops of hair flowing out of his ears and nose like algae. Our conversations typically lasted five minutes and then he spaced out. When he looked exhausted I'd ask if he wanted me to go, but he hardly ever answered me directly. With his big eyes whitened like those of a blind horse, he would glare at me as if he were trying to recover an elusive memory. Then he'd start swatting at the crushed flies decomposing on the blades of his window fan. "I haven't felt like myself," he'd say over and over again in a deep, gravelly voice, all the while ripping pubic hairs out of the snaps of his royal blue pajama bottoms.

When he was well enough to leave the hospital he moved back in with us. Zandy's parents and my mother hammered away at my father about how Charley needed special care, private nursing, a place of his own. My father's face was expressionless when he said that Charley's illness was just one of those cerebral episodes that happened to people in life. But to me his eyes said that he, too, might someday be like Charley, and I had no trouble reading the panic in his face.

The morning after the funeral, Charley said to me in a dignified voice as I floored the gas in my Saab, "So, how was it?"

"What? The service?"

"Elliot," he said pleasantly, "the drive home yesterday. After you dropped me off."

A BMW fishtailed down the street in front of us. I glanced over at him. He was shoving the hair off his forehead. Then he smacked his hands together as if he were killing gnats.

"It was as easy as pie," I fibbed. "The roads were already sanded."

He coughed a few times and rolled his window halfway down.

I changed the subject. "You never told me what Dr. Rosenberg said."

"Nothing interesting," Charley said. "It's always the same story. Most of the time I think he's talking foolishness."

"Then indulge my curiosity for a change," I urged.

"Don't bully me," he burst out. I peered sideways at him and saw that he was grimacing at the flow of cars on Chain Bridge Road. He was chewing his lips. "You're worse than a wife," he added, rolling his window back up.

"You never had a wife," I said quietly.

"And would you want to know why, *boychik?*"

I shook my head, no.

"Of course not," he said stiffly, slamming his back against the bucket seat. "You're healthy!"

I laughed. "Jesus Christ, Charley. Don't tell me you're jealous of *me?*"

He grunted. "I suppose you and Zandy think you know what's best for me?"

"Yes," I said softly. "We do."

He belched.

Bleakly, I said, "You haven't changed at all."

"I've been unlucky," he said facetiously. "The Chosen People are terribly frail."

"Don't break my balls," I said roughly. "I can remember when you used to be the world's biggest optimist."

"I'm tired of this conversation, Elliot. You don't understand what it means to be my age."

We were driving back to my house. It was quite blustery out, and the small amount of snow that had fallen during the night was scattered in pathetic drifts. I glanced over at him. He was unshaven this morning and didn't look particularly well. His hands were scaly and red, and trembled in his lap. When he opened his mouth to speak, an odor like wet ground issued forth. At the gravesite I watched him carefully—the pinch of his charcoal-gray trousers with the light-blue stripes on the seams, the glow on his just-shined shoes, his creased brown tie, his bulging, ditch-colored eyes—and I was galled at the way he let other people's problems drag him down so much. The mourners, old men I recognized from Charley's apartment complex, were all dressed in ill-fitting black or brown suits and white shirts. In the wind the stubble stood out on their cheeks like Hebrew lettering. A square-necked loudmouth named Leo Skolnick passed out blocky silk skullcaps. A trio of sullen gravediggers sat smoking cigarettes in the dirt-filled cab of a dump truck.

Bluestein's only child, Ira, a urologist, was killed in a car wreck on the George Washington Parkway many years ago, and Bluestein's wife, Miriam—a woman, Charley reminded me earlier that morning, celebrated for her stuffed cabbage and cheese *pirogen*—had been dead for five years. A broad-shouldered nephew in a camel's hair coat had driven down in a Lincoln from Philadelphia to give the eulogy. It was painfully brief. The nephew, in an irritated tone of voice, left out fifty of Bluestein's years while dwelling on how shrewd a pinochle player he recalled his uncle had been. The nephew chewed on an unlit cigarette while he spoke. After the service Charley introduced me to the rabbi—a burly young man in a navy mohair sweater and Prince Valiant haircut—who'd arrived on a Yamaha. The rabbi stroked his full red beard thoughtfully while he listened to Charley proudly detail all the charities Lou Bluestein had supported. While they talked about the Anti-Defamation League, the West Bank, and the Cousteau Society—I heard Charley tell the rabbi that Louie had never missed a Jacques Cousteau television special—my attention was diverted by the changing of the guard at the Tomb of the Unknown Soldier. Following Bluestein's last wishes to the letter, his friends held hands and sang *Hatikvah* at the conclusion of the service. When we left, the rabbi put his hand on my back and told me to have a nice day.

At a traffic light on Massachusetts Avenue, Charley said, "Lou had a retarded older sister he treated to Rehoboth Beach for a week every August. Let me tell you, it was a terrible strain."

"I can imagine," I said, veering around a stalled Metro bus.

"Take a shortcut, Elliot. Make a left at the next light."

"I know how to go," I said sharply.

After a few more minutes he said, "Everything's settled now. We won't have to depend on each other anymore."

"What's settled?"

He sighed. "Our real estate cookie came through for us. She's located a big apartment not two blocks from the ocean. Elliot, she swears it's a steal."

My legs, beneath the steering column, felt like they'd suddenly gone to sleep. The sky was a turpentine color, the clouds seemed to flounder in the distance like fattened seals. "You promised to reconsider," I said.

"I did," he insisted. "At least a thousand times. And then last night we went over it again, and decided nobody needs the winter anymore. I'm sick of the cold weather. Even the rabbi thinks we should go for it. He said it was an 'awesome idea.' "

I glanced at him. His eyes gleamed with mischief. "I don't know, Charley—"

"What's there for you to know? Look, we want friends our own age, warm weather all the time. This condo's got twenty-four-hour security, oxygen, a nurse on duty around the clock. Maybe I can ask a nice widow out for a fancy supper once in a blue moon, buy box seat tickets to spring training, play shuffleboard year round. I'll look for a job as a floorwalker in a shopping center. I hear they're hiring *alter kockers* like me to work fifteen hours a week. You know how I love the smell of the ocean. Why are you making such an issue out of it?"

"I'm not making an issue out of anything," I said unconvincingly. "You're just naturally depressed over Lou. Your thinking's a little gummed up."

I heard him start to pant, and felt very ashamed.

"You talk to me like I'm an idiot," he shouted. "I deserve more consideration."

"I'm worried, Charley."

"Don't make me laugh, Elliot."

"It's not easy for me," I said. "For any of us."

He made a grating noise in his throat. "*So?* Go on."

"Never mind," I said.

He struck the dashboard with a chopping motion. "You brought it up, smart guy. What's on your mind?"

I started to answer, then sighed.

"You're a sweet boy, Elliot. But you shouldn't worry so damn much, you'll get an ulcer yet. Sleep on it, okay?"

I stiffened my neck and mumbled, "Agreed." Saying it seemed momentarily to affirm some powerful belief I had in Charley's inner strength. In the same breath, that belief was shattered at the sight of Charley's reflection in the windshield. It was more like a shadow passing across my line of vision, and I was shocked by his distorted image. My right eye began to twitch then, and I felt something thick flowing through my bowels. I straightened my spine but the pain in my belly grew only sharper. Listening for a few minutes to his hard breathing made me think of rusty machinery. I experienced—wrenchingly, I freely admit—a yearning sensation I can only describe as homesickness, an avid longing for the deep-felt warmth of affectionate surroundings. I struggled to calm myself by focusing on the pale-gray horizon. It didn't work. Sadly, I felt—it hit me, for the first time in many years—the enormous ache of regret. I simply didn't want Charley to go.

I managed to get my bearings back after a few minutes of concentrated breathing, and when I exhaled, my stomach felt better. The pulse in my neck had stopped its frantic beating, and the pain in my ribs had subsided. I skidded onto River Road from Little Falls Parkway and passed an ambulance spinning its wheels in a ditch. I asked Charley when he expected to leave.

He wasn't paying any attention. I repeated the question.

In a voice free of harshness he replied, "Very soon."

He spent the afternoon making phone calls and writing lists. The kids were at school and Zandy had errands to run. I went for a swim at the Jewish Community Center in Rockville after Charley dozed off on the sofa. Jagger, Zandy's schnauzer, snored at his feet.

When I returned, around five-thirty, Charley was talking to Josh, my son. "Your old man was a decent bunter," Charley was saying as I entered the kitchen. "But a lousy glove man."

"Radical," Josh said, his hands full of Fig Newtons.

"You're confusing me with my father," I said. "I was chicken. I always stepped in the bucket, remember?"

"Yeah, sure," Charley said immediately, but his eyes seemed to be saying something different.

The first thing he said to Zandy when she got home was "Did you put on a few pounds, darling?" He must have realized what he'd said because he added, "You have a lovely figure for your age, Zandy. Just lovely."

"Who's hungry?" Zandy snapped, jerking open the fridge.

"Don't knock yourself out on my account," he said.

Zandy spun around, her dark irises churning at me. Her eyelashes, fringed with ringlets from her recent perm, beat like tiny feathers. She went to the stove and turned on the broiler. Beneath her peach-colored exercise leotard, her underpants were visible.

"Where's Paula?" I asked.

"At a Student Council meeting," Zandy said, getting lettuce and beets from the vegetable bin. "They're planning an old-fashioned sock-hop."

"At this hour?" Charley asked. "Doesn't she have things to study?"

Zandy looked at me and made a scornful mouth. "Do you eat beets, Charley?"

"A pleasure," he boomed, kneading Josh's shoulders.

Zandy started to sauté some cauliflower. Peanut oil sizzled in the electric wok. I sliced the beets and green onions, peeled a cucumber, tossed the lettuce. Paula phoned and said she was going out for pizza with her friends and a couple of teachers.

"You let her go out on school nights, Zandy?" Charley said.

Zandy, her face bent over the wok, said, "If you've noticed, Charley, she's not a baby anymore."

At supper he didn't care for the way his steak was broiled (we liked ours Pittsburgh rare and he wanted his ruined), he insisted the diet Thousand Island dressing tasted sour, said the cucumber seeds got stuck in his dentures. "Nothing personal," he told Zandy twice.

"I hope not," she grumbled.

In my mouth the food tasted like dust.

"Did everything go all right today?" Zandy asked.

"Great," I said, with my mouth full of salad.

Charley bent his head and pointed at me with his fork. "What's so great about a funeral, Elliot?"

"I didn't mean it like that," I said.

"Lou Bluestein had two different degrees from Columbia," Charley told Josh. "Did you know that Lou Gehrig graduated from there? Just like Elliot and your *zayde*. He played at Baker Field. Gehrig was German, so I don't especially trust how he felt about Jews. Not too many of us made the bigs, but when we did we could carry our weight. Hank Greenberg, Al Rosen, Koufax—those Jews could play ball with anybody, crackers or colored guys, it wouldn't matter. Back to what I was saying, Louie Bluestein rode the subway every day from Flatbush to attend classes. He even belonged to the glee club. The man could carry a tune like a regular cantor. Would you believe he knew *Kol Nidre* by heart?"

I tried to look surprised.

"Is that so?" Zandy said.

"He certainly *did*," Charley insisted. "And the past few years he even took some night courses at Catholic University. Mostly economics. To pass the time he fooled around with the stock market and made a little spending money. I swear he never missed *All Things Considered*. The guy absolutely loved education."

"Teachers pass away like everyone else," Zandy said, trimming her meat carefully.

"Charley's got an announcement," I said.

Zandy stopped chewing for a moment and asked, "Oh?"

"He's moving to Florida," I said deliberately.

"All right!" Josh yelled. "Do some jai alai!"

"Josh, be quiet," Zandy said. "What for, Charley?"

Charley gazed at me for encouragement. "He wants to change his lifestyle," I said. "You know, switch gears and all. Be a swinger."

Behind her contact lenses, Zandy's eyes seemed magnified. She fiddled with the band of her gold wristwatch.

To me she said, "Do you need me to draw you a picture?"

Josh wanted to know if he could fly down next year over Easter break. "That's when all the fine college foxes are hanging around, Charley," he said.

"Good idea, pal," Charley laughed, patting Josh's arm. "Maybe we can go pick some up together."

"He can?" I asked.

"That's between you and your wife, Elliot. *Ask her.* Not me."

"We all need to reach some kind of sensible decision," Zandy said. "As a family," she piously added after noticing our blank faces.

"Uh, wait a minute," Josh complained. "Charley said it was solid, Dad."

"We'll discuss it later," I said.

"How come?" he demanded, salad dressing trickling down his chin.

"*Later*," Zandy warned. "I'm not discussing it with you now. Finish your dinner and go do your homework."

"But I am," he answered back.

"Go to your room," she shouted. Her face was red.

I looked at them both—gloomily. "Go, *please*," I said in a low voice.

"I'm going," he said with a huge effort.

"This is terribly inconsiderate of you," Zandy said to Charley after Josh had left. "*You* amaze me, you know that?" she added ambiguously.

"*Me?*" I asked.

She gave me an unforgiving glance.

"And you," Charley said to Zandy, "ought to lighten up a bit."

"I beg your pardon," she said indignantly. She stood up and began clearing the dishes.

"C'mon, honey," I said. "Nobody's at fault here."

We heard Josh's bedroom door slam, and in less than a minute his stereo came on full blast. The entire house vibrated with "Thriller." With her cheeks puffed out like an adder, Zandy asked "So when are you splitting, Charley? When's the lucky day?"

Almost awkwardly he replied, "Is a Tuesday afternoon good?"

"Tuesday's great!" I brayed.

Zandy pivoted around like she was playing hopscotch and planted both feet on the floor simultaneously. "Tuesday?" she gasped, grabbing her elbows with her hands. "Jesus H. Christ, Elliot!"

I felt my ears buzz like static. "Charley, Charley," I prompted him.

"Do you go to Weight Watchers on Tuesdays?" he asked her.

"I can't stand it!" she shrieked, and started stamping her sneakered foot.

Charley screwed up his face, scratched his head, and tapped his breastbone with his index finger. "I wasn't aware you harbored such resentment towards me," he said.

"Don't tell me what I'm feeling," she scolded. Then she shot me a pleading gesture and said, her composure suddenly coming back, "Are you doing this on purpose, Elliot?"

"I know there's something I'm not getting here," I said, twirling one of the walnut salad spoons between my fingers.

"Haven't you been listening?" she asked.

"Of course I've been listening," I replied bitterly.

Charley shook his head in agreement. "Excuse the expression, darling, but you sound very *farblondjet*—all fouled up."

Zandy waved her arms in total exasperation and dropped back into her chair. She picked at a crumb on the tablecloth with her thumb, and some flakes of copper polish chipped off. She looked so furious I felt like comforting her. "This is killing me, Elliot," she said hoarsely.

We sat there silently for what seemed like ten minutes, listening to Michael Jackson. Then Charley leaned forward and rubbed the back of Zandy's hand. "Not this *coming* Tuesday," he said. "In three, maybe four weeks. You should bite your tongue for thinking what I realize you've been thinking about. Paula is my angel."

I stared at her pitifully. "You thought he—*we*—forgot Paula's *Bas Mitzvah?*" I asked.

She immediately denied my accusation with a snort and left the room.

That seemed to settle things, at least temporarily, or so I thought. Later that night, after Zandy shoved my hand off her behind, dramatizing her rancor by shifting her whole torso away from my side of the bed, I told her what I knew of Charley's plans.

She cut me off. "It'll be a pain in the ass," she said coldly. "I'm giving you plenty of warning."

"That's unfair—"

"The hell it is," she insisted, giving me a wearied expression. "You're incapable of dealing with Charley rationally. There's no balance or sense of proportion when it comes to him. I'll never convince you of this, but Charley's how you keep your grandfather and father alive. In fact, I think you're more frightened of his death than he is."

I ran my fingers across the top of her nightie. "Anything else?" I asked, smiling.

She flushed. "There is, as a matter of fact. I'd feel better knowing he's only twenty minutes away by car than in some Miami Beach crash pad with a bunch of old fogies as sick as he is. Who's going to keep an eye on him? My God, the man's imposed himself on you and your family for decades. If he goes it'll cost you, Elliot. And I'm not talking about money."

"Then what?"

"Go figure it out for yourself," she said.

I reached for her but she eluded my hand. Had I gotten hold I might have twisted her arm into a hammerlock, and I think she knew it.

"Let's just cool it," I said mildly. "Charley's made of iron, Zandy. Pure iron. He knows what he's doing. And I don't appreciate all the pop psychologizing—"

"Bullshit, Elliot!" she shouted.

She took her pillow and went to sleep in the den.

I went downstairs for a beer and pistachio nuts and paused in front of the rec room. I knocked, and peeked in. Charley was on the sofa, wrapped in a Hudson's Bay blanket, watching *St. Elsewhere*. Josh was flipping through cassettes. He gazed up and asked Charley if he could use the VCR. "Having fun?" I asked, crouching down like a catcher.

Charley pointed at Josh. "He's making a social studies project, Elliot."

"Nice," I said.

Josh cocked his head and gave me a petulant smirk. He was still pissed at me for not taking up for him.

I peered at the TV screen. A guy in a tie-dyed muscle shirt with rolled up sleeves was humping a microphone. Banners and flags were flapping in the breeze behind him. The stage was crowded with saxophone players and farm equipment. I sighed heavily and plopped down on my butt. "Man, do I feel out of it."

"You are," Charley said, passing me his Sen-Sen's.

"It's on the post-Bruce era, you know?" Josh explained. "That's B-R-U-C-E. I'm calling it a 'Rockumentary.'"

"Lenny?" Charley wondered, scratching his chin. "The comic with the filthy mouth?"

"He means Springsteen, Charley. Right, Josh?"

Josh was on his stomach, taking notes on one of my legal pads. "Yeah, really, Dad."

Charley cracked his knuckles and said, "What do I know from such wild music? Is he Jewish?"

Josh turned and grinned, his braces almost glowing in the brilliant light of the TV screen. "That's incredibly spaz!" he crowed.

Charley leered at the screen for a long moment and then picked up the *Post*. I told them not to stay up too late, and said good night. They both nodded disinterestedly at me, and Charley waved me away. I backed cautiously out of the room, feeling almost like a thief in my own home, and pulled the heavy sliding doors shut with an airtight hiss.

"Oh, *Dear!*" Doris yelled when she saw Charley enter the reception hall. He was escorted by four of his cronies.

Zandy said she was going to murder him. "How could he?" she asked me at least a dozen times in front of Mrs. Fingerhut, Paula's *Haftorah* teacher. Doris suggested I call the cops. "Who knew," I asked them repeatedly, "he was going to bring his pals?"

"You should've anticipated it, Elliot," Doris said. When I tried to intercept Charley I myself was seized from behind, by the waist, and a raspy voice rang out my name. "Buddy, how are you?" I asked. The voice belonged to Buddy Preminger, one of the men who'd be moving to Miami. I hadn't seen him in a few months, and in that time he'd grown a walrus mustache and bought a pair of silver wireframe eyeglasses. Dandruff crusted over his thinning hair like lice. "Nice tan, Buddy," I said.

"A quality sunlamp, kiddo. It'll make your skin shine like a million bucks."

Then he gave me the once-over, blowing out his cheeks like Dizzy Gillespie. Buddy had blistered grooves where the glasses pinched his nose. He reached out and palmed the lapel of my suit. "Worsted?" he asked nasally. "A poly-cotton blend, perhaps? I used to know garments like the back of my hand, Elliot. Hickey-Freeman, Stanley Blacker, all the big names. I belonged to the ILGWU. Years ago, you hear what I'm explaining? Never mind, you look ultra contemporary. Very snazzola." Buddy's adenoidal squeal made my skin crawl.

I caught up with Charley at one of the buffet tables. He was studying the pyramids of chopped liver and chicken salad. He said something to a waiter bearing a tray of *knishes* and tiny franks that caused the waiter to crack up. "Charley," I said softly, not wanting to make a scene.

I heard his rapid breathing, and his chest rattled under his vest like a greasy bike chain. He hugged me and I smelled his chlorine breath. "I know what's troubling you, Elliot. Don't have a heart attack, I'll square it with your in-laws."

I smiled pathetically, aware that people were watching us. Charley's other friends—Mickey Wishnograd, Moe Floss, and someone

I had trouble placing—came over to wish me *mazel tov*. The man I didn't recognize wore a Moshe Dayan black eye patch, had enormous breasts, and looked like a redneck bartender. I was shaken to find out it was Solly Jupiter, one of Charley's oldest friends; he seemed to have put on at least a hundred pounds since I'd last seen him. Solly used to be an amateur ventriloquist, and for years he entertained the temple youth groups during *Simchath Torah* and *Purim*. When he performed he always wore a Tyrolean hat and bright lederhosen.

After showing me his Ed Sullivan imitation for the hundredth time, Moe Floss gave me an airmail envelope with Paula's name written in red ink on the outside and told me it was from "all the boys." He said I should let Paula buy whatever she wanted. I thanked them all profusely for coming, and drifted away. My belly burned, and I wondered if the caterer had any Maalox.

When Charley found me I was finishing off a club soda at the bar. He had bloody spots in his eyeballs and he was pointing suspiciously at the table arrangements. "It really floors me that Ezra went in for this kind of high-priced outfit," he said, gesturing at the waiters milling aggressively through the crowd.

"Ezra's not the boss here," I said.

"Yeah, I understand," he said, ordering a ginger ale.

Before I could tell him that he didn't understand anything, my father-in-law, a big, sloppy textile manufacturer, was giving Charley one of his phony handshakes and a stupendous grin. Ezra had oily white hair and a cigar stuck between his dark little gums. His mustache was damp with dribbled schnapps. They made elaborately polite small talk with each other for a few minutes. Ezra kept nudging Charley in the ribs every few seconds, glancing down as he did so to check his gold pocket watch.

"*Shmutz*," Charley said when Ezra had left and he and I were sitting on swanky velvet armchairs. I couldn't disagree with him; Ezra was the kind of businessman who'd built his fortune on the ruins of other people's failures, and had enjoyed doing it that way. The band Paula wanted—five anorectic teenagers in turquoise Mohawks and fishhook earrings—were playing hard rock from the sixties. I scanned the room and saw Moe Floss downing highballs at the bar. He was slavering over the women dancing *horas* in their stockings and bare feet to "Under my Thumb." I felt sick when I saw him dig brutally at his crotch.

"Hungry?" I asked, pointing to the platters of food.

Charley shrugged and stood up. "This is typical," he said loudly, startling some friends of Doris's who were fox-trotting nearby. I waved at them and grinned. Charley picked up and sniffed a panatela, and I watched his mouth water over the diamond-shaped buffet tables. "That guy Pritikin would go nuts seeing this kind of food. *Shmaltz* wherever you look. They fill you up on hors d'oeuvres at this type of affair, there'll be plenty of leftovers. Trust me, the caterer gave that *zhlub* Ezra a royal screwing."

"*I* paid for everything," I said defensively. I felt the heat under my clothes like a steaming shower. "Just be quiet and eat something already."

After filling his plate, he turned and gave me a pained look, his reddened eyes bursting with grudge.

Rabbi Flanken pushed through the imitation rice-paper panels that separated the adjoining halls and grabbed Charley's elbow. Flanken was the Jewish chaplain at the state prison, and he taught courses on social psychology to the inmates. He spoke in a high-pitched voice and was reed-thin, a vegetarian. Charley, his mouth full of dry turkey, shouted, "You can't get a *minyan* for services up there, I'll wager. Elliot"—now he turned and faced me—"seven, eight *Yids* in the pen tops." Before I could interrupt him and change the subject, Charley had pivoted as gracefully as a second baseman and was facing the speechless rabbi again. "Go on, *rebbe,* tell Elliot here how things stand in the mob. Those hoity-toity dons are nothing without an old-time consiglieri. We're not so well known in the gangster business anymore, though I read in the *Post* that those Russian Jews in Brighton Beach are tougher than the Sicilians or Puerto Ricans any day of the week. But there's no more Lepke Buchalter, no more Bugsy Siegel on our side. That Meyer Lansky was a pip-squeak compared to those scary guys. Lansky was a nobody, a lousy accountant." Flanken, a man about my age with incredibly sad eyes, looked doubtfully at his hands and said he was going to ask the band if they could play "Five Hundred Miles" by Peter, Paul and Mary. Before going he said something vague about how the damp weather we were having could affect your mood.

"What a lightweight," Charley said as soon as Flanken was gone. "His sermons are from outer space. He's not aware that he puts the entire congregation to sleep?"

I protested mildly. "Oh, he's not so bad, Charley—"

"Hah!"

"What is it? Second thoughts about leaving?"

He heaved his shoulders forward and said, "Who knows?" His eyes swam at me through their cloudy lenses like iridescent fish. Then came his worried look, his pale lips twisted like a pretzel.

"You don't remember, Elliot," he began, listing sideways like a dinghy in the wind, "but there was a time I thought nothing could stop me. Problem was, I didn't piddle around, or loaf enough. I never relaxed, I never bothered to take stock of my situation in life. I didn't know how to ease up, I never learned how to smell the roses—like your grandfather told me I should. Truthfully, I'm the kind of guy who pissed away his natural talents on idle schemes. Are you listening, Elliot? I was a pie-in-the-sky kind of *shlemiel*. I didn't learn from my mistakes, like most people. I'll give you some free advice on human mentality I hope you'll put away and never forget: don't be so nervous all the time. It's like when I tried to learn how to switch-hit. I believed it would change the world for me, you catch my drift, make me not stink so much of the time. But if you're not a DiMaggio or a Ted Williams, don't break your chops trying to be. To tell you the honest truth, I don't get so much pleasure from baseball anymore. I don't know, the owners, the players, it's all wisenheimers in thousand dollar suits now, bigmouths who build condominiums and own shopping malls. All these money guys, nobody respects the game itself anymore. They know nothing about history." He paused and massaged his chest as if it hurt.

I tried to contradict him but he waved my objections away. I felt divided, and terribly confused. My head throbbed and the muscles in my neck were as tight as piano wires. Something was kicking inside my diaphragm.

"I'm proud as hell of you, Elliot," he said. "And I know your grandfather would be too."

I smiled. "I used to have dreams about you, Charley. After my father died."

He laughed nervously. "They must've been nightmares, kid."

"Uh-huh. I can't remember them exactly, but I think you and I were playing catch in Crotona Park after my grandfather's stroke. You'd lob me the ball, and I'd drop it. Some dream; just like it was in real life, right?"

"All boys have dreams like that, Elliot. Even pros."

I could have wept watching him pick at the whitefish and nova. He ate daintily, as if the food were an extension of Ezra's way of life and therefore lacked sincerity. He dropped his knife and flashed his crooked teeth at me. They were small, like chipped gravestones. He removed the commemorative pink *yarmulke* he was wearing and a grapey vein in his forehead seemed to throb in segments. I wrapped a huge hunk of cake in aluminum foil for him to take back to his apartment—he requested pieces with Paula's name in icing on them. Then I was distracted by a commotion in front of the band—I heard Rabbi Flanken's piercing voice above "Tambourine Man"—and by the time I broke up the fight and returned to our table, Charley and "the boys" had gone.

I was shaving on the Wednesday morning Charley was driving south when Zandy got me out of the bathroom to answer a call.

"Something's happened, hasn't it?" I barked in her drowsy face.

"Don't get excited," she said, handing me the receiver.

"Hello!"

"Yes . . . uh, Mr. Elliot Sachs? I'm Will Nathanson," a half-wheezing voice replied.

"Charley?" I asked. "What about him? Is he all right? Where is he? Don't lie to me!" I was gripping the phone so hard my fingers ached.

"No question about it, Mr. Sachs."

The hospital was squashed between an auto wrecker and an abandoned Sunoco station filled with spools of rusted industrial cable. In
front was a series of old-fashioned phone booths with the glass
panes smashed out. A perfumy receptionist told me through a blast
of cigarette smoke to go up to the third floor. I took the elevator
with three laughing interns and a pregnant woman in a wheelchair.

Old men soaked in sweat packed the humid corridor. Bedpans and
hospital gowns were stacked on gurneys. A couple of orderlies were
playing catch with a whiffle ball. I jogged up to the nurses' station
and announced I was the nephew of the critically injured old man
brought up about an hour ago. I inhaled deeply and tried to put a
good face on my anxiety. The floor reeked of ammonia, the walls of
wet paint, the corridor of pureed fruit. The nurse on duty, a round-
faced, vaguely Eskimo-looking woman with a shaggy growth of
blonde hair on her chin, glanced up at me from a pinging computer
terminal.

"Where's Mr. Palestine?" I shouted, pacing like an attack dog.

She yawned and stretched and said, matter-of-factly, "*Quién?*"

I went crazy making wild gestures with my hands signifying an
old man with a fractured skull. The nurse pointed aimlessly in the
direction of a room down the hall. Another voice, a man's this time,
yelled from somewhere I couldn't see that I'd better wait for the
doctor to come back from the cafeteria.

I went and peeked into Charley's room. He was covered in sheets,
and there were tubes in his mouth and nose. I jumped back into the
corridor. I staggered over to a wicker bench and felt pinned there by
a force greater than gravity. I knew I'd have to push all this away,
that I'd have to find a way to stop it from dragging me down into a
place so deep and dark I'd be decades digging myself out. I took a
slow breath and walked back to Charley's room. My knees were shaking and I felt dizzy all of a sudden. As I began inching the door open,
a fierce-looking Sikh in an off-white turban and red bow tie grabbed
my elbow and said in a ringing tenor voice that he was the attending
resident. He had tremendous eyebrows and pitted skin. When I told
him who I was, he smiled warmly and suggested we sit down.

"How's my uncle?" I asked.

The Sikh scratched his enormous nose. "Veddy, veddy bad," he said glumly.

His beeper went off and he excused himself. I phoned Zandy and told her that Charley was in bad shape. There was something in her voice when I said she shouldn't come down here, uncertainty perhaps, maybe even guilt, though I doubted that.

To calm myself I went downstairs to the cafeteria for a cup of tea and a bran muffin. When I got back, Charley's face was turned to the wall. A group of people I didn't recognize were standing around his bed. I couldn't bring myself to enter all the way, and just stood at the partly open door. A woman in a peasant dress came over and introduced herself. I drew a blank, but smiled nonetheless. Then she thanked me for coming. Before I could ask her who she was, she turned to the others and introduced me as Dr. Reep, the liver specialist they'd been waiting for. A groan like a car backfiring went up from the bed, and the sheets, coiled like a swarm of snakes, shifted. I looked down; it wasn't Charley.

When I tracked him down he was in the emergency room getting his wrist and arm taped. He had a few stitches in his cheek. His friends huddled around him, poring over a Triple-A map of the East Coast. Moe Floss and Mickey Wishnograd argued over whether or not they should stick to 95 the whole way down. Solly Jupiter pounded on a Sunkist machine, vines of kinky hair bristling from his huge ears. I raised hell with Will Nathanson for not telling me the whole story. His head was too small for his body and Buddy Preminger warned me not to be fresh.

"Elliot," Moe said, a colored toothpick in his mouth, "do me a favor and tell this stubborn mule here he doesn't know from nothing when it comes to modern parkways. He always drives like an old woman. Never above 50."

"Who needs a goddamn speeding ticket?" Mickey asked me. "The cops down there hate Jews." After all these years he still looked exactly like Jack Benny.

Charley lifted up his swollen arm and sighed. His face was black-and-blue. "Let's get the show on the road," he said.

"You'll be fine," I told him in the parking lot. "But don't sit in the sun without protection. Remember to take your walks inside a mall when it's too hot out. Did you pack your Giants hat? And drink plenty of water and juice. Where are your pills?"

He tugged on his scarf. "Is this a quiz, Elliot? Washington is hot. Miami is three times hotter, take my word on it. Let's not kid ourselves." His breath was visible in the cold.

I shook hands all around and nodded graciously at the invitations to come visit with the family once they were settled. Charley looked frail in the pale winter light. He stood absolutely still, as if he were trying not to sway in the wind.

He blew on his fingers and said, "Try to keep in touch."

"Lucky for you I wasn't there when you tripped. Otherwise you'd be home now, having noodle soup or taking a hot sitz bath."

"Hah! You think so?" A nerve jumped in his face.

"I know so," I said, placing a hand lightly on his shoulder. "Some habits are hard to break."

"Enough already, Elliot. You're telling me?"

I held him for a minute and kissed the top of his head. "I'll see you next fall, Charley. For *Rosh Hashanah*. You'll fly up."

He adjusted his glasses and said, "Next fall is next fall. Please don't worry."

I must have left my gloves in the hospital, so I went back for them after the "boys" finally took off. They weren't on the bench outside the room where I thought I'd first found Charley. Going back down in the elevator, I felt my composure ebbing and my legs got so weak that I thought I would need to sit down. My hands were shaking slightly. I was at a loss—could this be the start of a massive panic attack? An old woman with a pink ribbon in her white hair seemed to notice the difficulty I was having standing erect and offered to push the elevator's emergency button. I wondered if she suspected that I was a patient from the psychiatric ward allowed out for a stroll, or perhaps an alcoholic with the D.T.'s.

"Low blood sugar," I lied. "I just need some orange juice."

She dug into her shiny leather pocketbook and fished out a Nestle's milk chocolate candy bar. She peeled away the inner whitepaper wrapping a third of the way down like Charley used to do, and ordered me to eat it. "I can't stand elevators," she told me. "And airplanes. They ruin my blood pressure. I went to a head shrinker for it. He even tried hypnosis, but nothing did the trick. My grand-children live in San Antonio, and I certainly can't drive to Texas every time they have a birthday. So I just grin and bear it—like everything else at my age."

"What else is new," I said, and she sighed in agreement.

I thanked her for her concern and the chocolate bar, but when she wanted to go find me a nurse in order to have *my* blood pressure taken, I told her that all I needed was some fresh air. And once I was outside, the misty air did seem to help momentarily, though I still felt morbidly anxious. I remembered my missing gloves, but didn't have the nerve to go back for them. I decided I'd just call the hos-pital lost-and-found later in the day. I went to find my car and ran into the family I'd intruded upon earlier coming out of the hospital. They looked ghastly. A man in a fur-lined coat stepped forward ten-tatively and patted my back.

"It's all right, Dr. Reep," he said. "We were prepared for the worst. My dad didn't want any heroic measures. He was ready to go."

For an instant I thought the wind would flatten me. They were all expecting me to say something. I stared at the sky's quivering slate-blue light, my mind a vacuum. The woman in the peasant dress tilted her head, waiting.

When I finally opened my mouth to speak, instead of sounding compassionate, I came off as terribly pinched and pompous—as if I were a real physician and not merely a clumsy impostor. "I wish I could have done something for him, but medicine, like life itself, has so many limitations," I said. "Please call my answering service if I can lend you any further assistance."

"This is a difficult time," the woman in the peasant dress said through her pursed gray lips. She seemed to be choking back tears, and her cheeks were mottled and red from the wind.

"For all of us," I said, without thinking.

"I know this is better for him, going quickly. But I miss his presence already. My father was a simple man, but he had a lot of charm."

A few of them started to sob then. I exchanged looks with the woman in the peasant dress, and she smiled wearily. Her soft eyes had no sparkle in them; the disklike pupils were like tiny black ink-drops. Not knowing what else to do, I smiled back at her. At that very moment a fierce and intimate attachment to her spread through my body like an immutable blush, as if I were suddenly closer to her than to my own wife and children. Nearly light-headed, I was on the verge of asking her out to drinks and dinner—my shortness of breath and trembling legs told me I was on the threshold of begging her to run away with me—when the man in the fur-lined coat took my clammy, gloveless hand in his and squeezed it. It came to me then that each of us carried impossible and unyielding burdens, and that we hungered after these unforeseen though merciful intercessions of fate to help us travel across those rickety bridges just beneath which all our intractable fears are churning away in a harrowing whirlpool, their innumerable disguises finally unveiled. My disheveled equilibrium restored for the time being, I escorted them then—single file, our heads lowered against the swirling snow—up the concrete ramp of the towering garage. In a few minutes I began to be warmed by a strange exhilaration, their footsteps like durable heartbeats on the fractured ice behind me, my face sawing against the bitter wind.

If you could lick my heart, it would poison you.
—Yitzhak "Antek" Zuckerman, leader of
the Warsaw Ghetto Uprising

I died in Auschwitz, but no one knows it.
—Charlotte Delbo

The Quarry

I

The forbidden quarry was no more than a brisk two- or three-mile walk beyond the dusty apple orchard in back of the local chapter of the Monroe County Elks Club. Although our mothers warned us not to, my friends and I ate the mealy green and yellow apples off the ground and then chucked the wormy cores at blue jays and magpies and mangy dogs. A hand-painted billboard, nailed crookedly to a telephone pole across the pitted asphalt road from Ditenhafer's Ice & Dairy, announced to travelers that they had just entered the limestone and applesauce capital of the world. (The Empire State Building, on Fifth Avenue in Manhattan, for decades the tallest building in the world, was fashioned from pearly limestone cut and blasted in this part of the state.)

A week before Halloween, the Elks would sell tart apple cider and chunky apple butter in Mason jars and apple dumplings from a bunch of knotty pine roadside picnic tables spread with newspapers. There were always chattering, frilly-sleeved church ladies in gold and blue straw hats with bright red ribbons on them walking about, rolling out piecrusts, pulling berries from thorny currant bushes, smearing orange and lemon marmalade on buttermilk biscuits, or ladling hot bubbling rhubarb out of squat iron vats on corn fritters and buckwheat cakes. The yellow jackets and carpenter bees and bluebottle flies were vexing if the weather had remained both dry and warm since the middle of September, and frequently a child, idling barefoot in the sword grass or pulling at the loose railroad ties that vanished into a thick stand of copper beeches, got nipped on his heels or the soles of his feet. Lazy brown Jersey cows, milked by the Ditenhafers, grazed in the dilapidated, scrubby fairgrounds nearby, and you could just see, poking out of the lavish poplar hills north of town, the thin white spires of the rebuilt Calvary Baptist Church.

Public records in the library indicated that New Brooklyn Township, the county seat, was first laid out in 1879, its simple design a joint capitalist venture by miners and bankers and the Illinois Central. Disenchanted sodbusters from the Ozarks crowded in to work the quarries. Sharecroppers from Alabama and Mississippi, on their way to enormous smelting factories and blast furnaces in Gary and Hammond, remained to cut stone. In the twenties there was a growing market in the country for construction limestone, and New Brooklyn's population more than doubled in ten years. Legend had it that the town took its name from the birthplace of its first elected mayor, a fat wily Dutchman with a thick walrus mustache, though I've never found any public documents that either confirm or deny that.

The Elks Club itself was quartered in a big house of whitewashed brick, with gables and dormers and pegged-maple floors. It had been a bequest from a childless circuit court judge in South Bend who had grown up in it. The judge, who'd died a few years back after coming down with diphtheria, had played the defensive line for Knute Rockne at Notre Dame. My proletarian father had always loathed bourgeois affiliations like country clubs and fraternal orders. He said that they were intended to exclude certain members of society (it didn't take a genius to know he was talking about us), that they were perfect for gossipy and intolerant people, people fixated on hearsay and slander and conformity and petty suspicions. His own philosophy was no doubt forged by *his* father, an immi-

grant from Bohemia who labored fifteen hours a day on an iron ore
boat that docked in all the Great Lakes.

Papa first settled in Michigan City, near a rendering mill, in a
cramped frame house enveloped by a screen of soot and smoking
horseflesh. My father told me that during the suffocating summers
the hazy sky over the chemical plants and petroleum refineries was
saturated with a greasy green dust. He said that my grandparents
would sit in their blue bathrobes each evening after supper and
swing in the burlap hammock hung in airless shade between two
withered plum trees, talking in whispers about their relatives and
friends left behind in the vast Carpathians. They would eat sliced
tangerines and grapes and sip scalding Russian tea out of thick-
bottomed glasses, and watch the ruby blossoms of fire from the East
Chicago smokestacks spread over the gin-colored lake in a murky
glow. Black-hulled freighters were smudges on the horizon.

My grandfather Samuel fought his way up in the world. An austere man, a demanding patriarch constrained by his knowledge of
brutal work and poverty, he refused to immediately follow his four
older brothers and move his family to one of the safe North Shore
suburbs until long after the scrap metal business they had gone into
was bringing in plenty of dough. My father worked long hard days
for him during the summer, and for meager pay. When Samuel finally felt secure, when the Heller Brothers Scrap Metal and Cement
Company at last had five times as many customers as it needed to
be prosperous, he put down hard cash and bought an attractive
split-level in Skokie, and later on became a bigwig in a large conser-
vative synagogue, endowing a yearly three-week trip to Israel for
worthy *Bar Mitzvah* students and sponsoring the temple basketball
league. Each night after supper he drank homemade slivovitz and
smoked two White Owls, and he played pinochle every Thursday
with his brothers and took my grandmother and his children out
for Hong Kong spareribs and chop suey and egg foo yung at Tung
Hoy's, in Evanston, every Sunday evening. He sent my father and
my aunts to Northwestern. He himself enrolled in night school; he
took some accounting and business courses at Loyola and struggled
to improve his English. When they all went under during the crash,

Samuel fed and clothed the entire family with the thousands he had kept hidden in a Wells Fargo safe in the leaky basement of his Skokie house.

Located in the south-central part of the state—not three hours by car from Fort Knox, Kentucky—New Brooklyn, Indiana, as I remember it, was a proper, patriotic, and ardently Republican town of narrow, sycamore-shaded residential streets and modest shops, and eight thousand or so civic-minded, churchgoing souls. A substantial freight depot had been hastily built at a now-defunct spur of the Vincennes and Wabash to transport limestone and gypsum to Kansas City and Chicago and points farther west and east, roughly at a place where the plucked barren cornstalks finally gave way to a solid curtain of dark green hills. When I was still in grammar school a number of sudden Indian summer tornadoes had ripped through the peaked tin warehouses, crushing porters and stray cats and dogs, even an occasional copperhead or rat snake, or a small red fox, and shearing thick, flat-bedded freight cars loaded with quarried stone in half. A mud-brown, perch-filled tributary of the Lost Pigeon River meandered through the bottoms, a wide, circular tract of cottonwood trees and fuzzy cattails just beyond the northern edge of New Brooklyn—a joyless conclave cynically called Smokey Glen by the bankrupt farmers and angry stonecutters who lived there in seedy shacks and trailers. Spooky chickens pecked at the mushy red soil. The kids who lived there were big and mean and noisy and had bruises and pus-filled cuts all over their white legs. They smoked cigarettes and cut school and started fights all the time when they came. Nowadays almost all of the old quarries are simply worked-out: they are stark, flooded pits filled with burnt lime and contaminated water. After a spell, important companies like Otis Elevator and Westinghouse finally came in to take their place.

The forbidden quarry could be easily found down a deeply rutted cinder road off newly paved Route 37, hardly fifteen minutes by bicycle from the gray stone World War I Memorial in front of the large courthouse square and American Legion Post. Each summer for as far back as anyone I ever knew could remember, someone had slipped at the quarry and cracked open their skull or broken their legs on a jagged slab of rock, or had drowned in the foul brown water. In a vain effort to dissuade the juvenile trespassers, the county had put up one of those wobbly cyclone fences that seemed to go to rust overnight, flimsy diamond-shaped wire with barbed-wire tops that anyone could cut through easily enough with pinking shears. The secluded quarry was a dark crater with a squishy mud bottom, full of bloated needlefish and lightning bugs, and my sister and I, unlike the wild kids from Smokey Glen, were not permitted to swim or play there. Sleek-winged crows and red-tailed hawks settled on the murky water, fighting over orange rinds and potato peels. At night in hot weather you could hear the whistling rattles of flying bats.

Hearsay had it that most of those who died in the quarry were hobos who slept in vacant hog sheds and cow barns and deserted sedans, that they were mostly impoverished veterans who picked corn and pumpkins and strawberries at one of the dark and desolate farms a few miles south of town. At recess, I'd tried to listen to the country hardnoses when they milled around the baseball backstop marked out in the weeds and talked about these men in low, respectful voices. They said that they'd come back from fighting the Japs and Nazis for Roosevelt, and now they couldn't earn a living because there were so many bohunks and coons and sheenies around landing all the good jobs. I had no idea, at that time, what a bohunk was, but I had no trouble understanding what sheeny and coon meant.

The hardnoses said that these men dressed in denim work pants or grimy gray union suits with holes in them, that they belted down rotgut bootlegged whiskey and cheap Tokay wine and arm-wrestled on a huge flat shelf of limestone that jutted out over the water, and that they bathed themselves and rinsed their soiled underwear and socks in the many shallow pools where the pebbled water lay stagnant and foul. I knew of a tramp in a leather eye patch who'd cut his foot open on a piece of dirty barbed wire and gotten lockjaw; another one was chewed on by starving rats as he was washing in the quarry and died of blood poisoning at the medical center in Indianapolis a month later. A forlorn drifter with sagging cheeks and dirty whiskers and a filthy plaid neckerchief came around our house every few months and swept the coral-colored mission-tile roof and pruned the magnolia trees and washed and waxed my father's pale blue Studebaker till it glowed. This man went stark raving mad from a black widow bite and jumped in front of a freight train filled with alfalfa and horse fodder and farm machinery. Despite losing both arms and legs and part of his skull, he somehow survived close to ten years, before choking to death on a piece of cashew-filled butterscotch taffy that was too big and sticky for him to swallow. My father had visited him four or five times at the V.A. hospital asylum up in Kokomo. He brought the man hair tonic, some flannel shirts and sweaters, a heating pad. He said the man sat on a small padded chair in front of a locked and gated window and never uttered a sound, not even a grunt.

It was common knowledge that these pariahs lived in a predatory state. They ate squirrel and weasel and were covered with lice and fleas. They suffered from incessant diarrhea and chronic skin inflammations. They brawled with each other over women and cards, armed with forks and rusty steak knives and barber's scissors they'd filched from Woolworth's, the dark evidence visible in the clusters of dried blood that had leached into the cool ropy crevices of the burnished stone. Occasionally you read in the Monroe County *Herald Telephone* that one of them had been arrested for public drunkenness, or lewdness, or burglary. People in New Brooklyn at that time soon after the Second World War didn't, as a rule, lock their doors at night, so a crime of any kind made everyone edgy for weeks, even if what the thieves stole was mostly cured pork chops and flour and bacon and dry firewood. These bewildered souls were as skinny as squealing newborn lambs, and like a starving beast a man without grub was capable of anything. I never knew of a neighbor ever getting clubbed over the head, and "rape" was not a word you heard mentioned too often, and when you did, only in a discreet tone of disbelief.

Vagrants were often found sleeping off their benders in tarpaper outhouses and corncribs and root cellars, but only rarely did a prowler try to break into one of the grim old farmhouses down on

Jumper's Hole Pike. Those places kept fighting dogs, snarling bull terriers with mangled ears and tails, and the clannish, brooding families who lived in them knew how to use hunting rifles and long carbon steel knives for disemboweling livestock. Usually the intruder was attacked and bitten into unconsciousness by the vicious mongrels—a perfect object lesson for the growing criminal element wandering loose among us, my father said somberly, peering at me and my older sister, Dara, over the newspaper at breakfast.

Those were bleak years for my father. After the war he found himself teaching biology and chemistry at the state college in New Brooklyn, a new branch of the vast state university an hour's train ride north, and raising two unruly children by himself. My mother had caught the measles from a neighbor's child when I was twelve. Her symptoms—extreme neurasthenia, intermittent vertigo and nausea, a low-grade temperature, coupled with stabbing pains in her pelvis, lower back, and jaw—were ambiguous. Doctor Slezak, an irritable old man with grainy brown warts on his hands who had delivered both my sister and me in the very four-poster my mother was now feverish in, examined her closely. He suspected that she was merely experiencing a not uncommon systemic allergic reaction to something she had eaten. With my father's consent, he gave her an injection of epinephrine. Her pale hands and knees shook all day, and her heart rate and blood pressure both rose. But by the time she missed her next period a speckled pink rash had broken out over her neck and chest. The doctor did some rudimentary calculations in his head and estimated that she must have been pregnant for at least seven or eight weeks, meaning that the hour of conception had most probably occurred at about the same time she started to feel ill. He closed his heavy-lidded eyes and placed his hands tenderly on my mother's meager belly. With his raised and wrinkled face cleansed of impatience, he could have been a Holy Roller blessing my parents' unborn child. Before my father could ask him what we needed to do in order to ensure her swift recovery, Doctor Slezak told him that we should read the Bible and pray, for everything was now in Jesus' benevolent hands. You can imagine how reassuring that sounded to all of us.

She was confined to her bed for months, a course of treatment designed to strengthen her and save the baby, but which only made her sicker. She'd suffered through whooping cough as a child, and her scarred lungs weren't in the best of shape to begin with. For some reason, the air around her bed and comforter reeked faintly of malt, or vinegar. We were alarmed when she suddenly grew afraid of drifting into sleep alone, as if she'd had a premonition that her death was imminent. To quiet her fears, I sat on the window seat and kept her company while she napped on the davenport in the back parlor, her head propped up on beige needlepoint pillows trimmed with rosy lace rosettes. Barely stirring myself, I listened to the ball game broadcast on the radio from Chicago or St. Louis or Cincinnati, half-asleep on the antique beechwood rocker my father had purchased at a flea market down in French Lick. When she was bored we played gin rummy and hearts on the green felt bridge table. There was an infection in her bladder that penicillin wouldn't heal, and I soaked her badly swollen feet and ankles in a zinc basin filled with Epsom salts, garlic powder, and scalding water. Doctor Slezak gave her a bottle of rancid smelling medicine that made her vomit for hours. My mother had always been the kind of person who rarely spoke to someone without touching them. Those days she could barely lift a finger to run through her thinning red hair. Her appetite was fading and all she ate was stewed peaches and black cherries, and a loathsome jellied broth made from salted calf's liver, bone meal, and buckwheat groats—her paternal grandmother's remedy for gout, mumps, lumbago, and sties. In the middle of the night she was awakened by leg cramps that made her cry out. Her pale gums bled like thick red fountain pen ink, she had a retching sensation in her throat that wouldn't go away, and a pasty fungus on her palate had caused her mouth and lips to ulcerate and whiten.

When my father finally pinned him down for a prognosis, Doctor Slezak said he was stumped. He confessed he couldn't find anything visibly wrong with her—anything, that is, he could readily treat with conventional medications—and contended that her puzzling symptoms were the foul harvest of an agitated nervous system. He said she needed some months in the mental sanitarium over in Terre Haute. I bet old Jesus will be there, too, Dara whispered to me. My father grimaced in my direction and then asked him to withdraw from the case.

The new doctors he found ordered all kinds of tests for her in the regional hospital in Seymour, and their serene optimism gave my father and sister hope. Notwithstanding the doctors' good intentions, I knew in my heart that the simple truth was she was tearing apart at the seams and that nothing could curtail the progress of her decline. The measles had set something terrible loose in her body, something that was far beyond human understanding. In turn, eminent specialists from the university medical center were consulted, dry, brooding men in pin-striped suits and polished shoes. They shook their heads solemnly and took samples of her urine and blood and told us it must be a cancer they couldn't find. Most likely an endocrine tumor, something affixed to her adrenal glands or thymus, or a malignancy at the base of her brain. A famous neurosurgeon with stiff white hair in his nostrils wanted to operate and take a closer look, but my father, a reserved and kindly man whose resolve to see her cured at all costs was gradually softening, couldn't bear the thought of her being in such needless pain.

Nearly every day after school I sat on a cushioned hairpin chair next to her bed and read magazines to her, soothing her by running my smooth fingernails up and down her delicately veined wrists until her melting, slanting green eyes, which had enormous black rings around them, like a panda's, slowly closed. She had me gently knead a yellowing eyelid cream around them. In the tips of my fingers I could feel that her bones were dissolving. Each morning the crumpled white tissues on her cedar bureau were streaked with a thin bloody discharge. I shampooed her hair every other day, working freshly squeezed limes and brown soap and a tablespoon of buttermilk into her brittle curls. Once she kissed the knuckles on my free hand while I was combing it out, and I felt something sharp drag inside my chest. A sudden swell of helplessness told me she was beyond mending. Soon after my father had finally worked up the nerve to tell her that the baby she was carrying was no longer alive, she stopped taking food and water and refused the painkillers her doctors had prescribed for her. In a matter of days, she stopped speaking as well.

My father's cheerful stoicism had suddenly deserted him. He was never a man given to feeling sorry for himself—about anything—but the worst that could have happened to him had happened. It wasn't very hard to guess how he was feeling since Dara and I were feeling much the same way, and it was soon unmistakable to both of us that he was losing an elusive, interior struggle with himself. He'd been devoted to my mother since they were in grammar school together, with an immeasurable passion he could feel beneath his skin, as if the two of them had shared a common nerve pathway. (I'd heard him say that—and countless other things about their life together—to my squint-eyed maiden Aunt Raizel and her widowed sister-in-law Froma at my grandparents' house in Highland Park, where we'd retreated to after the brief funeral to sit *shivah* and stuff ourselves with starchy food and share our grief for a week.) My parents had taken ballroom dancing and accordion and sketching lessons together from a cross old Hungarian lady in Evanston, and during the steamy Chicago summers they'd peddled pulpy lemonade and vanilla sugar cookies and colored Italian ices from a varnished pickle barrel, and they played ringalievio together in Grant Park, near the glimmering yachts rocking noiselessly at anchor in the shadow of the high-rise hotels and apartment buildings hovered above the steely lukewarm lake.

Given my father's affection for her, I'm sure he had felt unremitting shame that he had been unable to shield my mother from such implacable suffering. For months, his gentle hazel eyes were an anguished chasm of mazelike passages. At the time, we had thought, both Dara and I—this decades before our own less than unblemished marriages and adulthoods—that we saw, serenely mirrored in our father's ominous face and in the discontented shuffle when he walked, all we would ever need to know about the ephemeral quality of life. How quaint it must sound to the exuberant and self-absorbed people of today to hear, if they hear it at all, that men and women from their grandparents' generation had often fallen deeply in love as children and then managed to stay deeply in love during their entire adult lives. We live in a time when everyone wants to disregard the past, in essence projecting their rootlessness and displacement on the generations yet to come. People have no clear sense of who they are anymore and where they came from, and they have foolishly squandered something essential to themselves. What a bitter inheritance that must be.

For a time my father managed to get from one week to the next by doing all the necessary things—that is to say, he went to his cluttered campus lab each day, gave his lectures, paid the bills, mowed the grass, even dissembled interest and glowered at our scribbled essays and sloppy arithmetic. I went grocery shopping at the A & P and made our salami and cheddar cheese sandwiches for lunch. Dara did the wash and strung it outside to dry on clotheslines in the backyard. Then, as if he'd been stricken with an illness himself, without a single word of explanation he simply ceased shaving and cooking meals, and he wore the same wrinkled tweed clothes to teach in for days at a time. He stopped watering and weeding my mother's huge vegetable garden as well. The plot was divided into tidy grids by wooden posts, and it was lush with leeks and chives and radishes and thick stalks of red-leafed, dusty rhubarb and baby watermelons the fearless skunks gnawed on. By summer, hairy caterpillars were devouring the mint and marjoram.

He was a light sleeper, and my mother's harsh barking cough, like the croup I had had the previous winter, kept him (and us) awake. In the middle of the night he took to swaying on the padded wicker swing that hung on rusted chains from the slanted eaves of the L-shaped sunporch. My father chain-smoked Chesterfield after Chesterfield, and with my window open a crack I could hear his rapid asthmatic breathing. I parted my bedroom curtains slightly and watched him. His long-fingered hands were before him, gesturing, shaping some message or question to the remote constellations. If he heard what sounded like an airplane, he shone his flashlight in a sweeping arc toward the dark evergreen hills in the distance. For some reason I imagined my mother and father in their old bed when she first became ill, hushed, beyond mere words, silently watching each other.

He had apparently grown mindful of the certainty that there were limits to everything, including the will to live. As my mother got frailer and frailer, his compliant eyes took on a fatal look, as if he had made some dreadful mistake, or stupid error in calculation, something ghastly that had brought all this wretched calamity about. We are what we are—trembling creatures of concealment— and soon I too was inconsolable, silently enduring the illusion that *I* was ultimately responsible for what had happened to my beautiful mother. And then, of course, I was disillusioned. My family had little fortitude for feigned innocence back then; the German killing machine in Poland had erased forever any notion of the evolving benevolence of human nature. I had always loved my mother tenaciously, and I was rapidly learning of the suffering that often comes with such love.

I unburdened my heart to my father one smokey morning after a night of having lain awake listening to his wheezing. He looked at me guiltily, leaning his grieving face into his palms, and forced a smile. Cicadas were screaming in the huge Asian willow. Weeping, I told him about my recurring nightmare—of being sick with a drowning sensation, and entangled in a net, while frozen flies and spiderwebs swirled in icy blue space and heavy yellow candles burned in filigreed glasses. We'd been watching the steamy August mist rise like a sodden blanket from the ground, uncovering zinnias and wild sunflowers and the small black-eyed Susans my mother had planted the previous year. The bright dew, evaporating in the pale, buttery haze, was rank with the aroma of crushed sassafras, and in his black hooded sweatshirt my father made me think of the gloomy paintings of Franciscan monks I'd seen at the Art Institute in Chicago. He looked shaken, even dazed—all at once his inscrutable eyes were trained on something behind me, over my shoulder—and he nodded in the direction of some pine needles, which dangled like penknives from the badly clogged rain gutters. But the most he could do to console me was to lean over and pat my knee with his dainty fingers spread apart. Then, without so much as a single word passing between us, as if suddenly distracted by the fright he knew he had heard in my voice and seen in my tears, he simply turned away.

As if out of despondent shame, as if she couldn't stand witnessing anymore the changes taking place in her husband and children, my mother finally gave up. Her last weeks were filled with bottomless sighs—sounds so deep they seemed to have come from the center of the earth. The weather had suddenly turned drizzly, and an angel-haired mist lay over the pachysandra and asparagus ferns. Even the leaves on the lyre-shaped elms had already started falling. You could smell the change of season in the air—the calabash and pumpkin-seeds and clots of decomposing vegetation, the worm-eaten black plums and Winesap apples along the roadside. And for some reason I'd started dreaming about an abandoned Nash with a wide running board I'd imagined I'd seen parked outside our house the winter before, its heavy windshield and chrome-plated mirrors smashed, its gray-felt interior filled with soft snow and spears of glass.

Dara came home from school hoarse with laryngitis one day, and by the next afternoon my mother had a sore throat and a raging fever. I imagined her floating in a brilliant orange lake, her brain wreathed in fire, heat waves rising around her. Her lank hair spread in a scarlet fan across her pillow. She was lying on her side, her skin slick with sweat. My father filled the bathtub with ice cubes and cold water and placed her in it. While she shivered, large beads of per-spiration rolled down her cheeks. Dara and I just stood there, watch-ing him struggle with her scrawny, tormented body; his voice as he spoke to her was velvety and rolling, like Bing Crosby's. He ran a frayed chamois washrag over the hairline cracks in the skin around her mouth; he dug cautiously at her faintly barbed ears. When she stepped out of the tub, all collarbones and kneecaps and ribs, not really a body any longer but merely a spine, shriveled pink flanks shuddering with cold, her breasts pared to bone, he threw a large patchwork quilt around her shoulders. I had never seen her naked before, and it all started pouring out of me then, thick strangled sobs, gagging sounds that swept up and down my body like a flame, and I embraced her fiercely. I had already begun to grasp fully the dreadful power her pain had held over the three of us, and even after all this time I cannot help but wonder how much of what I was feeling was simply my own desire to be spared the sight of her misery.

I have no idea how long I held her there, though I know it mustn't have been for more than a few seconds. What still sticks in my memory is the brittle shadow of iridescent half-light that was filtered through the delicate cobwebs on the opaque bathroom window. Is it now disingenuous, or merely deceitful, to say I don't clearly remember what I had expected from her back then, what I so desperately needed? Beleaguered by sorrow and regret, and by my appalling dependence on her, I knew I desired some kind of decisive solution to all this suffering and dread—I knew, even then, that I craved something that would have made all this despair seem more like an illusion, a perverse trick of my ghoulish imagination. But when I looked up at her that night, her lyric face offered me only the ghost of a vanishing smile.

We took turns nursing her—changing the Noxzema-smeared pillowcases, coaxing her into having a small cup or two of my father's bland crab chowder, giving her soapy sponge baths when it hurt her spine and hips too much to sit in the tub. She had her beautiful hair cut short around her head like a boy's. Without telling either my father or Dara, I carried her scant wastes to the weed-choked garden in layers of wax paper, hoeing them under the tomato stakes and beds of acorn squash. Whenever she asked me to, I rubbed eucalyptus oil on her shoulders and back. She would linger on her stomach a few minutes, and I could see the tiny blonde hairs in the small of her back move when I gently blew on them, cooling her. A papier-mâché mobile that had once hung from my cradle—dancing polar bears and otters and lilac reindeer—now hung from the triple-bladed ceiling fan, and moved with the slightest current of air. She napped fitfully most of the time, her troubled sleep a chorus of feeble murmuring—evidently engaged in whole conversations in her dreams—and her nourishment had finally dwindled to sipping candied raspberry tea through a glass straw that a retired bachelor pharmacist across the street had brewed for her. Her liver had obviously begun to fail; the whites of her eyes had developed a pale jasmine tint, and there was no sparkle in them anymore. Her vision, it seemed, was growing dimmer by the day. She had trouble seeing me if I moved more than a few feet away from her. She grew steadily more placid, her languid body sinking into death, till an acute bout of double pneumonia brought on by scarlet fever carried her off in November, a few days after Thanksgiving.

I had kept a kind of private vigil over her those final unhappy days. I felt remorse for what I can only call the helplessness of the well in the presence of the hopelessly ill. At first Dara had sat watch with me, but she soon became too disheartened. I knew well the genesis of my sister's dark looks, when she was beginning to whirl downward into one of her dreadful blue moods. By nature reticent, Dara had always been vulnerable to despair—even over trifles. A neat, timid person with precise habits, she was unhinged by disorder. Something as foolish as a misplaced sock could ruin her day. Dara had been a fidgety child, reserved, reclusive, given to frenzied nightmares that left her sobbing for hours. An early and avid reader, she withdrew to her room and played with microscopes and erector sets and memorized the periodic table. Musically precocious, she had begun playing the cello at four. My mother would proudly boast to relatives that she had a Marie Curie on her hands. What she really had, unfortunately, was a budding manic-depressive.

In the decades following my mother's death, Dara assailed my father unremittingly, blaming him for things as wildly divergent as the McCarthy witch hunts and, later, something she ruefully called the "Watergate mentality," even the inevitable decay of spirituality in the West. Restless, she gave up her scholarship and dropped out of Brandeis during Christmas vacation her junior year. While visiting at a college friend's home in Savannah, she hitched a ride to Miami Beach, and after a few crummy jobs—as a valet parking attendant at a Coconut Grove nightspot, lugging groceries and doing laundry for retirees, being a grease monkey for a small-time race car driver—she moved back north to Greenwich Village, to a tiny cold-water flat on Cornelia Street, above a noisy tattoo parlor and Lebanese deli, and she waited tables in a drab painters' bar on University Place. The next thing we knew she was a blissful Hare Krishna with sallow pimply cheeks and dirty ears who forgot to flush the toilet the lone time she journeyed back to the Midwest for a visit. I couldn't imagine the drugs she had been using, and I studied her thin arms for needle tracks. For more than ten years she spent her days haunting commuters in Grand Central Station.

Infrequently she wrote me aggressively condescending letters, first baiting me about what she called my intolerant Midwestern chauvinism, and then moving on to knock the Jews and Catholics at every turn. My father reasoned that Dara's disaffection and estrangement was rooted in her muddled conviction that he had always held a grudge against her. After the Hare Krishnas, she borrowed money from me and went to Israel for almost three years, living on a *kibbutz* near the Mediterranean and harvesting avocados and olives. When we saw Dara back in Manhattan's Little Italy a few months before she drifted west to San Francisco with her old Brandeis roommate Hermine (a former debutante from Lexington, Massachusetts), she was petulant and broke and kept referring to herself in the second person, as in "you are an expatriate," meaning *she* was. When my father went to the john she lifted a wad of bills from his wallet. He never once made an issue about it to me—like why didn't you stop her?—so I always assumed he had put some extra fifties in there, snugly sandwiched between the tens and twenties, doubtlessly hoping she would steal them.

Dara had dyed her curly fawn-colored hair orange, and both of them (my father had asked her to invite Hermine along) carried sheathed hunting knives underneath their bright woolen serapes for protection. During dinner they told us in grisly detail about all the assaults and robberies that had occurred in their miserable tenement. Listening to this, my father appeared terribly alarmed. When he quietly suggested that they should consider moving to a safer neighborhood, to Long Island or Westchester perhaps, Hermine giggled and said he "blew her mind," and Dara gave him a scowl that could have been engraved onto her face with acid.

In the insolent and incandescent sixties Dara did her share of picketing and rallying and vigiling, of jamming the rifle barrels of dead-eyed National Guardsmen with carnations and roses. She was in Mississippi with SNCC for Freedom Summer, at Berkeley for Vietnam Day, was in attendance, it seemed, at every teach-in and sit-in and peace-in and grope-in and be-in and loot-in California had to offer. In turn, there were flirtations with the Moonies and the Scientologists, and an infatuation with a blind and wheelchair-bound ex-Pentecostal minister with pomaded hair from Oakland who took her on an evangelical mission to Yellowknife, in the Canadian Northwest Territories, and then to Alaska. For fifteen months she was an acolyte of Brother Godfrey and lived an ascetic life in an Eskimo hamlet along the Yukon River, reading Ayn Rand and Alan Watts. She even eloped with a bad-tempered abstract expressionist, an odious little man twenty years her senior with a prosthetic hand and three ex-wives who taught her how to be a serious boozer and whacked her around. She left him after a year or so and moved back to Chicago without telling us. An old friend of my grandmother's wrote to say that she had seen Dara in Wilmette, not far from the Baha'i Temple, walking a couple of Great Danes. My father paid a private investigator a bundle to find her, and then he drove up to Chicago to see her, but she refused even to speak with him.

A few years later she was busted for shoplifting a leopard-print evening gown and a couple of pairs of Capezios in Marshall Field's. She had stolen credit cards in her purse, as well as a small vial of amphetamines and a few joints. And this wasn't the first time she was in trouble with the law. A few years earlier she had forged some checks. Dara phoned me in Detroit (I had begun my legal career there a few years earlier, apprenticed to an ambitious, tough-talking federal prosecutor) to give me the good news and ask for my advice, and I called my father. He straightaway flew to Chicago and made her bail and hired a renowned Chicago criminal lawyer who cut a deal with the district attorney and miraculously kept her out of jail. The judge suspended her sentence, and placed her on probation, provided she received court-approved psychiatric counseling. My father also offered to pay for her therapy and medication, and he had hoped that she would see all this as a modest gesture of commiseration on his part, that it was an opportunity for them to end the harrowing discord in our family, a chance to come to some kind of fresh understanding. In response she ranted at him. Dara wasn't interested in any fabricated acquiescence or cosmetic harmony. She told him bluntly that she had always resented his disapproval and that she would never cease from holding him accountable for our mother's death.

My father came back from his visit with Dara very dismayed. He said she was profoundly morose, surviving on a diet of stale croissants, Gouda, and Thunderbird wine. She squandered her energy on dope, discothèques, and blasé liaisons with total strangers: it broke his spirit that all our exertions should have been rewarded with so much animosity. He was at a loss. She was renting a small carriage house in Wilmette, a dank stone cottage with a black iron fence and barred pebbly windows that was attached to an enormous estate with terraced gardens and a padlocked tennis court. It had been renovated into gloomy living quarters after a fire gutted the inside. The owner, an aristocratic matron in her nineties who spent her winters in the Drake Hotel, had met Dara through her grandson's daughter Adele, a sorority sister of Dara's from their Brandeis days.

Dara had been looking after Adele's Great Danes when my grandmother's friend had seen her that time. My father said that Dara had flown into a rage the moment she saw him getting out of the taxi. She rapped on the windshield with her knuckles and ordered the Greek cabby to wait, telling him that his fare was leaving in less than a minute. Her skin was puckered and there were tears on her cheeks. My father told me he thought she was going to slug him; her large green eyes seemed to throb with tension. He reached in and gave the cabby a twenty and told him to get lost. They talked briefly, and I tried to imagine my gravely meticulous father in his baggy blue trousers beneath the paper-thin chestnut tree blossoms, the Midwestern sun curving down like a burning orange penny—his hushed voice full of solace, soothing, searching for a crooked path toward reconciliation. He told me that she had felt abandoned when our mother died, and horribly frightened, and her powerful wrath was merely the spontaneous expression of her persistent misery and lavish grief. She was still, even in her mid-thirties, in a blind fury that he hadn't been able to prevent what couldn't have been prevented. It had made *him* appear impotent, and that only fueled her recurring fear of desertion. Then it got distorted even further, and she was sure that he had always blamed her for our mother's death, her passing an indisputable consequence of Dara's having brought home that strep throat from school. Her anger, he said ingenuously, had probably helped keep her from feeling crushing shame, perhaps even from killing herself. Finding fault with him kept her alive. He said that her days were lit with regret. He was still a big softie, an easy mark for anyone with a gripe. It didn't make him a lousy parent because he had refused to accept without reservation that the path to Nirvana had to wind through all the chapters of the *Kamasutra*. What was the point in my reminding him that her unabated reproach and censure was irrational, and her estrangement deliberate? And that her blind obdurateness had spoiled any lingering chance she had had for a decent life.

I see Dara now and again—at our yearly *Chanukah* party, at Passover (for the first *Seder* only), and on the Fourth of July, when she comes to my house for skewered red peppers and lamb kebabs, Waldorf salad, fresh hot pita, and, for dessert, homemade tapioca pudding and real pistachio ice cream. She always brings two bottles of muscatel that no one drinks. Before nightfall all of us—Dara, my wife Helen, and our three college-age children, Naomi, Leah, and Noah—drive to the Edgewater Beach Hotel to watch the fireworks from the parquet bridge of Helen's brother's sleek 45-foot cabin cruiser. Jerome is an insurance company V.P., and he makes a couple of hundred thousand dollars a year. Tired and hot, we (this includes Jerome's wife Judith, their four kids, and both sets of grandparents) wear ridiculous patriotic straw hats and wave our names in the air with sparklers. And once a month the two of us meet for steaming cocoa and prune Danish in a dreary cafeteria near DePaul.

For a very long time Dara went through all kinds of desperate losers like a femme fatale, often seeing three or four men at the same time. During only the last few years she's made a concession both to age and the threat of disease, and has mostly stuck to dating affluent professional louts whom she lets belittle her in public, in front of strangers or friends. Her most recent steady was a criminal lawyer in private practice who specialized in defending pharmacists and physicians who had been arrested on drug charges. He got them released on bail and they were never heard from again. From Dara I learned that Ismail drove a salmon-colored Porche and sky-dived for relaxation. He took her skiing in Aspen and whaling in kayaks in the Gulf of Alaska. Helen and I had met him only once (he was with Dara and another couple) and even then only for a few minutes while we were standing in line for tickets to see *Midnight Express*. They had just finished a *paella* dinner and were on their way to hear Dexter Gordon in a new jazz club on Rush Street. A short, hairy, black-eyed, acne-scarred Turk in a vicuña coat, Ismail had a loud grainy voice and his face seemed to emit a pungent minty aroma. He yanked me aside and whispered in my ear that Dara was an Earth Mother. Waving goodbye, he dragged her across the street as if she were a little girl. She dumped him only a few weeks later, after he had suggested, as a prelude to marriage, that they go and live with his family in Ankara for the summer.

Though it wasn't always the case (Helen and Dara were like oil and water in the old days) she now gets along quite famously with my wife. Sometimes they slip away together for long weekends, lodging at rustic country inns and shopping for antiques in Wisconsin. And Dara's always been the adoring spinster aunt. When my children were young she spoiled them with luscious sweets and birthday presents she couldn't afford, and when she was around she always came to applaud wildly for them at their school plays and band concerts and swimming meets. We talk mostly about her nephew and nieces and the past, our fractured memories of our long-dead mother. We see each other on the condition that I never mention our father.

At first we argued bitterly over this blackmail of hers, and afterwards we didn't speak for months. But then my fretful father had cautioned me that I ought to check on how Dara was fashioning her way in the world. He told me I should never overlook the fact that she would be my only solid link—my only tie after his death—to a broken and irretrievable childhood. He understood, or so he had led me to admit, that she had been shattered by the death of our mother and that her only psychic remedy had been to separate herself from her remaining parent. In his opinion, making him accountable for what had happened to our family just wasn't enough for her. He said that Dara had needed to construct some impenetrable edifice of detachment, mercifully secure only in her isolation from the two of us. *Empathy*, he implored me again and again. And generosity. Without empathy, genuine compassion is unimaginable and life loses its fragile cohesion. None of us wants to slip away unnoticed, he said sagely. With a pleading expression he counseled me repeatedly neither to judge nor to neglect her; he said that she was drowning in her ferocious envy of me. Envy of my satisfactory marriage, of my wonderful children, of my many friends, of my robust health. And, most defiantly, she was acutely jealous of my self-discipline, what he so elegantly and curiously called my "accommodation to loss." I surrendered to him meekly when he said that. I've learned with much hard practice that one gives in to loss in much the same way one bravely gives in to passion—rapturously, even gracefully, but with humility.

Last year Dara developed a painful condition called orbital cellulitis, a severe infection of the soft tissue in the eye socket, and she took to wearing Ray-Ban sunglasses twenty-four hours a day. In recent months her short angular body has looked malnourished to me, her lined, moon-shaped face anemic—as if she's never out in the sunlight. Her kinky, milk-colored Afro is as dry as parchment. She has grown very morbid over the years—she has always been high or low on some lethal combination of prescription drugs—and has drifted through her gloomy life without any purpose, brimming with malice toward everyone, as if it had been etched into her spirit with a sculptor's chisel. She's only very lately attached herself to some far-out fundamentalist sect in Zion, and proudly wears a huge ivory crucifix with the inscription *Got Saved—All Else Fades Into Insignificance* on a gold chain around her neck. She dresses like a stoned waif—denim peasant skirt, leather sandals, pink dove barrettes in her hair—much as she did some thirty years earlier.

Any conversation we have nowadays inescapably turns to my failure to accept Jesus Christ as anything other than a bemused Trotskyite *rebbe* with a scruffy beard and a very high opinion of himself. But instead of acrimony, she offers me countless doses of "Born Again" piety. Jesus loves me even if I remain a pagan. Fair enough, I tell her. Thank him for me. Dara's a cocktail hostess now, in an acclaimed Chicago restaurant and bar atop the slowly revolving roof of a Michigan Avenue skyscraper, and she lives alone with her voracious guinea pigs and her diaphanous angelfish.

Without overstating it, there was an absolute sweetness to my mother's last hours. How gray and frail she looked—almost a silhouette—against the white brocade curtains and bedspread. Barely conscious from all the morphine she had been given, and beyond any visible signs of distress, she faded quietly away in her own warm bed, surrounded by familiar photographs of her family, a faint smile on her wasted face. The yellow fringed shawl my father had given her for their tenth wedding anniversary was loosely draped around her shoulders. Her pale cool forehead was without wrinkles. The small camphorwood writing desk gave off an odor like castor oil. My father's gaze kept shifting from my mother to the oak-beamed ceiling. Although he never dwelled on it in conversation, it was clear to me that he was stunned that all of this had actually come to pass, and so quickly. He looked decrepit; within weeks he had turned into an old man. A line of white had appeared in his hair; he dragged his feet. His need for her was so great that her dying would seem to him like the passing of his very own self.

I knew the imminent prospect of living without her had staggered him, and I wasn't at all confident that he would ever be able to muster the energy it would take to reconcile himself to her loss. He seemed so helpless to me there, immobile somehow, staring into his soft empty hands, looking so much like a frightened animal caught in the glare of headlights. His striped necktie coming apart at the knot, he lowered his head to her ear and calmly talked to her about the everyday things she wanted to know about—his talented, hard-working students, the very late blooming goldenrod, her beloved catalpa tree, planted when I was born, the sweetness of the last ripe tomatoes in her garden, the way the thin juice ran with sugar. His arm beneath her back, he lifted her slightly and held her close before going downstairs to help Dara stuff the veal roast for dinner. Concentrating, I closed my eyes and tried to alter the course of fate and will her ravaged body back to health. Her dry lips parted in a smile, and she pressed my fingers against her smooth cold cheek. She told me her skin hurt when I touched her. But I kept on touching her because I knew that her discomfort meant she was still breathing. I had never understood what my father meant when he talked to me about the body and the spirit, and I didn't understand it any more now. What little was left of her radiant hair fell to one side of her slightly bent head, over her ear, like a veil. I laid my head on the pillow beside her and breathed in her breath, its sour-sweet smell, and ran my hand through her hair. Her eyelashes had turned white; there were cracks in her lips. She breathed and stopped and breathed and stopped. Her blurred face darkened. The starved shape of her body rose and fell; it began, slowly, to bend. I waited for her to breathe again. The silver moonlight streamed through the half-open shutters and collected on the floor in unswerving rails. Her treasured bedroom slippers—the flat ones laced with yellow silk thread my father had brought back from Europe—were sticking out from underneath the bed. I went to her mahogany dressing table and found the egg-shaped bottle of toilet water I had given her for her birthday. Her lambent eyes lowered in a wink. She tilted back her head, and I let the pearly drops of scented liquid trickle down her neck. Her lips trembled faintly, and she started murmuring what sounded like "Summertime," from *Porgy and Bess*, her favorite opera. In minutes that faint rhythmic music came pouring through the darkening silence of the night, eddying beneath my desperate efforts to conceal my rising grief. I kissed her and kissed her and told her how much I loved her, and then she drew this peaceful descending breath, and then she was gone.

Thus I found myself—a widower with two young children—intoxicated with grief. Without any warning, my balance had been disrupted—as if I were in the grip of an acute inner ear infection—and I would instinctively perceive the need to clutch something solid if I didn't want to crumple to the floor. Eve's untimely passing had left me reeling—it had left all three of us reeling. In truth, I had never prepared myself for the worst, not that I would have had the least idea how to have done so. Eve left no written instructions concerning the final disposition of her remains, though she had often told me previous to her illness that she wanted both of us to be put to rest near her parents' home in Highland Park, just north of Chicago, in a spacious Jewish cemetery off Sheridan Road. I didn't argue with her—what was I supposed to say? If it meant that much to Eve, it was fine with me.

My own parents had both been gone by then for almost ten years—my father stricken with his second massive heart attack, my mother dying from pancreatic cancer. My father dropped dead on the sidewalk at fifty-seven, after having eaten sable and steamed eggplant with his older brothers Ezra and Simon in a cousin's delicatessen on Wabash Avenue, in the Loop, while he was showing them an antique jeweler's eyepiece from Radom, Poland (the birthplace of *their* father) he had picked up for a song at an auction of Polish and Lithuanian artifacts at a Jewish Community Center in Milwaukee. My mother passed away when Eve was seven months pregnant with Mickey. Thank God she went downhill fairly quickly, and with relatively little suffering. It was one, two, three—she woke up one morning with terrible indigestion and an upset stomach, and in two weeks she wasn't among the living anymore. That's how it goes sometime, my nephew Sidney, who's an oncologist at Billings, told me outside her hospital room. The malignancy reaches a critical mass, and everything inside stops working. Total organ failure, he called it. I had been worried about my father for months, and urged him numerous times to go see the cardiologist about his shortness of breath and hoarse dry cough. His tough-guy Chicago response was that the heart specialist in question had a girl's handshake and a personality like flat seltzer. I had warned him over and over again that whatever he had could quickly turn into bronchitis or pneumonia overnight, when what I had been really worried about was congestive heart failure. Whenever I'd nag him he'd wave my concern away and ask mockingly, "Are you going to run my business? Who has the time to worry about a little cold?"

Though proud of our Jewish heritage, neither of us were religious people, and up until the moment Eve told me what she had wanted me to do with her I had always assumed we would be cremated, our children and grandchildren mournfully scattering our ashes over a sun-drenched Lake Michigan. When I told Dara and Mickey about their mother's wishes, they looked puzzled. "Why there?" they both asked at once, and I had no good answer for them. I told them that perhaps it made the darkness more visible for her, having her parents so near, or some such nonsense to that effect. They had had ample time to adjust to the certainty of their mother's passing, they understood that a rapid end to her hopeless suffering was something to be desired, so I just assumed their calm demeanor was merely an expression of how adeptly they had come to terms with the inevitable. At the time, it had never occurred to me that their composure might be a symptom of how deeply depressed they had become over the past few months.

I had tried to keep my eye trained on Mickey; even Eve was especially concerned about his sudden fervent attachment to her during her sickness. She had always thought (wrongfully) that he was the more needy child. At times she said she should have demanded more self-reliance from him, though I don't quite see how that could have been managed. Mickey would come around, I told her, he was merely full of mischief and confused, like most boys his age. It was a stage. In my way of looking at things, it seemed obvious that Dara would surely need her mother more, to help guide her into womanhood. It was clear to me even then that Dara would suffer without her mother. She had always kept things to herself, it had been hard for Eve and me to know what was going on behind her tense evasive smile. Being her father, what could I do for her? Except to give her affection, to tell her over and over again that I loved her, that her mother would live on in her. Dara had a way of holding still, of watching and waiting with rigid concentration, that made me feel the spitting electricity, the grease and foam of my nerves, inching along my spine. This would be a whole new world for us, and I wasn't convinced I was up to it. I had always supposed that like most Jewish husbands I would die first; why should it have even entered my mind that mother nature had other plans for my family?

Chicagoland already had tons of fresh snow on the ground. Overhead, the dense gray clouds were boiling up for another early winter storm. Maintenance vehicles were out sanding the slippery roads. From the Outer Drive, the city looked like a baroque finger painting on a wall, it looked sealed-in, awash in a kind of sinuous silver light from the drifting snow. The swollen, steel-blue lake was dazzling, the giant waves fierce. Clumps of grimy slush splashed off the hood and bumpers of my old blue Studebaker. The bare trees shimmered with daggers of ice.

In Highland Park we endured *all* of it—the influx of weeping relatives and old acquaintances, the heaping platters of baked chicken and brisket and pastrami, the large jars of pickled herring and stewed apricots and borscht and *knaydlach* soup (we were mourners literally *starved* by our loss), the mist-white candy dishes always refilled to the brim with flat chocolates sprinkled with white dots and sugared fruit in half-moon shapes with a white line around the arc, even the nearly deaf mortician, a second cousin of Eve's older sister's husband, a millionaire undertaker who looked like a giant stork and sweated through the hairy pores on his big nose.

While we awkwardly sat on maroon crushed-velvet wing chairs in his garish West Rogers Park office, Cousin Mordecai—Bibby, everyone called him—steepled his manicured fingers and lectured us on the various splendid caskets at our disposal. His wife, Cousin Shana, carried in a copper samovar and a bronze serving tray piled with glasses and spoons and lemons and bismarcks and chocolate eclairs. We listened politely as Cousin Bibby gave us his *spiel* about the special family fund that had been set up years ago by Eve's grandfather to make low-interest family loans for education and funerals and the like, but I couldn't see the wisdom in laying out too much cash for an elegant coffin, and so, in the end, despite her mother's and father's aggrieved protests, we buried Eve in the same unadorned pine box she'd traveled in on the train ride to Chicago. Her parents prided themselves on being fully Americanized, and that meant a viewing of the corpse sunk in the faded pastel padding of the coffin for three excruciating evenings, and day lilies and Hebrew prayers at the burial plot. Though I suspected that these arrangements would have appalled Eve—her sobbing mother and aunts in their big dark hats with dotted net veils, her cousins and uncles grumbling about the lousy weather—in the spirit of compromise, of not wanting Mickey and Dara to witness a scene, I docilely consented. I can still see Eve's casket, aboveground under its soaked green canopy, and her blue-lipped father sitting with his gray fedora in both gloved hands, between his knees, turning it like the steering wheel of a car as the casket was finally lowered into the ground. As the pensive rabbi recited *Kaddish*, the ice-pelted wind sent small spirals of snow and dead leaves up around our ankles.

Unable to sleep, I wake alone in the winter night, snow blasting at the fragile panes of my bare windows. The snow has in it a silky phosphorescence, diffused and velvety, and I wonder: Who can account for the dead face of the past? Nursed by intimate misfortunes, our memories, it seems, have powerful lives of their own. Time and reason are our adversaries, and like the opulent wastes of star-filled space, they mutely distort the meaning of things. Though I had spent so much of my early years thinking otherwise, I now believed that change was the essence of all living things. Awake, I can barely remember what Eve looked like, though an image I know to be hers frequently haunts my dreams. When I examine old photographs it seems like I'm staring at strangers, people whose features have long since receded into the tenuous misremembered past. All I have left is my impoverished *memory* of what happened to my wife, and *that* is an illusive thing indeed. She didn't belong to me anymore—she belonged to what had *happened* to her.

I know as surely as I know that I am sitting here writing these poor words that my brain has been quietly at work reconciling the past to my feelings about it. The unconscious can perform retrospective miracles, it can occasionally compensate for loss. Now and then I relive those final painful weeks of Eve's life, including those days right after she died—the unrelenting nausea, the monotonous smoking and pacing on the porch in the middle of the night, the gloom on the faces of my children as they drifted into despair, the glancing reluctantly down at her smooth powdery face and peach-colored dress and neatly folded hands in the coffin—but even in my uneasy sleep I know that there is something not quite right about all of this, that I've lost my bearings, as if something unforgiving and cruel had tampered with the way things really were, and the something in question was the heartless work of my slumbering mind. When I try to rearrange everything in my wandering imagination, when I seek to mend what the passage of time has permanently obliterated, I come violently awake—howling out nonsense words, pure gibberish, a mad clatter of grunting half-sounds that have little meaning to an indiscreet old man spared nothing in his dreams— my shortness of breath and worsening angina like a gouged toenail clawing inside my chest as I sob and reach for the nitroglycerin pills on my night table.

The ravaged Europe my father remembered was a teeming graveyard, an indifferent and unforgiving place where the living as well as the dead were lost. When I was still young, and by young I mean the idyllic time before my mother passed away, he rarely spoke of the things he had witnessed during the war, but within a few short months after her death he sat me down one night after his glass of tea and lemon meringue pie and told me everything. His shirt and trousers were badly rumpled and he had dark circles under his eyes. We huddled in that cluttered and unpainted back parlor where I had watched over my sleeping mother during the last weeks of her life. A thick moist creosote odor came from the unused brick fireplace. He wanted me to understand that science had taught him that the things of this universe were governed by natural laws and logic, but that the monstrous war the Germans had waged against the starving and defenseless Jews and Gypsies of Central and Eastern Europe had settled in his troubled mind as a bitter reminder of the vast abiding failure of the human species. He said it could never be anything less.

My father had managed to come through the war with nothing more serious than a dreadful case of infected foot blisters and a badly dislocated thumb. Our whole family was graced in that respect. None of my grandfather's brothers' sons were killed or maimed. Uncle Reuben, one of my father's two younger brothers, who later became a prominent North Shore ophthalmologist (among his many local celebrity patients over the years were Mayor Richard Daley and Ernie Banks, the great Cubs shortstop), survived tropical genital ulcers as well as a serious leg wound and gangrene in the steaming mangrove swamps of New Guinea and came home a hero with two Silver Stars and two Purple Hearts. He went to the University of Chicago on the GI Bill, and did his residency at Johns Hopkins. The other one, suave Uncle Isaac, a liar and a notorious cad, my favorite out of all my parents' brothers and sisters, who, after spending three soft years as a motor pool staff sergeant on the airbase in Lake Charles, Louisiana, playing poker and getting laid and making money trading in black market jeep and truck parts with the local Cajuns, had dropped out of sight. He had slipped out of our family's smothering Chicago orbit for almost ten years before eventually returning home to the Midwest with his battered suitcases full of hundred-dollar bills. He surfaced initially in Texas and Oklahoma, and then drifted to Las Vegas, working first as a roughneck in the oil fields and ultimately as a pit boss in a number of big casinos. No one ever asked Uncle Isaac where all the dough came from, and he never said. He later owned a prosperous Cadillac dealership in Lake Forest, among all the haughty, overbred Presbyterians, and made a small fortune investing heavily in cosmetic companies like Avon and Helena Rubenstein.

My father had survived Bastogne and the savage combat in the freezing Ardennes without a nick. He'd told Dara and me about the huge, dreamy, birch-mottled landscape, the daily midnight patrols behind the collapsing enemy lines, the roaring windstorms, the blinding, serpentine light from the swirling snowflakes. The bottle-green Ruhr lay under a vast pall of soot. Throughout the winter, the Allies had been hounding the battered regiments of the German army for weeks, capturing half-frozen and fearful young boys and trembling old men too weak to carry any weapons or ammo. The seemingly invincible *Wehrmacht* was finally vanquished, he told me; their goose-stepping days were over. "The master race," he sneered; "the master butchers would be more like it." They came limping out of the forests and farmhouses and the twisted rubble of shelled towns and villages, waving their puny white flags, frostbitten, famished, many of them cursing their revered *Führer*, a once-imperious enemy now grateful they were surrendering to the swaggering American conquerors and not to the vindictive Red Army.

In May of 1945, only a few days before the official German surrender, the large concentration camp near Enns, in Austria, on the north bank of the Danube, a mere sixteen miles from the city of Linz, the hometown of both Adolfs, Hitler and Eichmann, was liberated by American forces. Months earlier, my father had been transferred to one of the mammoth armored divisions sweeping into Germany from the west. For some time already there had been disquieting rumors about this particular camp. He said that alarming reports of mass killings had been circulating among diverse partisan intelligence operatives who had penetrated Gestapo headquarters—especially reports concerning the murders of captured Anglo-American and Dutch flyers. It had long been known that Russian POWs were routinely shot immediately upon their arrival. After the war, a Czech inmate of the camp, an eyewitness, testified at Nuremberg that the airmen had been clubbed and kicked to death while carrying huge stones on their backs. My father said that when the Americans entered the camp they found masses of sick and dying people lying helpless or else roaming among the putrefying dead, bewildered skeletons in their gruesome, maggot-stained pajamas. He said the bodies were stacked like blackened cordwood. The mild spring breeze had the fragrance of burnt sandalwood and rotten meat, and the grass was waxed with blood. There were branch-covered trenches piled high with tangled corpses. Grizzled veterans were throwing up all over the tanks. His eyes as he told me all this were filled with urgency.

"We found hundreds of bodies decomposing in open freight cars. I saw GIs give their pistols to prisoners so they could kill the *kapos* and the handful of SS sentries. We handed out Lucky Strikes and

C rations and Hershey bars. Prisoners scuffled with each other over cigarettes. It was like watching skeletons fight. They gulped leftover Army chow and drowned in their own vomit. I could smell the stench of that place in my nose for months. Are you able to understand what I'm telling you? Can you imagine what it looked like?" He ran his bony hand through his vanishing silver hair. "I couldn't move, I was gasping for breath. It was a revelation of hell."

There was a long silence. What could I say? How could anyone imagine it? He stood up and moved around gingerly. I had never heard him use this tone before, even during my mother's final descent. He was taking noisy, deep inhalations, as if he needed to absorb all the oxygen in the room. He then told me that there were smoldering warehouses of shoes and clothes and eyeglasses and even teeth and women's hair, everything arranged by size and color and value, of the people who were murdered there. The ovens of the remaining crematorium were still warm to the touch when the deliverers reached there. While the frightened remnants of the Third Reich were dropping their rifles and marching with trembling hands clasped behind their heads into Allied lines, the SS were still burning people.

I asked him if he could remember what he had been thinking about during those hours.

"It's all so hard to explain," he said. He paused and shifted his weight. "It's confusing. I gave a young woman water from my canteen. She was sitting against a broken cart filled with pulverized rocks. There was a granite quarry there, and the prisoners had to drag heavy blocks of stone up a steep winding grade to the camp. We were told by the Red Cross that people were crushed to death beneath plummeting wagons all the time. Or they were worked to death. Or tortured. Or hanged. Or strangled by hand. Or electrocuted. Or clubbed with an iron pipe. Or shot. Or suspended from meat hooks in freezing cellars. Or they were forced to stand naked in the snow, and their feet would stick to the ground. We even found mutilated bodies at the bottom of the quarry. A local Austrian doctor told us that Jews too sick to work were bound and gagged and booted off the crest by the sadistic Ukrainian guards, prisoners themselves who had been trained by the SS to carry out many of the murders. This girl I saw didn't even have the strength to swallow. The water dribbled out of her mouth, and I wiped her lips with a filthy handkerchief. Her fingernails were badly smashed. She had wet fecal matter and green flies on her feet. A young woman who looked like one of those stick figures a child draws, all straight lines and circles."

I couldn't help it, I wanted to hear more. "Did you talk to her?"

"*Talk?*" He stiffened. "We didn't talk in the ordinary sense of talking."

"What was it, then? Did you do anything?"

"I shaded her face against the glare of the sun," he said softly, as if startled by my question. "It was no more than three fingers above the horizon." His breathing had suddenly slowed. "I felt like I was choking on something. Her starving eyes were piercing and alert, still alive somehow, among all this carnage. And her breath smelled of cloves. I couldn't figure it out, but then it came to me: cloves. When she leaned forward slightly to get more water, I heard her spine pop like a dry wishbone. Then something happened to me, far down deep inside me, something that stopped me from taking it all in. As if I were wearing horse blinders, and could only see what was directly in front of me. It was so confusing, and awful, and I wanted to forget everything I had seen. It made me feel so ashamed, all of it. I wondered if she was once pretty, if she had a husband, children, brothers, sisters, grandparents. I had no idea how old she was, she could have been sixteen or sixty. Would anyone from her family still be alive? Would they be looking for her? Did her home even exist anymore? God help her, think of how abandoned she must have felt. It gives me a hollow feeling to know that I will dream of those things forever."

I wanted to keep him talking; it made me feel, for the first time in a long while, that he was still capable of feeling, even if it was only grief. "Do you know what happened to her?"

He glanced at the hail ticking loudly against the beveled parlor window. When he turned back to face me, he leaned forward and placed his elbows on his knees. "I lost track of her somehow. Or I just don't remember. She probably died. Hundreds of them were dying."

"You sound like you think you were responsible for her. None of that was your fault."

"No, I suppose not," he said, nodding gravely. He put his hand on his breast. "I can remember the racket in here. My heart was racing, pulsing in my throat. Mickey—your father was not a very brave soldier. It was Socrates who said that a man who is not afraid to die is not really alive. I had a wife to come home to, and children. I did my job, followed orders, avoided heroics. I fired my carbine in the direction of the Jerries and prayed to God that I had killed the bastards. Murder was the decisive part of their schooling, the cold heart of their intellect. Homicide is the oldest kind of human knowledge. But *this?* This mad spectacle threatened all of creation."

Listening to him go on and on, I heard of the plight of my fellow Jews in terse, unsparing images. The war in Europe first came to members of my generation from Fox Movietone Newsreels, then as lyricized history, the rarefied domain of professional historians, as sanitized as Gettysburg or Gallipoli, or the Punic Wars. But he was *there.* When I told him all those years ago that I wasn't quite sure what he was getting at, he sighed heavily and said the day would surely come when I would long for such innocence again. And then he said something I could not have imagined coming out of his mouth. He said his belief in the sacredness of life had been forever poisoned by what he had seen that day. He was not ashamed to admit it; he had been elated when he heard that Truman had dropped the bomb on Japan. Even relieved, as if some vast moral weight had been taken off his shoulders. Without question, the bloodbath was horrible. But he said he was consumed with raw spite, with the insatiable craving for revenge. He had wanted to do something cruel and unspeakable to soften his sorrow and grief. He said he only felt bad that the bomb wasn't dropped on Berlin or Munich, in the diabolical heart of Wagner's Bavaria. He said he had desired a multitude of meaningless deaths to avenge the misery of that dying young woman he had offered water to in the deepening shadow of rotting cadavers. He said there had been no way to give her the justice (the retribution!) she surely deserved. A millennium of trials and executions would have still left her deformed and dispossessed soul in torment. He leaned across the space between us and stroked my hair. His face was closed, his mouth grim. Everything that had mattered had sunk to the bottom, he said.

I wondered if he was thinking of my mother now? Did he ever mix the two of them up in his troubled dreams, the young woman he offered water to and his wife? I got up slowly and put my arms around him as tight as I could. We sat there holding onto each other, in silence, for what seemed like a very long time. He felt so light in my arms, as if his bones were filled with air, and I experienced something I can describe as both durable and perishable, something charged I now think of as a beguiling shock of intimacy—as if for one brief paradoxical moment I were absorbed biologically into his being. He felt weightless, empty of substance, like my mother and that young woman must have felt to him. Our warm slow breathing had deepened and lengthened. Except instead of Hiroshima, he said despairingly, tearing away from me, his somber eyes narrowed into tiny gray pits, they should have flattened Auschwitz. They should have incinerated the whole evil place. And by incinerated he meant cleansed, and by the whole evil place he meant the entire continent.

II

July's heat was equatorial. Polio weather, my father said. That's what all the newspapers had called the blinding, pitiless sun and smothering humidity of the first summer after my mother's death. We cooked under an umbrella of wet tropical air. It pressed down on people's brains. It moved in sudden bursts of sticky wind. Gnats were swarming over everything. They stuck to everyone's eyelashes like curd. The shrubs and mustard-colored crabgrass seemed to hover on the edge of igniting. At twilight, the chalky sky was whisked in smudged color like a bloodstained egg. The tabbies sleeping on porches seemed drugged with heat. Only hand-cranked coffee ice cream slathered with chilled raspberry sauce and pleated white cups packed with shaved ice and colored syrup made people feel some relief. The streets and stores were deserted, the single movie theater in town was always close to empty. Even vibrating electric ceiling fans cutting in monotonous circles were thought by some to have helped spread the disease. Everyone was fearful of catching the malignant germ that had put our late president, Franklin Delano Roosevelt, in metal braces and a wheelchair.

A boy from Smokey Glen named Scooter Talgo I had played Little League baseball with was slowly suffocating in an iron lung machine in Indianapolis. In the city it was commonplace to see wasted people with short arms and withered legs hobbling down the street with canes. Though the tenant farmers farmed and field hands shucked the corn, most parents kept their stir-crazy children locked up in the house. Or those few lucky families who could afford it went on month-long vacations to fishing resorts on the Upper Peninsula of Michigan, or near the Minnesota and Ontario border, north of the Mesabi Range, to rent tiny log cabins above antler-shaped lakes as clear as rippled glass, their shorelines covered in white stones and pine needles, where people ate carp and pickerel every night and gladly put up with the mosquitoes and biting blackflies because they believed the chilly blue air was free of pestilence.

Since I was forbidden (especially now) to skinny-dip in the quarry with my friends, I passed the long mornings reading Robert Louis Stevenson and Sherlock Holmes and looking out my window at the feathery white blossoms of a frangipani tree and breathing in their jasminelike fragrance. I listened to my father's Benny Goodman albums, and for a while I practiced my clarinet twice a day. I actually thought I could hear the strides I was making. My father was a very good clarinetist, he often played "Rhapsody in Blue" and "Greensleeves" when my mother was alive. He was in the school orchestra at college years ago. Occasionally Dara and I played duets in the steamy back parlor, she on the baby upright Steinway with the embroidered lace runners our mother used to play. In the endless stretches of late afternoon heat we amused ourselves with gin rummy or war or Old Maid. Now and then we played a game of chess, which she always killed me at. Eight or nine moves is all it took her to checkmate me. Most of the time, however, she rinsed her hair with lemons and then went straight to bed after eating her supper alone. I cleared the table and washed and dried the dishes and put them away. My father repeatedly asked her to lend me a hand, but I told him it was no big deal. He let Dara get away with murder—she had him eating out of the palm of her hand. He should have put his foot down when he saw things going from bad to worse. She made no effort whatsoever to cope with her grief. I resented her (and feel crummy still about it) succumbing so easily to her despair.

In the evenings, while Dara dreamed of the dark side of the moon and my father took his pipe and cherry tobacco to his study, I went to the attic and climbed out the trapdoor leading to the roof. Our attic was stuffed with grocery cartons filled with high-school yearbooks, college notebooks, magazine clippings, yellowing letters from family and old friends, a steamer trunk of my mother's old clothes, and thick jars of preserved fruit and navy and pinto beans that looked blotted with rust and mold. Cautiously, steering myself with my clammy fingertips, I scaled the slick brown shingles. Straddling the chipped brick chimney with my sneakers, I tried to catch a breeze and cool off. I was unsuccessful. Summer locusts rang in the darkened treetops. Strangely—though the sky was densely powdered with glittering constellations, and bleached light spilled from the moon—even in relatively dry weather the air itself was like a viscous sap. From the roof I could clearly see the storm-damaged elms, sharply coiled strips of scorched bark peeling like burned skin off the blackened branches. From below, the sweet pale smoke from my father's pipe fanned out against the night. For hours I listened to the feathery black moths smashing themselves against the windowpanes.

It came to me late that August that my father never slept. Whenever I came back in the house and went to bed, the light in his study was still on. He stayed up all night most of the time, reading history until dawn or pacing and writing in the diary he had started when my mother first got ill. Though I was curious to see what he had written in his diary, I never stole a look. I figured his privacy was his privacy. The soft clear music from the mahogany Victrola—

usually Schubert or Schumann or Mendelssohn—glided under the door and curled up the stairs. When I asked him in the morning why he wasn't sleeping, why he didn't get some sleeping pills from the doctor, he kept tightening the belt on his bathrobe with an unsteady hand and said he took long naps in the afternoon on the leather couch in the living room and didn't need more sleep. He said you couldn't force sleep and he didn't want to get involved—dependent, he said—on sleeping pills.

His gray-flecked eyes were smudged with red, his flakey hair oily with tonic. He gave me a dry look that I understood to mean I should mind my own business, but he never flew off the handle—that just wasn't his style. I knew he was not given to feeling sorry for himself. He had gotten the short end of the stick, and that was that. At this point he wasn't about to unburden his heart to me in so blunt a manner. The lines at the corners of his eyes had deepened over the past few months, and I knew he was paralyzed by the risk and uncertainty of the next day. But what could I have done? Sure, had I had the composure and presence of mind—had I been the educated and experienced man that I am today—perhaps I could have jolted him out of his trance and told him that I couldn't bear it anymore, his unquenchable grief like a fishbone caught in his throat—in my throat, too. But what came out of my mouth instead was a pathetic flood of pointless nonsense about the baseball season, and my wondering if I'd ever get the chance to go to places like Ebbets Field and Yankee Stadium.

I guess you could say we made it through that sultry summer in one piece. I was relieved when the fall semester at the college had finally rolled around. I was ready to be back at school. Those long nights alone had done something to my father. When my mother was alive he had never been one to preach to anybody. He had evolved a restrained yet still dignified and scholarly style to his conversation. He could even tell a corny joke fairly well. I had once heard him refer to himself as avuncular. Live and let live—that was his private, as well as his public, motto. But suddenly, and very much out of character, he was inspired to impart wisdom to his offspring. Dara said she couldn't handle any of it, and simply excused herself whenever he went off on a subject she didn't care to hear about. God forbid she should have shown even a smidgen of interest in him and what he said. I thought he was merely lonely, and just needed somebody to talk with.

But after a few weeks I dreaded his lectures. He thought he was being helpful—passing on whatever insights he'd managed to accumulate over four decades. Designed to instruct, they merely wore me down. And then his repetitious questioning started to depress me. He asked me what I thought the secret of the universe was. I told him, quite cheerily, that I didn't realize the universe was hiding anything from us. His eyes widened in disbelief when I said that. A biologist by training and a skeptic by temperament, he nonetheless told me that all the evidence collected by science—the plain objective facts of nature—was still no nearer the essential truth of human existence than poetry was.

He then said he knew he would have been dreadfully unhappy practicing medicine. I told him I thought he was being too hard on himself.

He took his small dimpled chin in his fingers and rubbed it. "It's ludicrous—how most physicians are trained by their mentors. They are taught to feel so absurdly self-infatuated. And then, when they have diseased people on their hands, real sickness and real suffering—men and women in terrible pain, begging them for relief—they are helpless and mistaken so much of the time. The disenchantment must be galling."

He wondered if I remembered that he'd read verses to my sister and me when we were small and had trouble falling asleep. I said I needed him to do that now. Poetry, he wanted me to understand, was much more precise in evaluating human dilemmas. "Poetry should be required reading in every medical school," he said meditatively. "Doctors only understand death in medical terms, and that is very limiting. They miss the big picture that way. Less gross anatomy and more poetry for a change. How could it hurt anyone? You think any sawbones understood blindness as well as Milton? Or mortality as well as Keats?"

I told him what he said sounded good to me.

One day he came home with a slip of paper from the Dean's office asking him to please come out to his house after classes the next day. He went and rummaged among the scattered papers on his desk, looking for a misplaced notebook where he kept a daily calendar of his appointments. He thought he perhaps had inadvertently skipped an important committee meeting, a felony in the Dean's eyes. Given his nature, my father was worried. "I have no black marks against me," he told Dara and me over orange layer cake in the kitchen.

There were loud thunderclaps in the distance, and the yellow chiffon curtains my mother had made just last year blew in and out of the open window.

"Then why fret?" Dara said coldly, shuffling to the refrigerator in her fleece-lined moccasins to pour herself another glass of milk. Her dark braided hair hung like a noose.

When Dara had left the table, I reminded him that his colleagues—mostly friendly fellows with big sardonic grins and soft, napped patches on the elbows of their hound's-tooth sports coats— had all been solicitous and sympathetic during my mother's illness. Their wives had ceaselessly delivered pot roasts and ham steaks and steaming casseroles and runny cherry pies to our front door. I told him I thought he had no reasonable basis to feel so anxious. Even the Dean's wife, a laconic woman with failing eyesight and an enormous bust, had baked us angel food cake and sesame sticks on more than one occasion.

"But isn't this quite out of the ordinary?" he said, glancing up, suspecting my apprehensive tone of voice. "The Dean's not an easy man to read. He's a stickler."

Since I knew I would be unable to simply wave away his misgivings, I told him I would be happy to tag along and keep him company when he went there. I thought I heard the thunder rumbling south, toward the rolling amethystine hills. He gave me a quick kiss on my forehead on his way outside to have his evening pipe before the storm came. I watched the radiant flashing outside the window illuminate our street—the swaying larches, the glistening hunter's moon, the globe of his head and the swooping tangles of his vanishing hair. When I joined him in ten minutes, the rain had already begun to come down in sheets. The scent of burning leaves was in the air. They made a sizzling sound in the rain.

———

My father's last class the following day was finished at 3:45. A breezy, opalescent afternoon had unfolded in delicate swirls of high cirrus clouds. The leaves on the lyre-shaped elms were turning. The tops of the trees were undulating in the gentle wind. At the limestone chapel on the southern edge of campus—a funnel-shaped tangle of fallen branches, moldering leaves, and vine-wreathed trails carpeted with gourds and slimy apples and black plums swelling out of their very skins—we turned out onto a winding country road and followed it for about half a mile. The sour odor from a septic tank fouled the air. My father had run cross-country and the mile in college and had always fancied himself a good judge of distances. He estimated that we had about another mile to hike. I saw his tired face. The wrinkled circles under his eyes were puffy from lack of sleep. I can remember that the October sky was incandescent, the brittle leaves waving at the sun. We walked past stark old homes and rusted hog troughs and open barns reeking of silage and manure. On the sandy shoulder of the pebbly road a trio of squawking crows picked at the bloody carcass of a rabbit. The large muddy fields were separated by rotted fences and tree stumps, and they were abundant with winter squash and clover and colonies of nesting birds and quicklime and green garter snakes and patches of late-flowering pale-blue asters. Despite the unseasonable temperatures of the last few weeks, there was scarlet and gold in the trees.

The Dean's house was on a curved lane shaded by a huge three-forked oak. Columns of thick ivy climbed up to the sloping stucco roof. An Airedale, or a retriever of some sort, studied our approach from the lawn, where he was leashed to an entrenched croquet wicket. I walked over to pet the slobbering dog, and my shoes sank into the spongy soil.

My father rang the bell, and we heard a melody that sounded like a xylophone playing Hoagy Carmichael's "Chimes of Indiana."

The heavy door eased open. "It's me, sir," my father said. "Jacob Heller. And my son, Mickey."

"Yes, of course, Jacob," the Dean said, opening the door all the way and offering *me* his freckled hand to shake. "And it's nice to see you again, Mickey." Then, to my father, "Jacob—I appreciate your coming on such short notice."

The Dean was wearing a tuxedo and slippers, and his fuzzy red hair was set in curls on his low forehead. Nero-style, my mother used to call it with a smile. He motioned us into the house and asked my father if he cared for a cocktail. "I'm drinking Bombay gin, extra dry," he said.

"I don't drink," my father said. "Whiskey upsets my stomach."

The Dean looked chagrined. He led us down a long brick-lined foyer that smelled of mint and was lit with brass chandeliers. An empty birdcage hung from the ceiling. Behind us, a balustered staircase rose to an upper floor. We trailed the Dean into what appeared to be his study or den. It was painted a kind of dark undersea color. There were stuffed owls on the inlaid cedar bookshelves; antique pistols and gleaming muskets hung from iron hooks above one fireplace. The maple floorboards were covered with woven Persian rugs. He showed me a huge tank filled with tiny orange turrets and what he said were two Siamese fighting fish. Behind wavy curved glass, and framed by a moss-green serpent, was a large portrait of an old man in a Navy uniform whose chest was covered with medals and who bore a strong resemblance to the Dean. Buffalo horns and a puma head were mounted above the other mantelpiece, and a small log fire glowed in the hearth. Without asking, he poured me a goblet of tepid ginger ale.

The Dean pointed to a sofa and asked us to please make ourselves comfortable. The faded brocade upholstery was soft, and the lemony scent of furniture polish was in the air. He went and sat in a hand-carved, leather easy chair. My father looked dispirited, his thin mouth rigid in a sober line. The Dean shifted in his seat, stirring his martini with his pinkie, and the chair creaked. He was probably a heavy drinker; I had noticed the greasy fingerprints on the vermouth decanter.

"Jacob, you must be wondering if I spend my days dressed this way," the Dean said, going to the bar and pouring himself another drink. "I assure you, I don't. Miranda and I are going to a chamber music concert in Columbus as soon as we conclude our chat." He swirled the drink in his hand in a dreamy way. His long yellow fingers reminded me of candles.

"This is quite a place you have," I blurted out. "And who's that?" I was pointing at the portrait.

The Dean took a pack of Old Golds off his desk and offered my father one. When he told the Dean he didn't smoke either, the Dean shoved the cigarette back in the pack, breaking it.

"That's my grandfather," the Dean said, his voice furry with gin. "My mother's father. Admiral Raymond Marquand. What a doozy he was!" He put his glass down carefully and laced his fingers across his chest. "After the Navy, he became a great scholar and minister of God. This was once his home, and my great-grandfather's as well. Grandpa Raymond was a martinet, if there ever was one. And since you're so curious, Mickey, in his day my own father was a celebrated anthropologist. Then he came down with a kind of sleeping sickness soon after a research trip to Central Africa. After the progressive apathy, he lived out his days in a private asylum in Evansville. He drowned in the Ohio River many years ago, during a picnic, when I was still a boy. I can remember things he said to me, but I can barely remember him."

"Do you have any children?" I asked. My father seemed to have shrunk in his chair.

"My son Duncan is retarded," the Dean said perfunctorily. "He can't count to ten."

It had crossed my mind to ask him how high Duncan *could* count, but I knew if I did that it would have put my father in hot soup. This whole business had the air of crisis for him, a danger barely withheld. So we sat there in silence for what seemed like five minutes. I felt ridiculous for some reason—my neck was sweaty and hot— and I couldn't get the sound of my own breathing out of my ears.

The Dean leaned forward and I heard the leather sigh. He put his elbows on the arms of his chair and looked my father in the eye. "I know how you're feeling, Jacob. It's terrible to lose somebody close. Lionel, my youngest brother, a wonderful pianist, died at Guadalcanal. A Jap machine-gun bullet in the mouth. I saw Lionel's corpse at the mortuary in town; he was as gray as a sole and most of his jaw was missing. They had him lying in state like some governor. It sent my mother into a tailspin she never recovered from. You've managed to put things behind you?"

Barely, I thought.

"Everyone's been very considerate," my father said. "Things take time getting used to."

"Certainly," the Dean said. "Certainly." The dog started barking then. The Dean quickly stood, pivoted, and skittered a few steps in my direction. "The secret to a successful life, Mickey, a good life, is patience. No need to go running about searching for life. Life has a way of finding you." He smiled amiably then, or tried to. His teeth were filled with gold. He sipped at his gin and ran his fingers through his hair. It moved; he was wearing a toupee.

"My mother always said that I should just stay out of trouble and use the common sense I was born with," I said.

"Your mother was a sensible woman," the Dean said. The dog barked again, this time at what sounded like a passing tractor. "Stupid bastard," the Dean said, grimacing.

I knew my father was edgy, and I wished he had worked up the nerve by then to ask the Dean what in the world we were doing there. But my father was slow and logical and content to wait. His eyes looked almost glazed in the firelight. I heard some muted yelling from another part of the house.

The Dean lit up a cigar, rolling the tip in the match flame. He inhaled, and blew smoke through his nostrils. I noticed that his hand trembled slightly. "I'm told by people that you're of the orthodox persuasion."

"Hardly," my father said grimly.

The Dean's smile grew thin. "Oh?" He flicked ash from his trousers.

"I wasn't raised to be an observant Jew," my father said, "but to know and be aware all the time of what it *meant* to be Jewish. There were whole blocks of elderly Polish Jews in my immigrant Chicago neighborhood, very religious men and women in black coats and wide-brimmed Talmudic hats. One of my uncles was the sexton at a small synagogue. He was a despotic little man with a pointed gray beard."

I'd heard all this many times before. My father told him how the sidewalks were filled with junk dealers and peddlers and groups of noisy yeshiva students in side locks and shabby clothes. They were all penniless and scrawny and intimidating, and also scorned by other, less fervent Jews. All the small shops had signs above their striped awnings printed in Yiddish and Polish and Hungarian, and the asphalt gutters were smeared with the flaky balls of golden manure that had dropped from worn-out horses dragging dray carts. Both of my father's parents had come over from Europe, and my grandmother had kept a kosher home only out of respect for *her* parents, but my grandfather wouldn't hear of skipping his ham and bacon sandwich for lunch. They spoke Yiddish and Polish to each other and to their brothers and sisters, and a tortured, broken English to my father.

"My father loved to call himself a modern person. What an optimist. When he didn't have a dime to his name he used to say that things could only get better. A true American. When I was thirteen, just weeks after my *Bar Mitzvah,* we moved out of the city, to Skokie, 'to fresh country air,' I can remember him telling me. He thought we had finally escaped all the anti-Semites. My father made a very good living and worked himself into an early death."

"I see," the Dean said. "A genuine Horatio Alger." The muscles were bunched in his square face like clay. "I'll level with you, Jacob. I have a matter that needs careful handling. *Experienced* handling."

"How's that?" my father asked.

I wondered if the Dean had detected the displeasure in my father's voice. Probably not. He slanted his filmy eyes and gave me a slimy smile. "Tell me," he said, sipping his drink. "How was the war? For you, I mean. *Personally.*"

My father looked momentarily incredulous. I'm convinced he thought, as I did, that the kooky Dean was looped. I remembered that I had heard him telling my mother that the ranks of his college were filled with notoriously hard drinkers, and I know for certain that this worried him. People who drank were unreasonable, and unpredictable, and my father believed deeply in reason and order.

My mother had often told Dara and me how she would rub Polish vodka on our erupting gums when we were teething. She never gave us crushed aspirin in our bottles, afraid it would upset our stomachs. The vodka was more effective than slivers of ice dipped in brown sugar, and it helped to knock us out. My parents had been raised by their parents to be very timid when it came to alcohol. In the dead world of their forebears, only Gentiles were *shikkers*. In fact, the drunkard is almost unknown in Jewish literature or legend. It was considered taboo for parents to drink in front of their children, and when their children weren't around they didn't need it. As a result, my mother and father avoided faculty parties when they knew the main entertainment would consist of vindictive gossip and watching drunken couples make passes at each other. We never had any more than a bottle or two of mild kosher wine for Passover around the house, and a gold-tipped flask of Portuguese brandy in the tall chestnut highboy, for when any of us had a stubborn sore throat or an earache. When I think of my mother today, I can close my eyes and imagine her small whorled fingertips working their soft healing pressure in my tender mouth, putting me to sleep. Thinking of her mothering me like this makes me drowsy— even as I write these words.

My father smiled and tried to make an obvious joke out of the Dean's remark. "Europe was delightful, contrary to what you've read in the newspapers. And the accommodations were excellent, especially the cuisine." Something like a restrained grin passed over the Dean's thick face. He walked over to the credenza and leaned on it with his elbows. His manner was suddenly subdued, as if he were absorbed in thought. I looked at my father and he shrugged.

"I'd like you to meet someone," the Dean said, half turning. The cigar protruded from his fist like a gun barrel.

"Who?" my father asked.

The Dean's voice dropped conspiratorially. "A Jewess. From a DP camp on Crete or Cyprus—one of those places, I believe."

My father looked flustered. "How's that?"

The Dean scratched at the pitted, pink scars on his cheeks. "Are you hard of hearing, Jacob? I thought you might be able to help us out here."

My father remained expressionless. "*Us?*"

By now the Dean was obviously drunk and annoyed. Little drops of sweat shone on his nose. He lowered his depthless eyes, smirking, and lost his balance for a moment. Recovering himself, he went on to explain to us that the college had recently been petitioned by some relief agency like the American Friends' Service Committee to lend a helping hand to a few refugees relocated for the time being in Indiana. He said he had been led to believe that these DPs had relations of some kind near Milwaukee. "A Catholic priest—Father Gideon Rook—is in charge of their transition from being displaced persons to not being displaced anymore," he said fulsomely. "What I mean to say is that if they're here now, they're not displaced anymore, correct? I want you to work with Father Rook and help these people, *your people*, get acclimated."

"Is *that* what this is about?" my father said.

The Dean nodded.

My father, who, like myself, had been sitting all this time, stood up and took a few steps toward the Dean. For a moment I thought he was going to sock him in the eye. "No, no," he said.

The Dean made one of those vigorous theatrical flourishes with his arms like a trapeze artist and told my father to calm down. He flashed me a furtive look. "Cool off, Jacob. This is not such a big deal. I thought you would have wanted to get involved with this business. Jesus—it's humanitarian. And there's a boy involved, a kid not much older than Mickey. It'll be good for the whole family, you know, doing something fresh. What's the point in living like a damn hermit anymore? It'd be a challenge for you and your children. Christ knows it's an honor."

"I don't think Christ knows a thing about what these people went through," I said.

The Dean glared at me with enormous anger, his drinker's nose growing very red. I'm sure he wanted to say something to me about my insolence, but he was too furious to speak. He held himself stiffly and was fighting to draw breath, though his mouth was closed.

My father gave me one of his earnest affronted looks before telling the Dean he would do whatever was necessary to help these unfortunate people. His eyes were wide and red and gloomy. I could tell he felt terribly trapped and disheartened. In his mind, I'm sure he felt he had few options. My father withered in the face of conflict, and he certainly couldn't brush the sloshed Dean off, even reluctantly. And given the Dean's well-earned reputation for treachery and nursing a grudge, and then getting even, my father didn't ever want to be in his doghouse.

I heard my stomach growl. Evening was coming on; the orange rays of the sinking sun were knifing through the tips of the yellowing trees. Out the paneled windows I could see plump gourds and rotting apples and stacks of new lumber piled against a sagging brown shed, and an updraft of soft fallen leaves. For his part, the Dean seemed listless, and he let loose with a few strenuous laughs, as if they caused him discomfort. He was sulky and crabby and his chiseled face colored slightly as our eyes met. He was nothing but a vain sidewalk bully, tuxedo and expensive gin and all, and he understood perfectly that I hated him at that moment.

———

I may be all washed up by now, a dull-witted, churlish old nobody who bores people half to death with his aimless chattering, but I've lived more than eighty years in a world fueled with fraudulence—a counterfeit world that easily mocked noble intentions—a world where only love and evil have proved to be enduring. On the contemplative walk home from the Dean's house that balmy late fall afternoon all those many years ago, an obscure passage from Heidegger had strangely filtered through my reflections. If I can recall (and I don't trust my memory here) it had something to do with the possibility of meaningful human freedom residing solely in those gestures executed in opposition to the barbarism of the past. All else was imposture. All else was a dazzling chimera. All else was bedlam and a cold mosaic of illusion. In the curt vernacular of the street-corner philosopher, actions spoke louder than words. Does it help anyone to dabble in these kinds of abstractions? Self-knowledge could be, most certainly would be, perilous.

Obtusely, and with my normally staid voice cracking, I told

Mickey that Dean Riverside's brand of decorous bigotry was the most pernicious kind of all. Instead of gauging Mickey's own response to our conversation with the Dean—instead of remaining calm, alert, and wary, instead of trusting Mickey's shrewd, civilized instincts—I lost my temper momentarily and really let the Dean have it. I couldn't help it; the trace of ridicule in all his words was unmistakable. Those refugees, I explained to Mickey, weren't *our* responsibility, they were *his*. The man talked as if the Nazis were an aberration, a fluke, a menace only for Europe's Jews—never mind the rest of the world. And here *I* am, I said, a glum pushover for the job. I told my son that in due time he would learn all about these vain, dissolute blue bloods and their impeccable legacy of faintly restrained rage and patrician corruption. When they turned the other cheek, Hitler buried us alive and disguised their dirty work for them. Murder with impunity, the blood crimes and brutal glamour of killing. Imperious, soused, and wound up tight as toy poodles, they treasured their fond memories of a Jewless Harvard.

That very night, while we scratched our suppressed consciences around the butcher block kitchen table, Mickey unburdened himself and asked me bluntly why I had minded becoming temporarily involved with the DPs. We were having baked fish and boiled cabbage and corn for supper, thick, gray-skinned mullet I had gotten at the A & P. In Mickey's view, I was blowing everything out of proportion. Rubbing my dry palms together, I felt the heat radiate through my hands. The very last thing I wanted, or needed, was another disgruntled child. It was obvious that he had been disturbed by my wild outburst on the walk home. I simply told him that I wasn't ready to become involved emotionally with anyone outside the three of us. Kiddingly, I said I wasn't a trained social worker, and asked him if I could possibly be mistaken for Eleanor Roosevelt. He cradled the sugar bowl in one hand and ran the other one through his wavy hair. He looked forlorn, and I sensed that he felt I was in peril of breaching some moral imperative, and doubtless he was onto something. But I felt encumbered enough at the moment, barely afloat myself, and I didn't want to be drawn into anyone else's anguish. The magnitude of my own despair was just then becoming clear to me, and the worst thing was not knowing what was true and what was false about any of this. I reminded him that his gloomy sister wasn't even speaking in complete sentences to me yet. Her explosive wrath had somehow receded into an ever thickening silence.

The most I had managed out of Dara the past nine months was a grunt now and again, or, at best, a frozen stare of utter derision and defiance. After Eve's death, I felt her grief should be accommodated, her silences and solitude respected. But things never let up, she never came out of it. Even Mickey said he didn't think Dara would ever get over it. Her indictment of me was evident in all her sardonic gestures—slinking past me like a mime in the narrow hallways of the house, eyes glued shut, intensely pawing the air in front of her face with her pink, down-turned palms, mocking, there was no question about it, what she saw as my colossal blindness; or her disingenuously lifting her thin, penciled eyebrows whenever I said something to them or someone else that reeked even in the least little bit of *shmaltz*. She hardly ever had a meal with us anymore, and seemed to subsist on stale Uneeda biscuits, Welch's grape jelly, and tinned sardines and anchovies. When I dragged her to the doctor for a physical, she smiled teasingly at him and, with her freckled face relaxed and draped with playfulness, pretended that nothing was wrong. With the doctor she was garrulous, she rambled on about school and her friends, and for a few fleeting seconds I let my guard down, allowing myself to feel consoled. It strikes me now that, given how much all this misfortune weighed on me like a stone, perhaps I was simply looking for a sentimental solution to my ruined sleep. Once back home, however, Dara's imploring eyes came swimming at me, and the luminous pitch of her unappeased resentment erased any hope I had clung to that her bereavement would soon be over.

Psychoanalysis was rapidly coming into vogue at the time. Like its metaphysical analogue, German phenomenology (what soon became known on our side of the Atlantic as existentialism), it had caught the attention of many prominent writers and artists. Each year these avant-garde intellectuals spent many hundreds of thousands of dollars for the opportunity to recline on a plush leather sofa while painstakingly tracking their elusive migration from blissful child to wretched adult. But I scornfully looked down on psychiatrists. I thought they were mostly guilt-stricken quacks with unresolvable riddles of their own to solve. Besides, I just didn't have the stomach to put Dara through all *that* mumbo jumbo then. In hindsight, perhaps I was merely afraid that I would lose her permanently, that she would slip deeper and deeper into the deranged root of her despair. Curiously, especially in light of the way Dara and I were pulling apart at the seams, I had great confidence in the restorative power of our *own* minds. What a grievous, smug delusion! By avoiding pain (*hers? mine?*), by palliating what I knew in my melancholy heart to be true, my worst fear had come to pass.

In addition, I had surely neglected my students for months. I was ill-prepared, undiplomatic, and grouchy in class. I either misplaced or forgot to mark lab experiments, my lectures were addled, my scribbled comments on their examinations incoherent. I was a mess, and everyone knew it. No one came to see me during office hours, and who could blame them? There were those days when I even contemplated ending it all. When I said I wanted him to understand that I still needed more time to organize things at home and at work before I could even think of helping anyone else, Mickey said no matter, that *he* was looking forward to meeting these fortunate survivors of Hitler's mad crusade.

Fortunate? At his tender age he could not understand that the muddled world was considerably more than our mind's own troubled creation. Things were not always as they seemed, I told him. My Mickey was a good son; there was no pity or desperation or callowness in his inquisitive, good-intentioned heart. And that's the kind of man and father he grew up to be.

As a boy he understood intuitively that it took only simple virtue to extend a cordial hand to those shriveled souls defaced by the darkness of history—a darkness which had been remorselessly enacted upon them without respite—their harrowing voyage from the scum and muck of blood-soaked Poland to the American Midwest a stunted bleakness beyond our trite imagining. But I was still rattled with numbing sorrow, my own grief an undeflectable, draining sore, and I was shamefully unable to help my embittered daughter, or even myself. At that point in time, I had no space in my mangled heart for expiation, or healing.

We did not meet the DPs for another ten days. It turned out that the son was still recovering from a bout of pneumonia. My father had called and spoken to Father Rook, who told him that the DPs had had an inclement ocean crossing. They had experienced heavy weather all the way into New York Harbor. Most of the handful of dejected refugees in the cramped steerage compartment were quite ill with various degrees of seasickness, diarrhea, and dehydration. Their rations were meager (they were used to that, the priest told my father with mordant irony) and the son had caught a heavy cold on the battered freighter. A kindly Negro steward gave him some Vicks VapoRub to smear on his chest and nose, and aloe cough drops for the hacking. The crowded train they had caught to Chicago, with stops, had taken two whole days. By the time Father Rook met him and his mother at Union Station in Indianapolis, his condition had markedly worsened. Father Rook immediately took them to Riley Children's Hospital, where the feverish boy was thoroughly examined, x-rayed, and admitted. He was given medicine and fluids intravenously, and spent four frenzied nights there, in a steamy pediatric ward filled with gasping asthmatics. Esther, his mother, understandably vulnerable and derailed with panic, when she wasn't at his bedside had a room in a dingy hotel filled with traveling salesmen across the street from a pharmaceutical company. Father Rook said that the boy had a raw tearing cough but that he was slowly recovering, that he was being treated with codeine and penicillin.

Father Rook lived in a small whitewashed cottage less than a mile from the barren limestone quarry, directly across a paved macadam road from his yellow-steepled church. I had bicycled past this church without reflection hundreds of times on my way to Little League practice at Flint Park, or to pick freestone peaches and huckleberries at Quail Valley Farm, but only now, in response to my question concerning its rather modest proportions, did my father inform me that there were only a handful of Roman Catholics in our county. My limited knowledge of Catholic churches, orthodox or otherwise, was confined to those I'd walked past or peeked into while visiting my grandparents in Chicago, and they all seemed to be Byzantine cathedrals with silver spires and gaudy towers, or huge onion-shaped domes that caught fire in the sun. According to him, there were not that many more Catholics around here than Jews. "The Pope's no icon in this neck of the woods," he said. "We're all awash in a vast sea of Methodists."

My memory of the day we met them is indelible. It was the first Saturday after Uriel, the son, had been discharged from the hospital in Naptown. The air smelled like moss, and thunderheads blotted out the early morning sun. For breakfast, my father had made us fresh squeezed grapefruit juice, buckwheat cakes, sausage patties, and chocolate milk. We arrived at Father Rook's place shortly before noon. My father had wanted to stop at the Elks' roadside table on our way out there to pick up some brown betties and a gallon jug of apple cider for the Mermelsteins. For days, he had been skittish about this encounter. All week long I had caught him chewing on his pale, ribbed fingernails and staring out the kitchen window at the pair of flaming Japanese quince my mother had planted just a few weeks before she fell unexpectedly ill. He was normally a very private and bashful man, and I clearly recognized that his meeting this woman and her son had put him on edge. For someone who had longed above all else to avoid conflict and disputes and to live what could be labeled an *unhaunted* life, reality had certainly been infused with more unanticipated dread than he had been schooled to take on. He had never done particularly well in novel situations; in fact, he had often shrunk fearfully away from them, and had taken it for granted that my mother would break the ice with strangers, something she had always managed with great ease. I knew this wouldn't be a cakewalk for any of us.

Father Rook was waiting for us at the front door, sucking on a cigarette. A hawk wheeled in slow circles above a field of pumpkins.

The priest was very tall and very thin, almost skeletally thin. I guessed he was at least six-three or four, probably a star pivot man back on the abbey intramural team, and he was wearing worn denim work clothes stained with transmission oil and axle grease, and low-cut black sneakers. He pumped my father's hand vigorously after first wiping his own on a big smudged rag he had pulled from the rear pocket of his pants and, quickly turning sideways to let us pass into the house, gazed down at me sympathetically. He was probably somewhere in his late fifties. His large front teeth were nicotine-yellow and peaked; his flat, dainty ears faintly barbed, like a fawn's. The priest had a long, cadaverous face, like a famished wolf's—a medieval face, my father said later—very long arms, and his extruding charcoal-gray eyes were piercing and alert. Those were eyes, I could tell, like a ferret's, eyes that had evolved to work especially well in the dark. Willowy white hair, parted crookedly in the middle, fell in wisps on either side of his pointed head. I noticed that he wore a thick ring of keys on his belt.

The mother was sitting in a caned hickory rocker when we entered the house, and she quickly rose to greet us. Her dark clothes hung on her in folds, and she shuffled when she walked, as if one of her feet were deformed. There were guttering ashes in the fireplace behind her, and a crude woodcarving of a thistle-crowned, weeping Christ hung over the brick mantel shelf. Father Rook took her by the elbow and made the introduction in a grainy, emphysemic voice. It was obvious that something grave was eating through his lungs. "Esther Mermelstein, I'd like you to meet Jacob Heller. And his son, Mickey."

"I'm very pleased to meet you," my father said, extending his hand. They shook hands and he smiled broadly.

"Me too," I said. I held out my hand and she took it in hers and squeezed.

"Esther—may I call you Esther?" my father said.

She offered him only the ghost of a smile and let go of my hand one finger at a time.

Mrs. Mermelstein appeared weightless. She had a gaunt, sallow, heart-shaped face, and a jagged streak of silver flared through her coarse gray-black hair. While Father Rook went to the cast-iron stove to boil water for tea, the three of us sat down, my father and I on a small, chintz-covered chesterfield, Mrs. Mermelstein back to the rocker. I looked around at the furnishings. The priest had a blue ceramic head on a white walnut butterfly table (I later discovered it was a representation of Saint Anselm, celebrated in Christian metaphysics as the designer of the ontological argument for the existence of God), a few gooseneck floor lamps with fluted, mauve, blown-glass shades, cream burlap curtains, what appeared to be a lute in disrepair. There were scoured milk pails and a butter churn on the scrubbed planked floor next to the stove, jars of pickled tomatoes and wax beans and peppers and beets in a glass-fronted cupboard above it.

My father asked her how the living accommodations were, and she told us they were sufficient for their needs, but that she had heard mice scratching in the walls. Her melancholy blue eyes, as she spoke, were trained on me; they were spectral and globular in their milky sockets. Her lips were tightly compressed. There was a thin white line where her eyebrows had been. She had a finely sutured scar which dipped brokenly along her upper lip and vanished inside her mouth. My father smiled at her, and her half-closed lids rolled down. For a few seconds my mind drifted back to what he had told me about that dying girl in the sun: the scissoring of her emaciated legs, the starlike cartilage of her wasted hips. Over his shoulder, Father Rook said that Mrs. Mermelstein and her son had been in a DP camp on Cyprus.

My father said Dean Riverside had already told us that.

"And before that," Mrs. Mermelstein said softly, "from Bergen-Belsen. And before that, Majdanek and Auschwitz."

"Good Lord," my father said.

Father Rook brought us teacups and saucers and sugar and milk in a small pewter pitcher, and lemon cookies on a delicate square plate embellished with pansies and morning glories. "Rose hips," he said. "Excellent for the digestion." He poured the hot water from a copper teakettle. My father seemed to drink his tea down in one steaming swallow.

"It's a miracle that you managed to get to America in one piece,"

I said. "My father was in the Army and he told me what it was like over there."

My father's face reddened slightly as his eyes met hers. God knows what she was wondering my father had told me. She lowered her eyes. "Yes," she said. "And I always prayed we would come to this country."

"How are you and your son adjusting?" my father said.

She paused then, and dropped her eyes. "We are feeling our way, Professor."

"The selection process for emigration, or repatriation, is absolutely magical," Father Rook said, almost in a growl.

"At least you have family over here," my father said. "The Dean said they live in Milwaukee. Have you been able to contact them?"

"Cousins," she said. "They were cousins of my husband's. From Vilna. Two old women, sisters, who never married but had the good sense to leave Europe before Hitler. I think they are no longer among the living by now. I never knew them. Only their names. Rose and Gussie Zygielbaum."

My father looked incredulous. "And you have no other family here? Does the relief agency know that?"

"Now they do," she said. "In Cyprus I lied and I lied and they finally believed me for some reason. Maybe we were processed by a Jewish clerk. The British wouldn't let too many of us go to Palestine, they didn't care to make the Arabs crazy. We were lucky, for a change."

"I guess you could say that, considering," my father said, his tone markedly guarded. "What do you think, Father Rook? Is *this* all a matter of chance, or divine intervention?"

"Gideon, *please*," Father Rook said, lighting up a fresh cigarette from the butt of his last one. "I don't ask questions that are unanswerable. To me, the existence of God is not an inquiry. The universe is rational despite our senseless cruelty. We are a miserable pack, yet a pack capable of subtle vision. What redeems this ghastly world are miracles—the minor miracles of fellowship and compassion. Yes, yes—suffering is an inherent aspect of human life. The world we live in is inexplicably evil, wicked beyond all probability.

Children die needlessly or are murdered or even purposely cause others to perish. But the world can, on rare occasions, be mysteriously beautiful and just. We live for that state of grace, no?"

"In my way of looking at things," my father replied, "the concentration camps cancel out both the idea and meaning of God. The existence of God is forevermore irrelevant."

"Perhaps it's the idea of man they annul," Father Rook said stonily, checking his wristwatch and stubbing his cigarette out in a porcelain ashtray decorated with angels. He lit up a fresh one.

My father leaned back on the chesterfield and sighed, gathering his thoughts before counterattacking. Perspiration beaded his high forehead. His elastic mind could often be a deft instrument of analysis. He could burrow to the core of an abstraction with corrosive logic. For the moment his perpetual dark mood had receded. He was, despite himself, having, if not quite a good time, at least a better one than either he or I had expected. This was just the tonic he needed to get his mind off his loneliness and Dara, some intellectual sparring with a loquacious, pedagogical priest. He then asked Mrs. Mermelstein if she needed anything—a washstand, some bedding, cooking utensils, towels—to tide her over while she and her son got more settled. Something—a nerve, a muscle—jumped in her face. To this day I'm bad with ages, but she couldn't have been much past forty, if even that; yet if it weren't for her supple boneless neck, she could have passed for sixty. There were hairline cracks in the flesh around her mouth, and her rough fingertips had the texture of sandpaper.

Though everything about this situation dictated prudence and restraint, if not compassionate silence, it was soon apparent that I was unable to tame my impulses. As a result, my avid adolescent self went rushing in where angels would surely have feared to tread. And, as I had somehow managed but little more than a week before at Dean Riverside's house, I ineptly switched the subject—and to one that was absolutely no business of mine. "Where's Mr. Mermelstein?" I blurted straight out. "Is *he* still a DP?"

My poor father shot me a withering glance.

Blank-faced, Mrs. Mermelstein seemed to infold upon herself.

"Lost, presumably," she said, her eyes expressionless. "They're still trying to locate him. In Warsaw I met someone Pintor knew from Frankfurt who thought he was tortured by the Gestapo for selling black market medicine in Cracow. Then a reporter from the BBC told me that he was probably deported to Siberia. Another man at the DP camp said something else. Who can know the truth of these terrible things?"

There was a short lull in the conversation. Twice there were moments when I was convinced she was getting ready to resume talking, only to witness her briefly pause and glance down at the varnished plank floor. I then somehow managed to curb my curiosity, and hesitated chattering on myself for a few seconds, uncertain if Mrs. Mermelstein was merely gathering her strength to continue speaking about her unfound husband or whether she was feeling some kind of constraint or embarrassment. She excused herself then and went to the bathroom, leaving the three of us alone for a few minutes.

My father put his hand on my shoulder. "Mickey—all your personal questions are embarrassing. It's prying and rude. You needn't be so impulsive and say whatever comes into your mind. You must learn to control yourself."

"I have a big mouth, I know," I said.

Father Rook smiled and frowned at the same time. "Easy does it, Jacob. The boy just needs to learn how to be more discreet."

I stammered an apology and promised to check my nervous tongue. Father Rook then explained how he had been counting on me to befriend Uriel, who was only four years older than I was, after he was fully recuperated. Then he told us that Uriel was supposed to be some kind of watercolorist, and that my father should try to locate a faculty member in the art department at the college to evaluate his paintings and sketches. Maybe there were some classes he could even take.

My father looked like he had the wind knocked out of him. He cleared his throat and told Father Rook that he needed to beg out of this. He explained that despite his sympathy he had no time for these people, that he had his hands full at the moment, what with a full load of classes, committee responsibilities, and a child at home who was still terribly bereaved, pining for the mother she would only see again in her dreams. Halfheartedly, without conviction or force, he said that he had absolutely no natural talent for this sort of thing. His wife had been the easy mixer, the one who had always made friends effortlessly, the one who had radiated warmth, the one strangers had liked immediately—*not him.*

Father Rook thumbed out his half-smoked cigarette in an enamel ashtray by the fireplace. "But what you have is firsthand experience of what things were really like over there," he said. "You're an educated man. I'm sure you'll manage to make everything work smoothly."

I saw her shadow on the wall a second or two before I heard her voice. "I took care of everything," she said softly, "and didn't ask anyone for anything. Now I'm asking a small favor."

My father faced her and said, "I've been up to here with work," and pointed to his chin.

"You have nothing to explain, Professor," she said. "I'm sure you are a busy man." She looked at me nervously, licking her lower lip; my heart turned over.

"Everyone's on a tight schedule these days," Father Rook interjected.

As I turned around, she drifted by me, and her pale, almost translucent eyes settled on the row of red geraniums in green glazed pots on the windowsill. She held her head like a lily.

"Ask away," my father said resignedly.

I went over to her and looked in her face. "Your son draws?"

"Yes, yes," she said wearily. "Uriel paints."

"Did you or his father paint?"

"My husband always wanted to be a painter, but he wasn't good enough."

"My mother loved to sketch children's faces," I said.

She turned away from me slowly, swaying slightly, and touched my cheek. Her crooked fingers were wet. Her small chin had a few white hairs on it. She seemed to be keeping her face from falling apart by focusing all her energy on me. Her dry lips were moving, and I had the impression that the effort to control her feelings at this moment would soon become unendurable. Those damp misshapen fingers gripped her black dress. She looked up at my father, her face closing like a fist. "How can it hurt you to do this small thing for Uriel? You have a son and a daughter, you appreciate how I am alone."

He moved his hand as if to erase her words from the air. "I know, I know," he said forlornly. "Perhaps we can show Uriel's work to a painter I'm friendly with on the faculty. No—I'm *sure* we can handle that."

He touched her arm—an anxious gesture of apology. Then he gave me one of his fishy looks. I didn't know what he wanted, or expected me to say. It suddenly occurred to me that perhaps he was anticipating that I would make an attempt to dissuade him from this dubious course of action. I could tell by the discontented hang of my father's narrow shoulders that his untiring imagination was busy squeezing him into *her* shoes. I could also tell that he was wrestling with mistrust, all the brittle, improbable things that penetrate our unglamourous lives like a burning sword.

"I gave them nothing," she said fiercely, shaking her head. "Uriel only wants to be himself. But you will understand he is different from other boys of his age. The camps, wandering all over Europe, frantically searching for his missing parents. We told him to be very strong and to survive, to do *whatever* was necessary to stay alive. I have no illusions anymore, Professor Heller. Your son can show him what it means to be an ordinary American boy. I want Uriel to be *ordinary* again. All he does now is dream about his father. He wakes up in the dark choking."

Father Rook suggested that I go outside and introduce myself to Uriel, who was tramping around in the pumpkin field behind the church. When I looked at my father for permission to leave, he shooed me away with the back of his hand. Mrs. Mermelstein smiled with those widely spaced front teeth and said that Uriel was looking forward to meeting me.

In back of the church a twisted gate, choked with burdocks and wild blackberry canes and swung half open, was sunk back firmly on its large broken hinges. Here and there were patches of ragweed and pallid phlox and stubby coarse grass. A scythe and an ax and some firewood were piled against a blacksmith shed with rotten hasps on its doors. Everything smelled of compost and cider. A small turkey was squatting on a post, sunning itself. When I found Uriel he was sitting on a stump, his spine in a bow, stringy legs sprawling, peeling a Bosc pear with a horn-handled pocketknife in one continuous strip, like my mother used to do. A brindled cat slept on its side at his feet. About fifty or so feet behind him a small grove of chinaberry trees encircled a dark pool of water. I could see a pair of geese gliding on the smooth surface. There was rich pastureland a hundred or so yards away, then a greenish-white stand of what my mother always called "quaking" aspen.

I called his name as I approached him, but he didn't lift his drawn, bearded face. I tried calling him again, much louder this time, and he raised his head slightly. Shading my eyes from the flat strips of early autumn sunlight, I felt myself forcing a smile. My heart fluttered and sank. I had the uncomfortable sensation that he was looking clear through me. His hair was wet with sweat, and he stood up suddenly, maneuvering around the stump. He was quite tall and thin and his overalls hung on him in folds. I had the notion that he could wrap his long skinny arms completely around himself. His beard was a knotted reddish-brown growth, mosslike and quite bristly.

As I got closer he visibly stiffened. I mentioned my name, and that I had just been talking with his mother. I saw that he also had a scar on his face. His was more in the shape of a right triangle, with the hypotenuse extended in a straight line from the corner of his thickened eyelid and running down across his cheek. In time the beard would cover most of it. His heavy nose looked as if it had been broken more than once, and the scaling flesh at his wet hairline was dotted with raised, wine-colored spots.

"I have this for you," I said, and held out a pocket Webster's dictionary in one hand and a silver-blue Sheaffer fountain pen and inkstand in the other.

He lifted his brows, and his hard gray eyes took on a vacant expression. They looked drowsy with fatigue. His head bobbed ever so slightly as he watched me. His posture was quite rigid, and I noticed that he had a fever blister on his mouth. I put the gifts down and extended my hand. We shook; his grip was quite powerful. In peculiar contrast to his bony torso, his thick, pink-palmed hands were like slabs of meat, a stevedore's massive hands.

I felt embarrassed for some reason. Grinning, I said, "What do you say if I come by your place on Tuesday? How's half-past four? We can talk about school, maybe shoot some baskets at the Y."

I thought I detected a movement in his eye, the uninjured one, but he just stood there without answering me. What was I doing wrong? What was bothering him? Like my father, I was never much good with first impressions; like him, I routinely misjudged people and they oftentimes misread me. And I had little tolerance for mystery or surprises. I was rapidly becoming an expert on alienation and anxiety, and as I grew into manhood my flair for coarseness and impertinence found expression in gauche behavior. I was both too bashful and too clumsy to get away with aimless, petty chitchat with strangers, and I refused to discuss lawyering outside the office. At cocktail parties I usually preferred to drink my Jim Beam alone and as quickly as possible, and to pretend disinterest while our hosts remarked to Helen about what a quiet fellow I had turned out to be after everything they had heard about me; or I was the life of the soiree, full of earthy limericks, vulgar one-liners, and indecent anecdotes—anything to avoid talking about myself.

So Uriel and I stood there for a few minutes, eyeballing each other like gangly welterweights poised to duke it out, and it struck me as strange that he had long pale eyelashes, like a girl's. "Great," I finally said, putting a hand on his shoulder. "I hear you're interested in painting. My mother, who died last year, loved to draw. I couldn't make a straight line if my life depended on it."

He withdrew, shrinking, despite his height, beneath my arm.

"Look," I said, now not bothering to mask the exasperation in my voice, "I know this must be very strange to you. Heck—it's pretty strange to me also. I can imagine how different you must feel here. Let's at least talk to one another; in time, maybe we can even be friends. I'll show you the ropes around here—what do you say? Teach you all you need to know about Indiana. It's a nice place to live, friendly. Can I bring you or your mother anything? Soap, thread, needles, socks, scissors? I bet I could convince my sister, Dara, to bake you a raspberry *babka*. With walnuts. My mother taught her. C'mon, you can trust me—I'm a Jew just like you. See?" And then, opening the collar of my shirt, I showed him the gold *mezuzah* on a chain around my neck.

He slumped down inside his overalls and stared at me with those somber gray eyes. His white shirt was damp and tight under his arms, and his big head continued to move involuntarily as he watched me.

Desperate to reach him, I tried another approach. "You're not making this easy," I said. "I know you had a bad time of it, but now things are looking up. Tell me what's wrong so I can help."

I must have shown my displeasure in my face as well as my voice, because he grimaced when I finished speaking. I was momentarily gratified that I had finally evoked a response from him. I sensed that he clearly needed to be shaken up, that he needed to learn that there were people in the world other than his mother who meant him no injury. It came to me then that all of this would be much harder work than I had imagined. As I opened my mouth to suggest that he come home with us for supper, he abruptly turned his back on me and walked away.

Like his mother, he shuffled when he walked. Could it possibly be that *I* wasn't the right person for this job? I had a short fuse and limited patience, and I was just beginning to get a clean taste of what my father had been driving at when he said that being involved with these people would give him insomnia. I trotted after Uriel and grabbed his elbow. Before I could apologize for my fit of temper, he pulled away and began wailing.

The wailing grew deeper, slower, harsher. I was unexpectedly reminded of *Yom Kippur* every fall in Chicago, the unshaved, sour-smelling old men in rubber-soled shoes and small black skullcaps, rocking and praying with my grandfather and his older brothers in an airless basement *shul*—a roach-infested firetrap reeking of tallow, sawdust, and stone, with rusted metal benches, a wooden ark, and, behind a transparent muslin partition, a modest section for the kerchiefed women—a windowless sanctuary down a flight of iron cellar stairs from a kosher butcher and a Chinese laundry. Watching Uriel, I stood absolutely still. Notwithstanding my deafness to social niceties, I had immediately sensed that it would be prudent on my part to allow him to vent whatever anguish he was experiencing. I half expected him to fall to the ground, and, like an epileptic, with his head knocking and his teeth clacking, slip into frenzied convulsions. His sounds were garbled, as if they came from an animal struggling to speak. A large pulsating vein ran up the center of his forehead.

When the wailing suddenly died down, I again placed my hand lightly on his shoulder. "Uriel—what is it?" I said gently. "Talk to me, I'm not here to do you any harm. I'm on your side."

Biting a knuckle, he turned slowly around and slumped down even deeper inside his clothes and looked at me with sullen, disbelieving eyes. I heard the breath go out of him. He opened his mouth as if to speak and showed me. The Nazis had mutilated his tongue.

Everything you have read thus far in this imperfect memoir had happened just the way my father and I had experienced it all those many years ago. In our minds we had taken the liberty to presume that you had given us some meager concessions for our infrequently deficient recollections. After all, the margin between the truth and distortion, like the one between mirth and misery, can be blurry and ill-defined, and what we remembered about the past may, of course, be more *significant* than what had actually happened.

Since he'd last been able to contribute his detailed impressions to this meditation, my father, like my grandfather before him, had fallen victim to a killer coronary soon after eating his lunch, and had passed away a few days later. He had, thanks to beta blockers, vaccines, and antibiotics, lived an active life almost thirty years longer than my grandfather had, and seemingly his only concessions to age were the benign polyps in his nasopharynx, the premature tremors of Parkinson's disease, and that he needed a magnifying glass to read the editorials and funnies.

He was alone at the time he was stricken. Lena, his sassy Jamaican housekeeper, had found him slumped over a half-eaten plate of belly lox, Bermuda onion, slices of Jarlsberg cheese, and black olives. She gave him CPR until the paramedics arrived, and they somehow managed to restore an acceptable sinus rhythm to his irregular heartbeat. He must have been very muddled, since his dentures were floating in a glass of iced coffee by his head. This cardiovascular business is messy as hell and can run in the genes. Even my own internist, a natty, sober young man as rawboned as Gandhi, has warned me that down the road one day I'm probably looking at angioplasty, or even worse, especially if I don't make the effort to shed a few pounds, avoid needless disquiet, and make the time in my hectic schedule for vigorous walking or swimming. He has showed me gory pictures of rubbery and fat-clogged hearts, and of pudgy-cheeked men with zippers from their navels to their sternums. He has encouraged me to eat more fish and raw fruits, says my urinary and bowel complaints are very common for men of my age, and wants me to enroll in a yoga or *tai chi* class at the Jewish Community Center. Laconically, I have reminded him that we softbellied *Ashkenazim* are shackled with an insatiable sweet tooth for smoked and salted and pickled foods. "Give me *halvah* or give me death," as my father used to say. My doctor has me come in to his raucous office twice a year for treadmill studies and blood chemistry profiles. My liver and gall bladder and prostate gland are functioning normally, but despite my avoiding eggs and ice cream and red meat, my cholesterol levels drive him bananas. He wants to snake a catheter up a blood vessel in my groin and get a close-up look at my coronary arteries.

My father had a few semi-lucid days in the hospital before his kidneys began to fail, and on one of them, while I shaved his stubborn neck stubble with a straight-edge razor, he shoved aside the oxygen mask covering his mouth and nostrils and urged me to conclude this story on my own, to sort out the truth of our past lives as best as I could, a daunting, vain, and unavailing commission.

I wish I could say that my father and Dara had come to some sort of mutual understanding, some sort of meaningful accord, but sadly I cannot. She ultimately boarded a commuter flight at Midway to come see him in order to say farewell, but he was already in a coma and fading fast. By the time she had answered the plea of filial obligation and had arrived at his high, cranked-up bedside, he barely had any blood pressure. The rumpled resident managing my father's care put his stethoscope on his hollow chest and waited, listening to his failing heart. The doctor turned his head in my direction and said he only had at most thirty minutes left. Dara sat there, her drugged, shrunken, underwater face like a harness of pain, and watched him drift into oblivion. She kept on crossing and recrossing her freckled legs, her fingers quivering with tension. For almost five hours he breathed and stopped and breathed and stopped. Once, she leaned over him and wiped the clotted saliva out of the corners of his mouth.

Like the uncompromising realist he had always been, he had previously left precise instructions with both me and his team of physicians that he was not interested in any heroic measures to keep his ancient and ravaged body alive. If circumstances dictated it, I was to pull the plug on the respirator. He told me, over and over again: "Please, Mickey—when nothing more can be done, no feeding tubes in my belly and throat." Then, in what can only be described as a final display of guileless caprice, he offered up his perfect eighty-three-year-old corneas to the middle-aged family man who had shared his semiprivate room, a peevish, powerfully muscled plumber named Angelo with glaucoma undergoing radiation therapy for Hodgkin's disease. My father was a man who saw life as it really was—damaged and disarmingly sad—scrubbed clean and purged of debilitating illusions, and in desperate need of simple generosity. I can only hope that I am as prepared to meet my maker as he was.

At the abridged memorial service Dara's low-key, submissive disposition caught me off guard. For weeks I had been gearing up for the worst possible spectacle—derision, scorn, even a spasm of wrath at the burial. But she was congenial and compliant and very distracted instead. I never found the fortitude (believe me, it would have taken some) to ask her what she would have said to him had he miraculously emerged from his unconscious state. In this endeavor, as in so many others that have afflicted and bewildered us in this limitless

veil of tears, I must retrieve from the vortex of obscurity the dis-
continuous scaffolding of time, allowing my inept and impaired
imagination to rearrange and reconstruct the compressed details
and consolidated entirety of our remembered experience. I have
nothing lurid to confess and no one I want to confess to. My
amended thoughts and intruding dreams transform themselves,
physically, into language. But as an impartial witness, staring hard
and deeply into the periscope of memory, I can testify that what
follows is all invention—albeit faithful to what actually happened.

The only way I can touch the Mermelsteins now is in the
misremembered past, by way of my deficient memory. The past is
never dead; it is not even past. We pretend to cut ourselves off from
the past, to cease keeping watch over absent faces. We each devise
our means of escape from the unendurable. Sometimes we can even
fantasize it out of existence. But there is no protected state—escape
is illusionary. No safe interlude or sheltered interior space where
dreams remain unhaunted. In my fitful sleep I confront the dreadful
spirits of the dead, I can hear the gathering of their distant grieving
voices. Just having their eyes flicker across my consciousness makes
my heartbeats lag.

Over the next few weeks we learned more than we really needed
to know about these people. Pintor Mermelstein had been a docent
at the university in Frankfurt, before he was deprived of his posi-
tion by the Nuremberg Laws. He was an art historian, an expert on
Saxonian woodcuts. He painted, we were told, for his own diversion, yet offered private lessons after his unforeseen dismissal in
order to earn a small living. *My husband was clever with a brush,
but he never took himself very seriously,* Mrs. Mermelstein had
said to us. *To be really good you must take the work seriously.* She
said that Uriel would sit and watch his father paint for hours. She
told us it was the most pleasure he had as a child.

Esther had been a history teacher in the *Gymnasium.* She had
first met Pintor Mermelstein when they were students in Leipzig.
He had been born in Lublin, but when he was nine or ten his fam-

ily had moved to Frankfurt, where his mother soon died from sepsis resulting from an infected hip. His father was a well-respected scholar, a curator in the Rothschild Museum there. Professor Mermelstein had scorned those Jewish colleagues of his who had sought to flee Germany for England or the United States. He had, instead, deduced that the national infatuation with Hitler and his harebrained ideology would soon turn to disenchantment once the austere economic distress caused by the war and its acrimonious aftermath had abated. After *Kristallnacht*, the Gestapo had forced him and his assistants to catalogue the priceless artwork they had confiscated from pillaged museums and burned synagogues. *Fat Göring's plunder*, she said Professor Mermelstein had called it derisively. Göring thought of himself as an art collector, when he was nothing more than an ill-bred thief and fraud. An outspoken critic of Nazi political philosophy, Professor Mermelstein was quickly sent to Dachau when he wasn't useful anymore, along with Pintor Mermelstein's three older brothers, and they were never heard from again. It was a mystery to Esther and Pintor why he wasn't arrested along with his father and brothers. A drunken clerk's oversight perhaps. A serendipitous blunder. A letter finally reached them from a Dutch communist who had befriended the Mermelsteins in Dachau, who said that they had been deported to a labor camp in eastern Galicia, near Lwów. The communist told them about the rumors he had heard about the shootings and gassings in special vans. He had heard of a town where all the Jewish men were rounded up and crammed into a synagogue that was then doused with gasoline and set on fire. Some months later another letter arrived, this time from an old student who had written his thesis under Pintor Mermelstein at the university. The student wrote that he had heard from someone he trusted in the Polish underground that his mentor's father and his three brothers had all been shot in the back of the head in the Pietrasze Forest, a vast, empty, secluded woodland district outside Bialystok. And that was the last word they ever heard about the fate of Pintor's family.

Esther's family had moved to Mannheim from Cracow when she was still an infant. For a year or two they had lived in a small house with an aunt and uncle who had left Vilna a few years earlier in order to make a better life, a more enriched, progressive life, they calculated, in Germany. A life without the threat of pogroms. Esther's mother had told her that all societies breed their own unique kind of derangement, but that anti-Semitism to the cultivated Germans was not the chronic raving mania it was in Jew-hating Russia or Poland; among Germans, it was more like an intellectual abstraction. Later on her mother would call Nazism a transient vulgarity, a nuisance, something that would eventually pass off, like a nagging cough. That agitator Adolf Hitler, in her estimate, was nothing more than a crude street hoodlum, a political leper, a provocateur. Her mother's paternal grandmother had grown up in Berlin, and she had taken great pride in German institutions and culture, wet nurse to Goethe, Schiller, Heine, Bach, Mozart, and Beethoven. Her mother fondly remembered her summer vacations there, the museums, the concerts, the theater, and she always said it was a paradise compared to Poland. She thought Germany was a beautiful country, and the mass of Germans were exceptional people, sanguine, inventive, ever industrious.

Her family had thought that they were on the threshold of an auspicious voyage. And for a short time, things had improved. Her father had been a talented clock maker, but it had always been difficult for him to make a decent living in Cracow. A resilient man, he made some money in Mannheim, dressed his wife and children in nice clothes, drank fine amber beer. He had forgotten temporarily what shame had felt like after having been beaten up by guzzling peasants. The children ate robustly and attended excellent schools. His wife was happy and she sang Schubert *lieder* with a women's choir at the music hall. He lost a foot in Flanders fighting for the Kaiser, and won an Iron Cross for his heroism. After Versailles, the long journey to a more prosperous, more suitable life had quickly turned dark. The economy was in a shambles, the swastika was suddenly everywhere. In Richard Wagner's Teutonic Bavaria the strutting goons and looters were running wild in the streets, clubbing and kicking and spitting on Jews, shattering shop windows, desecrating cemeteries, searching for beards to pull—as if they were pious, besotted Cossacks in their loose red shirts, pursuing poor Jewish dairymen and cobblers and fishmongers with sabers in a *shtetl* in Ruthenia or Bessarabia. Esther's mother and father, her older sister and younger twin sisters, her brother and his pregnant wife, her aunts and uncles and cousins, her nieces and nephews, her three remaining grandparents—all were deported to Warsaw, and in less than two years all of them wound up riding loaded transports to Treblinka. She alone of her family had survived.

My mother and father and grandparents did not see the urgency of the situation. They were lulled into thinking that they were honorable and faithful Germans first, Jews second. And the Germans counted on that. They would do what no one else could imagine. What was happening was the unthinkable, and so my parents did nothing, until it was too late. It was impossible to escape, impossible to disguise themselves as Christians. I saw my older sister and her daughter in Warsaw when Pintor and Uriel and I first arrived there. Everyone else was already smoke. I heard her tell all this to my father one night. They were drinking apricot brandy and smoking cigarettes, and my father was rapt. His attention had already narrowed in on something I was blind to. *Believe in what I tell you, I saw all there was to see. The frightened Poles did not weep over the vanishing of their murdered Jews. They knew we were starving to death in the ghetto, and much worse. People were jumping off buildings, dying of fevers in the filthy gutters, living on rats, hiding in the sewers. And the Poles were still killing dazed survivors a year after the war had ended. We are still hated over there. Even in our absence they want to exterminate us. In the face of such obscene madness, what can one feel except humiliation and despair?*

———

Uriel remained silent inside himself, a perfect mystery, or riddle, like the Sphinx. He had been denied the simple gift of speech, and his silence was part (the largest part) of his immense power over me. I wanted to read the words on his face, but he remained expressionless, inscrutable. There was something in the way he stared at me those first few weeks that made me feel ashamed of myself. His chest seemed partly caved-in on one side, as if his ribs had been removed. Mrs. Mermelstein had told me that he was continually afflicted by frightening nightmares that made him groan and scream in his sleep. She'd said that he was struggling to stop dreaming of those times when he was tortured by the SS. *It is so arduous to come back to a normal life,* she told me.

When I talked to him he seemed to look away dully even while he was looking straight into my face. Those hard granite eyes of his had a kind of listless, unfocused quality. It's clear to me now that I was gravely inept on at least two counts: I was simply too vain and too ineffectual to measure the painful repercussions of the adversity he must have endured; and I possessed no unclouded sense of how easy it could be to conceal the deepest wounds. Despite my best intentions, the topography of his soul was utterly beyond my inadequate reach. My instincts, for whatever they were worth, told me that there was a great emptiness within him I wouldn't be able to penetrate. I'd learned from Mrs. Mermelstein that Uriel—even more than his bitter hatred of the SS—had despised the stupid and sadistic Ukrainian camp guards who had volunteered to round up and torture and kill Jews for them. But in time I became convinced that Uriel had, above all else, detested feeling so completely dependent on us—that he and his mother had ultimately become the objects of what he no doubt saw as pity.

We followed a set routine for a while, meeting three late afternoons a week. I told him about our town and state, I showed him how to dribble a basketball, and taught him how to play horse and around-the-world. His coordination was shot; he could barely catch a simple bounce pass with two of those gigantic hands of his, and he couldn't jump an inch off the ground. When I made a joke of it in front of Father Rook, the priest told me that Uriel had broken his ankle in the DP camp. He limped because the bone hadn't healed properly. My father and I took him to a few high school basketball games, but he seemed disinterested in all the rah-rah stuff and ill at ease with the bright lights and noise.

I brought home vocabulary lists from the consolidated county school and read the words aloud to him. His mother had assured me that he read and understood English quite well, and I knew he was way ahead of me in math and science, so those subjects weren't a problem. We did jigsaw puzzles and played Chinese checkers and chess (I was no competition for him; like my sister, he could always polish me off in less than seven or eight moves). But when I asked if I could see some of his paintings or drawings, he shook his large head half-heartedly, and so I dropped it for the time being. My father had warned me to be prepared for what he strangely called a paralysis of the will. When I pushed him for an explanation, he said that Uriel might be immobilized because of what he had experienced during the war. My father told me to imagine what it must be like to live without a tongue, to not be able to say what was in you to say, to not be at home in the world. I had no idea what Mrs. Mermelstein's future plans were for Uriel's education—what she thought he might do one day for a living in this country. Whenever I sensed that we were getting nowhere, that we were merely passing time, sitting on the porch in gloomy silence in the mild October breeze—myself in a straight-back chair, and Uriel in the big leather armchair my father had given Mrs. Mermelstein as a housewarming gift, his sweaty face unfocused, his dull eyes sagging—I left before I was overcome by his mood.

That mild autumn happily dragged on in flashing colors. We went fishing for sunnies a few times down near the mudflats, and took long hikes into town, where he was a curiosity to many people. We rode our bikes (he borrowed Dara's) down to leaf-strewn Brown County, climbed steep undulating trails carpeted in fiery maple leaves and crackling pine needles as stiff as quills, and we rinsed our grubby faces and necks in a fast-moving creek that swirled beneath a one-lane gravel roadway toward the misty laurel hills farther east. We had breakfast and lunch a few times in Ladyman's Cafe, and Uriel gulped down the Denver omelettes and grilled pork chops and flakey buttermilk biscuits smothered in blueberry syrup.

By then everyone had heard of the Mermelsteins, the survivors from the Nazi camps whom Father Rook had taken in. Sometimes children would walk right up to Uriel and touch his sleeve. For his part, Uriel seemed bored by their interest; he merely looked down and smirked acidly at them, his mouth drawn to one side. Friends of mine from school had wanted to know from me if the Mermelsteins had a particular kind of body smell, if they had eaten cats and bugs where they came from in backward Poland, if they carried fleas and ticks—if they really saw, like we saw in the grainy newsreels, big concrete rooms heaped high with tangled naked arms and legs, with heads and hands sticking out. Sukie Chester, a pigtailed girl with bulging thyroid eyes, wanted to know if all their body hair had been shaved before they were gassed. She'd heard the hair was put in pillows and mattresses for Nazi soldiers. Peggy Crooms said her mother had told her that a Christian man looked different than a Jew because of an operation with a knife Jews had to have down in their privates to be considered a real Jew by their angry God. Jesus, Peggy's mother said, wasn't interested in that kind of disgusting operation, though he was tricked and had one himself by mistake, before he realized he was the son of God, a good Christian. But since he was Jesus it hadn't mattered all that much. He could grow back whatever the Jews had stolen from him at any time. Mrs. Crooms said that there was no telling what the people from over there in Poland really believed in, so there ought to be a law against them until we found out. Otherwise they might well bring their indecent ways over here and do it to others. Other kids had then agreed that bad things were done all the time in Europe, where the foreigners came from, where the world's troubles always started. Rennie Alford, a honey-skinned boy with a rutted face, said in a sulky voice that his father told him the Germans made lampshades and lye soap and beeswax from Jewish skin. When I told them they were all simpletons, that human beings were just human beings, he sneered and said I ought to return with them to whatever backward place they were born in—that instead of causing problems over here in a free country we could take the place of all those people who were killed in the war.

My father had warned me to not be surprised by any kind of foolishness I might come across. "It takes all kinds to make the world go 'round," he said, "but ignorance can be an incurable disease." He told me that many people in this part of the Middle West could trace their family roots back to places like Prussia, and that those same people had blamed the Jews for the Great Depression and Prohibition, for electing President Roosevelt and starting World War II, for the destruction of handsome Deutschland cities. He'd told me that there were many superstitious and mean-spirited people in the world, people who hated us simply because they had been taught that Jews had tricked the Romans into crucifying Christ. Many of them still believed that Jews murdered Christian babies and drank their blood during Passover. Others felt that Jews were all atheists or Bolsheviks or both—thick-nosed, big-lipped, rapacious outsiders. Even the Klan, at that time still a potent force in much of Indiana, spread lies that Jews defiled Christian women, that they manipulated the government and controlled the banks, that they advocated interbreeding between the races. Following an impulse that seemingly arose from thin air, I defied once again my father's long-term standing edict and brought Uriel to the abandoned quarry not far from Father Rook's church, and he seemed to like it there. I read to him from my mother's worn copy of *Leaves of Grass,* and we listened to the rasping crickets, the croaking bullfrogs. The cool stone was choked with yellow weeds and nettles and spreading roots, and the surface of the brackish-smelling, murky green water was alive with skittering dragonflies and praying mantises. We took off our shirts and sunbathed on the ridge. His marbled flesh had pallid bluish crescents, and though I clearly understood that Uriel had lived through things that were a great deal worse than anything I had ever imagined, I felt the mysterious desire to reach out to him at that moment. How could we ever be real friends unless I showed him that I knew what it meant to be cruelly dispossessed, to be deprived of a beloved parent? In truth I wanted to claw something out of him—recognition, esteem? Looking at him in repose for a few minutes, it was as though I were facing my own tapered reflection in the depths of a somber and immense mirror.

Having taken it for granted up to that point in my life that nothing was inexplicable, and that it was always possible to uncover a way to empathize with the world's random victims, I could not accept—I could not *understand*—that certain historical events were quite possibly beyond any kind of absolute resolution or redemption. In my naïveté I believed that Uriel would never be able to reveal to me in gestures that I could understand (obviously never in words) what life was *really* like in the camps—what it constrained of ordinary people to endure one's very own being. And so, with my stomach turning over, I heard my reluctant voice tear through the cloak of memory and bitterly I told him everything about my mother's infirmity and its grievous effects—her ghastly suffering and Dara's mordant despair; how I had flinched at my cringing father's ephemeral good cheer, his startled obsequious smile, the bruised-looking bands of exhaustion and despondency under his mopey eyes; how I had disobeyed him time and time again, and ridden my two-wheeler to the abandoned quarry when she first fell sick; how I had lingered there well past nightfall—I always waited for the winking fireflies to hover above the crushed buttercups and yarrow before pedaling home—with the muggy looming moonlight sifting in all around me like a lattice of fog; and how it had taken so many agonizing months for my mother to finally release her tenacious grip on life, enabling her to repossess, during those dreamy evanescent days before her death, a trace of genuine solace; and why, when the end mercifully arrived, amid the passing sobs and silences of my father and sister and grandparents, the well-intentioned prattle of meddling relatives and disregarded friends, I felt oddly neutral—engulfed by an acute sense of detachment and dislocation, a scathing consolation.

They became devoted to one another—my father and Esther Mermelstein. While I tended to Uriel, they had tended to each other. I could not understand the implications of this at the time, but their harrowing losses had not been able to master their power to generate intimacy. In hindsight, I realized that none of this should have come as any big surprise. As a boy, however, I knew nothing, really, about the physical and emotional desires of a man my father's age, of his need for female companionship. If I had, I'm not sure what I would have done with that knowledge, except to keep it to myself. And I have no good reason to doubt that their attachment was ardent—at least on his part. For some reason I cannot recollect the precise moment when I first became conscious of their mutual attraction, but it must have *happened,* as surely as I am scribbling these words in black ink. Dara and I were able to register a change in our father's eyes not long after the first anniversary of our mother's death. They seemed brighter, as if they were reflecting more light, though I know that sounds silly. I can, however, remember perfectly the unfamiliar sensations I had during those few pivotal days—a feeling of imminent eruption, as if he were going to split apart, though he was particularly quiet over the course of that week—distant, restless, private. At the very last minute (our battered suitcases and the car were already packed, we were about to walk out the front door) he changed our long-standing plans and told us he wasn't quite up to driving to Chicago that weekend in order to have a rabbi mumble a Hebrew prayer to a God he didn't believe in at my mother's delayed unveiling. He looked agitated when he asked me to phone my apprehensive grandparents and tell them we weren't coming, to tell them a white lie—that we had all come down with a touch of food poisoning in the middle of the night and that we would spend a whole week up there in the spring, during Passover. Naturally, they were distressed and disappointed.

It was late November, and the weather was still unseasonably mild. In town, people were walking around in shirtsleeves and light denim jackets, you could hear the whiffling leaves in the balmy gusts of wind. In the damp chilly mornings, big hazy spools of fluffy white clouds seemed caught halfway up the dripping yellow birch and evergreen slopes to the southeast; then, as the pale sun warmly burned through the fog, they nimbly lifted off in vast roiling scarves. The paper said it had been the warmest Thanksgiving in almost forty years. My father had roasted a fresh-killed turkey for the three of us, Father Rook, and the Mermelsteins. We had mashed yams laced with molasses, pecans and raisins, and butternut squash and wax beans and toffee apples and tangy wild rice dressing and cucumber salad and brandied cranberry sauce that Father Rook had made from the cranberries he had picked himself. We ate and ate. At one point my father said, sniffing, that he smelled something burning. In seconds we all smelled it. Father Rook ran to the stove and opened the oven. The Parker House rolls were on the metal rack, charred and crumbly, oval loaves shrouded with soot. Frowning, Father Rook removed them and scraped them into the sink. My father told him we had more than enough to eat, that we could manage to survive without them. Dara had followed one of our mother's favorite recipes and had baked a lemon meringue pie we ate with peach ice cream.

The four of us Americans ate like hogs and later toasted marshmallows in the hearth. I wondered how the Mermelsteins had felt, seeing all this food and gluttony at one meal, more food than they had seen for a whole year in the camps, but I somehow kept myself from asking. They appeared comfortable, and Uriel, to my surprise, devoured his food with great relish, refilling his plate at least three times, though Mrs. Mermelstein was subdued and showed little appetite. Always the worrier, my father was quite solicitous—he asked her if something she had eaten had disagreed with her. He even walked over to her and placed the back of his palm on her forehead, checking for fever. I recalled that she had once told us many survivors had ruined stomachs because of the rotten turnips and stale moldy bread that had comprised their diet. Mrs. Mermelstein smiled at him from beneath her hooded eyes and thanked him for his concern. Father Rook offered his advice as well. He recommended that she drink at least two full glasses of tomato juice a day, and that she needed more midday naps to regain her strength, to combat her lingering fatigue. She made a little rippling motion with her fingers and said that she was merely feeling a bit winded from getting settled in a new place.

My father looked at her differently somehow, but I made nothing of it at the time. I had no ear for the unspoken speech beneath their conversations. We all wondered when the first frost would arrive, the first dusting of snow. I can remember hearing the tin wind chimes I had given my mother for her birthday a few years earlier tinkling in the wind. Dara and I cleared the dishes from the table and then she and Uriel went into the kitchen to wash and dry them. Father Rook smoked a corncob pipe and grumbled about the trim peeling off his springhouse roof, of having to sand and refinish the maple flooring in the church. He then tried to amuse us by trading philosophy with my father, who seemed distracted.

"Living under the constant threat of death makes human behavior more—not less—important. Men cannot act as if nothing matters, but as if everything does. Jacob—what do you think?"

I could tell my father wanted out of this conversation. His voice was reedy, caustic.

"I have no idea. It's pointless to generalize. People do what they need to do in order to survive. You want to make an intellectual exercise out of it, but the camps defy your religious need to impose order on history. You ache for moral clarity in a world where there is none. You yearn for something to mute the impact of the slaughter, to see it as a sign or promise of future glory. It's your calling to discover transcendence, but there isn't any. Does it help to ask all these kinds of questions? I think not. Reason is feeble and words fatal. Your intractable faith is your way of distilling purpose out of chaos and lunacy."

Father Rook looked mortified; he refilled his pipe with fresh cherry tobacco.

I watched Mrs. Mermelstein as her small blue eyes moved back and forth from the priest to my father, and I thought of my beautiful young mother dead these past twelve months. I remembered her in her bed when the undertaker and his hard-looking men arrived at our house: the spotted sheets, her bare, withered calves, her discolored feet and fingers. How far had any of us budged toward quietly reviving some quotient of balance to our lives? Or would our unrestored grief be more like an immutable seal, preventing us from ever going beyond our ephemeral memories of what could never be unchanged?

Mrs. Mermelstein raised her long skeletal hands out toward both of them.

Father Rook—there was no protected place in the camps. We were poor wretches living in a vacuum. In a tunnel. Informers were everywhere. Prisoners would bribe their torturers for a piece of dirty bread, for a frozen potato. I saw decent people betray their friends for some extra soup. Men smeared their lips with urine to ease their thirst. Everyone was disappearing down a well. We were like straw. When a kapo *slaps you in the face and puts his boot on your neck in the mud because you asked if you could run to the toilet because you have cramps from the coffee, nothing is ever the same anymore. You hear me? Nothing is ever the same anymore. No one is there to help you know what to do. You are someone who can be slapped over and over and over again. What's worse, you come to want to be slapped, because the pain is the only thing that keeps reminding you that you are still human, still capable of feeling what it means to be a person, even in a place like that.*

I'll tell you what the camps were like. I watched with amazement a group of manacled prisoners—not Jews, not Russian soldiers, not partisans, Jehovah's Witnesses, I think they were—go on a hunger strike, to protest to their disdainful German taskmasters about their barbarous treatment at the hands of the Lithuanian and Ukrainian guards, and the treatment all prisoners received in general. Can you imagine this? A hunger strike, there? And other prisoners begged them to take their bread and slop and then give it to them. There was even rivalry among the SS men. They even had favorites among the prisoners, women they felt attracted to, were jealous over. They didn't mind sleeping with pretty young Jewish girls— first letting them wash all over with lemon soap and hot water and then giving them gifts of French perfume and rouge and lipstick to put on—and then gassing them in the morning. I knew of an SS man who had a sculpture of a naked woman made by a Jewish sculptress. Then she was sent to the gas. To the prisoners, these were men who walked between snowflakes, between raindrops even. I was told by the other women in my block not to complain or cry out if an SS man, or even a stupid kapo, *wanted to do something to me. My body was not mine anymore, they said. I was told that they hated it if you made them feel shame or pity, and that's how you could stay alive. Never make them feel pity or shame. They wanted to kill us with a clear conscience. That was very important to them. They needed to know that their hands were clean. They admired strength alone.*

When I first arrived there I thought I would have the power to

*live and die on my own terms. But I made myself a good friend
with a woman in my block, she was tall and good-looking and still
healthy, and she had a reputation for being a good organizer. She
was connected to the black market in the camp. She would find a
way to get an extra ration of bread, some lard, a piece of hard
cheese. We sat at sewing machines all day and repaired military
garments—we fixed torn uniform sleeves and zippers that weren't
on straight. We were walking to our workshop one morning when
she was pulled away from the* kommando *and raped by an SS man
behind a building. We were forced to stand outside in the harsh sun
until he was finished with her. I remember that it was a beautiful
morning, the sky was blue and cloudless, and there was no burning
smell in the air for a change. We could hear him barking orders at
her in German as he was raping and beating her. He was like one
of the heartless Ukrainians, a wild animal. What did they want
from us? We were dirty and skinny and hairless. They called us
filthy Jew pigs. They said it made them sick to look at us. Our bodies stank. Our breasts hung from our chests like chicken skin. If I
touched myself there I felt nothing. They had their fat-faced Czech
and Russian whores in the camp brothel. The raping and beating
went on and on, and all the time he was shouting at her in German.
Appalling words. Then another SS man joined in. We stood there
like helpless cows, quietly awaiting our turn to be milked. They
taught us this dumb obedience—that was the heart of their madness. They trained us to cling to our illusion of hope, that we had
choices in this inferno of theirs.*

*I thought I would be next, I thought we would all be next. I didn't
think I could do this and live normally again. It's impossible to believe but I was still modest. I was still my mother's daughter, my
husband's wife. And when I looked into the bright sun the light was
like an explosion in my eyes. At that moment I knew that I would
die that day. Or the next day. Or the next. I was certain of it. And
I was also certain that I had no control over what happened to me.
There was no way out. I didn't know what to expect from one moment to another. And it didn't matter what I thought. And who
knew what behavior would be favorable, and what would send you*

to the tin chimneys? And I felt for only a brief moment this clear understanding that even if I remained alive for a hundred years I would not have survived the camps as a human person after this terrible morning. But this tall woman who was my first friend in the camp, my protector and teacher, she was very strong, she said nothing, she didn't fight them, she wanted to live a while longer. She gave them no reason to have shame or pity. The handful of us standing in the sun were making little fearful noises, our eyes were gloomy, we felt shame, but we heard nothing from her. Not a whimper, not a murmur even. Nothing. She wanted to stay alive so she gave them back her silence. She had nothing else of value. Then when they were finished with her they dragged her back in front of us. The blood was running from her mouth and ears, her face was a bulb of purple flesh, her rags were torn away from her, her breasts were blue from all the biting, she was naked and trying to cover herself with her hands, and each of them put a bullet from a black Luger into the back of her neck.

These SS men looked so young. Like schoolboys, really, but with dimmed eyes that could make you shiver by looking on them. And they had this great rage, this immense hunger to kill. Then the one who first took my friend away to begin with started screaming obscenities at the rest of us in German, and I told some of the Dutch and Polish women later that night in the barracks that he was saying that we Jews were to blame for the war, and that one day we would all be grass. At least now we understood why this was happening to us, this was our deserved punishment for starting the war. To them, murdering innocent children wasn't murdering at all. I saw them tearing infants in half, and then bashing their heads against a wall. I saw them hanging children in front of their mothers. Before they shot members of the Polish resistance they filled their mouths with cement so they couldn't sing their national anthem. They stole everything from us, even our speech. Normal words had no meaning there. We both existed and didn't exist at the same time. And still there were people who prayed every morning and evening. I saw women who blessed the electric light bulbs, who tried to make yortzeit *candles out of potato peelings and margarine. Everyday I felt my heart clawing its way out of my chest.*

When the camp administration broke down at the very end, when we thought they were going to kill all those remaining, everything was much worse. The SS and the guards were coming and going all the time from the camp. People were dying from typhus every hour. I had a fever and there was a terrible smell in my urine. I thought I already smelled something dead inside my body. I had water bags on my feet from wearing wet clogs. My flow had stopped in the camp for a long time already and I thought that maybe my female organs were full of pus. I couldn't go to the toilet for ten days, two weeks. There were yellow corpses decomposing in blocks, and the rats and spiders were attacking people's toes and ankles. We had no water, no medicine, nothing to eat. When the guards were off somewhere, starving prisoners went into the fields and ate rotten cabbage and mice, and some of them ate cats and dead goats and worms, and some of them died of food poisoning. People couldn't eat anymore, they were so weak from hunger; their bowels were bloated and ran loose and bloody all the time. Your front teeth fell out when you bit into a spoiled pear. Prisoners were blind and deaf, many of them couldn't stand up. And our tormentors loved us all so much they came back with a train and took as many of us as they could back to Germany with them when the Red Army finally came.

Her hands were alive. That's what he told me when I became a man. *Her hands were alive.* I can see my father and Esther in her weatherworn cottage—the iron bedsteads, Uriel's charcoal sketches of barracks and barbed wire on the otherwise blank walls, the roller towel, the woodbox, the water buckets near the deep enamel sink, the faded green rag rug with a radiating hole in the center, the kerosene lamps softly glowing, the faint odor of resin and turpentine in the air—clinging to each other, as if the essence of their shared torment and the dense foreboding of the unknown territory they had embarked upon were somehow lessened by the unfeigned contact of warm human flesh. They could feel the cold metal of the bed frame through the thin mattress. My father could make out her mother's Swiss jewelry box on the white pine bureau, the swan barrette Esther had removed from her hair before she came to bed, a jade paper doll. They were the only things she had managed to smuggle in and out of the camps; they were all she had left of her family, save for Uriel.

Her face drooped over her steepled fingers. My father's melancholy tenderness enveloped her like a shroud. His hands seemed so large on her, he thought she was as delicate as a blue-tipped lotus. He said he felt he had wanted the wrong thing, that he thought he had wanted her to be absorbed into his being. They could smell the splintering heat from the woodstove. They heard nothing, save the rustle of their rough clothing as they undressed, and the sharp pattering nails of squirrels and mice in her cellar and walls. She had been spooked the first time she heard the sudden creaking of a loose floorboard, so he had explained to her that the boards of a clapboard house contracted with the change of season. They were deaf to their own shallow panting. From the blackness outside her window, a spectral moon climbed out of the weeping beeches. Snow like spilled sugar shadowed the darkened hills.

He said it was awful, what your mind will do to you.

You are wrong, my darling. The body lives for a much longer time than the mind. The SS understood all this very well. Without the mind the body can still do work. At night in that stink I put myself to sleep remembering the smells of my grandmother's kitchen. On Shabbes she wore a white silk scarf around her head, and she would place two candlesticks on a freshly starched white cloth and light the candles and pray as it grew dark. She closed her eyes and passed her smooth palms over the burning candles, always toward herself. She told me she asked the Almighty to preserve her family, its health, its honor. I can remember the yellow wax dripping down into a thick heap at the base. She had made two perfect loaves of braided challah, carrot stew and potato latkes, and chicken with watercress and parsley in giant simmering pots, and poppy-seed cake and lemon tarts with hazelnut sauce, schnecken with cinnamon and chopped almonds. If I had a cold in my lungs she fed me roasted kasha and pinto beans and massaged my eyes with eggshells to ward off the evil eye. Her wrinkled hands always smelled of bird's milk and rose hips. Those odors kept me alive. I wanted nothing else but the chance to eat those thing again, to stuff them into my mouth and feel them make their way to the hole in my stomach. I am hungry all the time now, but I cannot taste or smell or swallow food. I am no longer a prisoner, but there is only the stench of excrement and quicklime in my nostrils today. Now I feel like I am hiding in a cesspool. The thought of food makes me want to retch.

You will vanish if you don't eat.

I want to vanish, deep inside, in a place I cannot touch. I want to shed my dead skin like a snake.

That winter passed slowly. The temperature never went above freezing for weeks. The cold clawed in through the storm windows. We were snowbound most of the time—thanks to a couple of roaring blizzards forty-eight hours apart a few days after New Year's—imprisoned in a vast, unending mansion of luminous white. The raw sky brimmed with moisture. Snow-webbed ice had descended to the marbled roots of broken-fingered oaks, the wailing squalls blew thick coarse snowflakes through the vaulting branches of glowing trees. The roads were impassable, and the Army was helicoptering in food and fodder to the isolated farms south of town. The newspaper reported that a farmer had found one of his missing rams in a tunnel of ice.

Many weeks later, long after the brutal winds had diminished and the clanking snowplows had piled the snow up in drifts along access roads, I fixed a thermos of hot cocoa, wrapped some thick meatloaf and tomato sandwiches in waxed paper, and took Uriel cross-country skiing over the blustery country club links, and ice skating at the abandoned quarry. Icicles made the shingled limestone glisten. A chain of feathery clouds was scudding overhead, and the sluggish sun burned without heat. The wind was up, and the heavy branches of the hemlocks and blue firs sagged, the soft snow showering down upon us. I heard a bird rapping in the woods. We stumbled into some country boys there I recognized from town as troublemakers. They called us *kikes* and pummeled us with slush balls filled with small stones. I told Uriel to just pretend that they weren't there, that they would soon grow bored with their sport and leave us alone. He pushed me aside and pulled a long kitchen knife from his navy peacoat. Looking into his face, I had no doubt he was ready to go chase after them. There was a pained intensity in his dispassionate eyes I'd never seen before. He opened his mouth and bellowed at them in mangled words. Squinting, he took off the visored herringbone cap my father had given him and raked his greasy hair back with his fingers. Before I was finished pleading with him to use good judgment and put the knife away—I said there were too many of them for us to tangle with, and they were known to carry hunting knives and snub-nosed revolvers—the stonies had left, laughing and calling us names as they vanished into the frosted woods.

We sat down on a low stone wall and watched a pair of dark gray rabbits bounce through the red-stemmed thornbushes. I pointed out the alder and juniper to Uriel, but he looked away from me. I tried to explain to him why I felt that ignoring them was the smartest and safest thing to do—that they were malicious boys, capricious and crass. I told him it was common knowledge around school that these brutal thugs would lurk in the shallow grassy ravine below the rusty footbridge and take potshots at nesting ravens and robins and ring-necked pheasants with their .22s and BB guns. But I couldn't bring myself to tell him that I was terribly afraid of all physical confrontations, and that I knew absolutely nothing, in fact, about how to defend myself.

He stood up and looked at me with terrible bitterness, his raw face all scrunched up and fierce, and took off his red woolen mittens and smashed his ice skates—*my* ice skates—onto a frozen shelf of crumbling limestone, breaking the blades. He put his rubber boots back on and kicked at the packed, heaped-up mounds of snow. His eyes now had a strange glittery cast to them, as if his long girlish eyelashes were coated with angel-hair tinsel, the kind you always see around Christmastime. Then he caught me off guard. He unzipped his fly, took out his penis, and sent his steamy urine in a golden crescent out onto the snowy ground beside me. It glistened in the fading light. If this was a demonstration of his disgust, then who was he pissing on—the country boys or me? I tried to imagine that his eyes were snow-blind, and that nothing bad would come of all this. I wanted him to forget that it had happened, I didn't want it to come between us.

Just the other week, and without any prompting, Dara had said to me that sooner or later something would happen to one of us that the other one would be unable to understand, and it would drive us apart. She said we came from different worlds and that I was a fool for believing I could do anything for him. I told her I wasn't trying to *do* anything, other than be someone he could count on. She smiled and said I'd have to learn the hard way. I was annoyed at her for thinking that—I allowed that she was just being spiteful and envied my growing friendship with Uriel. But the truer truth is that I felt some of what Dara was hinting at myself, and I was desperate to shield myself from any more disappointment. I got up and walked over to him. He looked at me and then looked down at the huge white palms of his hands and started giggling. I studied our half-turning shadows in the snow. With his cracked lips pinched together so that his mouth vanished, he cautiously ran the blade of the knife beneath his throat. Before I could say anything more, he turned and limped away from me, his damaged leg dragging behind the other. I went and stood on the low stone wall and watched him follow the meandering trail back to the frozen duck pond. He paused there for a few seconds and took his bearings—the gravel bypass to the highway was just a quarter mile up the path—then he hobbled across the old iron footbridge.

Uriel eventually showed me his drawings and paintings. They were all pretty much the same: electrified fences, grim dilapidated barracks, the emaciated face of a man or woman in pitiable attire. When I suggested that he try painting the landscape around his new home, he looked at me blank-faced and grunted something that sounded German, full of the letter z. Father Rook had managed to get him a part-time job nailing on heels and soles over at Bailey's Shoe Repair in town. (Mrs. Mermelstein was already taking in clothes to be mended.) On Tuesdays and Thursdays I could always find him in the back of the store, his large head buried in a mass of disordered brown leather. His overalls were baggy and had holes in them, and with a scraggly beard and huge forearms he could have actually passed for a stonecutter. He did his job and kept to himself, and Chick Bailey, a large friendly man with woolly gray hair and a hard swell of belly, told my father that he was a good, honest, careful worker. Mr. Bailey said the very same thing to me, and then he felt the need to further explain that people like the Mermelsteins "wasn't as advanced over there in Europe as we are." When I asked him how he knew we were so advanced, what he actually meant by it, he gave me a dry shifty stare and disappeared into the dark stockroom without answering.

Whenever I dropped by to say hello, Uriel always stared at me as if he had never seen me before. His flat gaze managed to make me feel like I was still a stranger to him (I probably was) and he to me. I would say a few words to him about what I was doing in school, about possibly getting together the coming Saturday for supper and a movie and popcorn. Before I left I would give him a brown paper bag filled with two Mars bars and a large bottle of Orange Crush. He loved the soda and could drink it off in one clean swallow. At that time I had no idea if he knew our parents were sleeping with each other, and I had no intention of letting on what was happening between them if he didn't first give me some sign that it was something he knew about and didn't like. How could he have not known? It was going on right under his nose. But what could he have done? Drawn me a picture?

What am I doing in my fertile dreams, if not struggling against the sheer erosion of time to breathe life back into all of them?

My father had told her that he wanted her, that he would protect her and never leave her, and she echoed him teasingly. *Jacob—there is no never, no shelter. Your kindness and your need to comfort me is like a miracle.*

Then they both wept—bereft, grateful.

You do your best to make believe that you can go on. I am two

people now, and will be forever. Or I am not even one person. I try
to put everything away so deeply in my mind. I told you that Uriel
wakes up screaming every night. Only he doesn't come awake. He
sits there in bed screaming. But they aren't screams you can hear.
Or only I can hear them, as if they are my own.

Her tortured body had caressed him back to life. Touching her,
he pretended that he had been drained of crushing remorse. She had
put the bouquet of tiger lilies he had given her on her night table.
Her damp, matted hair had unraveled across the stained pillow. He
was lost in the jungle of her hair. He rolled his blushing face in it,
he drew it back ravishingly in his hand. He gripped her frail aching
shoulders. She turned over and pulled him down, locking him in.
He moved his mouth along the flowerlike scar on her belly. He
wondered how she got it but wouldn't ask her. Her body was an
oven. Sweat streamed down his rigid spine; her pensive, cobalt eyes
were tensed in perplexity. With her lying on top of him, he felt no
weight, no substance at all, as if her bones were hollow. He was
astonished that someone could feel so slight, so airy. He brushed
the strands of hair from her transparent cheekbones. Beneath her,
the heat of his breath warmed her pale flat breasts. With soft, mes-
merized fingers he stroked her shriveled nipples, her pallid thighs.
In my dreams I wondered if he ever smelled my mother on her
milk-white skin? Did he ever hear my mother's morning voice in
Esther Mermelstein's unrestrained sighs? Were their feelings for
one another merely another kind of desperate irresolution, another
form of dispossession?

They kissed and made love like normal people in that sad, unpainted room, and something elemental tore open inside my father's core. He knew he was beyond mending.

He had forgotten that there were limits to everything.
(That's how I came to think of it.) The blossoms of comfort and
gratitude and passion were too fragile. They had become the salve
of each other's unassuaged heartache. I knew my deliberate, vigilant
father; he had always moved through the world gingerly, and now

there was urgency in his eyes. He was bewitched by Esther Mermelstein's tattered, damaged beauty, and now he wanted more than there was—more than he should have expected. I fancied them limping into one another's arms. Their undisturbed sleep was hypnotic, as if they shared one pulse—their yearning for closeness, for enlivening conversation, finally abated. No doubt they did what they could for each other and hoped for a better future, an enticing catharsis for their mutual despair. I imagined them in her narrow bed, silently watching each other, slumped down inside the twisted bedsheets. A question moved between them. He knew that there were secrets that could never be talked into clarity. He would never press her about them, never make her tell him about things she couldn't put into words. In time they felt condemned by unseen accusers, the familiar vocabulary of the unthinkable and inviolable. He told her about my mother, her illness, how he had loved her, and she told him about her bleeding dental abscesses in the DP camp, her infected nail and frostbitten toes, and showed him how her perfect false teeth spent the night floating in a glass of baking soda mixed with salt water. Whenever they wanted to be alone they sent me on an errand into town with Uriel. I knew he knew what had been going on between our widowed parents, but he withheld any sign of his awareness. His father was dead, as was my mother, so there was no duplicity, no betrayal. His mother was a woman slowly coming back to life, as was my father. Life was all about restoration, renewal. I thought that this was what Uriel had wanted, to watch them stitch the scarred and slivered fabric of their broken lives together. But the spirits of the dead were always with us in our dim and irresistible delusions. A second chance—was that the mirage they had clung to? There never was to be but one. Even *now*, my fingertips tingle as I am forced to consider what I have written.

———

The night wrapped itself around them. Esther lifted one of my father's tapered hands to her face and cupped it against her ear like a broken seashell. She told him to listen there, and be patient. What magic could he have heard? What sounds? Her sobs in Warsaw when she had been separated from Pintor? The memory of her son's voice? Her grandmother's prayers?

A filament of grief ran through her body like a wick. She told him that she was afraid of closing her eyes at night, that she kept reliving everything in her gruesome nightmares. She said she dreamt of agate-colored bonfires stoked with screaming babies; of strangled women in shredded rags and smoldering wigs; of *davening* old men, thorns like crimpled blue *tzitzit* in their shaggy gray beards, hanging stiff and pale and gutted and upside down from a gibbet by their black leather *tefillin*; of vast zinc basins filled with pulverized teeth, shorn hair, hacked limbs, melted gizzards; and of being snared, like a hare, in a deep dry hole, then driven into dim simmering boxcars and frigid cattle wagons. But she dreamt mostly of her missing parents in their dark fecund trench, great boiling rivers of blue-gray bone, the ripe solid mineral spore of decomposing matter, hearts and stomachs and kidneys and brains and livers, a garish spiderweb of extinguished faces, all the strewn impermeable cadavers disinterred by floods—millions of bleached Jewish skulls riding a cataract of muck and mud through the squalid Silesian countryside, all of them liquefied, succulent, unliving. Dispersed like seedless roots in a measureless, unredeemed pit, they rot.

She told him she had reached out for her parents, that she had heard their racked breathing in her sleep—their rolling heads protruding from the chalky earth, their moist excreting mouths nailed shut—but there was nothing in her groping hands but oily smoke. My father rocked her in his arms. He kissed her eyelids. Her hair was wet and tangled. The soles of her feet ached. When she said she was hot, he opened the window a crack. The lamp sputtered and went out. A few strands of moonlight slithered in beneath the dark shade and scrolled along their flanks. The cold air blew across their sweaty faces. Over and over she had told my father that she had no more space in her withered heart for hatred, that she did not want to surrender to all this despair. She was not enraged at her tormentors, save one.

I have such shame for human beings. It is too much to have. There is no pity in the world. Our hearts are empty and made of stone. When my older sister's family was being deported from the ghetto in Warsaw, my niece Vera was ordered to take out her earrings and remove her rings and bracelet. I had given them all to her on her last birthday. They were not worth much, their value was mainly sentimental. Vera was small and pretty and frightened, a sweet little girl with braided red hair, a soft round face like her mother's, like my grandmother's. She could not remove the earrings quickly enough, so the Jewish policeman tore them out. She bled some and cried and cried. Then this same Jewish policeman said to my sister in Yiddish: "Du Jude, Kaputt—You Jew, finished. Now you are leaving your beloved Warsaw behind and you will never return here again. Say farewell to your house and cheder and synagogue. The Jews are forever finished here. Poland is Judenrein. The Jews are forever finished in Europe. Tell me—who among nations wants the Jews? Find me someone who loves the Jews. Show me who is weeping for the Jews. Only the rebbes weep, only the virtuous yeshiva buchers weep. The world as you have known it has come to an end. There are no more illusions for the Jews. No more prophets to part the Red Sea, no more legends about a desert God, no more anointed messiah from the House of David to restore the Kingdom of Israel. The Jews are soon wiped clean from the earth."

I can hear his voice in my ears. He is the only one I would like to meet again. I want to force him to recount to me his life after all these years, all this time since my sister and her husband and children have perished from the world. Does he sleep well? Can he swallow food? What does he see when the light goes out at night? I want to tell him that I never saw Vera after this time. I never saw my sister again. This policeman is the only one I have vengeance against. He is the only one to whom I would like to creep into his contented dreams and make them wicked abominations. He is the only one I want to get retribution from. He is the only one I would plunge a knife into his breast and cut his evil heart out. Do you understand what I am explaining? He is all the little pieces of my grief. Because he had said that they would not be coming back to Warsaw and Łódź and Lublin and Lwów and Cracow and Poznań and Radom and Bratislava and Prague and Vienna and Berlin and Budapest and Am-

sterdam and Salonica and Vilna and Kovno and Dvinsk and Shavli and Riga and Minsk and Lida and Bialystok and Odessa and Kiev—to all the buried cities of Europe. And because he said it all in an inhuman irrevocable way, so that they knew they were already ashes in the flames, already dust released into eternity—because he said we had obituary faces. But mostly because he was a rapacious Jew without a conscience, believing he could save his miserable head from departing up the chimney by working for such monsters.

The summer before my father's death, he journeyed north for a rare visit a few days before I left for St. Louis and an ABA conference. At sundown on the Friday he arrived, the three of us packed ourselves into my Tempest and headed for Harbor Island to see the Fourth of July carnival and fireworks display co-sponsored by the Lions Club and the county volunteer fire department. This was the first year for as far back as I could remember when we wouldn't be celebrating the Fourth with our children and Dara and Helen's brother's family. Everyone was out of town at the same time, so my father's trip was propitious.

I backed the Tempest into a space alongside a huge billboard which read "Freedom" in the shape and colors of the American flag. Helen went to serve refreshments at the L-shaped booth operated by our temple's sisterhood. Harbor Island was an enormous municipal park on the eastern edge of town. It divided the commercial and residential neighborhoods from the bay. A broad isthmus of stone walled off the numerous inlets and shallow channels that slanted off like the spokes of a wheel from a complex of baseball diamonds, an ice skating rink, and ten red-clay tennis courts. Ringing the slate plaza was a kiddy land, complete with monkey bars, sandboxes, seesaws, chain swings, and an Art Deco carousel operated by an old man in galoshes and knickers. To the left of the plaza were the lockers and bathhouse, and down a steep embankment was the public beach—a rough track of white sand and smooth pebbles running like a horseshoe from a crooked leg of asphalt to a fishing pier built from barnacled timber pilings. Around nine-thirty—on the narrow cement walkway adjoining the small freshwater aquarium—the fireworks display would commence, officially concluding the week-long fair.

My father and I had joined the large crowd filing past the picnic grounds, and we detoured to get in line at a pink booth selling books of chances for the grand raffle. The proceeds, a fireman said, would go for new fire-fighting equipment. First prize was four days and three nights at Epcot; second prize, a VCR and a Sony Walkman. There were booths for face-painters and potters and animal carvers and snow cones and cotton candy. There were wobbly aluminum tables in a rectangle around a hook-and-ladder truck, where joking firemen in bib-overalls sold barbecue and corn dogs and chili and rotisserie chicken and slabs of homemade pie. A makeshift wooden plank stage was erected for church choirs and square dancing and jigs and patriotic speeches by the mayor and police chief and white-haired veterans of Iwo Jima and Inchon representing the VFW and American Legion. A few feet away from us a couple of shaggy Shetland ponies were giving rides to screaming children. The ponies moved crablike—hesitantly, a small step at a time— around a painted circle, their brown eyes wide and terrified.

He told me he wanted to look at the speedboats for a few minutes, so we doubled back for about ten minutes, to where the pier intersected the stone wall. Walnut-colored heaps of dog turds jigsawed the muddy field like dominoes; bottle caps and cigarette butts and bird droppings were everywhere, sprinkled like pollen among the bluebells and daisies. The mayor always complained that the county executive wouldn't budget enough money to keep the gypsy moths and Japanese beetles under control. My father pinched his nose and made a face. The place smelled like warm loam.

Gazing down into the cloudy water we saw fish heads skimming in pools of sludge. Cattails and reeds and spongy brush were glued to rocks and pieces of wood; a part of a car hull floated on its trunk against the inky seawall. Dead minnows glided belly-up in the pitch-colored tide. The water was green and creamy, fumy from leaking gasoline. Motorboats rocked at anchor. The cement barrier we were standing on was serrated on the edge like a saw, notched with reflected mica. About fifty feet out was a demolished bait-and-tackle shop, fastened with heavy braided hemp to logs and rubber tires that joined the refurbished dock a few yards from where we stood. The current gently stirred the mooring and caused it to reel slightly. Snapweed and golden asters grew in the wet sand. Beyond the whitewashed shack were the low hills of the town: laundry strung on lines, an animal shelter, the rear exits of restaurants piled with garbage drums. A local artist had painted a crooked mural along the glass masonry of the Lobster Shed Tavern—a queer eyesore with a steamship fronting and whale-shaped windows and paddles decorated like salt-and-pepper lobster claws.

My father looked at me with uncertainty, shading his eyes with his hand. A bright crescent of perspiration ringed his mouth. The air smelled smoky from smoldering incense punks, and the new tide rolled in wavelets of platinum fishbones and pale, bloated sunfish. After a few seconds during which he combed his hair with his fingers, he pointed to the mural and wanted my opinion of it. I told him it wasn't the Love Boat.

The painting was a seascape of a blazing passenger liner going down in a swollen trail of smoke and blackened sky. The ship's hull was done in the colors of the spectrum, and people were toppling or diving overboard. Their faces—lightly pigmented with touches of copper and gold—were contorted, burning in the creamy green waves, and sparks of fire leapt from their hair and skin and teeth. Silver sharks snapped them out of the air as if they were bait.

He said he wanted to win Helen a bottle of Chanel No. 5. We walked back to a booth where players placed their bets on a cracked oilcloth dotted with smudged numbers, and a man in a billed feed cap and a greasy vest spun a wheel which started out fast and came to a sudden stop. The prizes were mostly pints of Four Roses, Pabst Blue Ribbon and Hamm's beer mugs, gutting knives, fishhooks, softballs, Greek watch caps, kites, cologne and perfume and Wildroot Cream Oil, and airline-sized bottles of Canadian Club and Southern Comfort. The barker was as big as a moose, and he swept the money from the oilcloth into a straw sombrero held by his albino sidekick. Lord knows where the Lions Club found these people, but they were here every July, with their trick wheels, loaded dice, dancing dogs, and midgets who swallowed flaming swords and shook tambourines and climbed all over each other.

Losing made my father crabby, and he started to perspire heavily. An obese man with egg-shaped blackheads all over his face crowded in behind us, and he started giving the barker hell about the lousy spins. People elbowed for space and started booing. I looked over at a canvas-draped tent beneath which tattooed hot-rodders in ribbed undershirts, black silk shirts, and tight stonewashed jeans pitched lopsided baseballs at bowling pins. Stacked on racks above the pins were tubes of bubblebath, skin cream, and hand lotion, and containers filled with hairbrushes and barrettes and colored bobby pins. Girls with plantlike hairdos in halter tops and shorts giggled and smoked behind their boyfriends.

I told my father that I wanted to go, but he was dead set on winning something for Helen. Then a wide-framed woman in pedal pushers and open-toed sandals poked me in the ribs, nudging me aside. I nudged her right back, and a heavyset man in a garage mechanic's outfit shoved me against one of the stakes anchoring the booth into the sandy soil. I tripped and fell backwards.

I knew this guy could probably kill me, but I jumped up and gave him the finger anyway. He pointed at my nose and demanded to know if I thought I could take him. Before I knew what had happened, my father had blindsided him with a roundhouse right to his jaw. Spurts of blood flew out in streamers. The mechanic staggered on his heels, fell, and rolled on the ground. Then he vomited. The chattering albino, who had dark ears the size and texture of baby eggplants, slapped my father five. The leader of the hot-rodders, a big ex-Marine type with thick tanned muscles and a blond flattop slick with styling gel, threw a few quick jabs at my father and called him Sugar Ray Leonard. A shaved white miniature poodle sniffed at the garage mechanic's mess and then slipped in it. Finally reinforcements arrived—four hulking security guards in Fu Manchu mustaches. They had their hands full breaking up the secondary scraps that by now had erupted between rival groups of out-of-town hoods. The light was rapidly fading; thin fluorescent clouds were passing over the water. Ash cans and cherry bombs burst sporadically in the distance. Before we left, the barker leaned over and shook my father's hand. He gave him a bottle of toilet water for his sweetheart.

We entered a winding wooded area camouflaged by a slanting arch of drooping dogwoods. There were dark-green wrought-iron benches and bisecting nature trails there, carpeted with scented red cedar woodchips, and a tear-shaped reflecting pool filled with circling boneless fish and small brown turtles. We paused to rest for a few moments. He pointed out the pimpernel, wild iris, and orange hawkweed, the fringed gentian and some lilac shrubs whose toothy leaves he said gave off a rich vanilla fragrance after you rolled over them. The balmy ozone breezes from the sound stroked our skin. We found a nice spot to watch the fireworks on a grassy hillside covered in dandelions, spread our blanket, and waited there for Helen to join us.

He asked me if I ever thought of the Mermelsteins, and of that painful time so soon after my mother's death. He wanted to know if I had ever seen any of Uriel's drawings. He said he had not had enough time to get someone at the college to look closely at them. His memory was failing; we had talked of these things many times before. Was he becoming aphasic, frantically adrift in a sea of forgetfulness? Or was he more like a friendless tourist trapped in a foreign country? But perhaps speaking of that time made him feel fully grounded again, my memory apparently a conduit, a reliable bridge he could cross to the most critical days of his life. My father looked shaken, and I heard what sounded like the old reticence in his quavering voice. He lived like an ascetic. He had very few wants anymore, his needs were limited. I knew he was slipping away from me, and I also knew that I would spend the remainder of my life grieving for him. It pained me that he still felt so badly after all these years, that he was still shouldering the responsibility for something that was not his doing. I told him that I had seen Uriel's drawings many times, and that they were all the same. He wondered if Uriel would have had any future as a painter, and I said that

I had no way of knowing. But I couldn't believe what I said to him next. I told him I thought that Uriel would have had to have found a way to glance away from his own penetrating sorrow in order to find some permanent beauty in the world, and that I could not say if he would have been able to do that. What drivel, I thought to myself. What blather.

So we went through it all for the last time: the bitter weather of those final weeks, the colossal ice storms, and Uriel's long dark form—curved spoonlike and shadowy under the shallow gray ice at the abandoned quarry—his lusterless eyes as big as saucers, the black center of his irises clouded over. His lacerated mouth was open like a gasping fish. He was dressed in one of my father's plaid scarves and heavy cardigan sweaters, the lush wool as white as cream. There were chiseled cracks in the ice where he had fallen through, now crudely frozen over. A break in the temperature was promised by the next day or two, so the sheriff decided to hold off chopping through the ice to recover the body for at least twenty-four hours.

The wind rippled at our legs like surf. My father's gaze slid along the hard ground toward Mrs. Mermelstein. Her shoulders were drawn forward. In the platinum light he could see that she was freezing, that she wasn't dressed properly for the weather. Her unbuttoned coat hung on her in heavy gray folds, and she wasn't wearing boots or a hat. She lifted one of her feet and took a step toward my father. He went to her. Embracing her, stroking her wet, stringy hair, he asked her in a stilted voice if she could tolerate the delay. She wrapped her arms around herself, and started swaying; he could feel the pulse in her throat dancing against the hollow of his hand. She pressed her cheek to his arm and began, quietly, to weep. Her gummed eyelids were quivering like insect wings. Her mouth opened a little, but she said nothing. Then her eyes fell on me.

Uriel had been missing for days. At the time I had no idea what had happened to him, why he had left home without leaving his mother a note. He knew she would be upset and terribly worried. And he surely knew that I would feel burning shame.

A few days before his disappearance, he had been assailed by those same detestable hooligans who had called us hateful names at the abandoned quarry. He had just finished work, and was waiting for me on the sidewalk outside Ladyman's Cafe. We were going to have a Blue Plate Special there—black mushroom soup, breaded veal cutlets, succotash, roasted Bliss potatoes, slabs of mulberry pie—and then go see a Gene Autry double feature. Coming down the street, I froze when I saw the loitering hardnoses heckling him. I wanted to run to him, but my legs wouldn't move, and my voice was lodged in my throat. I closed my eyes momentarily in the hope that it would all begin to seem unreal, more like something I had dreamed. Unlike the last time, however, I was now hoping that Uriel would lash out savagely at them. I wanted him to land a few ferocious blows, to break a few jaws and knock out a few teeth, to send them whimpering back to wherever they belonged, cracked and smashed and bloodied, squealing like piglets to their foul-mouthed mothers and callous fathers. But he just stood there impassively, soundlessly, a grim stoic, *taking it*—no doubt remembering my counsel from the time before, until they were finished with their few minutes of cruel and stupid mischief.

When I pretended that I had just gotten there, he acted as he usually did, as if nothing out of the ordinary had happened. But I knew he knew that I did nothing to help him. I was a frightened bystander, just like any of the other faceless, well-intentioned spectators who stood around and numbly watched. I would like to think that I knew what was passing in his mind, that he thought he was making things easier for me, protecting me, lessening my humiliation somehow. Even so, I did feel very guilty. And angry. I still do. He seemed to me at that moment like a large elder brother, someone who had been groomed to take on the burdens of his ignoble and unreliable younger sibling. It was something that went unspoken by either of us, unexpressed, as if we were bearers of the same vile secret. Though it's impossible to be sure of this (in hindsight, perhaps even fatuous) I think I wound up divesting some treasured certainties that evening, and repudiating certain half-truths. For the very first time I saw myself for who I really was, a dismal, unremarkable boy disfigured by deceit—furtive, disloyal, devious—and not the dependable friend I had aspired to be. It all came crashing down on that sidewalk.

It had thawed that day—the day after he was discovered by a drunken stonecutter and his yapping beagles—and the following morning Uriel's bruised and bloated body was fished up with the aid of a tow truck. It had shifted during the night and now was face down on a slab of limestone. There was a shell of crusty snow and stiff roots over the ground. The sun was melting everything. Massive slate-blue fingers of ice had dripped from the spruce and locust trees in half-formed, unlikely shapes—menacing, half-woven giant sculptures scaled with ironstone and mica. Flat walls of scalloped ice moved slowly in the thick brown water.

Once Uriel was out of the quarry, the sheriff ordered his deputies to turn him over. Uriel's eyeballs were like flattened pink blisters on his face. His mud-caked fists were clenched in pain, like a sleeping child's. For some odd reason, he wasn't wearing any shoes or socks. He appeared to have (or I saw it that way) a crooked smile on his face, and the beads of ice caught in his knotty hair glittered like crystal. His large head looked as thin and fragile as an eggshell—he had a jagged red gash on his scalp. A single rusty strand of barbed wire spiraled out of his swollen belly. His marbled skin was so translucent we could see the delicate dark veins winding underneath it. They were the same blue-green as the numbers on his arm.

The gauzy mist swirled in silver tendrils around the police ambulance. Its road reflectors and whirling roof light painted throbbing red streaks in the narrow tar road. The deputies fingered Uriel's cold, sopping body; they lifted it, heavy as lead, onto the stretcher and covered it with a paint-stained muslin sheet. The slender, chalky stems of his ankles and wrists dangled limply, and the exposed cubes of his mushy, purple toes were like crocuses. I felt suddenly disoriented, even faint, and wished I could be on a stretcher myself. One of the officers tried to close Uriel's mouth; the other one slipped a strand of his glazed hair behind his ear—as if it mattered.

There was an autopsy and an inquest. He had a crushed chest and pelvis, and two of his ribs had punctured his heart. They found water and leaves in his lungs, but the coroner said it was impossible to ascertain whether he had jumped or stumbled or was pushed by someone. The police asked some questions around town, here and there, but nothing came of it. Always meticulous, my father kept wanting to know why Uriel wasn't wearing anything on his feet— he kept asking who takes their shoes off before killing themselves? But the sheriff said he wasn't going to be engaged in aimless specu- lation, and he seemed indifferent and bored with the case after only a week had passed. He said they had no leads to follow, no clues, no witnesses. His hands were tied until someone came forward with a solid piece of evidence. He brusquely deflected my father's badger- ing with disparaging banter. When my father persisted, the sheriff started to question him as to *his* whereabouts when Uriel first dis- appeared. He said that this was a small community, and people were starting to talk about him and the dead boy's mother. My father was enraged, but, for obvious reasons, he wouldn't say where he was. Uriel's death was finally listed as accidental drowning.

That afternoon I broke down and tearfully told my father and Mrs. Mermelstein what had happened in town the other evening. I told them about my lack of nerve, my fear of getting beaten up, of being punched or kicked into submission, of crying and wetting my pants. I told them that I despised my very image in the mirror, and that my wretched cowardice sickened me. But when I told Mrs. Mermelstein that I knew in my heart Uriel had destroyed himself, that he had thrown himself onto the ice because I had forsaken him the one time he needed me, she held me pinioned like a trembling sparrow in her thin warm arms and told me that I should not punish myself for something I could not help.

With the red silk scarf my father had given her woven around her neck like burnt skin, she then told me in an unsparing voice that Uriel had survived the camps by cleaning out the suffocated bodies from the gas chambers, by mopping out the blood and urine and feces, by pulling hidden wedding rings from blackened hands, by incinerating the dead and brushing their ashes and bones into trenches, and covering them with peat and lime. She said that he

grew powerful from such grisly labors, but that his desire to live
had been consumed from his spirit long ago. If he had killed himself, she told me, it was not because of something I had done to him.
She said I should try to put such thoughts out of my mind. More-
over, she knew he cared greatly for me, that he had come to see me
as his trusted friend.

Mickey, ask yourself—what has he survived? You cannot bring
the dead back to life. We are all tainted by death—this is the way
it is. Nothing can be returned to the way it was, nothing can be
repaired. Everything is too late for Uriel. I wanted him to stay alive
if he could, but the darkness, the silence, has a life of its own. If he
gave up, he gave up. He couldn't go back and return the gold to the
missing teeth, the skin to the wasted muscle, the eyeglasses and
combs and hair and hats to the missing faces. So don't lose your
way, my child, looking for a reason that reason does not know.
Please understand that there is no fitting end for people like us.

She said this bluntly—brown darts ringing her somber eyes, her
voice scratchy as a damaged phonograph record—while all the time
running her strong fingers through my hair.

I was permitted to be with Uriel as the silent morticians soaped
the soft gray mass of his body. They shaved his beard and smeared
some waxy unguent on his face that made his cheeks shimmer. His
tin-colored skin was translucent, like butcher paper, his wasted clav-
icles and vertebrae like bone splinters for a dog. With his big jaw
drawn back, the scattered, wavy-yellow strings of winter sunlight
angled through the tall arched window and into his open mouth.
There was gristle at the base of his severed tongue. It was pulpy,
mottled with amber clots of blood and mucous, the limpid fluid
pooling inside our permeable tissues. I knew there were frozen
pieces of ligament and tendon in there, in the smooth dark shafts
where the icicles had pierced his windpipe. The dense brown hair
on his caved-in chest was standing up for some reason. His spongy,
pearly-white navel stuck out like a champagne cork.

Watching the morticians work on him, I kept on picturing the
sporting trophies—the rich umber pelts and thick stuffed heads
that deer hunters would mount above the blackened fieldstone fire-

places inside their dens, the floating ivory crowns of razor-tipped antlers, the tawny velvet ears, the glistening coal-black eyes pressing through their pliant glassy membranes at the terrible moment before the moment of death. I chose to think that Uriel at the end of his life was not afraid of dying—that as he slowly tumbled all the terror was dispelled into the cold universe, the dreadful scream he had kept sealed in his throat all this time to bear things snuffed, like sluices of shimmering blue-white flames, at the end.

We buried him in frozen earth blanketed by powdered snow the color of brass, beneath a twisted cherry tree, in the austere graveyard behind Father Rook's small church. A fine silver haze was undulating up the snow-laced hills behind us. Just the other day Father Rook told me that he'd found two dead owls in the parsonage chimney, their lathered feathers putrescent, brittle and crumbly to the touch. He said that had never happened before—great horned owls dying in the rectory—and he wondered if there was some dread bird pestilence coming around to afflict us, some punishment for our duplicity and unkindness. My father said it was probably just a germ, and he asked Father Rook why he was thinking about catastrophe so much lately.

The air was crisp, the sky metallic blue—the sprawling pink clouds were like vapors of steam. In the ecstasy of my grief I thought of my mother descending into her dismal Chicago grave—her head dreamless on the pleated satin pillow, the wavy pastel light of mid-morning in a muffled snowfall, the black shroud of the lake still seeping out of a stark gray mist, churning in the wind. My troubled mind was already searching for a way back to her. Mrs. Mermelstein's eyes were opaque, her blank face the pallor of parchment. Her mouth was set to cry, but she held herself, unmoved, like a mask. My speechless father's skin was white as sand.

He went to her that night, a final time. It was flurrying outside, the spruce and ash creaked in the vicious hypnotic wind. He carried in some damp logs for the fire. There was a web of amber mold in the scored window frame where the beveled glass didn't fit right. He spoke as if time were running out on them and he had to get everything said at once. In the cold he blew on her hands, warming them. He got up to stir the embers in the small woodstove. He let the heat burn the backs of his thighs before returning to her. She understood him well enough—the declensions of silence are untranslatable. Their voices were low and intimate, and in the guttering candlelight he saw that her face had seemed to whiten. He whispered something and smiled, and she waved his words away with a flick of her numbered wrist, as if dispersing them. Her hands shuddered slightly, and he took her tired face in both his hands, touching it lightly as he would a child's. She knew what he was up to: he was trying to erase her memory, to force the darkness from it. He wanted to restore her. To repair time. He said he wanted only to live in the present, with her. She could feel the sudden tremor of desire in his long cold fingers. In a daze he leaned over and kissed her. Her mouth parted and he heard her gentle breathing. Her bony arms went around his neck and held.

They slept till dawn. Awake, he sniffed the chilled air and smelled the pink-veined wood sorrel in the plump glazed pot hanging over the enamel kitchen sink, the musty condensation in the rotting timber. He got out of the bed and went to stand at the window. Banks of black-grained snow were blown in drifts against the house. He could see the ropy fumes, faintly golden, from someone's chimney down the road. Shivering, he ran his fingernail in a crude circle through the shiny frost. A thin violet light had fanned out across the sky. Long sinuous combs of transparent blue fog had sifted through the thick-trunked Norway pines. He heard scratching, crunching on the roof. He imagined nails tearing off cedar beams, wood splintering, famished raccoons, bushy wolverines. Things were leaking; he pictured the sodden ground beneath the drafty root cellar funneling into a sinkhole of creepers and red clay. He stayed still like that for minutes, listening. When he took a step backwards, she slowly turned beneath the heavy quilts. Her eyelids fluttered, and in the refracted light cast by the kerosene lamps he saw her look of living emptiness—her husband was with her like a permanent shadow, and now Uriel. She swallowed, and mouthed the words silently.

*You cannot make us whole again. You cannot rescue us from our-
selves.* And then: *Do you love me, Jacob?*

It was getting dark. By now the hillside was already
crammed with jostling families—there were young children
swarming over people's picnic baskets and blankets, shooting squirt
guns at each other, playing tag, waving fizzling sparklers—so I
stood up and scanned the crowd, looking for Helen. I wasn't too
concerned; she had a pretty good idea where we'd be waiting for
her. My father tugged on my jeans. He said there was plenty of
time before the fireworks began to finish what we'd started. According to our familiar ritual, it was now his turn to retrieve something
from our mutual history. We'd played this perilous game for decades. In this way both of us would always be mired in the past, our
memories intact, unassailed. He looked spent, so I asked him if he
would mind if *I* reiterated the story he had told me those forty Pass-
overs ago.

As promised, we had finally come north to Chicago to lay pebbles
at my mother's granite headstone. It had stormed the previous two
days, and on that frigid afternoon we stood beneath wide striped golf
umbrellas in the swirling snow at my mother's grave, the crashing
lake behind us bathed in a languid bronze glow. The savage swells
were foaming up against the Outer Drive. He let out a broken
sound, but didn't move. His flushed face was flattened out, troubled.
With his fur-trimmed, double-breasted overcoat unbuttoned and
unbelted, my father—hatless, soaked through, teeth chattering—
walked heavily, lurching in the wake of freezing rain.

As I closed my eyes, his old words came to me.

Esther grieved deeply for Uriel, as any mother would grieve for her
dead child. I couldn't touch her pain; her hiddenness was like an
anvil buried in her breast. I could never have understood what she
understood. I could never have known who we really were to each
other. She wanted to come live with us, to marry me, to be a wife
and mother again. After Uriel had disappeared, she asked me over
and over again if I loved her. Why didn't I answer her question that

night? I had told her many times before then that I loved her. What was I afraid of now? What had changed? Why was I vacillating? Was my sickening remorse coming from my refusal to answer her, or from the reason why I did not answer? Who can make sense of all these things? I was diseased inside, floundering, drowning in indecision, in misgivings. She had told me intimate things, things never to be repeated—what you would do for a piece of potato when you were starving, what bread was worth when you had none—and how she had managed to survive. I thought I had wanted to care for her—I was sure of it. What sickening pride! What foolishness! But I did not answer her because I knew I had to choose my unknown future over hers. I did not want to build a new marriage, a new life, on the pain of our past lives. I did not want my children to be irreversibly drawn into her humiliation. I left her to save what was left of my embittered life. And when I said this to her, I felt both relieved and reproved. I was selfish—I was afraid for myself, not her.

Esther must have read the misery and regret in my face, because in order to allay my wallowing in sorrow and self-pity she told me not to feel accountable for her. She had no more tears. There was no such thing as a past she could go back to. There was no past— the past was the present and the future. She said I was as blameless as you were. She held her thin arms outstretched, and I melted into her warm body like an infant. Her generosity had survived the burning and she lavished it on me. She caressed me and said I had given her pleasure and affection, and that was more than she had ever expected. There she was, trying to make me feel better, and I could do nothing at all for her. How could she bear it? Watching her, I couldn't speak. Her voice was steady when she said she would return to Europe and once again search for her missing family. There are still corpses coming out of the forest, she said. Maybe she could reclaim someone among the ruined faces. Then, perhaps, a freighter to Haifa. She had an aunt there, a harpist or a cellist, she couldn't remember which, a music teacher from Kielce, in Poland, she thought escaped and took a boat to Palestine before the war. She said she would learn to speak Hebrew, that she would plant date palms, olives, and pomegranates in the Galilee. She said she was done forever with Germany and Poland. Done with murderers. She said she needed heavier clothes, thicker boots, woolen gloves—that the winter in Europe was like iron. I was dazed by an unexpected vacancy, a violent sinking and shifting. I knew she would never find anyone, that she would live at the bottom of her memories, at the boundary. . . .

Before I had finished his story my father took his fingers and pressed them to my lips.

"I thought it would be a relief to be away from her," he said, trembling. "Maybe I just needed more time. I wanted to outlive my memories, and I knew there was no outliving of anything for Esther—there was nothing to redeem, nothing to recover. So much was left unexplained and unaccounted for. There was no reassurance and I wanted some. It was a terrible mistake. I panicked—I gave up too early. And still I cannot erase the presence of the dead."

She had left in less than a week. My father was uncommonly formal with Dara and me that week. He looked haggard and worn out from within. His eyes were flat and distant. He had obviously lost weight—the light brown suit he wore to teach in was oversized and hung loosely on his slender frame. For hours at a time he would stand by the bay window in the living room. His long face seemed to eclipse the dull yellow sun knifing into the elephant-skinned birches. While screening his eyes from the white glare of the Midwestern sky with a newspaper or book, he would scan the bleak winter horizon. When he grew chilled he warmed his hands over the rippling blue flames of the gas stove. He said that if you stared at the flames and let your mind wander you would see schools of brilliantly colored fish swimming through them.

Father Rook came by and told us that Mrs. Mermelstein had gone first to Schenectady, New York, in order to try to locate the married daughter of one of her husband's cousins who had supposedly lived there before the war. She sent Father Rook a postcard with a picture of Niagara Falls on it, and wrote that she'd managed to find out that the cousin's daughter had gotten divorced and had moved to Miami with her children many years ago. When I asked him where she had gotten the money to travel with, I felt my father's shaky hand on my shoulder. He told me I shouldn't listen to conversations that didn't concern me. I said I wasn't trying to listen.

Father Rook told us that she had seemed more thoughtful than lonely those last few days, not particularly gloomy or troubled, and that they had spent a rather pleasant afternoon on the window seat in front of the fireplace idly drinking strong English tea and playing chess. He said that Mrs. Mermelstein had kept to herself that week, packing a few things in cardboard boxes secured with twine and giving the remainder of her meager possessions away. He then showed us a scribbled letter in pencil she had left for my father, in which she said she was leaving all of Uriel's drawings to me, his trusted and only friend. I have no dependable memory of whatever else she had written in that note, but I can clearly recall that she wrote in a tight script I had trouble deciphering.

"On top of everything else?" my father kept saying after he had finished reading the whole letter. His voice was deep and rough. "But why? This makes no sense to me."

Father Rook's wet eyes became soft and almost affectionate; he shook his starving wolf's face. "People are unfathomable," he said bleakly.

And that was the very last time we ever heard from her.

I never asked my father what it was in Mrs. Mermelstein's letter that had upset him so much, and he never came forward to tell me on his own. Perhaps neither of us had the heart anymore. For little more than a year his once harmonious life had slipped out of his control, and at that point his only credible response was to keep his mouth shut. I was sadly awake now to the grim knowledge that the pain of this unforgiving world was inescapable, and for the remainder of his long life I simply chose not to burden my father with my curiosity. Esther Mermelstein's fate and final thoughts, at least to me, have remained a perfect mystery.

On the other hand, I have been a steadfast sentimentalist these past four decades, discretely keeping Uriel's bleak drawings and sketches secured in an old leather satchel that once belonged to my grandfather. The satchel was badly scratched, and I generously coated it with linseed and mink oil twice a year—removing the drawings and sketches and looking at them, in private, only on the anniversary of Uriel's death. They were as dark and enigmatic as their creator, and always left me with a hollow, melancholy feeling. Then I burned them last year, impulsively, and sprinkled the meager ashes over Lake Michigan a few hours after my father's funeral. Please don't ask me why. There seemed no good purpose to my keeping vigil over them anymore. And handing them down to my children struck me as capricious, as well as morbid. Who knows about these things, really? Perhaps I was now ready to let myself off the hook, to forgive myself for my fainthearted and pitiable behavior on that snowy street corner almost forty years ago—to finally concede that even in my anguished dreams it was too late to change the past. I told myself that I was at the stage where no one in his right mind would say I was young or even youthful (in fact, I was clearly getting old), and that the time had come to leap forward. Life simply peters out—if you know what I mean.

When we got back to the Tempest, the fireworks were waning in quiescent leaks and shallow pulses against the sky. The smoke-colored air was stained with sulphur. The traffic signals at the rotary were dead, and two cops in leather hip boots and opaque visors directed the mad flow of cars as if they were drugged. We were like glazed marionettes hooked to strips of invisible string. Organ music—Aaron Copland's "Appalachian Spring"—streamed out of St. Thomas's Catholic Church on Fenimore Road. A convertible GMC loaded with drunken, hooting teenagers weaved in and out of the line of slow-moving vehicles. When I honked my horn at them, my father said that they were merely kids, and understood nothing about the fragility and preciousness of life. He appeared and disappeared and then reappeared out of the uneven darkness as the Tempest passed beneath streetlight after streetlight. I glanced at him through the rearview mirror and saw that his drawn face was etched with disenchantment. Without his wife, without Esther Mermelstein—had the whole sad struggle just been a folly and a mockery?

I imagined him whispering their names over and over and over again. My father had never had any use for fortune-tellers, but I wondered if he now wished there had been someone or something to help sustain him through this nebulous maze of human desire. Or had he finally determined that we were simply meant to act on absolute impulse alone? The past weighed on him—it weighed on all of us—like the mortar and stones of a synagogue. What, then, had all this entrenched unhappiness finally amounted to?

Catching sight of me, he tried to feign bemusement.

His unbrooding eyes as he looked out the window were utterly patient and enduring. He had lived his life the best way he knew how and the rest I could see was of no great importance. And despite what I knew about his rapidly declining health, I still saw him as impervious to ruin and decay. At a stop sign, he suddenly reached over and gripped my shoulders; his blunt fingers moved over me like slender vines, and I could feel the tenderness and composure in his supple hands. In the mirror he was grinning now, showing me a dark hole half-filled with crooked and jagged teeth. I read in his alert, merry, timid eyes a disastrous blend of fear and defiance and a profound resignation. I had once told Helen that he never spoke ruefully about his life, but that was misleading. He understood all too well that he was slipping into the shadows, but he refused to feel sentimental about the past.

Except for our brief time with the Mermelsteins, the dreary years following my mother's death were mostly the same. My father and Dara hardly spoke a civil word to each other. She wanted him to grovel, but thankfully he wouldn't (couldn't?) accommodate her. I had several close friends during adolescence, while Dara, at least through high school, was a loner and kept to herself. My father grew solitary after his deep wounds, solitary but never cold or hard, and never indifferent. Perhaps his wants were modest after everything that had happened. Or maybe his taste for taking anymore risks had dissipated. I cannot say for sure. Only that he never begged for a miracle, and nothing, regrettably, was ever resolved. After Dara and I had left home for college, he lived alone for the remainder of his life, never remarrying. If he was lonely he never let on. Did he squander his life this way? Had he tried he might have fallen in love and found happiness with someone else. It's not for me to say. For most of us there was simply no deliverance, no consolation—we dissolved like ghosts inside our impalpable, unspectacular lives, always on the brink of bereavement and atrocity. The fundamental truth of our attenuated existence—my father's and mine—was that we were forever treading in the unquiet footsteps of the dead.

For some peculiar reason I felt ashamed, and beyond that, obscurely spared of something I would have been at a loss to understand. I thought briefly then of my mother—her warm sweet breath, the radiance of her loose, flaming hair. I remembered something she had said to me during those last days of her illness, when I worried so about forgetting what she looked and sounded like before she had fallen sick. Filled with distrust, I feared that the muted fragments of my childhood would remain inaccessible, cloaked in the murky, amorphous rubble of the past. Invariably they would abruptly surface, only to be irrevocably erased. Even at that awkward, impressionable age I had already determined that this dismal mass of absence had a contour, an irreducible barrier, all its own.

Before dying she had disclosed to me her unbroken belief that memory was like an elusive hourglass, and all I had to do was keep turning it upside down before the salt ran completely through it, and the aftermath of time would be dismantled. I wanted to believe her, but I couldn't. *I didn't know how.* I couldn't abide the thought that my unpurged dreams of my mother might one day simply peel away and disappear forever. I was afraid, too, that I wouldn't be able to see her face directly in front of me, that I would merely be seeing a specter, a counterfeit, the sly artifice of my mercurial imagination. It has taken me a lifetime to thaw the grooved pieces of myself that had been anesthetized with grief. Only now can I acknowledge what she had meant.

The night was flushed with the golden plumes of Roman candles. A wave of shimmering fireflies surged across the windshield, like lacy snowflakes sweeping over the frozen shoal of a lake. The air was salty, blurry, and breezeless, the sky a magnesium-stained membrane of opal light. Thick columns of coarse, chrome-colored smoke drifted down between the darkened, anonymous houses.

"Did I forget to tell you that Gideon Rook passed away last month?" my father said. His hands were still massaging my shoulders.

"You mentioned it—don't you remember? He must have been close to a hundred."

"He made it to ninety-seven on one lung," he said. "Gideon was a very kind man. I used to have dinner with him occasionally—he'd bother to stew a delightful lamb fricassee—and then we'd play chess or hearts. He forgot who I was, who he was, but he always asked about you. Isn't that interesting?"

"I know, you've told me."

"Mickey—I want to go to the cemetery tomorrow," he said, his hands on the back of my neck now. "To see your mother's grave. And my mother's and father's. It's been a while."

"I heard it was supposed to rain," I said. "Can't it wait a few days?"

"We've gone in the rain before. A few days is a few days."

I took one last glance at my frail, exhausted father; his skin looked porous, and faintly pitted. It was gathered in spotted rumples at his temples. Deep lines ran down his cheeks, and his lips were tight with disdain. Helen, half awake, her pink mouth open so I could see the flawless porcelain crowns of her gleaming bottom teeth, was slumped against his shoulder, her cool white hand suspended like a tulip beneath his dimpled chin. She was wearing the tiny sapphire earrings I'd gotten her for our twenty-fifth anniversary.

"Let's go tomorrow morning then, Dad." I said. "We'll have coffee and prune Danish and go, rain or shine. Okay?"

A person not unacquainted with irony, my father saw me staring at him in the mirror and smiled, a dying old man waiting at the edge—his dismay and errors of judgment and irrevocable decisions and fatal deliberateness and blind indulgences washed clean. He looked into me the way most people peered into unfamiliar rooms. His eyes, confiding, untarnished, glittered like wet mercury. I watched his chest rise and sink, I listened to his slow, shallow, fibrous breathing. I felt the world tilt upon us, and for a charged moment I thought I understood it, *the whole thing*, life in all its tainted and turbulent dimension. I started to sob then, a soft, subdued, unspecified lament, and then a permanent boundless lament, something unveiled drawn reluctantly through me, like a frayed thread through a tiny needle—a shameful, shuddering little boy still bewildered in the sixth decade of life. My father hunched forward and embraced me. Without flinching, and in the same silky whisper I remembered him using during the last cruel weeks of my mother's life, he told me what was coming.

He said that he was ready—more than ready, in fact—and that there was nothing to worry about. *Not worry?* I reminded him that I was his son, and he made a grumpy face. He knew I would carry our shared memories inside me like a soul—that he would live in me after he died. We spoke very little after that, mostly about the lackluster pennant races, the rafting trip in British Columbia that Helen and I and some friends of ours were going on during the last two weeks in August, a few words about a biography of David Ben-Gurion he'd just finished, and when the traffic didn't let up I took a detour and drove my weary cargo home to bed, along plundered and debris-choked streets unsaddled by gloom—pitiless, lamp-lit streets humming with the secret, solitary power of untroubled sleep.

Harvey Grossinger lectures in literature at American University and in the Honors Program at the University of Maryland. His short stories have been published in *Chicago Tribune, New England Review, Western Humanities Review, Mid-American Review, Ascent, Cimarron Review,* and *Antietam Review.*

THE FLANNERY O'CONNOR AWARD FOR SHORT FICTION

David Walton, *Evening Out*
Leigh Allison Wilson, *From the Bottom Up*
Sandra Thompson, *Close-Ups*
Susan Neville, *The Invention of Flight*
Mary Hood, *How Far She Went*
Françǫis Camoin, *Why Men Are Afraid of Women*
Molly Giles, *Rough Translations*
Daniel Curley, *Living with Snakes*
Peter Meinke, *The Piano Tuner*
Tony Ardizzone, *The Evening News*
Salvatore La Puma, *The Boys of Bensonhurst*
Melissa Pritchard, *Spirit Seizures*
Philip F. Deaver, *Silent Retreats*
Gail Galloway Adams, *The Purchase of Order*
Carole L. Glickfield, *Useful Gifts*
Antonya Nelson, *The Expendables*
Nancy Zafris, *The People I Know*
Debra Monroe, *The Source of Trouble*
Robert H. Abel, *Ghost Traps*
T. M. McNally, *Low Flying Aircraft*
Alfred DePew, *The Melancholy of Departure*
Dennis Hathaway, *The Consequences of Desire*
Rita Ciresi, *Mother Rocket*
Dianne Nelson, *A Brief History of Male Nudes in America*
Christopher McIlroy, *All My Relations*
Alyce Miller, *The Nature of Longing*
Carol Lee Lorenzo, *Nervous Dancer*
C. M. Mayo, *Sky Over El Nido*
Wendy Brenner, *Large Animals in Everyday Life*
Paul Rawlins, *No Lie Like Love*
Harvey Grossinger, *The Quarry*